CH0060153Ⅰ

The Occidentals

The Occidentals

Caron Eastgate James

ASIA BOOKS

The publisher wishes to thank the Siam Society for its
assistance in the preparation of this book.

Published and Distributed by
Asia Books Co. Ltd.,
5 Sukhumvit Road Soi 61,
PO Box 40,
Bangkok 10110,
Thailand.
Tel: (662) 714 0740-2 ext. 221-223
Fax: (662) 381 1621, 391 2277

© Copyright, Caron Eastgate James, 1999

All rights reserved. No part of this publication may be reprinted
or reproduced, stored in a retrieval system, or transmitted in any
form or by any means, mechanical, electronic, photocopying,
recording, or otherwise, without prior permission in writing
from the publisher.

Printed by Darnsutha Press Ltd.

ISBN 974-8237-34-6

❖ *Acknowledgements* ❖

I would like to thank the following
for their contributions during the writing of this book:
The Siam Society, whose excellent library provided most of the
extensive research materials required;
Ian James, for continuing support throughout the project;
Howard Richardson, for leading me to Asia Books;
and, most importantly, my editor Richard Baker,
for his patience and dedication in making *The Occidentals*
the best it could be.

◈ *Prologue* ◈

The smell of cigar smoke still lingered in the dark, silent house, and he shrank back toward the sash window he had climbed in by.

What if the man were still here? The last thing he wanted was to cause a disturbance—never mind get into a fight—for he had come only to claim what was his. But then he recalled, of course, that she never allowed her gentleman callers to stay the night. Most of them were expected home, anyway.

It wasn't really stealing, he tried to convince himself. It was merely settling the score. He would certainly not be able to use it there—and perhaps not anywhere—but if he could not have it, then he wanted to make sure that she could not either. He would rather bury it in the garden for someone else's eureka, perhaps a century hence. In any case, she would never know for sure that it had been him. Rogues abounded there, and it could be anyone. He would go home with it tonight. Home to his wife.

If only she had stuck to their deal—their 'gentleman's agreement', so to speak—their secret stake, in her name, paid for by him, with profits to be shared between them. They had planned to escape together, for he would surely lose everything once he was discovered.

When he had found it, he considered it a fortuitous sign. But she had soon become distant. She began making excuses that she had to be elsewhere. She was seldom at home when he called, and finally she pretended not to know him in the saloon. She was rich now, and planned to open an establishment of her own. Not there, but somewhere pleasant. Somewhere with a better class of clientele.

She drank heavily each night after work, and he knew now that she would be asleep and would not hear him creep into her bedchamber. In the moonlight, he saw an empty bottle on the living-room table, with a half-full glass beside it. The other glass had overturned, and the red wine formed a dark puddle around it. He imagined her laughing drunkenly, not bothering to pick it up—and the man, in his urgency to have her, grabbing her and half carrying her upstairs. And she wouldn't have stopped laughing—because she thought men pathetic.

The smell of smoke became stronger as he climbed the stairs, but it was more acrid than tobacco. He crept quickly along the narrow passage—the familiar way to her room—and saw the smoke curl out from under her door like Minerva's snakes. He flung it open but immediately stepped back, gagging. The room was alight, and the flames had already engulfed the curtains round the four-poster bed.

As she reared up and coughed, wild-eyed, he saw the cotton sack on the low table at the end of the bed. She hadn't even tried to hide it. He stepped quickly into the room toward it.

When she saw him, she called out, choking, "Help me, for God's sake!"

Was it to be her or what he had come for? No one would ever know he had been there. On impulse he reached out and grabbed the sack with the tin container inside, hauled it over his shoulder, and rushed back to the door. But then he hesitated and turned back to her. Of course he had to do what he could. He put the sack down by the door and went back into the room, but the heat was too intense. The flames had already spread across the floorboards and had taken hold of the heavy velvet curtains over the windows.

She sank to her knees on the bed, her arms flailing desperately as the flames began to swallow her. In a moment the fire would be upon him too, and they would both die.

He turned, picked up the bag once more, and hurried down the hallway. As he descended the stairs and climbed out the window, pulling the sash down behind him, he felt consumed with guilt and cowardice. He moved furtively down the lane, and then looked back to see the top storey of the house completely alight. A moment later, he walked on through the darkness with the bag over his shoulder and didn't look back again.

Part 1

February 1868 – August 1869

◈ *Chapter 1* ◈

Gulf of Siam, February 1868

Edward Fairburn adjusted his stiff collar and wide necktie as another trickle of sweat worked its way down his back, soaking into his already damp shirt and waistcoat. The ship swayed and creaked, and he grabbed the railing once more, almost tripping over a sack of rice, one of scores that seemed to have been strewn at random about the deck.

He had discarded his heavy green jacket days ago, and he felt under-dressed without it, despite the cloying heat. But there, on a steamer in the Gulf of Siam, tossed by the waves and roasted relentlessly by the searing tropical sun, no one was concerned with the proprieties of dress. The other passengers were too busy themselves coping with the suffocating temperatures and the poor food and cramped conditions on board.

His checked woollen trousers, thick long-sleeved white shirt, and high-buttoned green velvet waistcoat were almost more than he could stand in the heat, and his fashionably-long side whiskers itched him irritatingly. He envied the Chinese and Siamese sailors their bare chests and their colourful cotton *panungs*—a sort of loose trouser that was wrapped round the waist and pulled through the legs and tied—but he could never have considered discarding his attire for theirs. He was an English gentleman, and was obliged to appear as one at all times, regardless of circumstances. Besides, his pale English complexion could not have withstood the incessant burning rays of the equatorial sun for any length of time.

He was glad of the protection provided by his felt bowler hat, although it, too, added to his sweltering discomfort.

It was the fifth day of the journey from Singapore to Bangkok, and for what seemed like the hundredth time since they had set sail on the grubby steamer Chao Phya, he wondered what had possessed him to make this journey to the mysterious Far East. He thought of his wife and daughter in Melbourne, and what they would make of his detour.

As always, he felt mostly guilt when he thought of Charlotte. She had suffered so much because of him. Would she be angry when she received his letter saying he was not returning to her by the most direct passage? But he already knew the answer to that question.

If he had travelled on the Devitt & Moore Line's celebrated new vessel, Sobraon, he would have been back in Australia within eleven weeks—and as a first-class passenger, would have enjoyed every luxury along the way. Instead, he had sailed to Singapore, and had been obliged to wait ten days in that crowded, humid outpost—where he knew no one—until he could obtain passage on the erratic steamer service to Bangkok.

He was accustomed to travelling first class, but on the decrepit Chao Phya, he might well have been travelling steerage. The accommodation below deck was filthy, and the air so foul and stifling that most of the passengers, even the ladies, preferred to spend the nights of the journey uncomfortably on deck, clearing a space between the rice sacks, ropes, and whatever else lay around, and sleeping as best they could. There was no provision for bathing or washing, and the food prepared by the Chinese cook was strange and virtually unpalatable to any of the passengers not accustomed to Asian spices. How they longed for a good English side of beef, with roast potatoes, peas, and a thick, smooth gravy.

Unlike most of the other Europeans on board, he wasn't seasick; nor did he suffer from any stomach ailment. Nevertheless, he would be delighted to bid farewell to the Chao Phya, although its master, Captain Orton, had been very obliging.

Most of all, he was concerned about how the tropical humidity would affect his expensive new photographic equipment despite the fact that his portable, folding-bellows camera had been constructed of teak instead of the usual mahogany. Teak, the W. W. Rouche company in England had assured him, was perfect for the tropics, being naturally adapted to resist heat, damp, and even insect infestation.

He wondered also how the chemicals necessary for photographic development would survive the rough voyage. Or were the bottles already smashed, leaving him with chests of leaking developer, collodion, cyanide, acetic acid, and the like? If any of it were damaged in any way, then he had made the trip for nothing, for the purpose of this Far East sojourn was to photograph the kingdom of Siam and its inhabitants.

It was all very well to travel the world in relative comfort to such places as California and Australia, but a journey to Siam was another matter entirely. It would establish him as an adventurer; a roving photographer in search of the world's most exotic subjects. One more miserable night on board and they would arrive at their destination, the captain had told him.

Here was Captain Orton now, sauntering toward him as if he were taking a Sunday stroll in the park, rather than negotiating the slippery hardwood decks of a rolling steamer.

"Do you see, Mr. Fairburn?" he called out, pointing beyond the starboard bow. "We've sighted land. We're approaching Siam."

Edward squinted and placed a hand on his forehead to shade his eyes. In the blinding white light, he could barely make out the shadowy strip on the horizon. "Yes, indeed. And a welcome sight it is too, Captain, if you don't mind my saying. Should we be landing tonight then, sir?" he asked hopefully.

The captain laughed with a loud snort. "No such luck for you, Mr. Fairburn. I'm afraid you're stuck on my humble vessel for at least another night."

"At least?"

"In order to reach Bangkok we have to cross the bar into our namesake, the Chao Phya River. It depends on the tides."

"I see," Edward mumbled, resigning himself to the continuing discomfort. "Well, at least we're within sight of our destination, Captain."

The captain strolled on, and Edward was alone once more. As alone, at least, as a person could be on a vessel which carried—as well as its cargo and eight other British passengers—some two hundred or more Asians of various nationalities, who spent their time huddled in tight circles on deck, gambling and smoking opium.

From what he could discern, several games were popular. Some were played with large decks of long, narrow cards illustrated with Chinese portraits. Another involved a brass cup and a wooden cube, which was painted half red and half white on one face. The 'banker' would place the cube on the deck, painted face up—without allowing anyone to see it—and then cover it with the brass cup. The participants would then place wagers on which direction the white half faced. Those with money on the winning side appeared to be well rewarded, while those with stakes on the other three sides lost them to the 'banker'—for whom the game appeared to be a most profitable enterprise.

"At least it passes the time," a fellow passenger—a Mr. Deakin—remarked to him as they stood watching the gambling. "Wouldn't mind joining them myself, if they'd have us. Mind you, they'd probably fling up their arms in horror and jump overboard if we even approached them."

Edward laughed. "Can you blame them for thinking us strange, Mr. Deakin? Besides, we'd look mighty unusual in our woollen suits, crouched down among a group of Orientals we couldn't communicate with. They'd have us, all right. They'd surely cheat us blind."

That night, on deck, he was able to sleep soundly for the first time during the voyage—despite the incessant snoring of Mr. Deakin nearby, and the continued, raucous gambling of the Asians. Perhaps it was the knowledge that he would soon be on land again, or perhaps his sleep was aided by a refreshing breeze that—for once—had lowered the temperature enough to leave him merely lightly perspiring.

But he awoke early next morning to find himself itching fiercely all over.

"Damnation!" he swore as he leapt from his resting place covered in biting, red ants.

Sometime during the night, seeking a more comfortable position, he had moved his head to rest on a sack of sugar cane that had been invaded by hordes of the insects. Having had their fill of the sack's contents, some had ventured on to the next interesting prospect: Edward. And despite his close-fitting clothing, some had managed to work their way inside. He could feel the prickly sting of their bites all over him.

"God save me!" he gasped, beating his trousers and pulling off his ankle boots and stockings. The other passengers stared at him in bemusement, but he was desperate.

"For goodness' sake, man, what's got into you?" the captain exclaimed as he strode over to investigate the commotion. His passenger appeared to be performing an insane war dance on deck.

"Ants, Captain," he explained as he continued to beat at his trousers. "The blighters besieged me while I slept. Never in all my life. . . ."

Captain Orton smiled. "Well then, you'd best go below and sort yourself out. My boy will bring you some water."

"Thank you, sir. Much obliged." Edward knew how precious fresh water was on the steamer, and it was not generally wasted on trivialities such as washing.

"On your way, then. The laddie will be down directly."

As Edward disappeared below, Captain Orton suppressed a smile. That one wouldn't last long in Siam, he thought. The landed gentry, by the look of him—and too accustomed to the comforts of life.

Despite Edward's claim that he had "roughed it" on the gold fields of California and Australia, he certainly wouldn't be prepared for what awaited him in Bangkok. It would be interesting to observe what became of him in that stifling and alien environment, the captain thought.

Melbourne, Australia, February 1868

There was a clatter on the porch, and then an impatient rapping at the front door. She heard her daughter's high-pitched squeals of excitement behind it.

"Mummy, Mummy, come quickly, let me in. It's come at last. A letter from Father."

The housekeeper, Mrs. Bains, opened the door, and Elizabeth almost tumbled through the entranceway and into the front room where her mother was sitting.

"Look, Mummy, it's finally come," she cried.

Charlotte set aside her needlework and took the letter. Elizabeth was right, it was his handwriting on the envelope.

To her daughter, the letter could mean only one thing: that her father was returning home to Melbourne soon, with chests full of gifts from England. To Charlotte, however, a letter from him no longer gave her a thrill of anticipation. She shivered with apprehension, for she could never know what scheme he would be planning next. Or even if he would return home at all this time. They had not parted on the best of terms.

He had been gone for more than a year already, insisting when he left that he must return to his parents' Yorkshire estate. Family business concerning trust funds and properties left to himself and his brothers by their grandfather, he had claimed.

"It's imperative, Charlotte, that I'm there," he had told her then. "I must ensure I receive my fair share. I wouldn't put it past my brothers to try to cut me out. You know we've never got on. To them, I'm the black sheep—the prodigal son gone bad who no longer deserves their consideration."

But he had left suddenly, and she was convinced it was to escape from the problems of their marriage, and from the monotony of his studio photography work in Melbourne. True, he had just returned from the gold fields at Ballarat, but he didn't talk about it much. After an enthusiastic start, he had quickly lost interest.

Seven-year-old Elizabeth was restless as her mother turned the letter over in her hands. "Hurry, Mummy. Let's see what he says. Maybe he'll be on the next ship, do you think?"

"We shall see," she replied, taking a carved ivory letter opener from its tray on a side table and neatly slitting the top of the envelope. She withdrew a single page.

"What does he say? What does he say?" Elizabeth hopped from foot to foot.

"Elizabeth. Please do sit down and behave yourself like a young lady. I shall tell you Father's news when you allow me a chance to read his letter myself first."

She did as she was told, jumping on to a large armchair next to the chesterfield where her mother was seated. Charlotte was slim and rather short, but the wide crinoline under her silk skirts made it impossible for her to fit into an armchair.

Elizabeth's eyes were bright with anticipation, but she clasped her hands tightly, and tried to distract herself by looking round the room. She loved the front room, despite the fact that she wasn't allowed in there alone. It wasn't a proper parlour, since it was the only sitting room they had, and so was not used solely for visitors. But Elizabeth thought it very grand, with the gilt-framed mirror hanging over the marble mantel above the fireplace, and the heavy gold drapes with elaborate grey tassels over the widows. But what she liked most was the rosewood cabinet with glass doors that stood in one corner. It was filled with souvenirs of their travels. Charlotte called it the "whatnot", and its treasures included ornamental elephants carved of ivory, a small rock with a thin streak of gold that her father had found on the Californian gold fields, and some exquisite pieces of heirloom china that had belonged to Grandmother Fairburn's mother. Charlotte always said that it was a miracle the china hadn't been smashed to pieces during their travels. She also said that one day, when they returned to England, Elizabeth would see what a really grand room looked like, because Grandmother Fairburn lived in a mansion.

Elizabeth turned back to her mother, who was still reading the letter. Actually, Charlotte was perusing it for a second time—to ensure she had read it correctly. She felt a hollow shock, yet at the same time was not really surprised he wasn't returning yet.

December 20th, 1867

Dearest Charlotte,

I am sorry I have not written for so many months, but there has been that family business to attend to: successfully, I might add, but with no thanks to Theo or Albert. I also made a short trip to Paris, to see the wonderful Exhibition, which you may have seen reports of in the Melbourne Argus.

While in Paris, my dear, I saw an exhibit that greatly intrigued me. It was the Siamese section, and it included the most unusual artefacts, rich silk materials, and most interesting of all, a set of photographs of the Siamese king.

The next news I have for you, dearest, will come as something of a surprise, perhaps even as a shock. You know, Charlotte, how serious I am about my photography, and you know well how I love a new adventure. On my return journey, I have decided to make a detour to Siam, and I hope to take similar photographs to those I saw in Paris for a future exhibition of my own.

I shall first sail to Singapore, from whence Siam is apparently a pleasant six days' journey by steamer. By the time you read this, my dear, I shall probably be in Siam, or close to it, so please do not worry.

I shall write again soon, but I am not certain about the efficiency— or even the existence—of mail services from Siam, so do not be surprised if it is myself in person who arrives home before my next letter. Give my love to Elizabeth.

It was signed simply "Edward", with no endearment.

She sank against the chesterfield with a sigh, and closed her eyes.

"Mummy, what's wrong? Father is all right, isn't he? Is he coming back soon?"

She sat up again and forced a smile. "Yes, darling, of course. Your father will be back as soon as he can. He has a little more business to attend to, that's all."

"Something else in England?"

"No, not in England, Elizabeth."

"Then where? What do you mean, Mummy? Did he go back to California?"

She glanced back at the letter. "No, dear. To a place called Siam, he says."

"Si-am?" Elizabeth grappled with the unfamiliar word. "But where's that? Is it in Europe or America?"

"Neither, darling."

"Then where? Why don't you tell me, Mummy?"

Charlotte looked across at her daughter's imploring eyes and sighed again. "I have to admit, I've no idea. Let's go and look at the globe in your father's study, shall we?"

❖ *Chapter 2* ❖

"*Farang! Farang! Farang!*" Everywhere he went in Bangkok, he was followed by the excitedly-whispered Siamese word used to describe white foreigners. And there were giggles from men, women, and children alike.

Westerners, especially those with fair hair and green or blue eyes, were ugly curiosities to the Siamese. These bizarre creatures with their long noses, huge ungainly bodies, and insipid colouring were unhygienic too. Sweat ran in streams down their red faces, and damp patches appeared through the clothing on their backs and under their arms. It was no surprise, for they insisted on wearing their ridiculous, heavy costumes that covered them from head to foot at all times of the day.

Neither did the *farangs* make any attempt to see that their teeth were blackened with betel-nut juice. No self-respecting Siamese—or Thai, as they referred to themselves—would allow his or her teeth to remain white. Some, particularly the wealthier women, used a black pigment to colour any spots that were not perfectly darkened, for—as the old Siamese saying went—"any dog can have white teeth".

Clearly, these *farangs* cared little for their appearance. Nevertheless, a passing European made for an interesting diversion, if not a source of humour and conversation for days to come.

Edward found Bangkok and the Siamese people equally fascinating. He had never seen or imagined a city quite like it. Aside from the fact that Bangkok was traversed by a network of canals rather than roads, its most intriguing feature, to him, was its markets. He was particularly captivated by the great bazaar at the city's southern end. There were hundreds of stalls, as well as ponds full of fish, sharks, and eels which were sold live or killed on the spot so the buyers could be assured they were fresh. There were strange fruits he had never seen or heard of before: the red spiky rambutan, the smooth-skinned green or yellow mango, the huge jackfruit, and the foul-smelling but highly-prized durian.

He was forced to hold his breath as he passed the displays of dried fish and squid, and there were piles of pork, chicken, and beef which were all left open to the stifling air and covered in grotesque flies that fed on, and laid eggs in the flesh. No one paid them any mind, and the meat was simply brushed off before being sold or made into curry that was cooked with coconut milk and the fiery little chilli peppers that were sold everywhere. Spicy pastes were added to the curries, and a strong sauce called *nam plaa*—made from the juices of putrefying fish—was sprinkled over other types of food. And of course, there was rice, several varieties, available by the sack-load, or in whatever quantity the buyer required.

There was little or nothing familiar to the Western senses of sight, smell, or taste. He was willing to try the food, but wanted to discover the exact ingredients before he bought anything from the vendors, who cooked their dishes in clay pots over hot coals. But his simply-worded questions were met only with open-mouthed stares or giggles of embarrassment. How he expected them to understand him was something only he could know, and they became even more incredulous as he began to gesticulate when his words failed. They had heard that the Lord of Life, King Maha Mongkut, could converse fluently with the *farangs*, who were now coming to Siam in their hundreds. But they were not certain they could believe the rumours. Why would the Lord of Life want to know the language of such beasts?

Sometimes he felt discouraged and lonely, and would sit in the saloon of Falcks's hotel, where he had taken a dingy room, wondering if he had made the right decision. He needed an assistant for his photographic work, and he had hoped, on his arrival, to employ a local boy who could understand English well enough to follow instructions and not get the developing chemicals mixed up. He now realised, after his experiences in the markets, that it would be impossible to find a suitable employee by himself. He resolved to ask at the British Consulate when he went there to introduce himself to Mr. Knox, the consul.

Two days later, he sat with Mr. Knox on the verandah of the consulate. Situated on the banks of the river between the Portuguese and French legations—but some distance from the American—the consulate was a large two-storey building raised from the ground and surrounded by narrow verandahs with intricately-carved Victorian latticework on both levels. The grounds and the sweeping paths that were bordered attractively with small rocks, were beautifully kept by several Siamese gardeners.

A light wind, cooled by the river, brought slight relief from the heat, and sweet-scented, flowered trees swayed in the breeze. Strange birds flitted amid them—squabbling, pecking at grubs, and catching insects—and Edward saw a large long-tailed lizard dash across the lawns.

A servant soon brought out a tray, and placed it on the cast-iron table in front of Mr. Knox.

"And you say your ambition is to photograph the king, Mr. Fairburn?"

The consul handed Edward a gin and tonic.

"Indeed, Mr. Knox. And as many of his subjects as will sit for me."

"Do you have some examples of your work? I'd be most interested to see more of this . . . er . . . 'art form' I'm tempted to call it. But I'm sure it'll never take the place of a good illustration, eh? Fascinating innovation, though. I understand the technological advances are astonishing."

"They are indeed," Edward confirmed, reaching for his leather portfolio which contained some of his recent work, and handing a selection of large prints to Mr. Knox.

The consul took the photographs and turned them over one by one.

"I took these shortly before I left England, in some of the new factories in Yorkshire. This set is called 'The New Age', and I hope they'll eventually be part of an exhibition."

Mr. Knox was perhaps more impressed by the obvious advancements in industry they revealed at home than by the pictures themselves, but he nevertheless pronounced Edward a proficient photographer. "Is your family involved in the factories?" he asked.

"No, my father is Sir Theodore Fairburn, the banker. But one of his friends in the textile mills gave permission for me to take these pictures."

Mr. Knox nodded, and then seemed to retreat into thought for a moment. "Are you really set upon photographing His Majesty, Mr. Fairburn?"

Edward suddenly felt doubtful at the consul's tone. "Why, yes. If it's at all possible, sir."

"Oh, I should think permission can be obtained. The king's actually quite taken with the idea of being photographed. He *has* sat for several portraits already. And there are so few photographers in this part of the world, so I think your chances are good. However. . . ," he said slowly, and paused, as if wondering exactly how to phrase his next comment.

"Yes, Mr. Knox?"

"Well . . . are you married, Mr. Fairburn?"

"Why, yes. My wife and daughter are in Melbourne, Australia. And awaiting my return, I might add."

"Ah, I see. Well . . . in that case, I'm afraid they may have a long wait. That is, if you wish to realise your photographic ambition. . . ."

The consul took another sip of his gin, and then leaned across the table, as if to share a confidence with Edward. "You see, things do *not* happen quickly in Siam. In fact, I may honestly say that they move at a snail's pace. The king has many pressing business and social matters to attend to—not to mention the demands of a huge household of wives and children. He may agree to be photographed this month, but then again, you may have to wait six months. One never can tell here."

"Six months!" Edward exclaimed. "I hadn't imagined that."

"Well, we shall see." Mr. Knox signalled to the servant to refill their glasses. "And by the way, a word of advice. You shouldn't expect *ordinary* Siamese to be thrilled at the prospect of being photographed. They believe such images steal a part of their soul from them. Nonsense, of course, but they're a superstitious lot, and it doesn't do to offend them."

Edward's eyes widened in surprise. He hadn't expected this to be nearly as complicated. "Indeed!" was his only comment.

"Where are you staying at the moment, Mr. Fairburn?"

"At Falcks's Bowling Alley and Billiard Hall. Not the most salubrious of lodgings, I'm afraid."

"Nor the most wholesome of company, I'll warrant. And not the sort of accommodation you've been used to, I dare say."

"Well, I'm only too pleased my dear mother doesn't know of my cockroach-infested room."

"Why don't you rent a house? I know of a vacant property close to here that would be quite suitable. Who knows, you might decide to stay."

"Yes, I'll certainly consider it," Edward replied uncertainly. "Meanwhile, Mr. Knox, I'd be much obliged if you could mention me to the king's officers. Perhaps an introduction may be forthcoming. . . ."

"Well, you won't get an audience, of course," the consul was quick to inform him. "But I'll see what I can do about getting you invited to any parties or receptions the king is holding for foreigners. In fact, if you're still here in August, you may be able to join an expedition to the South. His Majesty's an accomplished astronomer by all accounts, and has apparently calculated the exact time that a total eclipse of the sun will occur on the eighteenth of that month."

Edward nodded enthusiastically. "That sounds very interesting indeed, Mr. Knox. I'd be most grateful."

"I'll keep an eye out for a suitable assistant, too. You'll probably have to teach him English yourself. But don't worry, they're fast learners."

They talked more of the country and the other foreign residents, and Edward eventually took his leave, with thanks to the consul for his promised assistance. He went down to the riverside and was quickly able to hire a small boat for the short distance along the Chao Phya to the pier nearest his lodging. Fortunately, Falcks's hotel was located near a well-known temple, so he needed only to give its name—Wat Kaeo Faa—and the boatman knew where to stop.

As they slid through the greasy brown water, he gazed at the scene all around him, shaking his head in amazement at the variety of crafts and dwellings on the river. There were small, flat-bottomed vessels piled high with all manner of produce, mostly piloted by women or children, who rowed from house to house selling their wares. There were large, squat barges loaded with rice that sat low in the water waiting to be disgorged. Similar vessels that had already been emptied of their cargoes began making the return journey upriver, with their crews—the families who lived on board—lolling about the decks. And there were thousands of floating houses and shops. Most were made of bamboo, with pointed, thatched roofs, but there were some of polished teak constructed in the same style. They were all open to the river, and the residents seemed unconcerned about their complete lack of privacy.

Each houseboat was decorated with stylised *jovia* carvings that rose into the air at each corner of the roof like curved, raised, and pointed elephant trunks. Each one also accommodated a spirit house, a richly-decorated miniature Siamese home in which the spirits of the site were said to reside. The Siamese believed that whenever they felled a tree to construct a house, the spirits who dwelled there must not be made homeless. Thus, they were provided with their own home—which was always placed prominently on a pedestal at the front of the main house, or in a position where its shadows would never fall upon it. Offerings of food and drink were regularly placed on the spirit house, and if the main house was improved, so was the spirit house—for if the spirits saw that the human residents lived more comfortably than they did, they would take up residence in the main house, which could have dire consequences indeed for the inhabitants. The beauty of the floating houses was that they were moored in such a way that if a family wanted to move elsewhere, they simply unhitched their home and floated away.

Almost everywhere along the river, temples and *chedis*—the circular spires that marked the burial site of a monk or prominent person—rose from the verdant banks, and from amid the ramshackle wooden and bamboo houses. The *chedis* resembled glittering needles of gold rising into the sky, and the pointed temple roofs were decorated with green and orange tiles that shimmered like a snake's scales in the afternoon sun.

The most stunning of the riverside temples was Wat Arun, a 260-foot-tall, pagoda-like structure which was entirely embellished with a mosaic of broken Chinese porcelain shards. Further upriver were the spires and *chedis* of the Grand Palace itself, where the king lived in sumptuous surroundings of gold, jewels, and other treasures reputed to be more splendid than any Western ruler had ever known.

Edward looked down at the river. It was decidedly murky, with all manner of discarded objects floating on its oily surface—household refuse was simply tipped directly into the water—although he saw plenty of fish jumping, too. He had already heard that the king had issued an edict against "the inelegant practice of throwing dead animals into the waterways"—but if the number of dog carcasses floating in the river was any indicator, he concluded that even the Lord of Life's commands were not always heeded.

Bangkok was mesmerising, and he planned to begin his work as soon as a suitable assistant could be found to help him carry the more than one hundred pounds' weight of equipment necessary to take photographs in the field. And that would not be an easy task.

Several days later, he received an invitation to a party at the British Consulate—and he eagerly awaited the introduction to Bangkok's expatriate society that he had been hoping for.

$\diamond$ *Chapter 3* $\diamond$

As he walked up the steps from the pier to Mr. Knox's large brick house on the night of the party, he could hear the buzz of conversation and the tinkle of glasses. Several groups of people had gathered on the verandahs and were talking animatedly, or simply gazing through the flowering trees toward the river.

The scene that greeted him in the large ballroom was a welcome one indeed. Despite the heat, which had hardly dissipated in the night air, everyone present had dressed in the correct formal attire for the occasion—as Edward himself had done. The ladies added sparkling flashes of colour to the room, with sweeping silk dresses in delicate pastel hues of pink, mauve, buttercup, and light brown. Many of the gowns were fashionably low-necked or off-the-shoulder, with tiny puff sleeves. The men were more uniformly dressed, of course—most wearing white waistcoats, frilled shirt-fronts, black knee-length evening coats, and tight-fitting black trousers.

Even after sunset, the temperature was at least eighty-five degrees, but no gentleman could be seen to take off his coat and appear in his shirt-sleeves. It would almost have been tantamount to parading about in one's underwear. They never mentioned the heat, but from time to time the gentlemen used silk kerchiefs to mop their brows, while the ladies dabbed at their cheeks with lace-edged handkerchiefs, or used delicate fans to cool their faces. Several servants were charged with the laborious task of operating *punkah* fans, and many of the guests moved closer to the slight breeze they afforded. For the first time since he had arrived in the Far East, Edward felt entirely at ease.

Siamese serving girls carrying trays of drinks and *hors d'oeuvres* were present in great numbers. They wore traditional silk *panungs*, but so as not to offend the foreigners, they also wore European-style blouses. Siamese women usually wore only a wide sash draped across their chest, which did not necessarily cover the breasts—nor was it intended to do so. It was incomprehensible to them why these European women covered themselves completely at all times—even to the extent of wearing heavy gowns to bed that concealed their bodies from neck to foot. Was it any wonder that so many of their husbands looked elsewhere for pleasure?

Although she was Siamese herself, Mrs. Knox always ensured that her foreign guests were catered for with familiar food, and the consulate's supplies were continually replenished by ships arriving from Europe and Singapore. Edward had already heard that the consul had met his wife when she was a lady-in-waiting for his late friend, the *wang na*—or 'second king'—Pin Klao. They had married in 1854 and had two daughters.

Knox had fought with the British Indian army in the China Wars, and had arrived in Siam in 1851, at the request of Pin Klao, to help train its soldiers. He first joined the British Consulate shortly after it was established in 1857 as an interpreter—and had done well enough to be promoted to head of the legation as consul-general. It was whispered that, although he had friends in high places in both Siam and England, he was a trouble-maker, and many of the Siamese did not like him.

Mr. Knox and his wife saw that Edward was offered a drink, and then introduced him to a group they thought would interest him before they moved off to circulate among their other guests.

Among the clique was long-term resident John Chandler, who—twenty years previously—became the first person to journey up the Chao Phya by steamboat. He was the United States consul from 1859 until 1865, then became the official interpreter for the Siamese Harbour Department. He also established an English-language school, and tutored Crown Prince Chulalongkorn at the palace. After twenty-five years in Siam, he was due that year to retire to the United States, with a generous cash award from the king.

Also in the group was Captain John Bush, who had come to Siam in 1857 and was now harbour master and managing director of the Bangkok Dock Company. He was an old sailor with countless tales to tell of the seas he had traversed and the ships he had sailed.

There was also Joseph Shaw, a young Presbyterian missionary, who held a glass of tonic water and looked conspicuously uncomfortable at the turn the conversation was taking.

"Damned good idea, this pink ticket thing the wives have taken to, if you ask me," Captain Bush remarked. "Then no one has to fool anyone, do they?"

Edward noticed Mr. Shaw's face redden, and he wondered what the captain meant.

"I can see your point, but I don't know if such an arrangement should be condoned," Mr. Chandler added. "What about you, Mr. Fairburn? What do you think about the pink tickets?"

"I . . . I'm afraid I haven't the faintest idea what you're referring to, Mr. Chandler. But perhaps you might enlighten me."

Captain Bush laughed and broke in to explain. "Well, it's not exactly the sort of thing one can elaborate on too much in mixed company." He lowered his voice and leaned closer to Edward. "It's simply an agreement the foreign wives have with their husbands."

Edward was intrigued, but still a little baffled. He glanced at both Mr. Chandler and Mr. Shaw, who now appeared even more uncomfortable.

"Sort of turn a blind eye," Captain Bush continued quietly, "to any extra goings-on, if you understand what I mean." His voice then became almost a whisper. "They think it's better to agree to their husband taking a . . . second wife, shall we say, when he's away from home—or even a number of . . . ah . . . consorts."

Edward couldn't believe his ears. He glanced quickly around the room at the elegant women dressed in silks and adorned with pearls. "You mean to say that some of these ladies openly approve of their husbands committing adultery?"

"Well, I wouldn't say 'openly approve' exactly," Mr. Chandler rejoined. "More, 'discreetly agree to'—because it would happen anyway."

"That's quite extraordinary," Edward commented, shaking his head.

Mr. Chandler noticed Mr. Shaw's embarrassment. "Indeed, Mr. Fairburn. But then, I don't suppose we should be talking about such things in front of the reverend here."

"Oh, I don't have the honour of being addressed as 'reverend'," Mr. Shaw responded quickly, glad to change the subject. "I'm merely a teacher with a calling."

"And still a bachelor, too," Mr. Chandler added for the benefit of Edward. "No lucky young lady soon to become Mrs. Shaw?"

"No, I'm afraid not. There's very little opportunity here to meet suitable young ladies."

"Why don't you marry a Siamese woman, like I did?" Captain Bush suggested heartily. "They make the best wives in the world."

Mr. Shaw looked uncomfortable again. "Well, I'm . . . I'm not against marrying a Siamese woman. But she would have to be Christian, of course."

"Now that's making things very difficult for yourself," the captain said. "You missionaries aren't having much success, are you?"

"Well, we pray, and we continue our work. That's the best we can do."

"Escu' me, sir." A soft Siamese voice beside Edward spoke.

He looked around to find a serving girl offering a tray of *hors d'oeuvres*. To his relief, all the food was English—or as close to it as possible. As he took a scotch egg from the tray and accepted a serviette from the girl, he could not help noticing how attractive she was. Her deep brown—almost black—almond-shaped eyes tilted at the corners, and as soon as their eyes made contact, she immediately looked down, aware of his scrutiny. She did not giggle shyly as so many of the others did, but turned and walked gracefully and soundlessly away. The Siamese almost always went barefoot—

with the exception of the noblemen, who wore pointed slippers—and one rarely heard them coming or going.

The conversation resumed, picking up where it had left off, about the missionaries' work among the Siamese—but Edward could no longer concentrate. He suddenly asked himself why he had not seen before how beautiful the Siamese women were. Had he been blind? At first he had considered them uncultured, with their blackened teeth, bare feet, and strange, tufted top-knots.

But this young girl's sultry beauty had instantly captivated him. He began to look—as discreetly as he could—at the other girls around the room, now very much aware of their satiny skin, their petite bodies, their delicate faces, their lack of pretension, and—most of all—their beguiling eyes. He wondered if she worked at the consulate, and he wanted to know her name. It would, of course, have been quite impossible for him to ask.

In the kitchen, Kesri prepared another tray of food for the guests. There were no *punkah* fans, little ventilation, and it was stifling. She loathed serving these ungrateful *farangs*, despite the fact that her friends considered her fortunate to work at the consul's house whenever there was a party. She saw the foreigners at close quarters, they reasoned, was well reimbursed for her services, and wore a beautiful uniform—although they weren't impressed by the restrictive, *farang* chest covering she had to wear. But still she saw no dignity in it. And even though she was a paid servant now—and no longer a possession—it wasn't enough for her. When she returned to the ballroom, she circled with the tray of food close to the group he was with.

By the end of the evening, Edward had received invitations to dine at several homes, and had made some useful contacts for photographic commissions. He had also spoken to a number of the ladies present. Although greatly intrigued at the revelations made earlier in the evening, he made no reference, of course, to the alleged "pink tickets". He was, however, quite surprised at the women's adjustment to the conditions in Siam. Despite the heat, the swarms of mosquitoes, and the unavailability of many things taken for granted at home as part of civilised living, they seemed, generally, to be happy in Siam.

But as he thought more of this, he realised that it was not so surprising. Even those women who could not have been considered much above working class at home in England or America, were here attended by legions of servants. They rarely lifted a finger in the home, and spent their days socialising, or playing croquet and bridge. It was a life far above their true stations, and it applied equally to their husbands.

When Edward finally took his leave, it was well after midnight, and he wandered down to the small pier, where several other guests were waiting for boats.

"Would you like to come with us?" Captain Bush called. "You're staying at Falcks's, aren't you? It's only a little further up than us. My boatman won't mind." He indicated a handsome longboat with a Siamese oarsman that had drawn up beside the landing.

"Thank you, Captain Bush. Much obliged."

As he spoke, the slight, shadowy figure of a Siamese woman glided silently past him toward the pier. When she neared the steps, she looked back, and he recognised her immediately, even in the lantern light. It was the serving girl who had caught his eye all evening. She was wearing the same *panung*, only now she had taken off the European blouse and replaced it with a brightly-coloured sash that was loosely draped across her shoulders. He saw her breasts silhouetted against the light reflected in the water. An instant later, she turned and ran down the steps to her own tiny *sampan*, which was moored under the landing. She slipped into the little boat, paddled away, and disappeared into the night.

It was pitch black when he let himself into his room, and he stumbled about—drunk on the alcohol and the heat—until he found the desk on which stood a small kerosene lamp. He took off the glass cover, fumbled to light a match, and then found the wick, which quickly caught the flame. As he was replacing the glass and adjusting the dial, he became aware that he wasn't alone. Slowly, he turned to face the intruder—and was brought fully to his senses when he saw who it was.

She sat on the floor with her eyes cast down and her hands held together in a prayer-like position in front of her chest.

"*Sawatdee ka*," she greeted him softly, slowly raising her eyes to meet his.

◈ Chapter 4 ◈

February 28th, 1868

Dear Charlotte,

I hope this letter finds yourself and Elizabeth in good health. It will be winter by the time you receive it, and I know how much you feel the cold. But at least it does not snow in Melbourne, as it does in England.

As you will realise, I am still in Siam, and I must tell you that I have found it to be the most remarkable place. My work is progressing well and I have, in fact, set up a small studio here in the house I have rented thanks to the good offices of the British consul, Mr. Knox.

It is likely that I will be permitted to photograph the king himself, but I must await a royal summons, of course. Mr. Knox believes there may be an opportunity in August. His Majesty is a keen astronomer, and has apparently calculated the exact time and position of a solar eclipse which will take place during that month. A magnificent celebration of the occasion has been arranged on the coast in the Southern part of the kingdom where the eclipse will take place, and many of the foreign residents here, including myself as official photographer, have been invited to join the expedition. I believe it is 140 miles from Bangkok, and will take several days by sea.

My dear, this is a wonderful and exotic land, and to be perfectly candid, I believe I should like to stay for some time. I quite realise that my change of plans may greatly disturb you, but let me reassure you that I have the welfare of yourself and Elizabeth in mind, and I urge you to consider what I have to propose next.

Charlotte, we have not been without our difficulties throughout our marriage, and I fully understand your position. That is why I am suggesting that you perhaps would rather not join me in Siam. The climate and conditions are not well suited to English ladies, and many of those who bravely come here find it a trial. After a short time, they return home, frail and exhausted. If, however, you are set on joining me, I shall do my utmost to make your life here comfortable. You should have as many servants as you desire, and Elizabeth would be well cared for.

If you decide to come, please close up the house in Melbourne and terminate our lease. You may also arrange for our furniture and effects to be shipped here as well. Should you decide not to come, perhaps you would prefer still to leave Melbourne and return with Elizabeth to my parents in Yorkshire. You know well they would welcome the two of you, and that you would want for nothing there.

Let me know your decision, Charlotte, by the next ship. Please give Elizabeth a hug and kiss for me.

Edward

Elizabeth, who had become sombre and silent lately, wondering why her father didn't return, was almost too afraid to ask her mother what he said in the letter. She recognised the expression on Charlotte's face. "He's not coming, is he, Mummy?"

"No, precious," Charlotte replied, as cheerfully as she could. "He has a lot of work to do, and he's going to photograph the king of Siam. What do you think of that?"

"I think the king wouldn't miss a photograph as much as I miss Father. Doesn't he love me any more?"

Sometimes she spoke so maturely, Charlotte thought—and supposed it was the result of her being an only child and spending most of her time with adults.

"Of course he does, poppet. He loves you very much and tells me to give you a kiss from him."

She stroked Elizabeth's soft cheek, then made her decision. "In fact, he has asked us to go to Siam to live with him."

Elizabeth's eyes brightened and she jumped off the chesterfield. "Oh, Mummy, that means we'll all be together. And we'll never have to be apart from Father again, will we?"

"No, dear, never again," Charlotte mumbled to herself.

Elizabeth skipped off to play with her dolls' house, leaving Charlotte alone with her thoughts. She read the letter once more, this time to ensure that she had read correctly. She could only suppose that he was doing the gentlemanly thing; providing her with an escape from the marriage if she so desired it. Divorce was out of the question, but if she wanted to live apart from him permanently—and he from her—he seemed to be suggesting that this would be a way to accommodate that without bringing shame on their families.

But, despite their problems, she did not want that. She still loved him, and she believed Elizabeth should be brought up with two parents.

What was he thinking? She was doubtful, but knew only one thing for sure. If she wanted her marriage to survive, she must go to Siam—even though he had given her almost no information about the country in his letter. Had he been so convinced she would not want to come?

She decided to make an appointment to see Dr. Vickers.

Kesri hadn't worked for more than a month, and as she lay beside him with the morning light filtering through the bedroom shutters, she felt certain that her life was changing for the better. But still, she thought bitterly of the circumstances that had brought her there; of her father, swindled of what little money he had, compelled to sell himself and her mother into slavery to repay their debts.

Somtop had been a kindly tradesman who made spirit houses—until an unscrupulous Chinese merchant persuaded him to form a partnership, then absconded with the money from a year's worth of orders before the materials had even been paid for. In order to make good the loss—and to avoid a long jail sentence—Somtop sold himself and his wife, Ning, into slavery. Kesri, born into servitude, was their only surviving child, her three brothers all having died of cholera.

Her parents eventually died without having regained their liberty, but Kesri had always been determined to secure hers—by whatever means necessary.

And she had done so.

Not surprisingly, she dreamed of wealth, of marrying, and of owning her own servants. But without family, and because of her past, she had little hope of becoming *any* Siamese man's first wife, never mind the first wife of a man of wealth and status. And she knew also that to be a concubine—or minor wife—would be little improvement on the life she already knew as a servant.

But Kesri was possessed of a determined spirit, and she saw a way to fulfil her dreams by ensuring that one of these *farang* men fell in love with her. She knew that their strange religion permitted them only one wife, and she knew they were attracted to Siamese women. Many, of course, had mistresses, but that was of little consequence to her. The number of wives or consorts her husband kept meant nothing. Only that she be the first.

At first, she had found them extremely unattractive; repulsive even. The way they smelled was often enough to leave her feeling nauseated. The Siamese bathed several times a day, but these *farangs* sometimes refused to wash for days on end, despite the fact that they suffered dreadfully in the heat. But as she served at more consular parties, she began to see that not all the *farangs* were ugly. She was even able to tell them apart now, whereas at first, she considered them all alike. And the smell was something she thought she could learn to tolerate.

For a long time, however, she had not been able to attract any of them, despite her best efforts. None had given her a second glance. She was merely a servant; an invisible utility.

But that was until the night of the consul's party, when this new *farang*—this green-eyed, fair-haired man she had never seen before—had become entranced with her. Those green eyes, so bizarre to her still, had pursued her all evening—sneaking glances as she passed near to his group; watching her, she knew, from a distance; and gazing at her shoulders and hair as she served with her back turned to him. She dared not return his looks, but she felt them upon her at every turn. It was an opportunity that might not repeat itself, and she did not let it slip by.

It was more than a month now, and he had still said nothing about their future together. But she could wait.

"We haven't seen you for quite some time, Mrs. Fairburn," Dr. Vickers said brightly when she was shown into his Collins Street rooms a few days after she received Edward's letter.

"No, Doctor, I'm pleased to say."

"How have you been?"

"Well, Edward has been away all this time, since just after I saw you last. So, naturally, there's been no trouble with the old problem."

"And now?"

"Well, he wants me to join him in . . . in the Far East, of all places. I've come to ask you what sort of medical supplies I should take with me."

She said it as if she were resigned to carry out a recurring chore.

"The Far East, you say. Singapore?"

"No, Doctor. Siam."

His eyes widened. "Well, Mrs. Fairburn, you understand there are many health risks in such a backward place. I really would *not* recommend . . ."

"No, Doctor, I don't know anything about the health risks," she interrupted him—rather rudely, she realised—but she could not prevent herself. "And no matter what, I have to go." She felt close to tears.

He spoke kindly. "My dear, I understand you have no choice—and you won't be the first European woman to find herself in such a place. But I must stress, once more, the advice I gave you after the last time. You simply must not become pregnant again. It's dangerous enough for you to do so here, where medical practices are advanced, and where we have modern equipment. But to do so there . . . well, I cannot answer for your safety. Not only the baby's life, but your own life would be in terrible danger in the likely event that things went wrong again."

"I understand, Doctor. But it's . . . it's difficult."

The nausea she felt on the last occasion he warned her not to become pregnant again, returned now. There was much more she wanted to discuss with him, but she could not permit herself to talk of such private matters, even to her own doctor.

"Have you discussed this problem with your husband?" he asked.

"Of course. He says he understands. But it has. . . ."

She wanted to say that it had destroyed their marriage; that the fact she could not sleep with her own husband without always the fear of becoming pregnant again had ruined their relationship. Instead, she said only, "It has created some tension."

He didn't push her. "Well, as to Siam itself, all I can recommend is that you take quinine regularly, and use nets around your bed to prevent mosquito bites. They're much more than an irritation—they can so quickly turn septic in such a climate, and even poison the entire body. And I'd advise a tot of whisky each day to ward off cholera. It's much more prevalent there, of course, than in London—and London's bad enough, heaven knows. There is, of course, a vaccine for smallpox, which . . . yes, you and Elizabeth have already received, I see from your records."

He went on to explain other diseases they might be exposed to, including leprosy, dysentery, and consumption. Bubonic plague was rife in Singapore, and was thus only a matter of time before it reached Siam—if it hadn't already. The list was frightening, and he could do little more than explain the horrible symptoms of each. "I'm sorry to be so explicit but . . . are you still intent on going, Mrs. Fairburn?"

"Doctor, I have no choice."

But she did. Had he not said that she could return home to England if she so desired?

Home. Edward. Her thoughts wandered.

It seemed so long ago that she had fallen in love, married when she was seventeen, and set out with him for what she believed would be continual adventure—and continual happiness. She had been too young and naïve; too much in love to imagine that anything could go wrong for them. And she had thought nothing of the difficulties and discomfort of travel.

For a man, it was adventure. For a woman accompanying her husband overseas, it was something quite different. Most were pregnant within a few months of marriage, and then the weeks of morning sickness were spent rolling around in a cramped, airless cabin aboard a ship. A miscarriage at sea was far worse, and some women bled to death or died of hideous infections without adequate medical attention. But it was a risk she had taken often when she was younger. She was older now, and was prepared—determined even—to go through it again. If not for him, then at least for Elizabeth.

Dr. Vickers urged her to make her stay in Siam as short as possible, and then made out a prescription—which would be ready within the week—of quinine and other medical supplies to last six months. She thanked him and left the surgery feeling worse than she had since receiving Edward's last letter.

A week later, she terminated the lease on their house with some regret. They had lived in the two-storey, double-fronted residence throughout their time in Melbourne, and Elizabeth had been born there. She had come to think of it as her own home, forgetting that it was rented. She realised now that they had never owned their own property because Edward could never settle; because he was always lured away by the prospect of adventure.

Elizabeth too, seemed to have inherited her father's wanderlust. She had never lived anywhere else, but she didn't seem in the least upset to leave the house, even on the day they departed. And her eager, enthusiastic questions only served to further darken her mother's mood.

"What sort of house will we have in Siam? Will it be bigger than this one? Will Father be there to meet us?"

Charlotte prayed he would be, but she couldn't be certain. She wasn't even convinced they would be welcome.

"I sent the letter as soon as I knew what ship we'd be on," she told her. "We have to go to Singapore first, you remember. He won't know exactly what day we'll arrive, but I expect he'll ask someone to let him know as soon as the ship gets to Bangkok."

She walked round the empty house for the last time. Their furniture had been removed, the rugs had been rolled up, and all that remained were bare floorboards. The living room-cum-parlour looked cold and austere now; the kitchen had lost its friendly, welcoming air; and the dining room bore little resemblance to the inviting place where she and Edward had once held elegant dinner parties for eight.

She could not bring herself to go back up the stairs to the bedrooms: her own, which she had shared with him, and in which the joy of Elizabeth's birth had eased the sorrow of so many previous disappointments; and Elizabeth's, where her daughter had grown into an inquisitive and beautiful seven-year-old.

When she had lingered long enough, she briskly took Elizabeth by the hand and said, "Come, it's time to go."

April 21st, 1868

Dear Mother,

You must have been wondering what had become of us, it is so long since I have written to you. But I am afraid the truth is that I really have had so little news to tell you until now.

Elizabeth continues to grow, and is quite a young lady these days. However, you have probably seen a photograph if Edward visited you, as I asked him to do. He didn't mention it in his last letter, but then he did not mention very much at all. That is except for one rather unnerving prospect, which has caused me great distress, and brought upheaval to our lives once more.

He has gone to Asia, Mother, and writes to us from Bangkok, Siam, that he intends to settle there indefinitely. There is nothing for us to do but follow him, of course, as always. I must admit to you that I go with much trepidation.

We know little of the country, but I am sure that medical and other facilities leave much to be desired, so I shall have to pray there is no recurrence of my old trouble. I must also divulge to you, Mother, that Edward did give me a choice. In fact, he almost insisted in his letter that we return to his family in England. I am most reluctant to do that, naturally, but how I yearn for the rolling green hills, the heath of Yorkshire, and the shops of London. And your own dear company, of course.

I wonder what advice Father would offer if he were alive. He was always the epitome of good sense, was he not, Mother? I do so miss him still, as you must too.

I am enclosing the rather incomplete address Edward has given me in Bangkok. There is no house number, but the residence is on a thoroughfare called New Road. It sounds very ordinary, but I am sure it is not.

But I shall not burden you any longer with our sadness, and instead speak of lighter matters. I have heard that Mr. Singer's American sewing machine seems all the rage in the tailoring world. Nevertheless, I think nothing could replace your Mrs. Elder's tiny stitches. In any case, Mrs. Elder herself once told me that the sewing machine was a French invention, and so not to be trusted. I was also alarmed to see drawings on the ladies' page recently of the new fashion discarding the crinoline—with skirts trailing in the dust. It appears most unattractive. Has it truly caught on, Mother, or is it only a few radicals?

Do write back and let me know all the news, including that of the queen and her family. Does Her Majesty still lead a life of seclusion? Such a tragedy for her to have lost her husband in such circumstances. Such a shame though, too, for her to remove herself from public duty.

Siam, too, is a kingdom, and since Edward's letter, I have read a newspaper article about the Paris Exhibition—which highlighted the Siamese section and the magnificence of its display, and which drew Edward to the country in the first place. The Siamese king is, apparently, in favour of modernising his country, understands English, employs an English tutor for his children, and even corresponds with Queen Victoria.

Perhaps Siam will be more civilised than I imagine, although it is said also that he has scores of wives in a huge harem, and goodness knows how many children. I shall close now, Mother. The next letter you receive from me will be postmarked Siam, if they have such a thing there yet. I really have no idea.

Your loving daughter,

Charlotte

◈ *Chapter 5* ◈

Kesri stood outside in the hallway listening, and she could understand a good deal of the conversation. She did not know what "diligent" meant, but was certain it wasn't what she wanted to hear him describe her as. She had been right; he had called her his maid. And she was sure he had said that, given the opportunity, she might steal the jewellery. Her face burned and she felt hot tears brim in her eyes. She hurried down the hallway and back into the kitchen.

It was now more than four months she had been with him, and if she thought about it, she was little more than a servant to him anyway. She did his housework, cooked his meals, laundered his clothes—and shared his bed. Or rather, she had done until today. What would become of her now? And what would become of her unborn child? She hung her head in despair.

The only thing she could do was exactly as he wanted, and to wait. For instinct told her that she should remain as inconspicuous as possible. She knew he would not want his *farang* wife to know about her. Western women had peculiar attitudes about such things, and although she had spent eighteen months with the Protestant missionaries after she had gained her freedom, none of their ideas or beliefs had made any impression on her—or her compatriots for that matter.

But at least she had learned English from them, and it had helped her find work. It had helped her find Edward. But for how much longer would she have him? Or had she never had him at all? Or was the question, how much longer would he want her? Was she again just a slave and a plaything who conveniently filled the place of both servant and wife? Had she been fooling herself all along?

Charlotte too, had little reason to think well of Edward that day. It had been a long voyage, and as they had approached the tropics, she began to suffer even more in the heat and humidity. That morning, as the Chao Phya steamed along its namesake toward Bangkok, she had felt as if she were on another planet.

At mid-morning, they stopped at the village of Paknam, where vessels entering Siam had to gain customs clearance and surrender any guns on board. From there it was a three-hour cruise along the river to the city. A little further upriver, they passed some thirty or so decrepit royal gunboats, each one flying the striking, scarlet flag of Siam, emblazoned with its white elephant.

"Sad business, that," a British man, who had lived in Siam for five years, told them. "They belonged to the second king, Pin Klao, who ran the navy. When he died the year before last, they were left to go to ruin."

She gazed at the banks of the wide river, and was enchanted by the tropical foliage. The five other British passengers marvelled, too, at the scene unfolding before them, the discomfort of the journey quite forgotten in their wonder at seeing their destination for the first time.

"Look, Mummy, there are monkeys in the trees," Elizabeth squealed.

Charlotte looked up, and sure enough, Elizabeth was right. Chattering monkeys clambered and swung through the branches of the banana, coconut, and mango trees that clustered along the banks.

The wooden houses on stilts, open to the river, scrambled with the dense vegetation for available space. Children jumped naked from verandahs and rickety wooden piers into the murky water, their tanned skins glistening; women bathed serenely in *sarongs* or squatted as they washed clothes in the river; while youngsters sat on the wooden jetties, smoking, giggling, and teasing the skinny dogs that lay all around.

Boats of every description—small flat *sampans*, huge bulbous rice barges, dilapidated ferries, luxurious yachts, and modern cruisers—jammed the river, making the Chao Phya's progress slow, but allowing them time to take in the extraordinary vista. It was the "River of Kings"—life-blood of the entire kingdom. Brilliantly-coloured birds darted across the bow, and the people on the riverside waved to the strange *farangs*. The foreigners returned the greetings tentatively.

"Mummy, why is everyone so brown? Have they been sitting in the sun too long?"

Charlotte laughed. "No, dear. That's just the colour of their skin. You've seen Aborigines in Australia. And you saw the Chinese gold-diggers in Melbourne, remember? People have all different colours of skin, not only white."

"Aren't there any other people here like us?"

She smiled at her daughter again, appearing more confident than she felt. "Of course there are, darling. Not very many altogether, I'm sure, but quite a few near our new house. Anyway, perhaps you'll get to know some Siamese children."

The steamer rounded a bend in the river, and Charlotte caught her breath as the city of Bangkok came into view, a city that was as far-removed from—and as exotically different—as it was possible to be, from London, California, Melbourne, or even other Oriental cities.

Even as they had sailed upriver, she had hoped that the jungle might give way to something familiar, but there was little to reassure her. She realised with a jolt that she was very much out of her depth, and then wondered how long she would be forced to stay. Her gaze was drawn upward from the riverbanks to the elegant roofs and golden *chedis* of what seemed to be a city of temples.

The sky was a dull white-grey. It was the monsoon season, and although the rains would be heaviest in September and October, she could see already where the river had broken its bank in places, and sandbags were piled up here and there. Canals led off the river, and as the steamer chugged slowly past, she caught glimpses of ordinary life among the thousands of floating houses. In these tributaries, the activity was even more chaotic than on the river itself. People were everywhere—fishing, swimming, bathing, or washing clothes.

On the verandah of each house stood a huge decorated jar—sometimes two or three—used for collecting and storing rainwater. She would learn later that these were called *klong* jars. For at least seven months of the year—from October until April, or even longer—there was scant rainfall, and the populace had to rely on what they had collected in the *klong* jars during the monsoon season. By the time the hot season was at its peak in April, the water in the jars was slimy and foul-smelling. But at least it was cleaner than the river water, which by then was brackish, and a major contributing cause of cholera outbreaks. The very poor, however, were usually forced to drink straight from the river itself. That year, 1868, had been devastating, and thousands of bodies had piled up at Wat Saket—the temple where the dead were either cremated or butchered for vultures and dogs to scavenge.

But Charlotte knew none of this as they steamed along that early August day. She knew only that the sights that met her, although daunting, were also fascinating. She saw Siamese women wearing what Captain Orton called *panungs*. Many of the women were naked above the waist, although some draped a wide sash around their shoulders and torso that still allowed their breasts to hang free. She was taken aback at first, but then sighed with something approaching envy as she realised how much cooler they must be in the climate than she ever would. She hadn't even been brave enough to follow the latest English fashion and discard her crinoline, but she noticed one of the ladies on the steamer—who had just come from England—was without it. What relief it would bring to allow her skirts to trail on the ground, to be free of the steel cage that held out her dress.

A crowd had gathered at the riverside, and the Chao Phya weighed anchor midstream as the passengers prepared to disembark. Charlotte scanned the dock, searching for the face she had not seen in more than a year.

"Father will be there, won't he?" Elizabeth asked excitedly.

Charlotte continued to focus on the people by the quay and the riverside, but they were too distant to identify clearly. "He should be there," she answered uncertainly. "But we can't be sure he received my letter. It could have been held up at Singapore. It could even be aboard this ship, I suppose."

Rowboats transported them from the steamer to the wooden quay, and Captain Orton himself escorted Charlotte and Elizabeth. But her confidence diminished even further as she surveyed the scene more closely. There were hundreds of Siamese milling around, and only a handful of Europeans—there to meet the other foreign passengers. Edward was not among them.

"Your husband doesn't appear to be here, Ma'am," Captain Orton said sympathetically.

"I'm afraid he can't have received my letter. I don't even have his exact address. It's somewhere on a street called New Road. He didn't have a house number. The letter was sent through the British Consulate."

"Don't worry, Mrs. Fairburn. I've been to your husband's house a number of times. He's already well-known for his lawn parties. I know exactly where it is. And New Road is the only real street in Bangkok. The rest of the place is built along the canals. I'll send someone immediately to let him know you're here."

"Thank you, Captain Orton. But really, it's not necessary to send a messenger. If you could just arrange some transport for us, we're quite happy to go there ourselves directly."

"Very well, then. If you're quite sure. My victoria's already waiting." He indicated a small, two-seater, pony-drawn carriage with a driver perched up front. It waited some way off, where a narrow lane went up to the road. "Why don't you take that. I'll tell the driver where you want to go, and he can return for me later."

"Thank you, Captain Orton, that's so kind of you. And can you arrange for the luggage to be sent on?"

"Of course."

He walked with them up to the carriage, gave instructions in Siamese, and assisted them up to the seats. He watched them go, thinking how mistaken he had been about her husband. Fairburn had soon cast off his Victorian inhibitions—if not his woollen clothing—and had adjusted very well to life in Siam. Some might say too well. The captain wondered how Mrs. Fairburn would react when she discovered he had taken a Siamese mistress.

Elizabeth and Charlotte gazed out with apprehension as they rode through the narrow, muddy tracks. It was an unstable and uncomfortable ride, even when they came to what was, apparently, the main road—which was covered with puddles and pot-holes.

Charoen Krung, New Road, was constructed only a few years previously, in 1861, when the city's small European population had petitioned the king to have a road constructed so they could go about in their carriages. Until then, there had been no roads at all in Bangkok. Because the city was situated on a delta, and—as a result—flooded tiresomely for months during the monsoon, the risk of cholera was lessened if one lived on the river.

The Siamese didn't seem to mind the water at all, and were happy to simply wade through the floods whenever necessary. Charlotte had experienced terrible roads in Australia and California that turned to ankle-deep mud when it rained, so it didn't concern her unduly. But she certainly wasn't looking forward to several more months of rain. And she had never before seen such an array of refuse on city streets.

When she peered down the tracks that ran off New Road, she saw all manner of rubbish strewn amid the tangled, overgrown bamboo and broad-leaved plants. There was a ripe, putrid stench about the air, which emanated from the mounds of rotting vegetable matter. She noticed that there were no proper bridges anywhere to be seen, but there were plenty of simple, rickety-looking planks for pedestrians to cross the numerous canals. Best, she determined at once, to go everywhere one could by boat.

There were few shops as she knew them, but then again, she couldn't really discern what many of the ramshackle, dusty buildings were at all. As they progressed slowly, she was horrified to see a gang of forlorn-looking prisoners, all chained together, with heavy iron manacles and shackles on their necks, hands, and ankles. Elizabeth had fallen silent, and was merely staring open-mouthed at the strange scenes before them.

There were groups of Siamese here and there, squatting on the ground and either smoking or playing games to loud squeals of "*Euee!*" In unison, they stopped whatever they were doing and stared in utter astonishment at the European woman and her daughter. She felt hundreds of eyes follow the carriage. When they passed close to an elephant at the side of the road, she breathed in sharply, found Elizabeth's hand, and held it tightly. A giggling group of Siamese children fed bananas to the huge animal, while the mahout perched, grinning, on top of the beast's head.

But she had little more time to ponder the sights, for they soon drew up outside a two-storey house with a large expanse of lawn all round. Charlotte had noticed a few European-style houses on New Road, although none appeared to have any immediate neighbours. The driver pointed to the house and nodded, and almost before Charlotte and Elizabeth could remove themselves from the seat—no easy task unaided for a lady wearing a crinoline—he was off again. They were on their own.

It was a rather plain unremarkable house of dusky yellow stucco, of a modest size, with its pale green-grey window shutters all wide open, presumably to allow as much ventilation as possible. There appeared to be no glass panes in the windows at all, and as she looked up, Charlotte saw a small bird fly out of one of the windows on the second floor. It appeared well-kept enough, although the vegetation from an empty property next door was encroaching quickly on one side. It was really rather better than she had expected, especially given the accommodation of the locals. She would plant some flowers to make it more homely. She loved roses, but supposed they wouldn't grow well in the tropics. However, she had seen some beautiful flowers—orchids of every hue, apparently growing wild—among the trees on the riverbanks, and in the small tracks off New Road. She remembered seeing the same blooms—orange, purple, and pink—hanging from hooks on the houseboats and stilt-houses they had passed earlier. She wondered if there were many snakes, and then shuddered at the thought. She didn't mind insects or spiders—being well used to the plate-sized huntsmans in Melbourne—but snakes, she could not abide. It was best not to think of them.

"Is this our house?" Elizabeth asked.

"I hope so, darling." She took hold of Elizabeth's hand firmly, and walked with her up the front path. She was uneasy. A feeling of anxiety tingled in her stomach, and she wondered how she could possibly be nervous about meeting the man she had been married to for twenty years. It was some time since they had seen each other, it was true, and she wasn't sure how he would feel about seeing her here, but it was ridiculous nonetheless. She took a deep breath and knocked bravely, arranging her face into a smile of greeting.

A few moments later, the door swung open, and her smile faded as she spoke falteringly. "I'm sorry. I must have the wrong house. I was looking for Mr. Edward Fairburn."

The Siamese girl who opened the door smiled to conceal her own shock. So, *Mem* Charlotte had come after all. It was what she had dreaded, but had quietly accepted as an eventuality. She answered as calmly as she could. "Yes, this Mr. Edward house. Come in, please. Mr. Edward come soon."

Kesri showed them into the front room. Charlotte took off her bonnet and gloves and handed them to the girl, whom she assumed to be a servant. She also assumed she was fluent in English. "We should like some tea, please. And something light to eat."

"Yes, Madame." The girl smiled widely—revealing shiny, black teeth—then took the bonnet and gloves and silently left the room. When she got to the kitchen, she threw them on the floor. She had prayed they would not come, and now that they had, she had been treated like a slave. He would have to put this woman in her place. She considered herself his wife now. Had their union not been blessed by a monk? She didn't object to him having more than one wife—it was only right and proper that a man of consequence should have a number of wives—but to be relegated to the role of minor wife was simply a step back to her past. With Charlotte around, there was little hope of fulfilling her ambitions.

She went back with a pot of tea and a plate with the last of Edward's expensive English fruit cake, and knelt beside Elizabeth—lowering her head as a sign of respect—as she set out the refreshments on the low, Siamese-style table next to the sofa. "You tired, Madame? You sleep?"

"No, thank you," Charlotte replied coldly. "I'll wait for Mr. Fairburn."

She had hardly said this when footsteps were heard and all eyes flew to the window. He was walking up the path, his velvet jacket unbuttoned, whistling merrily. But from the outside, he couldn't see anyone in the dim interior.

Kesri immediately left the room, respectfully walking a few steps backwards before turning, and almost ran to answer the door before he knocked.

"Kesri." He kissed her lightly on the cheek. "You look as lovely as ever."

Charlotte, who could not see the entrance hall from the front room, thought this a most suspicious way to greet a servant.

Kesri didn't allow him to embrace her, as he normally might have done, but spoke formally and clearly for the benefit of the new arrivals. "Mr. Edward, Madame here."

He was puzzled at her tone and the way she had addressed him. "Madame? Madame who?"

"Madame Edward. Your Madame. And your. . . ."

His jaw dropped in astonishment. He had heard nothing from her since he had written of his intention to stay, and he had assumed she was on her way to England. He rushed to the front room and stood almost paralysed in the doorway, gaping at his own wife and child as if they were a mirage. Kesri closed the door but remained outside, listening to what was said.

Elizabeth ran to him and wrapped her arms around his legs. "Father, I've missed you so much. Promise you won't go away again."

Quickly attempting to come to his senses, he lifted her up and hugged her to him. "Dear little Elizabeth, of course I won't." He kissed her, then set her down in front of him. "Well, you're not so little after all. You've grown while I've been gone, haven't you?"

"I can read the newspaper, now, Father. Well . . . some of it, anyway."

He then looked again at Charlotte—still reeling from the shock, his thoughts in disarray—and didn't know whether to be pleased or sorry that she had come. But she had, and she was his wife. "Hello, Charlotte," he said gently.

"The letter must have gone missing," she replied nervously. He made a movement toward her, and in a second she was in his arms, feeling again the embrace she never realised she had missed so much.

"I didn't think you'd come."

"I didn't know whether you wanted me to."

"Darling, of course I did. You're my wife. And I could hardly bear to be away another day from my dear Elizabeth."

They sat on the sofa together, Elizabeth snuggled against her father's shoulder and his arm around her, as they all talked of the time that had passed—more than a year-and-a-half—since they had seen each other last. He told them about Siam, and what they could expect with the climate and living conditions. "I'll make your life here as easy as possible," he assured them. "You *will* find it difficult to adjust at first, but there's no need to worry unduly. Things will work themselves out."

"Who is the serving girl?" Charlotte interrupted lightly, almost as an inconsequence. Kesri's slim hips, dark eyes, and flawless complexion had not escaped her notice.

He felt himself blush as he detected her suspicion. "Er . . . that's Kesri, my maid. She's wonderful in the house, and she'll be a great help to you, my dear. And when you want to go out, she can look after Elizabeth."

"Really?" Charlotte said dismissively. "Is she trustworthy?"

"Absolutely, although I wouldn't leave jewellery lying round. You know what a temptation it can be for a girl like her."

"Yes. She does look awfully young, Edward."

"Well, yes, but she's very diligent, as you'll see."

The atmosphere in the room was still tense, and even outside, Kesri could sense it. It should have been a good sign for her that there was still some distance between Edward and Charlotte, but now as she stood in the hallway with her dream seemingly shattered, she could think only of the fate of her child. His child. The child he knew nothing of yet. He had said she was a maid, and probably a thief too. She ran back to the kitchen, the tears welling in her eyes.

Charlotte stood up. "Well, I think I shall go to our room and freshen up before I see the rest of the house. Can you have the girl bring me a basin of water?"

Edward also stood up, suddenly panicking. "Oh . . . yes . . . of course, dear. But . . . I'll just ask her to make sure our room is ready for you. . . ."

"What do you mean, Edward?"

He had to think quickly. "Well . . . I've been living as a bachelor for so long it seems, I'm afraid it's quite a mess. I often do my administrative work up there, so I'm sure there are papers and receipts and goodness knows what scattered everywhere."

"I see." She immediately sat down again, unconvinced. "Then I'll wait here until it's ready."

"Thank you, my dear, I won't be a moment."

He rushed out to the kitchen, where he found her sitting at a table.

"Kesri, my sweet, it's very important that Madame not know about you and me yet," he whispered to her, leaning close. "Please, move everything of yours out of my bedroom and into the back room." He pointed out to the servants' quarters. "It's only for a short time, until I tell her. Then you'll have a room of your own in the house." But he could sense what she was thinking.

She looked at him balefully—and knew he was lying. This straight-laced *farang* woman would never accept her husband's concubine, let alone allow her to live in the same house. She said nothing.

His next request was even more hurtful. "Kesri, could you clean the room? And Madame would like some water when you've finished tidying. And remember, please take everything of yours out to the back."

She simply made a gesture of acquiescence, and then stood up and left. When the time came, she would see to it that he gave her a house of her own. It would suit her better anyway. And then, slowly, she would entice him to spend more and more time with her, until he did not want to return home at all.

She did as he asked. Her few possessions were gifts from him; more than she had ever owned in her life, but still a meagre lot. She bundled them up in a sheet, and then hurried down the stairs and out the back of the house to the best of the maids' quarters. The tiny, dingy room had no windows or lamp, and contained only a worn dirty bed-roll, a scratched old desk with a few ill-fitting drawers that no longer closed properly, and an empty candle-holder. Next door was a trough for washing, and a lavatory set into the floor with a bowl of water and a scoop beside it. She had been used to this all her life, but had hoped she would never have to return to it.

When she had arranged the room and her possessions as best she could, she delivered the basin of water to Charlotte, who had taken Elizabeth upstairs with her to sleep off the discomfort of the steamer, Chao Phya. She then went back to the front room, where she found Edward sitting alone in an armchair. Without a word, she closed the shutters, and the room immediately became warmer as the breeze died away. Edward, deep in thought, did not realise what she was doing until she stood in front of him.

Without warning, she unbuttoned her blouse—which he insisted she wear in the house during the daytime in case they had visitors—and let it slip from her shoulders, revealing her firm, round breasts and her small, brown nipples, already hard and erect. Before he could protest, she had unwound her *panung*, and it, too, slipped silently to the floor.

She stood before him, naked, her small yet curvaceous frame highlighted in the shafts of light that filtered through the closed shutters. Her hands moved slowly down her stomach, through her soft black hair, and between her taut thighs.

He felt a surge of desire, but was well aware of the danger. "Kesri, for God's sake. We can't do this here. Not now."

She simply smiled and moved slowly toward him, deliberately letting her breasts brush against his face before she bent over to kiss his forehead with feathery lips. She then kissed him the Siamese way, delicately and briefly inhaling the scent of his cheek with her nose as her lips gently brushed against him. It was sensuous, and he was weak with lust and fear. He was powerless to stop her, even though Charlotte could have walked in at any moment. She straddled him, then quickly and deftly loosened the buttons of his trousers and slipped her hand inside.

"Kesri, not here," he whispered in her ear. "Let's go to your room. No one will find us there. We can lock. . . ."

But he couldn't finish the sentence. She had already manoeuvred herself so that he slipped inside her, and she began to move on him slowly and rhythmically. She raised her legs and linked them behind him, drawing him in even deeper.

When it was over, she immediately stood up, and he watched her put on her *panung* and blouse. She left the room as silently as she had entered, and he knew he could never give her up. She was the only truly erotic woman he had ever known. She took him far beyond his wildest imaginings. Her gift was one that Charlotte would never possess; the ability to give herself totally to sensuality.

He didn't blame Charlotte for that, of course. It had never been her fault. But since he had come to know Kesri, he realised how much he had missed in his marriage to Charlotte.

Somehow he would have to make it work so that he could keep both of them.

❖ *Chapter 6* ❖

Mr. Knox had returned to England on home leave, but the acting consul, Mr. Alabaster, had secured an invitation for Edward as the British Consulate's official photographic representative, with the promise of an additional photographic session with the king himself. The family were also invited, and they had risen before dawn to prepare for the long journey south to view the eclipse.

Edward had finally managed to hire an assistant, a boy named Narong, who spoke a few words of English, and who had once worked for a *farang* missionary family in his Northern home town of Chiengmai.

"Father, where are we going?" Elizabeth asked over breakfast of porridge and tea—prepared by their maid, Kesri.

"A place called Hua Wan, near the seaside. Mr. Alabaster says the king has cleared away part of the jungle to put up a temporary town and a palace. We'll have our own house on stilts while we're there. How does that sound?"

"Will there be any other children there?"

"Yes, I think so. Some of the king's sons and daughters are going. You might even meet Prince Chulalongkorn."

"Who's he?"

"He's the king's oldest living son, and they say he'll be the next king. He's fifteen, but some of his younger brothers and sisters will be there, too."

"But I won't be able to talk to them. I can't speak Siamese."

"Don't worry my dear. I've heard that the king's children all speak English. They had an English teacher for five years until last year. A Mrs. Anna."

"Eat up now, Elizabeth. We don't want to miss the boat," Charlotte said.

When they reached the dock, a large group of foreigners was preparing to board the Siamese gunboat, the Impregnable. Among those assembled were Mr. and Mrs. Alabaster and the other British Consulate staff; the American missionary, Dr. Bradley; and the American acting consul, Mr. N. A. McDonald.

Edward and Narong unloaded the considerable amount of photographic equipment from the carriage. The inventory included: the portable dark-tent, which fitted neatly into a wooden suitcase and in which the sensitising and processing chemicals were carried; a plate-box with two dozen plates; a case containing extra chemical supplies; two large tin cans to hold water used in coating the plates; a basket containing miscellaneous items such as towels, a glass funnel, filtering paper, a dusting brush, and a chamois leather; and a case containing the camera lenses, the camera stand, and the camera itself.

As he and Narong struggled with their loads, he wished there were a new technique whereby the developing process did not have to be done on location. If it could be done at the studio, he would hardly even need an assistant. What freedom to be able to travel with only camera and plates.

The voyage to Hua Wan was uneventful, and after only two days, the Impregnable reached its destination. As they were brought ashore to Sam Rot Yoi beach, Edward, Charlotte, and Elizabeth, along with the other Europeans, gazed in stunned amazement at the scene before them. For it was not the wild jungle they had imagined. Thousands of labourers, with the help of fifty elephants, had erected a town and palace extending along the beach-front for several miles. There were whispers among the crowd of foreigners gathered on the beach that the king had allocated a budget of tens of thousands of pounds for the expedition.

As they looked to the right, the magnificent royal pavilion stood surrounded by a fifteen-foot-high stockade draped in scarlet cloth. Some of the other buildings were pointed out by a Siamese courtier dressed in a shimmering, red silk *panung,* and a white muslin jacket—the jacket being a relatively new standard required by the king in one of his famous edicts, which were issued "by royal command, reverberating like the roar of a lion".

Adjacent to the royal palace stood the houses of the prime minister, then those of the royal children, the consular officials, and the other foreigners. To the extreme left, as they looked, were the accommodations of the French scientists, complete with a temporary observatory with removable roof for their telescopes. Ten accomplished astronomers had journeyed the 10,000 miles from France to view the eclipse from its best vantage point—this isolated beach in Siam. The French had arrived three weeks previously, and—despite every convenience and comfort being provided—were already complaining of a lack of co-operation. The Siamese, they claimed, had dispatched spies to ensure that astronomy, and not a plot to annex Siam in the name of France, was their object there.

King Mongkut, a keen and accomplished astronomer himself, had predicted to the second when the full eclipse would take place, his calculations differing from those of the French scientists by two seconds. Meanwhile, the traditional Siamese astronomers refused to believe there would be an eclipse at all. The event was due to take place on the morning of August 18th, and there were four days to wait, with all eager to see who would be proved correct.

The prime minister sent word to the master of the Impregnable, Captain Walrond, that Mr. Alabaster was to remain on the ship until the other visitors had disembarked, because His Majesty wished to welcome him with an official reception. It was a great honour.

The crowd watched in awe as—with much pomp and ceremony—the second foreign minister and other important members of the court greeted Mr. and Mrs. Alabaster at the pier. They then proceeded to the palace, where King Maha Mongkut— or, to the Siamese, King Chulachomklao—received them.

From his vantage point on the beach, Edward could see the king clearly. He was a slim, elderly man, taller than most of the other Siamese, although his height was hard to judge with certainty since his subjects prostrated themselves on the ground in his presence. He was, in fact, probably the first king of Siam whose subjects had actually seen him. Before his reign, it was illegal for members of the public to even look at the monarch. But Mongkut had been a monk for twenty-seven years before his coronation, and—as he said himself—he knew many people from that time. He wanted his subjects to line the streets, and he wanted to be able to speak with them if he so desired. They still, however, had to ensure that their heads were lower than his.

His Majesty was dressed fabulously in a richly-embroidered scarlet silk taffeta *panung,* and a dark blue jacket with gold braid at the cuffs, lapels, and Chinese-style collar. He wore a matching gold-braided hat and gold slippers. His wide smile revealed his new set of dentures, made for him by a Western dentist—a Mr. V. D. Collins—who had travelled from China via Singapore when he heard, the year before, that the king would pay 1,000 American dollars for a perfectly-fitting new set of teeth to replace his old ones made of red *sapan* wood.

Edward heard the story from other expatriates of how Mr. Collins had had terrible difficulties with the fit because the king refused to allow him to touch, or even look at his mouth, let alone to take a wax impression. His Majesty insisted on doing the job himself, the head being sacred to the Siamese, and that of the Lord of Life especially so. Several sets of teeth were made, but the fit on each one was understandably so bad that he could not wear them. The king eventually allowed the dentist to take an impression of his mouth, with excellent results, and paid him 560 dollars—which Mr. Collins accepted graciously.

Mr. Shaw said that Collins had then become quite an adventurer—afterwards making a 43-day journey with his wife to Moulmein by elephant and boat—and that he and the other missionaries had been particularly concerned, because the Collinses spoke no Siamese or Burmese, and the route they were to travel was virtually unknown to Westerners. Indeed, Mrs. Collins was the first European woman the villagers along the way had ever seen.

Edward noticed that one side of the king's mouth seemed to droop a little, as if he had suffered some malady, but that nevertheless, he had a warm, intelligent expression. He was old—in his sixties, but looking a decade older—and Edward felt he would make a most intriguing photographic subject. He was the first Siamese monarch to be photographed since the new art had reached the country.

His Majesty fired the seven-gun salute to Mr. Alabaster with his own hand—a very rare honour indeed—and the consular party then disappeared into the palace proper, where they were served refreshments in the vast audience hall.

The Fairburns were shown to their own house, a small but solid wooden structure that was more than adequate for their needs. A table was set in European style, and several servants were in attendance. There were more surprises to come. They learned that the finest European wines and champagnes were theirs for the asking; that a French chef was overseeing preparation of the food by forty Chinese and European assistants; and that an Italian *maitre d'hotel* would see to their every need. They were even more astonished at the extent of the king's hospitality when Edward ordered a bottle of champagne.

"Never mind if it's not chilled, my dear," he said to Charlotte. "I feel like celebrating."

The champagne arrived in a bucket of ice.

"It's unbelievable!" Charlotte gasped. "How on earth did they. . . ."

Edward laughed. He had known all along. "Shipped here from Singapore. Apparently the only thing in short supply is drinkable water. But then again, who needs water when one has champagne, eh?"

He smiled at his wife once more, and she thought that perhaps this excursion would help improve things between them.

Elizabeth hadn't seen them looking so happy for a long time.

The next day was a French celebration—Emperor Napoleon III's Fête Day—and everyone entered into the spirit of the festivities. The ships in the harbour were bedecked with colourful ribbons, and salutes were fired throughout the day—officiated by the French expedition leader, Monsieur Stephan.

Charlotte and Edward stood on the beach and watched the sun set, as one of the two bands brought in to celebrate the occasion played a popular romantic waltz. She hadn't felt so close to him since Elizabeth was born. It had been less than two weeks since her arrival in Siam, and already she felt more content than she had dreamed possible.

The following day, a far more distinguished guest than Mr. Alabaster arrived at Hua Wan: the Governor of Singapore, Colonel Sir Harry Ord, accompanied by Lady Ord and a large group of his officers and their wives. As their steamer, Peiho, appeared offshore, the king made arrangements to receive the governor immediately. He was disappointed, however, when Sir Harry asked to postpone the reception until the next day, because they had arrived on a Sunday, and he was a devout Christian.

The king granted the governor's request, and the following day he was duly received with a 17-gun salute and a royal audience, at which His Majesty was seated on a throne surrounded by two hundred kneeling princes and officers attired in gold silk jackets.

Edward was disappointed not to be granted permission to photograph the meeting, but the governor later allowed him to take a picture of Lady Ord and himself by the palace entrance.

Edward also learned later that the king would agree to appear in a group photograph surrounded by his foreign guests. He would have preferred to photograph the king without the Europeans—alone or with some of his wives, several of whom had accompanied him—but he felt reluctant to ask another favour. Now that the king knew who he was, however, he might allow Edward to photograph him alone at some future date. There was plenty of time, he reflected, now that he would not be leaving Siam in the foreseeable future. There was also the chance that he may even be given royal photographic commissions.

Edward spent the rest of the day setting up his equipment, assisted by Narong. Not the least important task was calculating the exposure time necessary in the overcast conditions typical of the monsoon season. Fortunately, his tint-meter, with the cumbersome name of Bing's Universal Self Registering Actinometer, was the most accurate device available for measuring exposure times.

Although he had warned the subjects to remain very still during the process, the first plate was ruined when the king made a comment—out of Edward's earshot—that caused laughter throughout the group. It was unthinkable that one of His Majesty's quips would pass unnoticed, and there was nothing for it but to discard the plate and start again. Edward took six photographs, after which everyone was relieved to move their limbs freely again.

The developing process revealed four of the plates to be worthwhile likenesses, and he decided to make prints for the king and for each of the other subjects. He had waited so long, it seemed, to achieve his goal of photographing the monarch, that the actual realisation was something of a disappointment. The photographs were not particularly interesting artistically, but their central subject had made them historically important. He took other photographs of the French scientists, as well as portraits of some of the important European guests.

But the one concern of all present throughout the preparations was the weather. It was, after all, the monsoon season, and menacing thunderheads had gathered above. They seemed to grow steadily blacker after the arrival of Sir Harry's party, and loomed still when the morning of the eclipse, August 18th, dawned.

The king and the *kalahome*—the prime minister—were said to be almost frantic with worry that the spectacle would not be seen at all. Nevertheless, people busied themselves setting up telescopes in front of the houses.

Dr. Bradley stopped to talk with Edward during the morning. "I believe your photographs were quite a success, Mr. Fairburn."

"That's very kind of you to say so, Dr. Bradley. I only hope the eclipse, too, may be successfully viewed. The king has set his heart on seeing it, I believe."

"With the Lord's help," Dr. Bradley commented as he glanced up at the sky—where the cloud cover was thickening and a drizzle was beginning to fall.

He walked on, leaving Edward smiling politely and thinking how ironic it was that an American missionary should be asking God to grant a Buddhist potentate's wish.

As it transpired, either the Buddha or God, or perhaps both, had listened to the prayers of the assembly—although initially, when the king fired a cannon to signal the start of the eclipse at precisely 10.22 a.m., nothing could be seen through the clouds.

Moans of frustration and cries of "*Mon dieu! Mon dieu!*" were heard from the French section, as the scientists began to fear they may have journeyed halfway around the world for nothing. But suddenly, as if on cue, the clouds began to break up, and the spectators on the beach were silent as the sky started to clear. Then, all at once, the eclipse was clearly visible in all its magnificence.

Dr. Bradley and his party of missionaries cheered loudly, as did some of the Siamese at first. But then, in awe, they fell silent. Some of the Siamese ran into their houses as the *kalahome* shouted, "Now will you believe what the foreigners tell you?" The king, beside himself with delight, danced for joy between his telescopes, and fired the cannon once more to announce his victory. Its boom was met by a blast of pipes and trumpets from his own people.

The spectators, still silent as they gazed at the phenomenon, heard the distant sound of drums being beaten in the nearest village. The Siamese believed that an eclipse occurred when the god of darkness—the evil black sky dragon, Rahu—attempted to devour the sun. In order to ward off Rahu, they beat gongs and drums, and crashed pots and pans together, lest the sun be completely consumed.

As the sun partially emerged, the French scientists quietly went about their calculations. They were relieved to have been able to witness the event at all, but were embarrassed that—for all their supposed superior scientific knowledge—the king of Siam had been more accurate in calculating the precise time of the total eclipse. Surely it was a fluke, each of them silently concluded.

As the eclipse continued to cast an eerie light over its path, insects and other nocturnal creatures began to stir, deceived by the onset of the false dusk. Edward slapped yet another mosquito that landed on his neck.

"Confounded creatures," he complained. "Don't suppose they do much harm, though. More of a nuisance than anything." Elizabeth's legs had been bitten, and Charlotte, like the other ladies, had covered her feet with a large brown paper bag, drawn up round her wide skirt. Even the king hadn't been spared from the bites, and Edward had noticed him scratching his arms during the photographic session the previous day.

The next day, they left in the Impregnable with the other foreigners—and despite the heat and the mosquitoes, Charlotte was sorry to leave. It seemed at Hua Wan that she and Edward had begun to communicate again; to appreciate the qualities in one another that had brought them together in the first place. At least it had seemed that way to her.

"In spite of it all, we're still the same two people we were when we married," she had said to him the night before, as they lay side-by-side in bed. But then she turned and saw he was not listening. He had fallen asleep, still holding her hand. She smiled in contentment, believing that she and her husband were perhaps falling in love all over again.

October 19th, 1868

Dear Mother,

All Siam is mourning the death of its esteemed ruler, or Lord of Life, as they refer to him, King Maha Mongkut, Rama IV. I do not know if you have read of this in the London newspapers, but it is such a tale of high drama that I shall describe it to you in detail. It is in fact—as you shall see—fortunate that I myself am alive to tell it, and it is also the reason I have not corresponded these last two months.

As you know from my last letter, we were to travel to watch the eclipse at Hua Wan. I have included with this letter an article from the Bangkok Recorder which describes the event much more eloquently than I could. The king certainly put those Frenchmen in their places when it was proved that his calculation of the eclipse was correct, and theirs wrong. We were more than a little proud, and pleased to ally ourselves with the Siamese contingent, rather than with the French, who are bent on gaining far too much influence in this part of the world, anyway.

We were amazed at the extent of civilisation in such an outpost, and especially at His Majesty's hospitality. The entire expedition is said to have cost as much as £20,000, and there was even ice for the champagne, can you imagine! Every important foreigner in Bangkok was invited, and the king paid for the entire entourage, as well as for thousands of peasants to clear the area and construct houses for the thousand or so guests.

However, all the trappings of civilisation in the world could not protect the visitors from the diseases of such a place—none of which discriminate between servants, Europeans, or Siamese royalty. The king, Crown Prince Chulalongkorn (now the boy king), no fewer than eight of the ten French scientists, and I myself, among many others, came down with what they call jungle fever. Some became ill as early as the return voyage, while others are still succumbing only now. This is a terrible illness, Mother, and is quite often fatal. At least eight have died, as well as scores of labourers and servants. It is, as the name suggests, brought about by the bad airs of the jungle, I believe.

The king suffered his first fever on August 24th, the day of our return. Having developed the fever myself—albeit in a much milder form—shortly after we landed in Bangkok, I can tell you it would be no way to pass into the Lord's hands. At first, one is burning hot, then icy cold, shaking from head to foot, yet still sweating in the extreme heat and humidity.

Dr. Bradley administered quinine to me, which I took religiously, and I seem to have recovered well enough. Elizabeth and Edward are quite well. I think my daughter takes after her father and is of strong constitution, unlike myself. The poor king, being elderly, I suppose, could not prevail, although Dr. Bradley says that he lived weeks longer than he should have by sheer determination.

Apparently, after first taking quinine and advice from his foreign doctors, and not making a quick enough recovery, he reverted to the traditional Siamese doctors, who are little more than witch-doctors— and nothing more could be done because he refused to see either Dr. Campbell or Dr. Bradley for weeks.

When, finally, Dr. Campbell was admitted, the king ignored his advice. The doctors believe that if His Majesty had taken quinine regularly from the first signs of the illness, he would most probably be alive today. Still others say he would not, for it is claimed he had made up his mind to die on his birthday, and did just that. Such a noble man he was, and we shall all miss him here, even though Edward and I did not know him personally. The Siamese are cremated rather than buried, but the king's cremation will not be held for more than a year.

Shortly after he finally succumbed to the fever, his highest-ranking son, Chulalongkorn, was proclaimed King Rama V, although because of his youth, being just fifteen, a regent has been appointed to rule until he reaches the age of twenty.

The young heir is a handsome, intelligent boy who, they say, has already voiced strong opinions as to the modernisation of the country, and the continuation of his father's good work in that respect.

Edward is sorely disappointed that he was unable to photograph the king alone, but only with a group of other royals and dignitaries during the eclipse. He believed he had made progress in that direction, and was even hopeful of soon gaining an audience. Now, as he says, he must start again with a new king, and not only that, but he must first gain an audience with the regent, which is just as difficult, he supposes. Nevertheless, his photographic images taken during the expedition must be quite valuable, as they are among the last ever taken of the old king.

Other than that, he has started to do quite well in his business. He has even gained a reputation as the "ladies' photographer", managing always, as he does, to somehow photograph his subjects from their most fetching angle, masking their less admirable characteristics. There are several other foreign photographers in the city, so he by no means has a monopoly on commissions, and must work hard for his clients within the limited expatriate community.

In addition Mother, I do not think I am breaching any marital confidences if I tell you that we are renewed together. Edward must spend much time with his business, of course, and is often away from the house, sometimes overnight if he must be at a late appointment and stay at his host's house rather than risk the dark lanes home. However, I believe he is happy and content with us here, and with our uneventful home life and our little lawn parties.

So do not fret for me, Mother dear. I am, as you see, quite content at present. I look forward to your reply.

Your loving daughter,

Charlotte

Charlotte thought it odd the way Kesri had just seemed to disappear. They returned from Hua Wan to find the house empty and the maid's room bare. Edward seemed distracted when she questioned him about it.

"Oh, didn't I tell you, dear? Kesri is no longer with us."

"Why? Where has she gone?"

"She . . . she had to return home to her family. Her aunt is very ill."

"I thought she had no family, Edward."

"Er . . . no close family," he answered quickly. "I believe the woman is really a distant cousin she calls aunt."

"Well, I can't say I'm sorry she's gone. She was a good worker, but sometimes I thought she was. . . ."

"Hmmm?" Edward mumbled, trying to sound as if he were not interested.

"Oh, I don't know, perhaps . . . well, I sometimes had the feeling there was more behind her smile than we realised. I don't think she enjoyed being a servant. Edward . . . did you hear what I said?"

"Hmmm? Sorry, Charlotte, what was that?"

"Never mind. I'll have to ask Mrs. Alabaster if she knows a girl who can replace her."

But Edward's thoughts were not on Kesri's replacement. He was still wondering how he had managed to retain a façade of normality throughout the entire trip to the South, especially after the news Kesri had given him only the day before they had left.

It had been her way of ensuring his return; of being certain that he would still want her. But she had been very wrong, and now he reproached himself about what he had said and done that day in the studio when she had come to him with the news. . . .

❖

It was only a week after Charlotte's arrival, and he had thought—when she let herself into the studio without knocking—that she was initiating one of their frequent, intimate interludes. Her revelation was a disaster.

"This cannot be true, Kesri. Tell me it's not," he uttered in shock.

"I tell you true," she insisted, her head bowed, understanding now that he was far from happy.

"Do you not realise this is the worst thing that could happen to us at this time?"

She said nothing. She needed his support—and screaming and crying would not achieve that.

"I thought you girls knew how to. . . ," he spluttered as she looked at him expectantly. "Well . . . I thought . . . I thought you knew how to stop these accidents occurring."

"In Siam, man not angry when wife have baby."

"But Kesri, you are *not* my wife. Charlotte is my wife, and it would bring shame to my family—cause a terrible problem—if everybody knew this child were mine."

So, he had finally said it. She was not his wife. She was a servant.

She lowered her eyes again, maintaining her composure in the face of his frustration. "But Edward, everyone know baby not Siam when he born."

"Kesri, that's why you must leave this house. Nobody must know."

She turned her eyes pitifully up to his. If she did not proceed with the utmost of care, her plans would be ruined. She would lose everything.

"Please, Edward, do not send me go," she whispered. "Do not. I do anything. Please, you think of baby. Our baby. Maybe son."

But all he could foresee at that moment was the catastrophe of Charlotte discovering the truth—and the public shame and humiliation if word were to spread, as it inevitably would.

Charlotte's suffering and devotion flashed before him, and only deepened his confusion. She had offered herself to him again, although she knew it could endanger her life. He had so far managed to rebuff her intimate advances, making the excuse that he was exhausted with the heat, and that the developing chemicals he had to use sometimes made him feel ill. But for how much longer could he deny her?

"I must send you away, Kesri," he continued. "I'm sorry, but there's nothing else to be done." He took her small hands in his.

"But don't worry. I shall still see you and the baby. I will look after you, and you'll have everything you need. But you *must not* tell anyone that I'm the father of your baby. You must go some place where nobody knows you."

Although there was still a possibility she would one day be with him, she was comforted little by his words. But, she thought, when he saw the baby, maybe he would change his mind. After all, Mr. Knox had a Thai wife, and no others.

"*Chai*, Edward, I do what you say. *Mai pen rai.*"

It was her only choice. She had to remain calm and allow him time to reconsider. Her alternative was to make a public spectacle of the affair. But what purpose would it serve? He would deny responsibility, abandon her, and likely leave Siam. At least this way she and the child would be taken care of.

"We're leaving tomorrow for Hua Wan," he told her, relieved that she was not going to make trouble. "When we get back, you must be gone. I'll see you have enough money to take care of yourself. You need not work. We'll return toward the end of the month, and you may send a messenger here, to the studio, to let me know where you are. I'll visit you."

"You not divorce me?" she asked fearfully.

Edward sighed, realising that their paths would never converge. "No, Kesri. I don't believe in divorce. And anyway, I can't divorce you because we are not properly married. You're not my wife."

Still she could not understand what he meant. If she lived with him, and if their union had been blessed, of course she was his wife. And if he was willing to have her live with him before, despite his *farang* wife, he must not believe the missionaries who said that a man must have one wife only. Why would he not admit it?

She wondered if perhaps Charlotte had discovered their relationship and had insisted she leave. But he had said it was because of the baby. A Siamese man would be proud in such a situation, because it proved his manhood. Why was he not pleased, particularly since he had only one other child? But he said it was the worst thing that could happen to him. It was beyond her comprehension.

◈ *Chapter 7* ◈

Porntip waited until late the night of the garden party. The last guests had departed hours ago, and when she saw the upstairs lamps go out, and she was sure everyone would be asleep, she slipped away down to the landing, her bare feet making no sound. She climbed into her tiny *sampan* and stealthily rowed down the Chao Phya and then off to the Thonburi side of the river into a narrow, anonymous *klong*.

A few minutes later, she moored her boat at another landing. Its stairway led to a floating wooden house, where a shadowy figure was waiting on the verandah.

"Come in quickly," Kesri whispered. "We've a lot to talk about."

Two months previously, in January, she had given birth to a baby girl after an easy, four-hour labour. It was not her first child—a secret she had kept from Edward—and she had known what to expect. She had immediately sent word to him with Porntip—her friend, and their new maid—but he did not come for a week. After the midwife left, she was alone with the baby. She felt deserted.

"His own daughter," she complained bitterly as Porntip sat down beside her on the rattan mat that covered the single room that was her home. It was, however, an improvement on the maid's room at the house. "And it's as if he doesn't want her."

Porntip tried to reassure her. "Of course he does, Kesri. But his wife barely lets him out of her sight."

"Then why doesn't he just tell her about me? Is he a man or not? Is he not lord in his own house?"

"I don't know why he doesn't tell her. I can't imagine. But Kesri, they don't often sleep together, so passion can't be his reason for staying only with her."

"He doesn't need to lie with her, because he has me. I'm his secret wife. The wife no one must know about. For some reason, he's ashamed of me."

"What will you do, Kesri?"

"I don't know yet. But I *will* do something. I'll not be cast into the background, my child not acknowledged as his. Not for long. Will you help me, Porntip?"

"You know I will, sister," she replied, using the Siamese form of endearment between close friends.

"Good. We need to plan this carefully."

Once she had fully recovered from her bout of jungle fever, Charlotte found that she had plenty of time on her hands. And because Edward worked such long hours, she needed something to occupy herself with. She had soon followed the other expatriate wives into charity work, which mostly involved visiting women and their children in poor areas, collecting clothing and other necessities for them, and advising them on health care and whatever education could be provided for their children.

Most of all, she wished the women would end their custom of "staying with the fire", in which the mother of a new-born child would lay with a brazier of burning charcoal beside her stomach for several weeks. When the woman could bear the heat no longer, she turned so that her back could be roasted.

King Mongkut had abhorred the custom, and it was said that his successor, Chulalongkorn did, too. Consequently, "staying with the fire" was no longer popular at the palace, nor among the nobility. Nevertheless, the poorer classes still believed that dreadful things would happen if they did not do it, the cessation of the practice having yet to filter down through the social strata.

It was March, and Charlotte was well established in her daily routine. In the mornings, before it became too hot, she would do whatever charity work she could manage, visiting mothers of sick children, and going to schools and temples to distribute food and clothing. In the afternoons, she would visit friends to play cards, to take tea, or to gossip, and then return home to meet Elizabeth after school, and to rest for several hours before dinner.

Although she knew she would always feel like a foreigner in Siam, and she would never become accustomed to the year-round heat, she at least found the country and the people fascinating. She eventually discarded her crinoline, more out of expedience than to follow fashion, and she travelled around Bangkok mostly by water-taxi—the tiny paddle boats that bobbed, along with thousands of others, on the river and the *klongs*. She never tired of watching the people going about their daily activities. Nor, in turn, did the Siamese ever seem to tire of staring back at her, the children always smiling and waving, wishing she would jump into the water with them.

The Bangkokians were used to foreigners now—they had been coming to Siam in more than rare numbers since the 1830s—but the novelty of them certainly had not worn off. Charlotte, sitting rigid in her high-buttoned long dress, holding a matching parasol to shield her pale skin, was an incongruous sight among the throngs of Siamese, colourfully dressed in their *panungs*, calling loudly to each other across the water, and crowded into every space on every tiny boat. A vessel barely more than three feet long might hold up to fifteen people. If it overturned, the passengers simply swam to the nearest landing, sat in the sun to dry themselves, and waited for another boat.

She went often to the residence of the consul, Mr. Knox, who had now returned from England. Mrs. Knox was a gracious, handsome Siamese woman who spoke excellent English and loved to talk with Charlotte about her children. Her son, Tom, and elder daughter, Fanny, were at school in Europe, but the youngest child, Caroline, now eleven, preferred to stay in Bangkok with her parents.

Although Edward's studio was on the property—in a room at the back of the house—he had his own entrance, and she knew he preferred not to be disturbed while he worked. Many members of the European community brought their families to be photographed, and as word of his talents spread, he even made customers of some of the suspicious Siamese.

It was only a few years previously that no Siamese would even have allowed their portrait to be painted, let alone be photographed. They believed that the reproduction of a person's likeness—whether on a coin, a drawing, a portrait, a sculpture, or photograph—would remove a part of their soul, and thus shorten their life.

Photography was introduced to Siam even before King Mongkut's time—during the reign of King Rama III—probably by the French missionary and adventurer, Père Larnaudie, who also happened to build the first rice mill in Thailand—but because of the common superstition, the presence of a camera could still immediately disperse a crowd, especially beyond Bangkok. Following King Rama IV's example, however, the wealthy and titled classes were now quite comfortable before a camera, and it was soon considered essential to have one's portrait taken.

Most of the professional photographers in Bangkok were Chinese, but there were a few Europeans. Westerners preferred, of course, to patronise one of their own, and so Edward soon found that he had more than enough business. In fact, he was often booked up for several weeks in advance. He was also hoping to lend his services to His Majesty and the government, in order to officially document the rapid advancements that were taking place in Bangkok.

Establishing contacts was a long, drawn-out process, however, and to do so, one had to secure invitations to the right sorts of social activities. That was why he encouraged Charlotte to work with the likes of Mrs. Knox, rather than with the missionary wives, who meant nothing to the regent but were merely tolerated.

While the regent, Somdech Chao Phya Sri Sriyawongse, did not favour foreigners, it was known that the young king was very enlightened—and was already planning to use the *farangs* to hasten the modernisations he wished to bring to Siam.

Nevertheless, because he would not gain his majority for some years yet, it was necessary for foreigners such as Edward to be patient, to wait, and in the meantime secure what private work they could.

Edward told her that he was still trying to gain an audience with the regent, but it was not easy. Sri Sriyawongse had many more pressing matters to concern him than the granting of his time for one English photographer with no political connections. It was rumoured that the French were preparing to colonise Siam, as they had Cambodia, and the hated French consul, Gabriel Aubaret, had been removed before King Mongkut's death.

But the French were still considered a threat—as, in fact, were the British, who now governed Burma—and Charlotte could not help but wonder at the ability of the Siamese to keep the great powers at bay. They possessed no navy to speak of, and could not possibly have defended themselves in the event of an annexation. Their diplomatic skills must be of the first order, she thought.

The lawn party guests that day had been a select few, invited for mid-afternoon to play croquet, to try their hand at archery, and to share an afternoon tea of tropical fruits and soft drinks cooled by water kept in a trough in the shade. Among those invited were the Alabasters, the Bradleys, and Joseph Shaw, who taught at Elizabeth's school.

Charlotte had met Joseph only a few times previously at school soirées, and although they did not know each other well, and had never had the opportunity to talk at length, she immediately felt him to be a kindred spirit; someone to whom she could talk easily, and in whom she sensed great empathy. Yet she also detected behind his kind expression and soft eyes, some sadness that seemed a permanent burden to him. They had never exchanged even the slightest of personal information before, but she found that the informal atmosphere of the party made her bold enough to enquire about him.

"I haven't met many of the English missionaries," she remarked as they stood in the shade of a large tree. "Most of them seem to be American."

"Well, yes, they do have a strong representation here," Joseph replied. "But, actually, I'm not really English. I'm from New Zealand. My parents are English, of course, but I was born in Auckland."

"Well, then you and I can feel homesick together for the Antipodes. We spent seventeen years in Melbourne. Elizabeth was born there."

"Oh yes, I remember your husband saying you'd lived in Australia. How are you settling in here?"

"Much better than I expected, Mr. Shaw. The heat is debilitating, of course, but with the shipments of food coming from England so frequently, we're really rather well looked after."

Indeed, life in Siam was much more agreeable than she had imagined it would be. Socially, it was almost as busy as Melbourne, and because of Edward's family background, they were accepted by the consular staff into their elite circle.

She had found, to her surprise, that the class divisions among the foreigners in Siam were almost as obvious as they were in England. Even by the early 1860s, the foreign community had split into four cliques, with the consular staff considering themselves rather superior to the merchants, the sea captains, and the missionaries. They were not strict divisions, however. An amusing or well-off sea captain might be invited to a consular party, perhaps, if he were considered to be of good breeding. And a consular officer might stoop to socialise with merchants and the like if he thought it could benefit him economically, or perhaps just for an amusing diversion.

Although it was far easier in Siam for certain people to fabricate backgrounds—and so, if they were guileful enough, be admitted to cliques they would otherwise never have been—true impostors were nearly always discovered. Charlotte heard of an English school teacher named Anna Leonowens, who had left the previous year after more than five years tutoring the royal children. Mrs. Leonowens, accompanied by her young son, Louis, had often attempted to gain access to the highest social circles among the British consular staff with her story of her officer husband, Captain Leonowens, with whom she had lived in Asia until, she said, he had died of sunstroke after a tiger hunt in Singapore.

But she had fooled no one, and the consular circle and the merchants ostracised her, even sniggering behind her back at her frequent—though minor—slips in etiquette. "She was no more a lady than Moll Flanders," as one young British attaché observed. Meanwhile, seeking friends but considering herself above the sea captains' wives, Mrs. Leonowens had been compelled to rely for social acceptance on the American Protestant missionaries, who felt it their Christian duty to accept anyone.

Charlotte, of course, did not suffer Anna's problem. Having been born to a family of reasonable social standing—if reduced means—and having made what was considered a brilliant marriage, she was immediately recognised by the British as a lady, a member of that class of landed gentry whose younger sons so often made their lives abroad, as Edward had done.

Charlotte could call upon the advantage, also, of having travelled abroad a great deal. She was used to things not being as they were at home, and was, in that respect, not as delicate as the Victorian ladies who arrived in the tropics straight from their English drawing rooms. She could hoist up her skirts and pick her way across a road ankle-deep in mud—as she had done around the gold fields on numerous occasions—without a second thought to propriety. In this way, she was admired by the other women of class in Bangkok, although a few thought her perhaps just a touch vulgar for it.

To add to her contentment, Edward seemed more satisfied than she had ever seen him. He made no demands of any sort on her, yet he remained mostly cheerful and considerate. Still, she did notice that he sometimes seemed distant and distracted, more ponderous than he had ever been before. They had a new maid, who was friendlier and more obedient than Kesri, although Porntip, as she was called, barely spoke any English and was not nearly as efficient.

But the climate was the one thing she found hard to tolerate. Although it was early March and the cool season seemed to linger still, the heat and the mosquitoes were unbearable. The loathsome creatures were everywhere, even finding their way through the nets covering her bed, and biting her as she slept. But despite the temperatures being much more comfortable in the cool season, particularly in the early mornings and at night, it still reached eighty or ninety degrees in the afternoons. And it was just such an afternoon as she stood on their lawn in conversation with Joseph.

"But tell me about yourself, Mr. Shaw. How long have you been here?"

"Six years, Mrs. Fairburn. Since 1862, in fact."

"Six years! Good gracious. Have you returned to New Zealand in the meantime? I presume your family is still there."

"Yes, they're still there. But no, I haven't been back." He paused, as if he were not sure what to say next.

Was she imagining it, or was there a wistful, melancholy look about him?

"You must have been quite young when you came here," she said to fill the silence.

"I was twenty-one."

"It must have been difficult for you—alone in a strange land, no wife beside you."

Joseph smiled a little and briefly looked heavenward. "I had help, Mrs. Fairburn."

"Of course. But what did your parents think of you running off to Siam to become a missionary?"

"Actually, it was my father's idea." A shadow seemed to cross his face for an instant, but then it was gone. "He's a minister, you see. He and my mother went out as missionaries to the Maoris in the thirties."

"How fitting that you're carrying on the family calling then."

"I suppose you could say that, but I hadn't thought of it that way before."

She thought that was a strange comment, but it intrigued her, and she persisted nonetheless. "But why Siam? Why did your father not keep you with him in New Zealand? I'm sure there's still work to be done there, is there not? Or perhaps somewhere else closer to home?"

Joseph hesitated, then spoke as if picking his words carefully. "I suppose he wanted to teach me to have . . . humility. You see, I don't believe we'll ever succeed to convert much of the populace here. Missionaries in the South Pacific have had such astounding success—almost the entire population has converted. Not so here in Asia, I'm afraid. So therefore we will, in a way, always be doomed to fail." He cleared his throat, embarrassed to have spoken so frankly to a woman he barely knew.

But he felt at ease with Charlotte, and he continued. "My father met some Presbyterian missionaries in America many years ago, when he and my mother visited California on their way to Hawaii. They were among the first to work there, but then the need for missionaries to go further afield seemed much stronger, and as New Zealand was part of the Empire, they decided it would be more patriotic to travel on. But they did keep in contact with their friends, and obtained a position here for me. Sadly, both those good people died of cholera last year. Within six days of each other. It was even worse here then, and I was quite lost for a while without them."

"Yes, Mrs. Bradley told me they've lost many of their recruits to illnesses since she arrived." She then lowered her voice. "Do you know that her husband has been here since 1835? His first wife died of consumption in 1845, so he took his three children, went back to America, and returned with her in 1850. He introduced the first smallpox vaccines here, and the first printing press. It's the stuff of novels, is it not?" She paused, looking slightly embarrassed. "But I'm sorry, Mr. Shaw. I'm forgetting myself. I'm sure you know all this already. And I'm sure you have no time for such nonsense as novels."

But before he could answer, Charlotte excused herself as another couple arrived at the party. She circulated among the guests, making sure everyone had a cool drink, but she couldn't help feeling curious about Joseph. She wondered why he hadn't married. He wasn't particularly handsome, but he was tall and straight-backed, with an intelligent face. He had only a small moustache and no side whiskers, and his straight, brown hair wasn't very well cut. But this seemed only to add to his look of sincerity and goodness. She felt he was someone who could be trusted. He would make a wonderful minister, she thought, wondering also why he hadn't been ordained.

Porntip came to Charlotte one day soon after the party, and said in the broken English she had learned since starting her job with the family, "Madame, friend me have baby. You come?"

Porntip had never approached her like that before, and Charlotte was quite surprised. "What's the matter with her, Porntip?"

"She no happy, Madame. She no have husband. She . . . I not know how say . . . she . . . *ther ngao maak.* Only her."

"Lonely? She's lonely?"

"*Ka,*" she assented.

"But she has friends, hasn't she? Family?"

"No family. Porntip only friend she."

"But why?"

"Baby *farang. Angrit.*"

"The poor girl." Now she began to understand. "And this English father—he's deserted her?"

Porntip looked confused, and Charlotte tried again, more simply. "He's gone? Man gone?"

The maid nodded.

"Very well. I'll come immediately. If the baby has an English father, that makes it a British subject. He'll have to do the decent thing by her."

But she was speaking to herself. Porntip understood nothing of what she said, except that she had gained Charlotte's attention, and that her task was almost successfully completed.

She took Charlotte downriver in her boat, and they soon arrived at a floating house, which Charlotte noticed was well-kept and clean. Through the open front, she could see a young woman with her back to the *klong*. The woman was holding a bundle in her arms and gently rocking it.

When Porntip and Charlotte climbed from the *sampan* to the house, the woman turned to greet them. Charlotte gasped when she saw that it was Kesri.

"Hello, Madame," Kesri said, her eyes cast down as she continued to rock the little bundle in her arms.

"Kesri! I had no idea."

"No, Madame."

Charlotte knelt down on the floor. "Kesri, I'm here to help you. You need not feel ashamed."

"No, Madame."

"Please. Let me see your baby." She was beginning to feel very afraid.

Kesri smoothed the wraps back from her daughter's face, and Charlotte looked down at the little girl, who was peacefully sleeping. At first she thought Porntip had made a mistake. It was a Siamese child, she was sure. True, the skin was not as dark as most Siamese, but then she was very young, and her complexion would most probably darken with age. But she had Siamese features: the tiny snub nose, the black eyebrows and eyelashes, and the fuzz of black hair on her head. But then she yawned and opened her eyes, and Charlotte was so startled she drew in her breath sharply. The child's eyes were the purest colour of green.

"She's . . . she's a very beautiful baby," Charlotte managed to say as a feeling of panic and despair shot through her stomach.

"Thank you, Madame. But I not think father want."

"Has the father seen her? Does he know about her?"

"Yes, Madame. He see, but have problem."

Charlotte knew what Kesri meant—and Kesri knew that Charlotte was beginning to fear the worst.

"Is he married already, Kesri?"

"Yes, and he say wife no want other wife in house."

"If I'm to help you, Kesri, you must tell me his name." But she was almost numb; stricken with fear at the prospect—the certainty—of Kesri confirming what she already knew to be true.

Kesri indicated a pile of triangular-shaped cushions, and Charlotte sat down against them awkwardly, unaccustomed as she was to sitting on the ground. Kesri sat beside her with the baby, and Charlotte noticed her very European-looking silver locket. "A gift from the baby's father?" she asked. But Kesri merely looked away and said nothing. Charlotte let it pass.

"Kesri, when was the baby born?"

"Two month, Madame."

She counted back the months, realising that Kesri was at the house when she had conceived. There could be only one explanation. She was almost shaking now, and her voice began to break.

"Was this . . . was this man a friend of ours, perhaps, who took advantage. . . ." But she was clutching at an impossible hope, and she trailed off as a dreadful sensation of nausea swept through her.

She remembered the way Edward had greeted Kesri that first day, and she remembered other things too; the looks between them, and Kesri's resentment toward her.

She was pale, and when she spoke again, it was almost in a whisper. "Kesri, tell me his name, I beg you. Tell me his name!"

Kesri lifted her head and looked straight into Charlotte's eyes, her chin held high.

"His name Edward Fairburn. This his daughter, Anchalee Kesri Fairburn."

◈ *Chapter 8* ◈

It began a few days after they set sail: the vomiting, the diarrhoea, the muscle cramps, the overwhelming weakness. She knew that she had cholera, and as the steamer lurched from wave to wave, her energy drained away. There was a British doctor on board, returning home to England after eight years in Siam, but he could do no more than sponge her with alcohol and administer a little opium to ease the pain.

"You must try to drink," he urged, holding some brackish water to her lips. Whisky was the only alternative, but he had tried that already. He could do nothing for her. Not there, in the middle of the ocean, and at that stage of the disease.

She took a sip, then immediately vomited again. Her tortured eyes opened for a moment as the helpless doctor gently wiped her parched lips. "Where is she?" she whispered.

"Don't worry about her, she's in good hands," he improvised, knowing nothing of her situation. "But she needs you, and you must try to get well for her sake."

It was futile but he wanted to show her some last kindness in her final hours.

She mustered all her strength to force out the faint words, "I'll never see her again."

Then she drifted back to that day when she had lost everything and everyone she had loved. . . .

◈

Edward had known there was something seriously wrong when she had stormed into the studio without knocking as she usually did. Intrusions irritated him, but he thought better of his reaction when he saw the anger and distress on her face. Jars of chemicals shook on the tables and shelves as the door slammed behind her.

Tears had begun to well in her eyes, but she managed to calm herself. "How could you do this to me, Edward? I'm mortified. How could you. . . ."

"What's this? What's wrong, for heaven's sake?"

She could only repeat herself, louder, shaking within, but staring at him intently.

"Sit down, Charlotte, you're hysterical."

"I'm not hysterical." Her voice was dangerously cold and quiet as she gritted her teeth to regain her composure.

"Well at least tell me what's wrong."

But he knew. Only, how could she have discovered it?

"I know, Edward. I've seen her."

"Seen who, dear?" he asked pathetically.

"Don't you dare call me that. It's obvious that I am not your *dear*, isn't it?"

"Well, whatever are you talking about?"

"You know, damn it." This time she shouted, and it was the first time he had ever heard her curse. "I've seen Kesri. And the baby. Your baby."

He took a deep breath, and sat down. "Is that what she told you? That the child is mine?"

"Yes. And I believe her. The baby has your eyes." She remained standing, her bonnet still on, having come directly from Kesri's houseboat.

"It could have been any foreigner. Green eyes aren't rare. These girls . . . you know how they lie."

"The only person who is lying is you, Edward. There's no doubt in my mind who the father of that child is."

He sighed. There was no point in denying it any longer. "I suppose you had to find out sometime, Charlotte," he admitted.

"But why, Edward? Why? In all our years together you have been a loyal husband." She looked straight at him. "Or so I thought. Maybe you have not. Maybe this has been going on for years, and I've been too blind to see the truth."

"Charlotte, I swear to you, this is the one and only time."

"I don't know how I can believe that, Edward. But tell me one thing. Supposing what you say is true, then why now? Why with this . . . this serving girl? Why?"

"Do you really need to ask?"

"What do you mean?"

"I'm a man, Charlotte, like any other. I'm not a priest. I can't be celibate. I need a woman."

"Edward, you have a wife," she uttered. Her voice was a shocked whisper.

"A wife in name only," he replied. "A wife whom I cannot lie with, for fear of the consequences. Kesri gave herself willingly to me, with no guilt, no sacrifice. She wanted me for myself. For her, it wasn't a duty."

Always, always the same thing. Their problems were ever the consequence of this one burden, this one disappointment, this one misfortune Charlotte saw as her great failure. His words cut so deeply, he might well have sliced her to pieces. There was only silence now, and he felt a familiar surge of guilt as she collapsed into an armchair.

They had remained in England only two months after their marriage, before setting out for California and the gold rush. But Edward was not an ordinary prospector. He had no need of the money that a gold find would bring. What he did need was excitement.

He could not bear the thought of joining his father's bank, as his brothers had done; nor did he have any desire to become an officer in the army—which was what his father had suggested when his son told him he wanted to see the world.

Charlotte was pregnant when they boarded the steamer for California, but she hadn't told him before they left—not wanting him to feel obliged to postpone his plans. But he was delighted when she did tell him, their first night at sea, and all went well until two days before their arrival in San Francisco.

In choppy seas, the deck was unstable, but that morning Charlotte was suffering so badly from morning sickness, that she had begged him to take her for a walk on deck. There was a sudden lurch, and they were both thrown to the floor. She fell heavily on her stomach, and retired straight to bed.

That afternoon, she awoke soaked in blood and suffering severe stomach cramps. The ship's doctor confirmed what she already knew. She had lost the child.

No sooner had she recovered in San Francisco than she found herself pregnant again—but she miscarried at four months, when Edward was away at the gold fields. She cried herself to sleep, alone in her misery.

Edward never did have much luck finding gold in California, but they had his private income, and they were never short of money or comfort. Then he discovered photography, and—after his investment in camera and equipment—did well enough, thanks to the steady stream of prospectors who were eager to have their "pitchers took" on their claims and with their finds. He had, at last, discovered a natural talent, and although they had no need of the money, he was thrilled that his new venture provided him with both satisfaction and a living income.

After her fourth miscarriage, Charlotte was advised not to become pregnant again. Nevertheless, she lost another child at sea in 1851 while they sailed to Australia to follow the gold trail. She carried the next baby—a girl—to full term, but she was stillborn. The marriage she had entered into with such joy, such passion, had become a bed of misery—although she still loved him deeply. She wanted so desperately to give him a child, and she felt she had failed him.

It was not until thirteen years after their marriage, in 1861 in Melbourne, that she finally gave birth to Elizabeth. As soon as she knew she was pregnant, she took to her bed—determined not to lose this child—and she stayed there for the full term, rising only for half an hour each day.

When Elizabeth was born, their marriage seemed whole again. Both felt the fulfilment they had so long been denied. But she also knew that she could never allow herself to become pregnant again. She was drained, physically and emotionally, and her face and body were a decade older than her thirty-one years.

He understood, of course, and they agreed that his "conjugal rights" should be taken only once a month—and each month she prayed she would not conceive. Her prayers were not always answered. She became pregnant again in 1866, and once more, she took to her bed. She watched herself grow with both mounting excitement and fear as the months passed, and he was filled with anxiety each day when he asked how she was. At twenty-five weeks she went into premature labour. The child—a son—was born dead.

It was the end of their physical relationship. He could not bear to inflict any more pregnancies on her, and she turned away from even his comforting embraces, sorrowful and bitter at what she saw as her failure to be a proper wife.

He left for England shortly after, and she felt it was mostly to escape her, and from the guilt he felt every time he looked at the lines of strain and disappointment on her face. But still, something made her want to try again, to save their marriage, and perhaps, in middle age, to become closer again. She wanted his love and his respect, not his guilt and pity. Her marriage vows meant everything to her, and she was willing to risk her life for them.

❖

And now, in the deafening silence of his studio, she still needed to know more. To know why. She spoke quietly and reasonably, hoping for an explanation.

"Edward, I offered myself to you without restraint. I told you I was willing to take the risk. I wanted our marriage to work."

"But at what cost?" he challenged bitterly. "Do you think I could live with myself if you died in childbirth simply because I could not control my desires? It would make me a murderer. Even if you were to have another miscarriage and live, I couldn't bear making you suffer so much again."

Tears of grief and frustration coursed down her face, and she could not speak.

He took his chance to try to explain. "Charlotte, darling, don't you see? This woman means nothing to me. I don't feel for her what I feel for you. I don't love her, but I need her, and she's content with that."

"Don't speak to me that way of your mistress," she cried again, her anger and disillusionment deep and draining.

"Charlotte, this is the way things are done here."

"What are you saying?"

"You'd be surprised at how many European men have Siamese mistresses. More often than not, their wives know about it. They give them what's called a pink ticket. . . ."

She could not believe what he was saying. "But it's wrong, Edward. It's wrong. They don't do it because they want to. They do it because their husbands bully them into it. Simply because you are here, doesn't give you licence to behave. . . ."

"Charlotte, can't you see reason? Having Kesri here would make our lives together more peaceful, more satisfying. There'd never be any pressure on you. You'd have all the status that went with being my wife, and none of the demands of married life that bring you so much pain."

She stood in dismay, stiff and unforgiving, and she stared at him for several seconds before speaking again. "There's neither status, nor honour, in being the wife of a man who'd ask me to accept his mistress. I've loved you for so long, Edward, but suddenly it's as if you're a stranger to me. It's as if that love were obliterated; had never been, and will never be again."

"You're tired and overwrought, Charlotte. Why don't you go upstairs to rest and I'll have Porntip bring you up some tea?"

"I don't want *tea*," she shouted. "Edward, do you not see? You *cannot* brush this aside. It's over."

"What do you mean?"

"I mean that I *cannot* and *will not* accept this woman as your mistress. How could you even imagine that I would? You must provide for the child, I suppose. But you must agree never to see *her* again."

"No!" Now he was angry, and he rose from his seat and stepped toward her.

"You've no right to forbid me to do anything."

"I have every right to ask this of you. To *demand* this of you. I'm your wife before God."

"And as such, you must obey me."

"So you'll not give her up?"

"No."

"Then our marriage is finished, Edward. I'll return to England, as soon as it can be arranged."

It took him by surprise. "Charlotte, don't be rash. Don't do anything you'll regret. Take some time to think this out. Please, darling, I . . ."

"I don't need more time," she cut him off quickly. "This won't change. I simply cannot accept her, or any other woman. It's high time Elizabeth went home to school, anyway. She's running round in bare feet, speaking Siamese half the time, and climbing trees. She'll be much better off in England."

"You're not taking Elizabeth with you. If you go, you go alone."

She had not expected that reaction, and now it was she who was caught momentarily off guard.

"You cannot stop me, Edward."

"Yes I can. And I will. You're a wife deserting her husband. No British court would award you custody of our daughter. Elizabeth stays here."

"And you're a man committing adultery," she responded. "What sort of life would she have here, with a father devoid of moral principles?"

"Better than the life she'd have with a mother who deserted her husband."

Now she began to panic. Fear engulfed her as she realised she would lose Elizabeth. "Please, Edward," she begged, as tears spilled from her eyes again, "I've done nothing wrong. Nothing. Why are you hurting me this way?"

But he was trying desperately not to allow her to manipulate his guilt. "It's you who's hurting me, Charlotte. A wife's place is with her husband, and he is the head of the family. Think what shame you'll bring on me by leaving this way."

"Shame? How can you talk of the shame I'd bring on you? You've brought shame enough on yourself to last a lifetime. You can explain my absence by saying I had to return to England for health reasons. In time, they'll find something else to talk about. Perhaps the ex-maid and her green-eyed baby."

"You're jealous, that's what it is. You're jealous of Kesri having a child because you can't have another. . . ." And as soon as he had said it, he wished he had not.

"You're insane," she replied through her shock and her tears. "You don't even deserve the dignity of a reply." She walked out of the room and into the burning afternoon sunlight, leaving him alone in his studio.

He felt a terrible guilt, like a gnawing pain deep in his stomach. It had been this way all their married lives. Would it ever stop? Would he ever be free of her pain?

It was Joseph Shaw's day off, and he was relaxing in a hammock that his houseboy, Somboon, had rigged up between two shady trees. He was taking to it more and more on his rare days off, despite his fear that a snake might one day drop on to him from the branches above. There were plenty of the reptiles around, including cobras, and five-yard-long pythons that enjoyed feasting on new-born puppies.

Here in his garden, Joseph was indulging in a pastime he was a little ashamed of, a pastime he felt would not be quite approved of by the more pious members of his church. He was reading a novel. George Eliot's excellent volume, *Adam Bede*—a story of a simple girl led astray from the man who truly loves her by a man she can never hope to marry—was one that he was particularly fond of. He had read the book before, but although it was now ten years old, it had not lost its attraction. His supply of new novels was exhausted, and he was reading again the best of his old ones— which he kept discreetly out of view in a teak cabinet in his living room—while he awaited a shipment from England. He hoped his next parcel would include something new by Anthony Trollope. In books, he could forget the sadness and loneliness of the real world, and become lost in a dream world in which he himself had no part, and in which he, therefore, could do no wrong.

He was engrossed in the book when Somboon arrived beside him, pointing to the house.

"Sir, Madame Fairburn here."

Joseph could speak Siamese well, but Somboon wanted to learn English, so they always conversed in that language, unless Joseph needed to explain something complicated.

He was quite surprised. "Mrs. Fairburn is here, to see me?"

"*Khap*," Somboon nodded. "She say must speak you."

"Of course, I'll come immediately. Please bring us something cool to drink, Somboon."

As Somboon ran back to the house, Joseph put his book down carefully on the hammock, took his jacket—which was hanging on a nail on one of the trees—and hurriedly ran his fingers through his hair. He walked briskly up to the house, and when he greeted Charlotte in the living room, immediately noticed how disturbed she appeared.

"Good afternoon, Mr. Shaw, I need. . . ." She was almost breathless. "I'm sorry, please forgive me for intruding."

He smiled warmly. "Not at all. You're most welcome any time. But you look a little flustered, Mrs. Fairburn—if you don't mind my saying so. It's the heat, no doubt. I've asked Somboon to bring some lemon squash."

"Yes, thank you, that's very kind. And you're quite right, I *am* flustered. In fact, more than flustered. But I'm afraid it's not the weather, Mr. Shaw."

"Can I be of assistance, Mrs. Fairburn?"

"To tell you the truth, Mr. Shaw, I don't think anyone can do anything to help me. But I wanted to talk to someone. I feel I can trust you."

"Of course you can. But please, take your time." He sat down on a chair opposite her. "You look pale. It's not Elizabeth, is it?"

"No, no, it's not Elizabeth. Well, that's to say, it's not her directly. But it does concern her."

"Go on, Mrs. Fairburn. Whatever's troubling you, I'm sure there's a solution."

"But that's just it, Mr. Shaw. There *is* no solution."

Joseph became alarmed. "Whatever is it, Mrs. Fairburn? Your health is all right, is it not? Mr. Fairburn is in good health?"

"Oh, yes," she replied cynically. "*He's* in good health."

"Then. . . ?"

"I may as well come straight to the point, Mr. Shaw." She hesitated only briefly. "My husband's having an affair with a Siamese girl."

Joseph wasn't completely surprised. It happened frequently, and he knew some of the wives even tolerated it. But he was sorry for Mrs. Fairburn, who seemed such a decent, honest woman. "Are you absolutely sure?" he asked.

"Yes, he's admitted it. But the worst of it is, they have a child. Or rather, she has a baby that she says is my husband's. And he doesn't deny it. In fact, he . . . he. . . ." She almost broke down, and had to take a deep breath before she could go on, dabbing at her eyes with a handkerchief. "He refuses to put a stop to the affair. He actually believed I'd consent to him continuing the relationship."

"That would be a most heinous way for you to exist," Joseph agreed, before pausing for thought. "You know, Mrs. Fairburn, your husband isn't a member of this parish. He's never attended a service, so I can do little to influence him, except to offer you my prayers."

"Mr. Shaw, I didn't mean that I wanted you to do anything. His mind is made up, and I doubt anyone can change it. He's not a religious man, unfortunately. I don't wish him any ill, and I don't wish to cause him any hardship. He's still the father of my own daughter. But I cannot countenance this relationship. The only thing left for me to do is to leave for England immediately."

"Mrs. Fairburn, I cannot officially condone your leaving your husband, you understand. But in private, may I say that I'm perfectly sympathetic to your decision. Is there nothing I can do to help you?"

His kindness almost made her burst into tears once more, but she took a deep breath and nodded. "There is one thing, Mr. Shaw, that's leaving a terrible ache in my heart—more so, in fact, than my husband's infidelity. He forbids me to take Elizabeth back to England with me. He says that as it's I who's deserting him, the law will uphold his right of custody of our daughter."

"I'm afraid he's correct, Mrs. Fairburn. Unfair as it may seem, unless you can prove his adulterous affair, which would involve a public court case, he's entitled to keep Elizabeth here with him."

"Oh, Mr. Shaw, I can hardly think of how meaningless life will be without her. But still, I cannot . . . I *cannot* stay. I will not. I don't want to stand by and watch my husband collect a harem. And equally, I don't want my daughter brought up among such customs. But a public court case is out of the question."

"Quite so. Is there *anything* at all I can do?" he offered again.

"There is one thing, Mr. Shaw. Elizabeth looks up to you. She thinks you're a wonderful teacher. Would you . . . would you watch over her? Could you talk to her from time to time—to be a sort of godfather, I suppose? I'm very sorry to ask such a thing, but you're the only one here I can trust."

"I'd be more than happy to," Joseph agreed instantly. "And if she ever needs help for any reason, I shall give it her without question. You can be sure of that, Mrs. Fairburn. I give you my word."

She sat with Elizabeth in the bedroom she and Edward had shared only briefly. A large trunk was open on the bed. She knew that the next day would be the saddest of her life; that it would be more desperate than any other. Her marriage was over and she was losing her only child.

"But Mummy, why must you go to England? I don't understand."

"Darling, I've told you. My health isn't good, and I must return to a cooler climate. Siam is an uncomfortable place for me, and I must get well again."

"Is it like when you told me you used to get sick before? And my brothers and sisters went to heaven?"

"No, Elizabeth, not quite like that. Just that I'm hurting inside."

"Will England make you feel better?"

"I hope so, sweetheart."

"Why can't I come?"

"Dearest, it's a very long journey. Besides, you have to go to school." For her daughter's sake, she fought back the tears.

"Does that mean you'll be away for a long time, like Father was?"

"Yes, Elizabeth. Perhaps longer."

Elizabeth began to sob. She could not understand. She looked up into Charlotte's eyes. "Don't you want me any more, Mummy?"

The tears that had been threatening all day, finally rolled down her face uncontrollably. She clasped Elizabeth to her. "Of course I do, darling. I love you more than anyone in this world. When you're older, you'll understand more why I had to go."

The next day, Elizabeth stood on the pier with her father, silently waving farewell to her mother as she boarded the boat that would take her to the ship waiting across the bar. He didn't wave, and still Elizabeth hoped that the vessel would somehow be forced to turn round and head back. But it wasn't to be. Her mother was gone, and Elizabeth thought she would never know why.

The captain had been through it before, and he knew the routine well. It had become something of a standard procedure, but it was never easy. He picked up his steel-nibbed fountain pen and began.

She had never really tried to fight it. She was thirty-eight years old and had given up the will to live when she left her only child in Bangkok.

◈ *Chapter 9* ◈

Each day she waited for her mother to come home. Might she not reach Singapore and then decide not to continue on to England after all? Her father was quiet these days, and would hardly answer her when she asked such questions. When she *was* brave enough to ask about her, his only reply was to tell her to stay quiet at the table, or to stop bothering him.

Less than a week after Charlotte had left, Kesri came back to the house with the baby.

"This Anchalee. Your sister," she said as she handed the child to Elizabeth.

Elizabeth thought for a moment. "My sister?"

"*Chai*. Your sister. We come back now, live with you."

Elizabeth was suspicious. "But how can Anchalee be my sister? My mother didn't have another baby. And if she did, she wouldn't have given it to you."

Kesri's expression darkened and she snatched Anchalee away. "I talk your father. . . ." And as she angrily left the room, she cursed in Siamese so that Elizabeth did not understand.

Elizabeth couldn't imagine what she had said to make Kesri react like that, but how could the baby be her sister? It didn't make sense. But she was sorry all the same, and she went out into the kitchen to apologise. She found only the maid there.

"Porntip, where's Kesri?"

"Go room she," Porntip answered.

Elizabeth started toward the back door, meaning to go out to the maids' quarters, but Porntip shook her head and held her back. "*Mai chai, mai chai*." She pointed to the ceiling.

Elizabeth laughed. "She won't be there if she's in her room, Porntip. Only our rooms are up there."

Porntip looked at Elizabeth, almost with pity, and Elizabeth wondered if the maid had understood her.

Finally, Porntip just nodded her head. "*Ka.*" The girl would find out for herself soon enough, she thought, and it wasn't her duty to tell her. She didn't know how to explain in English, anyway.

In fact, Porntip had already noticed that Kesri was treating her differently. No longer, it seemed, was she a trusted confidante, but more someone Kesri felt she could give orders to. Porntip was beginning to regret her part in the scheme. *Mem* Charlotte had been kind and undemanding, and she realised now that Kesri would not be so generous.

Elizabeth climbed the stairs two at a time, and when she looked round the doorway into her parents' bedroom, her mouth dropped open in astonishment. Kesri was lying on the bed, tickling Anchalee and giggling. She had pulled back the blankets and was lying across the bed on Mummy's white linen sheets.

Kesri looked up. "Yes, Elizabeth?" she said irritably.

Elizabeth was speechless. She didn't know what to make of the scene, only that it didn't seem right.

Kesri stood up, leaving Anchalee gurgling on the bed, and went over to the dressing table. "What you want, Elizabeth?" she asked again. "You want say sorry? So say. Then go."

She picked up Charlotte's silver brush and began to groom her hair, all the while watching Elizabeth in the mirror. When she put down the brush, several thick black hairs mingled with the lighter brown of Charlotte's. Elizabeth knew how much her mother had loved that brush. Her father had given it to her as part of a set when Elizabeth was born, and she wondered why her mother had left it behind.

Very deliberately, Kesri then took the stopper out of one of the little coloured-glass perfume bottles and dabbed the scent behind her ears. Elizabeth felt sick, and she hurried from the room, down the stairs, and into the front garden, where she lay in the long grass beside the fence, sobbing and not caring what snakes might lurk there.

It was in this condition that Joseph found her. He lifted her up, knelt beside her so that his head was level with hers, and wiped her eyes with a big white handkerchief. "Hush, hush. What's the matter, Elizabeth?"

"My . . . mother . . . has . . . gone . . . away," she stuttered, still shuddering from crying so hard.

"I know," he said. "And you must be very brave. Just remember that she loves you."

"If . . . she did . . . she . . . wouldn't . . . have . . . gone . . . away." She was sobbing less, but still distraught.

"I know it's hard for you to understand, but you must believe she loves you, and always will. And perhaps, when you're older, your father will let you go to England to visit her."

She found hope in his words. "Do you think so?"

"Why don't you ask him? Your father loves you very much, too, and I'm sure he wouldn't want to see you unhappy like this."

But this only brought on a fresh round of tears. "No, Mr. Shaw, he doesn't care about me. Whenever I talk about Mummy, he tells me to be quiet. He doesn't want to talk about her at all. And than . . . and than. . . ." She looked up at him mournfully.

He set her down on the lawn and sat beside her. "What is it, child?"

"I saw Kesri in Mummy's room, lying on her bed and using her brush and her perfume." But before Joseph could think of a sympathetic reply, she told him even more disturbing news—to which he could not respond. "And, Mr. Shaw, she told me that her baby is my sister. I don't understand. I don't know why she said that. She's telling fibs, isn't she?"

Joseph determined to speak with Edward as soon as possible. The child was so confused, she hardly knew where she was. He stood up and brushed grass from the legs of his trousers. "Well, Elizabeth, since I'm your visitor, do you think we should go inside and have some tea?"

"Are you my visitor? I thought you came to see Father."

"No, I came to see you."

She managed a weak smile. "I don't think I've had a visitor before." She slipped her hand in his as they walked into the house, and she asked Porntip to bring them some tea. "I have a visitor," she said importantly.

They went into the front room and chatted about her schoolwork and the subjects she enjoyed most. When Porntip brought the tea in, Elizabeth poured the cups herself, and they continued talking—with Joseph ensuring that Charlotte was not mentioned.

The conversation ceased when Kesri entered the room with Anchalee. *"Sawatdee ka,* Mr. Shaw," she said, surprised that he was alone with Elizabeth.

"Sawatdee khap, Kesri. How are you?" He remembered her from the mission, and from the party at the British Consulate.

"I fine, Mr. Shaw. This Anchalee." She held out the baby for his inspection.

He had no choice but to take the child from her, and was startled to see her bright green eyes. It was Edward's child, there could be no mistake. "She's very beautiful, Kesri." He held her for a moment and then handed her back. Elizabeth remained silent.

Kesri hugged Anchalee to her. "Are you come see Edward?"

"No, I'm here to see Elizabeth."

Kesri laughed to conceal her agitation. "Elizabeth? But she only girl." There was something dubious about the situation, and she didn't like it.

"Yes, but she's my pupil. And her mother asked me before she left to come to see if she was well from time to time."

Kesri gave him a sly look and spoke dismissively. "She fine. I tell Edward you come." Then she left the room without ceremony.

Elizabeth watched her go, and then whispered, "I don't know why she's so angry with me. I don't think she likes me."

How could he explain the situation to an eight-year-old? The truth was, he could not—and besides, it wasn't his place to do so.

"Perhaps I *will* have a word with your father before I go, after all," he told her as he stood up. He sent her off to read one of her school books in the garden, hoping it would provide some distraction, at least for a short while, and then went out to the studio, where he found Edward cleaning his equipment and preparing for a family portrait session later that day.

Edward greeted him jovially. "What can I do for you, Mr. Shaw? You haven't come to have your portrait taken, have you?"

"No thank you, Mr. Fairburn. I was in the neighbourhood, and thought I'd call by. Elizabeth treated me to a cup of tea."

"Did she really? She's becoming quite sophisticated in her old age, isn't she?"

"Indeed." Joseph laughed politely. "I also met Kesri. And the baby."

Edward abruptly became irritated. "Oh, yes. No doubt you've heard the rumours and were curious to see for yourself?"

"That's not why I came," Joseph replied quickly. "Actually, I hadn't expected to see Kesri here at all."

"I think of her as my wife, now," Edward commented almost casually as he went on with his preparations.

Joseph felt very uncomfortable. "Your . . . your wife? But you already have a wife, Mr. Fairburn."

"Not here, I don't, Mr. Shaw. Charlotte made her decision. It was she who abandoned her family."

"You didn't give her much alternative though, did you?" Joseph was shocked at his own forthrightness.

"And what interest do you have in all this?" Edward shot back, now visibly angered.

"I didn't come to moralise, Mr. Fairburn, if that's what you think. But I *am* concerned about Elizabeth. She's very confused. Did you know Kesri told her today that Anchalee is her sister?"

"No, I didn't." Edward was taken aback slightly, and the comment curbed his anger. "And she shouldn't have. Not yet."

"Mr. Fairburn, she'll hear the whole truth from someone, sooner or later. Or she'll put it together herself eventually," Joseph continued. "I realise it's none of my business, and I don't like to intrude, but she's also wondering what Kesri is doing in her mother's bedroom. Far be it for me to advise you on what you should tell your daughter, Mr. Fairburn, but I think you'll have to talk to her soon."

Edward *did* resent the intrusion, and—even more—the fact that it was the truth. But he was forced to relent.

"You're right, of course," he sighed, slumping on to the sofa. He gestured toward the armchair, and Joseph sat opposite him.

"I didn't want Charlotte to leave, you know. But things hadn't been good between us since she. . . ."

At that moment, Elizabeth knocked briefly at the open door and entered the room.

"Elizabeth, I've told you not to disturb me while I'm working. . . ."

"Yes, Father, I'm sorry. But a messenger brought this letter. It says 'urgent'. I think it's from Captain Orton on the boat." She handed the envelope to her father.

"All right my dear. Thank you. I wonder what Captain Orton can have to say that can't wait until he returns."

"Maybe it's about Mummy?" Elizabeth asked hopefully. "Maybe she's coming back."

Edward did not reply, but was certain that would not be the reason for the letter. Missives of this kind usually meant bad news.

April 20th, 1869

Dear Mr. Fairburn,

      It is with much sadness that I must inform you of the death of your wife, Charlotte Fairburn, on board the Chao Phya at 6 a.m. on April 20th, 1869.

Shortly after we set sail, Mrs. Fairburn developed a fever, and Dr. Matthews on board diagnosed cholera. He worked to save her through the day and night, but to no avail.

Mrs. Fairburn passed away quietly in her sleep, and she was given a proper Christian funeral service by myself, followed by a burial at sea.

I shall bring you the death certificate, completed by Dr. Matthews, personally on my return to Bangkok.

May I express my condolences, Mr. Fairburn, to yourself and to your daughter Elizabeth, and may your dearly departed wife rest in peace.

Yours sincerely,

Captain Orton

Edward stared at the letter, dumbfounded, the truth not sinking in. Without a word, he handed the page to Joseph.

Elizabeth noticed his expression and was alarmed. "Father, what is it? What's wrong? Why do you look like that?"

A numbness came over him, and a distant look entered his eyes. For a few moments, he could not seem to remember where he was. He saw a vision—like an old faded photograph—of a young woman on her wedding day, laughing gaily, as she looked into his eyes. She was young, and it was as if her life was just beginning. But then the edges of the picture turned brown and started to curl.

Elizabeth pulled at his sleeve. "Father, tell me what it says," she screamed, terribly frightened.

Joseph had also read the letter by now, and he, too, was reduced to a state of shock. But he knew he would have to be strong for Elizabeth.

Edward spoke unsteadily, and it was almost as if he were somewhere else. "Will you tell her, Mr. Shaw? I cannot." Then, slowly, like an old man, he walked from the studio back to the house.

"Mr. Shaw, tell me, please," Elizabeth cried. "What's happened? Is it my mother? Is she ill?"

Joseph also spoke listlessly. "Yes, my dear, it's your mother. Come, let's sit on the sofa together, and I'll tell you as gently as I can."

They sat down and he turned to face her. Her green eyes looked fearfully into his.

"Elizabeth, your mother is no longer with us," he began.

"Mr. Shaw, I know that. She's going to England."

"No, Elizabeth, I'm afraid she's not. Your mother was very ill, but she's at peace now."

"Then she's coming back?"

"No."

"Then she's . . . she's. . . ." Elizabeth could not bear to say it as she finally understood.

"I'm sorry, Elizabeth. Your mother died on the ship, of a fever."

She didn't bother to wipe her tears away. "It's not true. I don't believe you. My mother's coming back. She's coming back."

"No, my dear. As terrible as it may seem, she *has* passed away."

"But how? How did she die? And where is she now?" Elizabeth cried, not wanting to believe, yet understanding deep down that it was true.

"As I said, a fever. We don't know much yet, but Captain Orton says she was not in pain when she died."

He knew this was untrue, that the captain had attempted to spare them her agony. He had seen people die of cholera, racked with pain and exhausted from dry-retching when there was no more fluid left in their bodies to expel.

Cholera claimed so many in the tropics: missionaries, royalty, the poor, adults, children, Europeans and Siamese alike. There had been an epidemic only the previous year in Bangkok, and this year, things were not much better, although people said 1849 had been worse. Elizabeth sat there still and silent, but the tears continued to stream down her face.

Kesri was sitting in the nursery with Anchalee—rocking her to sleep—when he walked past in the hallway. Even in that brief moment, she saw that something was troubling him. When she was sure the child was well asleep, she followed him quietly into the bedroom, sneaking up as he lay face down on the bed. Softly, she began to massage his back in the way he always loved. But then suddenly, without warning, he reared up and pushed her roughly aside.

"Can you never leave me alone, woman," he shouted angrily.

She was shocked and looked at him in confusion, taking a moment to recover.

"You want I go?"

"Go, stay, do as you please. Just don't bother me. Not today."

"Edward. What wrong?"

He sat on the side of the bed now, his head in his hands. He looked up at her once more but did not need to say anything. His expression told her what to do, and she left the room as silently as she had entered.

Back in the nursery, she lay next to Anchalee, alone and afraid. Was he tired of her already? What if he rejected her? Had he met someone else? What would become of her and Anchalee if he had? And how would he react to her latest news?

She had planned to tell him today, but now she realised it would not be wise to do so. She could not risk her daughter's well-being for anything.

❖ *Chapter 10* ❖

She had already decided she should tell someone, a person who would believe her, and who would help her. Father had become ill-tempered over the last few months, and she was wary of approaching him for fear of making him angry. It wouldn't have been difficult. In any case, he seemed to have so little time for her now. He was either out on his photographic business, or busy in his studio most of the time.

Only a few days after it had happened, her chance came when Mr. Shaw arrived to visit her while Kesri was out. She told him what she had seen.

"Well, Elizabeth, that's certainly strange. And you were right not to keep it to yourself. I wouldn't like to guess the reason for it, but you have to be certain of these things before you make accusations. Do you understand what I'm saying? Are you sure that's exactly what you saw?" he asked gently.

"Yes, Mr. Shaw. Father always gives her money—whatever she needs."

"Then are you sure the money you saw her with wasn't given to her by him?"

She hadn't considered that. "No," she answered hesitantly.

She thought for a moment and then became more animated. "But she tried to hide it when she saw me. I don't think she'd do that if Father had given it to her. And I did see her take the silver things and come back without them."

"I do hope there's a logical explanation for this, Elizabeth. But I think what you must do is tell your father what you saw, just as you told me today. He should know about this."

She was silent and looked up fearfully.

"Are you afraid to tell him?"

She nodded. "He'll be angry with me. I know he will."

"Would you like me to come with you?"

She nodded again—uncertain of whether or not she was doing the right thing—and together they went over to Edward's studio.

She repeated exactly what she had told Joseph, and her father's reaction was just as she had feared. He was already annoyed at yet another interference by Joseph.

"I don't believe it, Mr. Shaw. The child's obviously making this up."

"Well, I don't think she is, Mr. Fairburn," Joseph replied firmly. "Perhaps you should examine the silverware case yourself."

Edward hesitated because he wasn't even sure himself what was in the case. There were so many small pieces that he'd be unable to tell if any were missing. It had always been Charlotte's collection.

"No, it's preposterous," he went on. "Why should Kesri need to steal and sell our silver? She can have whatever she wants. Shame on you, Elizabeth. You're either fabricating this deliberately, or you're beginning to believe your vivid imagination."

She now wished she hadn't said anything to anyone. "I'm only telling you what I saw," she pleaded miserably.

"I believe she's telling the truth," Joseph continued on her behalf. "Elizabeth isn't the type of girl to lie about something like this."

"Thank you, Mr. Shaw," Edward responded brusquely. "But I think I can deal with this matter myself, now."

"Of course," Joseph agreed. He turned to Elizabeth. "You've nothing to worry about as long as you tell the truth."

"Yes, Mr. Shaw. Thank you for helping me."

"I'll see myself out." Joseph nodded at Edward as he left.

"You have some explaining to do, young lady," Edward berated her sharply when Joseph was gone. "Just what possessed you to start spying like that?"

"But I wasn't spying, Father. I wasn't," she insisted. "When I saw Kesri take the silver the first time, it was by accident. She didn't know I was there when she came in. I wasn't hiding, I was there all the time reading. I was scared she'd shout at me if she knew I was there, so I kept quiet."

"Well, spying on someone and then telling tales to other people is not acceptable behaviour."

"I'm sorry, Father. I didn't know what else to do."

"What you *should* have been doing is paying less attention to your imagination, and more to your reading and your needlework."

"I'm sorry," she whimpered again.

"Off you go, then. And there'll be no more talk of stealing and secrets. Is that understood?"

"Yes, Father."

She went to her room and lay on her bed, confused and upset. She *had* told the truth, and he hadn't believed her.

But she remembered that afternoon vividly, sitting in the window seat in the front room, hidden behind the curtains. It was two months after they had received the tragic news of Charlotte, and she had accepted the fact that her mother would not be returning.

Her father had immersed himself in his work, and hardly spoke to her. He seemed to have time only for Anchalee—five-and-a-half months old, and a beautiful baby with dark, slightly wavy hair, skin that was perfectly balanced between the complexions of her parents, and startling green eyes.

As she sat behind the curtains, Elizabeth was thinking again of the day, less than a week after they had heard the news of Charlotte, when her father had explained that Kesri was no longer their maid.

"What is she then, Father?" she had asked.

She realised things were different since Kesri had returned with Anchalee, but she hadn't been able to work out exactly how.

"She's my wife, Elizabeth."

"But Father, she can't be your wife. Mother's your wife."

For some reason, she never called her "Mummy" now that she had died. Not to her father, anyway.

113

"Elizabeth, dear, your mother is dead, which makes me a widower. Do you know what that means?"

"No, Father."

"It means I no longer have a wife. I'm lonely without a wife, and Kesri and Anchalee need us. Don't you think it would be nice if they stayed?"

"Is that why Kesri was in your bedroom, using Mother's things? Because she wanted to be your new wife?"

"That's right, Elizabeth. And she'll be *your* new mother."

She understood then about the baby. "Is that why she said Anchalee was my sister? Because she was going to marry you, Father?"

"Yes, that's right. And I hope you'll treat Anchalee as your sister from now on."

Elizabeth found she actually liked having a sister, and it was true that Kesri had been friendlier toward her lately. She seemed to trust Elizabeth more, and allowed her to look after Anchalee for hours at a time some days.

But Elizabeth's recollections of the events of the previous few months were interrupted when she heard a noise in the room beyond the curtain. Someone had come into the room, and she peeked through a tiny gap and saw Kesri. She was about to say hello, to surprise her, when the words stuck in her throat.

Kesri went quietly to the "whatnot"—the rosewood cabinet her parents had filled with the souvenirs and treasures from their travels—and removed several small silver pieces. She put them in a small sack she carried, glanced round at the door, and then selected a silver candlestick from the crowded sideboard. She put it, too, in the sack, and then crept quietly from the room.

Elizabeth couldn't believe her eyes. She then heard the front door close, and from her window seat, saw Kesri go down the path, holding the sack. She sank back toward the curtains, hoping Kesri would not turn and see her. But Kesri didn't look back as she hurried off to the boat landing.

Elizabeth jumped up and flung open the curtains, looking incomprehensibly at the spaces where the silver pieces had been. Kesri hadn't taken much, and Elizabeth was sure no one would even notice the difference. But why? They were not dirty. Porntip could have cleaned them, anyway. They were not broken or in need of repair. Perhaps her father already knew about it. Perhaps he had told her to take them somewhere. She decided not to tell him just yet.

Perhaps because she was on holiday from school at the time—a result of the cholera epidemic—she allowed it to slip from her mind. Nothing happened for two more days. Kesri played with Anchalee, preened herself in front of the dressing-table mirror, and dressed up in the clothes Charlotte had left behind.

Elizabeth felt it strange. The dresses were far too big for Kesri, who wore them without petticoats, or even any underwear, and she was so slim, she had no need of a corset.

"You like dress?" Kesri asked one day as Elizabeth watched her from the bedroom door. She swirled the skirts round her.

"Isn't it too big for you?" Elizabeth answered honestly.

As usual, her comment sent Kesri into a black mood. "Go kitchen, look after Anchalee from Porntip. I go out."

Elizabeth did as Kesri asked—again feeling intimidated—but she was always content to look after Anchalee, anyway. She sat in the front room, bouncing the baby on her lap, laughing and giggling, and as she did so, it suddenly occurred to her. As she looked into the baby's eyes and saw again how green they were, she realised she knew only two other people with eyes exactly that colour—her father, and herself.

She stopped playing for a moment as she pondered the anomaly, and Anchalee became agitated. "Oh, I'm sorry, baby," Elizabeth hugged her closer. "Hush, hush, don't cry. You really are my sister, aren't you?"

But then she thought about it more. Anchalee had been born before her own mother died; before she had even left for England.

That meant . . . not the same mother? But it was all too much for an eight-year-old's mind to grasp.

She heard the front door close softly, and when she looked out the window, she saw Kesri, now dressed in her usual *panung*, hurrying down the path with the same small sack in hand. It jolted her memory, and she became suspicious again. She put Anchalee on the floor while she went to the sideboard and searched through it. Everything appeared to be in place, and nothing had been removed from the "whatnot".

She went through to the dining room and looked in the cupboard. There was a dust-rimmed space where a silver platter had been. She thought she remembered it from Melbourne. They didn't use it often, only if they had a large number of guests for dinner, and it would not be missed immediately; maybe not at all. She thought her father wouldn't even know what silver they had.

She played with Anchalee until the baby fell asleep, and after an hour or so, heard the front door open again, and Kesri's footsteps on the stairs. She decided to ask her about the silver platter.

She gently laid Anchalee in the little wooden cradle that had once been her own, and then climbed the stairs to her mother's room—as she still thought of it, despite Kesri having made it her own.

She had taken to going barefoot in the house, like the Siamese, so Kesri didn't hear her coming up. When she put her head round the open door, she saw Kesri reclining on the bed, counting coins from a small pouch. It was obvious to her now what Kesri had done.

Kesri looked up, not pleased to see her. "What you want Elizabeth? I busy." She hastily scooped the coins together and returned them to the pouch. "Why you look me, Elizabeth?"

She still could not quite pronounce Elizabeth's name correctly—saying something more like "Erisabet"—and at that moment, it made Elizabeth want to smack her.

"Nothing, Kesri. I'm sorry," was all she could say.

Sorry my father doesn't know you're a thief, she thought.

"Go play Anchalee," Kesri snapped.

"She's asleep."

Kesri paused for a moment. "So, go tell Porntip make *khao pat moo*. I hungry."

"Yes, Kesri." But she could not seem to move. Her legs were rooted to the spot, and she was staring at the little money pouch.

"*Pai, pai.*" Kesri gestured impatiently for her to leave—and Elizabeth ran off.

She brooded all afternoon, thinking of reasons why Kesri had stolen the silver, and why she needed money her father didn't know about. What secret was she hiding? She didn't like what she had seen, and she was convinced it was not right.

And so too was Edward. He hoped the matter could be left to rest, but the problem was—although he was reluctant to admit it—that what Elizabeth had revealed, troubled him greatly. He realised he did not fully trust Kesri.

After all, what did he really know about her, except that she had been brought up by missionaries after her parents had died? She had never volunteered any more information, and he had never asked for any. In fact, they seldom talked seriously together at all. Their relationship was based on sensual pleasures and little more. On the rare occasions he would initiate a sensitive conversation, particularly with any regard to herself, her family, or her past, she would smile beguilingly, slip off her *panung*, and that would be the end of it.

He reflected carefully and was forced to admit to himself that something was amiss. She had been moody and preoccupied lately, and she was eating more and gaining weight. When he had asked her if she were pregnant again, she denied it and changed the subject.

Perhaps she had a lover, he thought, suddenly panicking. He knew the Siamese women did not find the *farang* men handsome, but he had thought she might be an exception. Perhaps she was not, after all. Perhaps she meant only to extract enough money from him, and then to disappear with a young Siamese lover. He knew that some of the Siamese mistresses of expatriates even had husbands and families elsewhere, and that they regarded the foreigners as nothing more than a source of valuable income. Some self-righteous expatriates—most of them missionaries or scorned wives—claimed this as just retribution for the foreign males who, they said, used the Siamese women purely to satisfy their selfish and sinful lust. There was only one course of action left open to him.

◈ *Chapter 11* ◈

Narong followed at a safe distance, ducking into doorways or behind vendors' carts whenever it appeared she might look round. All he had to do was to follow, keep out of sight, and report back where she had gone and who she had seen. He was not, under any circumstances, to reveal himself. And he would not. Not with the promise of an extra month's pay if he completed the task successfully.

He followed her deep into Chinatown—a place she would not normally go—down the narrow, crowded lanes, past the tiny shops selling medicines, Chinese silk, all manner of bric-a-brac, and religious icons. They passed goldsmiths, where skilled tradesmen beat gold sheets into paper thin squares, and sold them to worshippers who used them to "make merit" at the Buddhist temples. And they passed gambling and opium dens, many with the doors almost closed on their dim, smoky interiors, guarded by large, grim-looking Chinese men.

When she reached her destination, she looked from side to side, then cautiously knocked at the door to a dirty, tumble-down wooden building. The door was answered by a European or American foreigner, which was something of a surprise to Narong, who now loitered at a stall selling noodle soup. The foreigner, too, looked warily up and down the street before ushering her in and closing the door quickly behind them.

Narong now knew that she was in trouble. He could not guess for certain what kind of trouble, but there were, however, only a few possibilities. She already had a *farang* man, so did not need another, unless she had lost a lot of money gambling and had been reduced to selling herself to repay her debts. But that seemed

119

unlikely. Siamese men were prolific gamblers, but the women rarely indulged.

Narong ordered a bowl of noodle soup and sat on a small, wooden stool next to the cart. His father was Chinese, and Narong spoke the language well.

"Who's that *farang*?" he asked the stall-holder in Cantonese, indicating the grubby building.

"Who wants to know?" The old woman eyed him suspiciously as she prepared his soup.

Narong grinned and said nothing more until he had finished eating, all the while keeping a careful eye on the doorway in case she should make a hasty exit.

When he went to pay the woman, he asked again about the foreigner. He held out his hand and the old crone leered greedily at the white porcelain hexagons and discs embellished with blue Chinese characters. They were *pee*—originally produced as gambling tokens, but also used widely as currency throughout Bangkok—and to her, they represented at least three days' clear profit or more.

"I might tell you," she hedged, as if not interested in the derisory sum on offer.

Narong dug deeper into his pocket and extracted another *pee*; another day's profit in his upturned palm.

"He's a doctor," she said, reaching out to grab the *pee* from his hand.

But Narong was too fast for her, and closed his fist, trapping the coins. "What sort of doctor?"

Now she was agitated and wary. "Who wants to know?"

"Just me. I may have a client for him."

"He's very expensive."

"Why? What does he do? Is he some sort of magic doctor? Does he deal with the spirit world?"

"No, but he does deal with the future."

"What do you mean? What sort of doctor is he?"

"Let's just say that he takes care of unwanted children."

Narong understood. But why would she have need of such a doctor? Unless, he thought, she had a Siamese lover to whom she had fallen pregnant, and—because she would not have been able to pass off the baby as Edward's—had to seek an abortion.

Still, he did not really care about such things, and did not think much more of it. His task completed, he loosened his grasp and poured the tokens into the old woman's impatient hands. He hurried directly back to the house, eagerly anticipating his own easily-earned reward.

When she arrived back home that afternoon, she found Edward in the front room, alone, waiting for her. He looked furious, and she prepared for the worst.

"Where have you been?" he demanded without any greeting.

She felt weak and disorientated, and she knew the ball of rags between her legs would be soaked with blood by now.

"I go market. Now sick, *mai sabai*. I go bed." As she spoke, she deliberately averted her eyes from his.

"First tell me where you've been. Tell me the truth, Kesri." His voice was cold and subdued.

She had never seen him like this before, and as she looked into his eyes, she understood that he already knew. There was a rushing noise in her ears—like the crash of waves on a beach—and a whispering in her head that she could not escape. "*Jai barb poo-ying. Jai barb poo-ying.* Evil woman."

"Tell me," he shouted.

She couldn't answer, and then—as if from a great distance—she felt his arms grip her shoulders and shake her violated body. All the blood and guilt inside her seemed to rise up to drown her, and she slumped from his grasp to the ground.

Later, he sat by the bed in a torment of rage, frustration, and confusion.

She was pale and weak, but pronounced by Dr. Bradley to be as well as could be expected after such a procedure.

He felt cheated. "Why, Kesri? Tell me why you did it? Why did you do this to our baby?" he pleaded. "Or was it not my child?"

She looked up at him, tears swimming in her dark eyes.

"*Chai*, yes, yes . . . your baby, Edward," she answered, almost in a whisper.

"Then why in God's name would you do this? An abortion in some filthy, back-street kitchen? It's lucky you're still alive; lucky that money-grabbing quack didn't manage to kill you in the process."

"I not think you understand why." She tried to sit up, but fell back against the pillows, exhausted. She closed her eyes for a moment and took a deep breath.

"Before, I have nothing. I not want Anchalee have nothing, too. One more baby make problem, and if boy I think you love more than Anchalee. Maybe you give son everything and Anchalee nothing."

"But Kesri, what you're saying doesn't make any sense." There was no sympathy in his voice. "It would still have been our child—and I'd love all my children equally. You must know that. There must be some other reason, something I can believe. What is it?"

She hung her head. "I scare' if have other baby, I not beautiful for you. Maybe you tired me, maybe you have other wife. Then you have more children with other wife and Anchalee get nothing. You have Elizabeth now, then maybe many son, and Anchalee same like me before."

Edward thought of his own brothers and knew there was truth in what she said. But he could not accept what she had done. It was murder. A woman belonged to her husband, and should not be permitted to destroy his child.

"Kesri, you lied, you stole from my house, and used the money to murder our child. I cannot forgive you."

"Please Edward, I do anything. Can have more baby."

"No, Kesri, there'll be no more children. Dr. Bradley says you've been too badly damaged." He looked dejected and weary now, and then stood as he said his next words slowly and quietly, as if to confirm to himself that it was the only course open. "There'll be no more of anything for you and me," he said. "We're finished, Kesri. Finished. I cannot love you any more. You've killed my child."

Tears slid across her cheeks and on to the white linen pillowcase. "Please, Edward. I do anything," she repeated. "You take more wife, anything. . . ."

"No, Kesri." He stopped her, not allowing himself to fall prey to the same guilt he had with Charlotte. "I don't want anything more from you. I'm sorry." He could trust her no longer.

"Edward," she cried, desperately clutching him with a weak hand. "Anchalee . . . how I take care Anchalee?"

He stared at her and wondered if he had ever really loved her. It had been nothing more than a shallow relationship, he knew now.

"You're right," he said at last. "None of this is Anchalee's fault. She's my daughter, and I love her. Nothing can change that. And she's a British citizen. I cannot allow her to go with you. You'll leave her with me, and she'll have everything I can give her. Everything, that is, on the condition that you leave and do not return. You'll have an allowance to live on—I'll not see you starve or go back to service—but you'll not see Anchalee or me again."

His words crushed her, and she could only moan in pain and despair as the tears seeped from her eyes which were shut tight in anguish.

But he did not relent. "As soon as you are well enough, you must take your things and leave. I rue the day I ever forsook Charlotte for you," he added, as much to himself as to her. Then he left the room.

Her fight was gone. Drained, irreparably damaged, and with nowhere to go, she realised that this one mistake had cost her everything she had dreamed of—and, for a time, believed she had attained. It was a terrible error of judgement. It was over.

In the days that followed as she lay there alone, recovering, she contemplated her future. She wanted her daughter to have the life she herself had never had, but she was consumed with thoughts of vengeance. Eventually, she vowed, her daughter would know the truth of what Elizabeth had done, of how Elizabeth's betrayal had ensured that Anchalee was left motherless. She would somehow ensure that, one day, Anchalee despised Elizabeth enough to want to ruin her.

Two weeks after Kesri left the house, he decided it was time for Elizabeth to return to England. And she complained bitterly when he told her.

"No, Father, please don't send me away. Please."

"Elizabeth, your mother was right. Siam is no place for you. You must return to England to school."

"But I love it here. I don't want to go to England. I've never been to England. At least let me go to school in Australia if you must send me anywhere."

"Elizabeth, we don't have any relations there to take care of you, and you can't go alone. In England, you can live with your grandparents, at least during the holidays. You'll go to the best boarding school we can provide, and you'll be taught how to be a lady. It's high time you stopped running around like a little savage."

"Won't I ever see you again?" she asked fearfully, thinking of her mother. She had begun to think that people did not return from long journeys overseas. Or if they did, everything was different.

"Of course, my dear. I shall doubtless make a trip home one day. And when you've completed your education, you may return here, if you like. Although by then, I'm hoping that perhaps Grandmother will have found you a suitable young man to marry."

But she was still upset, and thought only that he wanted rid of her. Since Kesri had left, he hardly spoke to anyone. It seemed that he was almost blaming her for the whole episode, and although she was not really sure what had happened, she was aware that it was something terrible. She began to think that she should have kept it to herself when she saw Kesri taking the silver.

"Will you send Anchalee away one day, too? Can she come to boarding school?"

"Well, if she wants to go to school in England, she can. But you'll be almost finished school by the time she begins. And remember, she's half Siamese. She may not want to go."

"Just as I don't want to go. Oh please, Father, I'll be good, I promise. I won't make a sound. I'll work hard at school, I'll stay in my room. I won't bother you. I'm sorry, so sorry about the silver, about Kesri, I never should have. . . ."

"That's enough, Elizabeth. It's final. You're going, and that's that. No more arguments."

And she did go, only one month later. Edward engaged a Miss Smith—a teacher returning to England—to escort her.

As Elizabeth waved goodbye to her father, and to Siam, from the deck of the Chao Phya, she tried not to think about the fact that it could be years before she saw him again; tried not to see the tall coconut palms gently swaying in the tropical breeze, the vendors in their little boats plying their wares up and down the river, or the naked children diving and swimming in the murky water. She was leaving Bangkok as a child, and she knew that when she returned, she would be an adult.

Part Two

April 1882 – November 1886

✦ Chapter 12 ✦

Sam balanced *Far East Adventures* on one hand, feeling its weight, and then opened it again at the foreword. He wondered what his father would have thought. He could imagine him saying, "Well son, now you're done with travelling, it's time to make some girl an honest woman. Come home and settle down. I've a nice little business here. You could do worse. . . ."

His father had never known about the book. In fact, he had heard little from his son over the last ten years. Sam had left home as a teenager, and he regretted losing contact with his father. And now it was too late. He read the introduction again.

Far East Adventures
By Samuel Taylor II
Foreword

Even as a young boy, I knew that an ordinary life was not for me. I would lie on my narrow bed in the living quarters above my father's saloon, dreaming of adventures in distant lands, and of life on the high seas. I believe I must have inherited this adventurous spirit from my father, although most people remember him as a steady, honest working man, rather than an adventurer.

Samuel Taylor I left England for California in 1848 in search of gold. He did not discover the riches he sought, but he did marry a beautiful Mexican señorita, my mother. I was only two years old when she died of scarlet fever in 1852. My father's wanderlust seemed to die with her, and he decided it was his duty to provide a home for his son. He bought a saloon in the then sleepy pueblo of Los Angeles, and there he stayed.

I studied hard and learned how to stand up for myself when I was called a "dirty Mexican half-caste". I was kept away from the drinking customers, but sometimes I would sneak down the stairs at night and sit outside the back door of the public bar, listening to the tall tales the men told. My yearning for adventure grew.

In 1865, during the Civil War, I finally persuaded the Union Army to let me join up. I lied that I was eighteen, but unfortunately, Lee surrendered to Grant on April 9th of that year, and I never reached the front. I returned home, worked hard, saved my money, and read every travel and adventure book I could lay my hands on. When I did reach eighteen, I said goodbye to California, and I have been travelling ever since.

This book is the result of the past seven years I have spent journeying in Southeast Asia, the Far East. During that time, I have mostly earned my living through journalism for publications in London and Europe as well as the United States. But there was so much more I wanted to tell about my experiences abroad, and this volume, I hope, will bring my readers a little closer to the world I have come to love. I will start with the city I have returned to again and again, perhaps the most Oriental of all cities: Bangkok, Venice of the East, the City of Angels.

Samuel Taylor II,
Bangkok, 1881

After his father died, there was nothing left for him in California, so he had arranged for the saloon to be sold. He would never have gone back to it. Siam was where his heart was now.

He leaned back in his chair and sighed with satisfaction. His book was finally published, and he was particularly pleased that his author's copies had arrived this week, when Bangkok was celebrating its centennial. His publisher said in the covering letter that he expected significant sales in both New York and San Francisco, and—later in the year—in Great Britain too. Furthermore, he wanted to know how long it would take Sam to produce a second volume of travel tales.

There was an additional, more personal note to Sam from his editor, with whom he had established quite a rapport, despite the fact that the two had never met: "*. . . If you have not done so already, you must read Mr. Butler's new travel book, 'The Alps and Sanctuaries of Piedmont',*" Jonathan Taite wrote. "*I have enclosed a copy, understanding the difficulty of acquiring new English volumes in your part of the world. You must be due for furlough soon, and I would enjoy meeting you in person.*"

Sam tapped out a quick reply to the publisher on his typewriter. He was particularly fond of the machine, although he had initially cursed the thing many times as one more heavy item of baggage he had to contend with on his travels. He had taught himself to use the Remington and Sons machine, eventually mastering the odd arrangement of keys, originally composed that way in 1873 in order to separate letters that often occurred together, and so prevent the keys from jamming as they struck the roller.

He sealed the letter in an envelope, and addressed it in large, clearly-legible print. The mail service was not particularly reliable. First, the letter would have to be taken to the American Consulate, where it would be hand franked. From there it would travel to Singapore, and then take a circuitous route to New York. There were rumours that the service would improve soon, with special stamps coming from Singapore, and more mail ships to and from Europe and North America. But for the moment, it was a matter of hoping for the best.

Sam put on his sports coat, left his room at the Oriental Hotel, and went down to the landing nearby to hire a boat to the consulate. It was only a short distance upriver, and he asked the boatman to wait to take him back.

Like most foreigners, he found the riverside activity fascinating, and when he returned to the Oriental after handing over his letter, he lit a cheroot and leaned against the wooden railing. He looked up at the plain, two-storey teak building with its verandahs and tiled roof—wondering if he could not perhaps secure more comfortable lodgings—and then turned and gazed down into the brown water below, marvelling that in all the filth, fish not only survived, but seemed to thrive.

A short distance out from the bank, the carcass of a dog floated by, half submerged. Not far away, children dived into the water, laughing and shouting, and a woman squatted on the steps of her floating house, using the river as the family laundry basin. On the landing itself, men sat together in groups, smoking and talking, and mangy dogs skulked around, looking for scraps.

"*Furlough*," his editor had said. It was a strange word for an even stranger concept. He could not even imagine what he would do on a vacation in California. Likely go insane, or become a raving drunk like most of the other failed adventurers who found their way there. No, he did not need to return home. What he needed, he decided, was some excitement.

The steamer was due in from Singapore today, and most of its European passengers would disembark at the landing. They generally preferred to stay at the Oriental because of its proximity to the British Consulate and its location next to the river, with its cooling breezes. In addition, many of the long-term residents lived in the area, and so would alight there with their trunks and wooden cases.

Soon, however, he was so engrossed in watching a beautiful Siamese woman bathing nearby—wrapped from neck to ankles in a *sarong* designed for the purpose—that he did not see the first boat of Europeans from the steamer until it was almost level with the landing. He recognised the man and one of the girls on board, Edward Fairburn—one of Bangkok's most prosperous photographers—and his daughter by a Siamese wife.

What was the girl's name? She must be twelve or thirteen, he thought, and she would certainly break some hearts one day with her perfect golden complexion, and startling green eyes. Still, even he drew the line at thirteen-year-olds. Now, if she were fifteen or sixteen. . . .

But he had never seen the other young woman in the boat before. She sat between Fairburn and his daughter, tranquil and composed, yet looking this way and that, as if rediscovering a scene she was familiar with but had not seen for a long time. As the boat pulled closer to the pier, she made some comment to Edward. Then he realised, she must be the other daughter, by his first, English wife. He couldn't recall her name either, but he looked at her with more than a passing interest. She would be in her early twenties, and he knew from local expatriate gossip that she had been sent away to school in England when she was quite young. The result of bad behaviour, perhaps? Looking at her now, he could scarcely believe the elder Miss Fairburn capable of any sort of misbehaviour.

She was pristine in her high-necked white dress, which was old fashioned in comparison with that of other young English-women, who now wore brighter colours. She held a white and pink-trimmed parasol above her head, and she wore a small hat, fastened beneath the chin with pink and white ribbons.

He wondered how she had managed to keep her dress so white during the long journey from Singapore. She must have kept it in a separate case, specifically for her arrival. She hadn't seen her father for many years, he guessed, so it was no wonder she wanted to impress him. Still, she appeared as if she had been dressed by her grandmother—straight-laced, with no sophistication or artistry about her costume. It was the outfit of a virginal young woman, he thought—which was almost certainly what she was. The English guarded their daughters as if they were the crown jewels.

As the boat drew up alongside the pier, the younger girl jumped out on the landing with ease. Edward helped his elder daughter from the boat, and she made a slow, careful exit on his arm.

"There are so many new buildings. I can hardly recognise Bangkok," Sam heard her exclaim as she looked around.

"It's true," Edward agreed. "But you'll soon get your bearings again. Really, not much has changed."

"Well, at least the Oriental Hotel is still here. That's one landmark I do remember."

"Yes, it's still here." He looked up at the decaying building. "Although perhaps due for some renovations."

The trunks were off-loaded, and as the three walked toward him, Sam noticed she was quite tall. She certainly towered over the Siamese women, most of whom were little over five feet tall. He nodded a greeting to Edward and tipped his hat to the girls as they approached.

"Afternoon, Mr. Fairburn. . . . Ladies."

"Mr. Taylor," Edward replied, shaking Sam's extended hand briefly. "You've met Anchalee before, and may I introduce my elder daughter, Miss Elizabeth Fairburn."

She looked at him, then quickly away again, and he smiled to himself at her flushed cheeks. Was it merely the heat—the result of the exhausting journey—or was it a blush?

When she looked at him again through long lashes, he was struck by the same green eyes as Anchalee's. Not as dazzling as her younger sister's, but serene and subtle.

"Charmed, Miss Fairburn. I hear you've been away for some time."

"Yes, Mr. Taylor. More than thirteen years, actually."

"Well, I trust you'll be attending some of the centennial celebrations?"

"I . . . I'm not really sure." She looked enquiringly at her father before adding, "I expect so."

There was a moment of silence before Edward ushered them on. "Come, Elizabeth, Anchalee. Excuse us, Mr. Taylor."

"Of course, Mr. Fairburn. We'll meet again soon, then," he called to her as she turned away, her cheeks scarlet again. He watched her intently as Edward escorted them to their waiting carriage.

A gang of rickshaw riders who were stationed at the landing, and could obviously see that the Fairburns had their own transport, laughed good-naturedly as they attempted to lure the foreigners into their vehicles for a reasonable fare to their destination. Edward waved off their advances without humour, and Elizabeth could sense that he had been irked by Mr. Taylor's presence.

Rickshaws had been introduced to the city in 1871, and enterprising Chinese operators continued to import them from other Asian countries—including Singapore and Hong Kong—usually after they had been rejected as too dilapidated for service in those places. There was a plethora of them available along New Road and its side lanes, and the Siamese had readily taken to riding in them for convenience, even for very short distances. They were used for every purpose; transporting household goods from one road to another, and for carrying pigs and poultry to market.

Foreigners, however, generally eschewed the rickshaws—most residents preferring to run their own carriages. It was an expensive investment, but labour was exceedingly cheap, so after the initial outlay for horses and carriage had been met, it wasn't difficult to maintain a stable with several employees.

Edward had two carriages: the larger one they were just getting into, which could comfortably seat four, and had room for luggage; and a smaller victoria he had owned for years, with room enough to accommodate only two.

Sam, however, wasn't concerned with carriages or rickshaws as he watched them leave. He was far more interested in one of the occupants of the departing vehicle. She had intrigued him. One word from a man and she was rendered almost speechless. There was no doubt in his mind that he would be compelled to seduce her.

But there was the problem of her father. Fairburn would never permit his daughter to become acquainted with a journeyman writer who had been brought up in a saloon, was of no fixed abode, who lived in hotels, and who had a reputation for enjoying life as a bachelor. Sam had known many women—but had been serious about none of them. None had managed to command his attention for much longer than it took to lead them to his bed. And that usually wasn't long. But this Englishman's daughter might require a little more attention and effort.

It was strange about her father, he thought. If the rumours he had heard were true, when Fairburn came to the city in the 1860s he had been no saint. By the time his wife and Elizabeth arrived, he had already taken a young Siamese mistress. The wife discovered they had a daughter, refused to share her husband, and left him—only to perish on the voyage back to England. Or so the story went.

Fairburn and his Siamese mistress had then apparently had a terrible argument, resulting in him banishing her, but retaining custody of their daughter, Anchalee. Almost immediately, he had sent his elder daughter back to England.

No one seemed to know exactly what had become of the Siamese mistress, although rumour had it that she died a year or so later.

After that, Sam thought, Fairburn must have been over-whelmed with guilt. Perhaps he believed he was responsible for the deaths of both women—which, indirectly, he was, it seemed. Whatever the truth, he had turned to the Church, and became increasingly involved with parish activities at the little riverside chapel run by the American Protestant missionaries. He had returned to England only once during that time, leaving Anchalee with a missionary family until he returned.

Sam wandered back up to his room, where he sat at his desk and contemplated the first chapter of his new book. He planned now to write exclusively of Siam, and intended to make the perilous journey north to Chiengmai, along crocodile-infested waters on overloaded boats, and on elephant-back through dense forest where the risks of tiger attacks, jungle fever, and venomous snake-bites were great. It was a journey totalling 500 miles, which could take many weeks, even several months, to complete.

Few foreigners went to Chiengmai, and he was convinced it would make for a first-rate adventure story. There were, however, a number of brave missionaries there, and Sam's friend, Louis Leonowens, also wanted to make the trip.

Louis had lived in Bangkok as a boy, when his mother, Anna, taught English at the Grand Palace, but he had left and spent some time, like Edward, on the Australian gold fields. In 1881, when he was twenty-five, he returned to Siam to become a captain in the army of his boyhood friend, King Chulalongkorn, but was now in Australia, again, to purchase horses from New South Wales to bring back for Chulalongkorn's cavalry.

Sam and Louis had been friends since their first meeting, and Louis had even offered his friend a commission in the army. Sam had admitted to himself that the generous annual salary was tempting.

"But Louis, I'm afraid I'll have to turn you down," he had said to his friend. "All that discipline, all that attention to detail, putting on a uniform every day, and all those men relying on me. It's not for me. Now, if you go into battle and need a correspondent, I'll be the first to volunteer."

Sam placed a sheet of paper in the typewriter and began. . . .

Chapter One: Bangkok

So much of Asia has been tempered, dare I say spoiled, with things Western, that the true adventurer is often disappointed when he arrives at some Oriental outpost only to find there many of the comforts of home. However, there remains at least one Asian port that has not suffered the effects of a colonial invasion; one that remains wholly Asian, wholly itself: it is Bangkok, the capital city of Siam.

Here, the visiting Occidental has never felt so foreign, so alien, or so overwhelmed by the Far East in all its tropical, spicy splendour. Here, the adventurer can. . . .

Can what? He got up from the desk and stepped over to the window. The publishers were keen to have another book right away. He had enough notes at least for the first chapter on Bangkok, and for several on Siamese life and customs. He had been to some of the country's beautiful Southern coastal areas in the seven years since he had first come to Siam, but the bulk of the book would remain unwritten until he travelled further into the hinterland.

As he looked out his window at the bustling scene below, the image of her face came to him again: her fine fair hair, her green eyes, the white dress and the white-gloved hands holding the matching parasol, and the unblemished skin that seemed almost as white as the dress until she blushed at his first glance. She seemed the antithesis of her equally beautiful younger sister. And he knew he must have her. Once the innocence had left her face, she would no longer interest him, he was sure.

"Damn," he swore under his breath. Like other authors, he liked to believe that he could work when required, that he did not have to search too hard for inspiration. There were few— only very few—distractions that could bring his work to a halt, and it now seemed that she was one of them.

The room was stifling, even with the window open, and he could feel the onset of a thumping, heat-induced headache. To prevent it taking hold, he needed some fresh air, a drink, and a diversion. He picked up his jacket from the back of the chair and slung it over his shoulder.

If he was lucky, perhaps he could still secure an invitation to the centennial ball at the British Consulate.

❖ *Chapter 13* ❖

"Who was that man, Father?" she asked casually as the carriage trundled roughly along New Road to the house.

"I introduced you. Samuel Taylor." His response was terse.

It was clear to her that he didn't like the man, and she wanted to know the reason. "Yes, but who *is* he? Or perhaps I should say, *what* is he?"

"A journalist, I believe. Quite well-known in his field. Why?"

"Oh, no reason, Father. I was just curious about him."

"Well, don't be. That man has a reputation for thoroughly enjoying the company of Bangkok's young ladies—Siamese and European—and you'll stay away from him. He's a philanderer and he's trouble."

That satisfied her curiosity and she could well believe it, if first impressions were any indication. He was tall, broad-shouldered, and olive-skinned. His mysterious eyes were almost jet-black, and his wavy black hair was longer at the back than most men wore it. He was a world apart from the insipid aristocrats she knew in England, and she was intrigued at what nationality he might be. He had spoken with an American accent, but he hardly looked American. He was dark, but he certainly was not Oriental. He looked more Spanish, or perhaps Italian, and she was soon wondering if he would be at the centennial ball, now hoping very much to see him there.

"And how is James?" her father quickly changed the subject of the conversation. She did not answer and he nudged her gently to rouse her from her reverie. "Elizabeth?"

"I'm sorry, Father, I was miles away. What did you say?"

"James."

"James?"

"Yes, James. Your fiancé."

"Oh, of course. James. Sorry, I'm not myself. It must be the heat and the long journey. James is quite well, thank you."

"Have you set a wedding date yet?"

But before she could answer, the carriage had drawn up at Edward's imposing, two-storey colonial mansion, and her attention was immediately drawn to it.

"This is wonderful, Father. Your description didn't do it justice, I must say."

The European-style house—built in 1880—was constructed of teak, with a white granite stairway leading up to the front door, and green painted shutters on each window. It was solid and comfortable, with five bedrooms upstairs, and a parlour, sitting room, billiard room, and dining room downstairs. In Siamese style, the kitchen was detached from the house, at the back with the staff quarters.

Compared to the way most of the population lived, it might well have been a palace. Elizabeth had noticed, as she had journeyed upriver, that the houseboats and rickety stilt dwellings along the banks had not changed in the years she had been away, only there were more of them.

She had noticed, also, several scorched areas where many houses had been burnt to the ground. Fires were frequent, and there was no concept of a fire brigade. Soldiers would be called to any major conflagration, but it was generally too late to prevent widespread damage. Flames quickly leapt from house to house via the tinder-dry, palm-leaf-thatched roofs, and hundreds of people could lose their homes and possessions within minutes.

Anchalee, who had hardly said a word during the carriage ride, jumped out ahead of her sister and led her quickly up the path, eager to show her around the house. Edward went out to the kitchen to ask the maid to prepare tea. The rooms were full of furniture that Edward had imported from Europe at great expense. There was a marble-topped tea table with curled, dark wood legs, a baby grand piano, Italian gilt mirrors, seven different types of wallpaper from England, and even a billiard table

Elizabeth was delighted to find, in the parlour, the old rosewood "whatnot" her mother had loved all those years ago, with the same pieces still displayed inside. "I didn't know this would still be here. How lovely." She ran her fingers along the wood of the cabinet lovingly.

But Anchalee wasn't looking. "We have lots of new furniture from England. Father's regularly summoned by the king to take photographs of the royal family, so he's become very successful now."

"I suppose His Majesty is quite grown up. When I left, he wasn't much older than you."

"Yes, and he has many children of his own now. And many wives."

"Oh, really," Elizabeth mumbled in quiet surprise. She had almost forgotten that aspect of the culture, and wondered how the Siamese women tolerated it.

Anchalee knew intuitively what Elizabeth was thinking. "Don't you like that idea?"

"What idea?"

"Well, in Siam it's prestigious for a man to have many wives."

"How can you say that? I'm sure the wives themselves don't like it."

"Oh, but they do. If your husband has other wives, you don't have so much work to do yourself."

Elizabeth laughed involuntarily, amused at Anchalee's precocity. "You didn't learn that at the missionary school. I forget sometimes that you're only half English."

Then she realised how insensitive that sounded, and apologised. "Oh, I'm sorry. . . ." she began.

But Anchalee seemed unconcerned, immediately taking Elizabeth's hand and leading her out of the parlour. "Come upstairs and I'll show you your room. It's the best one, and we've been saving it for you all this time. It's got a lovely view of the river."

Elizabeth smiled. She hadn't seen Anchalee since she was a baby, except in photographs sent by Edward, and it was still hard for her to believe that this dusky-skinned thirteen-year-old was really her sister. At twenty-one, Elizabeth felt more like an aunt or an older cousin. The only similarity between the two was their green eyes, and even she thought that her own looked nothing out of the ordinary, whereas Anchalee's were thrillingly exotic.

The room was as lovely as Anchalee had said, with a white lace bedspread, and masses of draped mosquito netting round the bed. There was a window nook with a seat that looked out over the water, and the dark teak floor was so highly polished that it almost provided a reflection. There was a dressing table with a large oval mirror, and a fine china basin and jug for washing.

Elizabeth was delighted. "It's perfect, Anchalee. Did you put all these lovely white orchids in here?"

"Yes. They're growing in our garden."

Elizabeth sat on the edge of the bed and patted the space beside her. "Come and sit next to me." She took Anchalee's small hands in hers. "It's been so long since I've seen you, Anchalee. You don't remember, but we played together when you were a baby. You were so beautiful and I loved you from the start. And now you're almost a young woman. We'll have to watch out when the men come calling for you."

"Elizabeth, you're so prim and proper." Anchalee jumped off the bed, giggling. "Is that what they taught you at school? I've already got a boyfriend. But don't tell anyone. He's Siamese, and Father wouldn't like that."

"Wouldn't he?"

"No. He says I have to marry a *farang*. He forgets who I am, sometimes."

"I think he's probably just concerned for your welfare, Anchalee. Anyway, you're much too young to be talking about such serious things."

"Lots of Siamese girls get married at fifteen—or younger."

"But you're not Siamese, Anchalee."

"Aren't I?"

"No. Your father is English and so are you."

"You're right, of course," she replied lightly, and then smiled, her small, even teeth gleaming white.

"And I'm glad to see you haven't started that awful pastime of chewing betel nut," Elizabeth said, in mock seriousness.

"I probably would, if it weren't for Father. But he'd die if I did. Anyway, the king doesn't like it and most of the younger people have given it up. White teeth are actually becoming quite fashionable now. Anyway, you must be tired. I'll let you rest. See you at dinner."

And with that, she skipped out like a child, leaving the door open behind her.

Elizabeth sat by the window, reflecting on the contradictions she saw in her younger sister. On the one hand she could be sweet and very immature. Yet on the other, she seemed earnest and precociously knowledgeable. She was sure Anchalee had only been teasing her about having a boyfriend. Surely she was much too young.

But how could she advise Anchalee when she, herself, had had so little contact with men—having first been taught privately at her grandmother's house by a middle-aged spinster, then at an exclusive girls' boarding school, and then at finishing school in Switzerland?

Her grandmother had held a wonderful coming-out ball for her when she was eighteen, and she had attended a fair number of functions since then, but she was always chaperoned, always under her grandmother's eye, and the young men she met were frightfully formal. It was at one of these balls that she had met Viscount James Claridge.

James, who was heir to his father's earldom, had fallen instantly in love with her, and had begged her to marry him only a few months later at another ball where they had managed to steal a few moments alone together in the garden. She accepted. After all, hadn't everyone told her what a marvellous catch he was!

And indeed, James was everything a woman could want. He was tall, handsome, wealthy, and titled. He was charming, witty, and he adored her. Her grandparents thoroughly approved of him, of course. But she had held off setting a wedding date, even though they had been unofficially engaged already for six months.

❖

"It's so hard to explain to you, James," she had told him then. "I do want to marry you, but there's something I must do first. I must return to Siam."

"I understand, my dear. But why don't we get married, and go there during our honeymoon?"

What he had said made sense, as always, but still she felt that she should wait.

"Don't ask me why, James, because I don't know myself. But I feel I must go back alone. I feel as if I've left something unfinished there. I'll not be a whole person, and I'll not be ready to marry you until I've been back. Can you understand that?"

"Not really, but if that's what you want, then so be it. We'll be married the moment you return."

She kissed him gratefully on the cheek then. "Thank you, James. You've been wonderful."

"But remember," he added, a hint of warning in his voice that she took to be a joke. "Don't stay away too long. I'm thirty and it's time I married. My father's getting old and he wants to see his grandchildren before he dies."

"James, I don't want to hold you to anything," she had said then. "We haven't made a public announcement about our engagement—only our families know. If you find someone else. . . ." And she had gone, promising to write as soon as she arrived in Siam.

At first, she had thought it might be a mistake, and that she would regret leaving. But she was filled with a sense of relief when she felt no pangs of homesickness—or of missing him. The feeling of freedom she had experienced as soon as the ship set sail remained with her, and did not leave. She began to feel, to her own surprise, that she had not been in love with him at all. And now that she was back in Bangkok, she truly felt as if she had come home.

Even though she had spent only a short time in Siam as a child, she had never forgotten the warm winds, the palms, the gentle people, or the easy way of life. She had always felt like a stranger in England, a guest in her grandparents' huge, sprawling mansion.

And now, as she sat in this new bedroom reminiscing, she felt herself blushing at the memory of another man. His dark good looks, and his confident, casual air were etched in her mind. She tried to busy herself opening drawers and closets, ready for her unpacking, but the vivid memory remained. She smiled to herself and leaned back on the soft bed. She was home.

As soon as her trunks arrived, she found her new pink silk skirt and blouse, and asked a maid to iron them before she washed and changed for dinner. She and Edward had much to talk about. She had not seen him since he visited England five years before.

"You seem to be very involved with the Church these days," she said to him at the table later, as their maid, Noi, served the first course of spicy seafood chowder.

"I am, indeed. Does that surprise you?"

"Well, to be frank, Father, yes it does. You always called them 'interfering busy-bodies' in the old days, as I recall."

He looked a little uncomfortable. "I found the Church late in life, it's true. And not before I'd made some regrettable mistakes. But I believe I'm at last on the true path."

Elizabeth coughed, and breathed in sharply at the now unfamiliar taste of chilli.

Anchalee could barely suppress a bout of laughter—caused by both her father's comment, and her sister's reaction to the spices.

"You sound like you're giving a sermon right here in the dining room, Father."

"Don't be impertinent, young lady," he admonished her. His words were harsh but his tone was not. Elizabeth could see that he adored her.

Anchalee laughed again, but nevertheless had to admit to herself that he was a happier man now. For a long time she had not heard him call out in his sleep as he used to for several years.

"And what of Joseph Shaw, Father? Is he still here, or has he retired back to New Zealand?"

"Retired? Good heavens, no, Elizabeth. He's younger than I am. He'd be only forty now. Retire? Whatever gave you such an odd notion?"

Elizabeth smiled. "Isn't it funny? When I was here, Mr. Shaw seemed so old to me. But he must have been only in his late twenties then. I always imagined he was about fifty when I was seven or eight. He must be married with a family, now, is he?"

"No, he's never married. But he's doing very well in his work. He's even brought a few converts into the fold."

"Is he a minister now?"

"No, he never seemed to pursue ordination, for some reason. But he's one of the Church's most valuable missionaries, and a wonderful teacher. The local people love him, even if they don't want to convert to the Church."

"They don't want to become Christians because they're already Buddhists," Anchalee pointed out matter-of-factly. "Buddhism is a much older religion than Christianity."

"Anchalee, simply because Buddhism is older, doesn't mean it's better—or the more correct path to the truth." He swiped at a mosquito that hovered directly in front of his face.

"But Father, you're always saying that with age comes wisdom," she responded quickly.

He couldn't muster an adequate reply, and instead resorted to his usual chiding. "Young ladies, Anchalee, should make polite conversation—especially at the table—and not try to outdo their elders and betters."

Anchalee, well-practised in the art of goading her father—or anyone else for that matter—simply smiled as the maids began clearing the table ready for the main course: a roast of beef complete with Yorkshire pudding and peas.

Edward wiped the sweat from his brow and swatted another mosquito on his hand. "Confounded things," he grumbled. "I hear one of the American families actually has a mosquito-proof dining room. They have special nets on all the doors and windows that allow in the air, but not the mosquitoes. Now they dine in perfect peace."

"No, they don't," Anchalee remarked. "Their maid's a dreadful cook. She's always burning the meat or undercooking the vegetables."

"Anchalee, how do you know these things?" he asked in exasperation.

"I have big ears," she replied. "And you forget, I speak Siamese. I hear the gossip from the maids."

"Well, you know far too much, if you ask me. And you shouldn't be listening to servants' gossip. Perhaps Elizabeth can teach you to be more ladylike. I've given up."

But he wasn't really angry, and Elizabeth noticed Anchalee smiling to herself for the remainder of dinner.

"Anyway, my dear," Edward addressed Elizabeth again. "How long do you intend staying with us?"

"I'm not sure, Father. I didn't have a set time in mind."

"But what of James? Is he in agreement?"

"Father, James isn't my husband yet. He has no say in the matter."

"But he's your fiancé. Surely. . . ."

"Not officially, Father. You know that. We decided to wait until my return."

"Why don't you write to him and ask him to come to Siam? You could be married here. It would be quite fitting for you to wed from your father's home. We have a lovely church beside the river, not far from here."

"No, Father. I'd rather wait. To tell you the truth, I'm not sure if I'm ready to marry James immediately."

"*What?* You're twenty-one, girl. You should have been married a year or two ago. *And* have given me a grandson by now. I can't understand why you've waited." He shook his head wearily.

"I can't explain it myself, Father. I can only say that the time wasn't right."

"Well, young Claridge is a patient man. There'd be many a woman—younger than you, I might add—who'd be only too ready to marry the Earl's heir. You'd be making a grave error to let him slip through your fingers."

Elizabeth made no reply, but steered the conversation toward less personal topics. "Anchalee tells me King Chulalongkorn is well established in his own right now?"

Edward could see that the subject of her marriage was no longer open for discussion, and he reluctantly began to answer. "Yes, he's doing wonderful things for the country. He's outlawed slavery, and decreed against people prostrating themselves before their superiors, including himself. Unfortunately, that custom's so ingrained, they can't help themselves and most still do it. But no one dares at official ceremonies when he's present.

"It's said, also, that he plans one day to travel to Europe. He's already been to Batavia, Singapore, India, and Burma. I think he's the most widely-travelled Siamese ever. He was to have gone to America and Europe about two years ago, in fact, but the trip was cancelled at the last minute. Still, he'll go eventually, I'm sure. In some ways, he's very enlightened."

Anchalee looked at her father sharply. "Only in some ways, Father?"

"Unfortunately, yes. We had hoped he would take a stand against polygamy. But I'm afraid he's as prodigious as his father before him. He has at least thirty wives—some say as many as ninety—and all manner of children, as you can imagine. And some of his wives are his half-sisters."

"Father, they'd be old maids if they didn't marry him. You know that Thai princesses cannot marry below their rank. And people who say he has ninety wives are stupid as well as liars."

"Anchalee, how many times must I tell you to hold your tongue? Especially at the table. Anyway, it's an abominable custom," he continued. "The king professes to be so modern, yet he still persists in this . . . this perversion!"

"I wish you wouldn't talk like that, Father. At least we Siamese are honest about such things. How many men in England are hypocrites who have one lawful wife, and who also keep a mistress—or two—hidden away? I believe the custom is especially rife among the upper classes."

"You, young lady, are English—and also much too impertinent for your age." He sighed and blushed slightly, feeling the conversation turning too close to home for his own comfort. "You'll not speak of such matters."

But she didn't relent, knowing precisely just how far she could bait him without making him genuinely angry. "It's only the truth. And I know some members of the church who keep Thai mistresses their wives don't know about."

Edward turned red. "Now that really is enough from you, Anchalee. You're simply showing off now that your sister is here."

But, he wondered, did she know the truth about her own mother? Or was this conversation just coincidence?

Sensing her father's discomfort, Elizabeth quickly changed the subject again. "And what of the former regent?" she asked. "I can't recall his name."

Edward was relieved to move on. "Yes, Chao Phya Sri Sriyawongse. Well, as you know, he relinquished the regency when the king turned twenty-one—in 1873, as I remember. But he's still chief minister, and although he's very old now, and not in good health, he's still a powerful man."

"And didn't something awful happen to one of the queens recently?" Elizabeth asked as she helped herself to some fresh fruit—pineapples, pawpaw, and roseapples—that Noi had set out. She loved catching up on all the news of Siam.

"That," Edward said getting up, "is a tragic story I shall tell you over coffee."

When all three were settled in the comfortable, overstuffed chairs in the sitting room, Edward sipped his black coffee thoughtfully, and then began. "Queen Sunanda was the king's favourite wife—and his half-sister, I might add. She was twenty-one and had a daughter, and was expecting her second child last year. Anyway, the court went to the summer palace at Bang Pa-In, and Queen Sunanda went with them, of course. One day, she and her daughter were travelling along the river when, without warning, their boat capsized. The queen and the child were drowned."

"But how?" Elizabeth asked. "The royal family never travels anywhere alone. There must have been many people there at the time."

"There were indeed," Edward confirmed. "Their attendants stood and watched as she died. They believed they could do nothing to help her."

"I don't understand, Father. Why not?"

"The sad result of yet another barbarous custom. No one helped her because, by law, commoners are not permitted to touch members of the royal family. The punishment is death."

Anchalee gave him a sharp look of disapproval.

"But surely in those circumstances, an exception could have been made," Elizabeth said, incredulous. "Or someone could have thrown her something so she could have saved herself."

"No, that too is against the law. The boatman must swim away. And if someone throws a lifebelt, he and all his family must be executed."

Elizabeth was even more shocked. "I can't believe it—it's preposterous. I'm sure the king wouldn't condone such a law."

"Maybe not," Edward agreed. "But the law is the law to the common people, and they dare not go against what they've been brought up to believe is correct."

Anchalee had been sitting quietly, but now she spoke. "Father, all these laws have a reason for existing, as English laws do. I'm sure there are old laws in England, too, that are not very sensible. It was very sad that the queen was allowed to die, and I'm sure the king would have granted a royal pardon had someone saved her. But you must remember, our history is long, and the people learn respect from a very young age. You can't expect them to change so quickly. They believed they had no option."

"Anchalee, you shouldn't take everything as a personal insult. And must I keep reminding you that you are as much English as you are Siamese? More so in my opinion."

"Which allows me to see both sides," she answered stubbornly.

They all fell silent for a few moments as they sipped their coffee—which was served from the same elegant silver pot Elizabeth remembered from her childhood. When she was finished, Elizabeth set down her cup and stood up, smiling at her father and sister.

"All this travelling has caught up with me. I think I'll retire for the evening, if you don't mind."

"Of course not. You must be looking your best for the ball tomorrow. The cream of Bangkok society will be there," he said haughtily.

"It's wonderful to be back," Elizabeth said.

"Goodnight, my dear. And don't rush to get up in the morning. Noi will bring you something on a tray."

◈ *Chapter 14* ◈

Elizabeth felt the room's gaze upon her as she entered the ballroom on her father's arm. She was in her element at a social function such as this, and although naturally shy, she had been trained to make an eye-catching entrance and to conduct herself with aplomb at any ball. And tonight, she knew she looked her best.

She wore an exquisite dress of pale blue-grey satin, ruched over a fashionably high bustle at the back, and falling to form a short train. The skirt was a mass of tiny rows of pleating in front. The neckline—her first décolletage, wide and low—was a special departure for her, and she loved the way it revealed her pale neck, extending to where her bust began to swell. It was the first dress she had bought without her grandmother's approval, and she felt daring and sophisticated, even though many women in the room opted for lower necklines than her own, some leaving little to the imagination. The long sleeves were edged with rows of lace, and she wore a double strand of pearls with an amethyst clasp at her throat. Her grandmother had presented the piece to her for her twenty-first birthday. Her fine, light brown hair was piled up on top of her head and threaded with grey satin ribbons.

"Mr. Edward Fairburn and Miss Elizabeth Fairburn," announced a page dressed in purple silk *panung* and white jacket with gleaming gold buttons.

A young, recently-arrived, single woman was always a source of interest in expatriate society, particularly of course, to those young men who were not yet married—but also to the women, who were keen to glimpse the latest fashions from Britain and the United States in reality, rather than in magazine illustrations that were many months old. Elizabeth was revelling in the atmosphere, but suddenly felt the attention drawn away from her. A stillness engulfed the room as if all in attendance were holding their breath as the announcer presented, "Miss Anchalee Fairburn."

In the glory of her own entrance, Elizabeth had almost forgotten that her sister was right behind them. And it was obvious why the other guests were so captivated. In her first ball gown, Anchalee was transformed into a beautiful, exotic Eurasian woman, and every man in the room felt his heart beat a little faster at the sight of her. She had chosen a simple emerald-green taffeta dress with a tightly-fitting bodice and ground-length, draped skirt. Her figure was developing fast, and her bust was accentuated by her nipped-in waist.

But it was her face that gained her the most attention. In contrast to every other woman there, she had left her hair undone, and it fell straight, dark, and luxuriant past her shoulders, halfway down her back. Her perfect complexion needed no rouge or powder, and her full lips were a natural, subtle shade of burnished rose. Even in the low gas light, her green eyes sparkled. She smiled at the guests, revealing her perfectly white, even teeth. Whispers of appreciation seemed to ripple through the room, and she graciously curtsied to them and joined her father and sister.

Edward had initially been reluctant to allow her to attend the ball, but she had pleaded and cajoled until he finally relented. Now he wondered to himself if it had been a good idea. He was well aware of the effect she would have, and did not want her maturing any faster than she seemed to be doing. Still, at least if she was here with him, he could keep a watchful eye on her. Noi had let slip that she sometimes went out for hours at a time while he was away, and he was concerned about where she was going and what company she was keeping.

The orchestra began to play the opening waltz, and Elizabeth danced with her father while Anchalee watched from the side. Within moments, a young British officer asked Anchalee to partner him, and Elizabeth was surprised to see how elegantly and confidently her sister danced.

"Where did she learn to waltz like that?" Elizabeth asked her father.

"An English woman runs a dance school for girls. I thought it would be good for her to go and meet some other young women. She spends far too much time with servants and anyone else who'll speak with her in Siamese."

"You'd never guess she's only thirteen," Elizabeth whispered.

"No, and that's what concerns me. In some ways, it might be best if she *is* married young. Then I wouldn't have to worry about her so much."

"Married!" Elizabeth exclaimed. "But she's only a child, Father."

"I know," he sighed. "But some Siamese girls are still married very young. It wouldn't be thought of as immoral if she were to marry at, say, fifteen."

"I suppose you're right. Even in England it's not rare for girls to be married so young. But why anyone would want to surrender their freedom at such an age is beyond me."

The waltz finished, and Elizabeth and Edward left the dance floor for drinks. They saw that Anchalee's partner had been replaced by another equally dashing young man, and Elizabeth wondered what either would say if they knew how young she was.

Elizabeth herself then accepted an invitation from the young officer who had just surrendered her half-sister to his colleague, but some way into the dance they were interrupted when a man tapped her partner on the shoulder and cut in. Elizabeth felt weak, and her breath caught in her throat as she recognised him.

"I knew we'd meet again," he said in a low voice as he held her closely—rather too closely for her liking. His hand seemed to burn through the flimsy fabric along her back, and she felt as if the room were resounding with her heartbeat.

"You're a very attractive young woman, Elizabeth. And especially beautiful tonight."

His words took her by surprise. She usually found the way Americans used first names so soon after introductions quite ill-mannered and distasteful. But with him, it somehow seemed appropriate. In any case, she was unable to object because she seemed to have lost her powers of speech. She could only look up into his dark eyes as he towered over her.

As they danced, the room seemed to spin, and all that mattered in the world was him. The music faded into the background until she was in a distant place, whirling with him in a misty paradise.

He smiled lazily and she noticed the wrinkles at the sides of his eyes; fine, white lines in his deeply-tanned face. Unlike all the other men in the room he was clean-shaven, without moustache or side-whiskers, which was considered terribly unfashionable. But to her, it looked wonderful. The black shadows on his upper lip and around his chin seemed strangely distinctive, and she imagined how rough his skin would feel on hers. The music stopped, and she was suddenly brought back to reality.

"Thanks for the dance. See you later," he said as he escorted her off the floor. And he was gone, as quickly as he had appeared.

She could only stand motionless at the edge of the dance floor, not knowing what to think; not knowing why he had left her so quickly. No man had ever treated her so casually. But she wasn't upset, only left bemused, as if it had been her alone who felt that way. Had she been so intoxicated by the combination of the tropical night air and a single glass of champagne?

"Elizabeth, there you are." Edward appeared again. "Would you like a glass of champagne?"

She felt flushed, as if she had been caught unawares in the midst of some guilty pleasure—which, in a sense, she had. She nodded, and he handed her a crystal flute. He rarely drank himself these days, preferring instead the tropical fruit punches.

"Having a good time?"

She nodded again. "Why yes, of course, Father."

"Have you met anyone interesting?"

"Yes . . . yes. But I think Anchalee is meeting more people than I am."

Anchalee was across the other side of the ballroom, surrounded by a group of handsome young men, sipping a glass of champagne.

"The little devil. I told her she wasn't to have any champagne. She's much too young."

"Anchalee doesn't seem to think she's too young for anything," Elizabeth remarked, and Edward looked at her quizzically.

"Well, she's not like other girls her age, is she?" she added.

"No, unfortunately not," he was reluctantly forced to agree. "But although she purports to be so sophisticated, I'm certain she's actually very naïve. That's what concerns me, Elizabeth. She could be vulnerable to the first young man who comes along. A handsome face, a few whispered compliments, and Anchalee could well allow herself to be. . . . Well, to be ruined, so to speak."

Elizabeth blushed again. Her father could well have been talking about her. She would have to come to her senses over this American, for she recognised the magnetism he held for her. If a single dance with him could render her breathless. . . .

"Elizabeth, what do you think?"

But she was too distracted to reply at first.

"Elizabeth. Why don't you join your sister over there, and do try to prevent her acquiring another glass of champagne?"

As she made her way round the room, she found herself scanning the dance floor, searching for him. She saw him dancing with a beautiful blonde woman, the young wife of a British consular official. He held the woman as closely as he had held her, and he wore that same charming smile. She could only wonder at what the woman's husband thought of the spectacle. Sam leaned closer to whisper something in her ear, which made her laugh and blush. Elizabeth felt a stab of jealousy and quickly turned away toward her sister, thinking that if he danced with every attractive woman in that fashion, then she could mean little to him. He had simply moved on to the next partner.

"Elizabeth," Anchalee called. "Come and meet my new friends."

She went over, and after they had been introduced, one of the young men asked her to dance. They took to the floor, but both the music and the man before her became distant distractions.

She moved mechanically, her feet automatically picking out the right steps, and she looked past her partner, trying to catch a glimpse of *him*. Again she found him with another partner, the sultry, dark-haired daughter of a Portuguese merchant. Her own partner smiled politely when the music ended, but did not seek conversation, nor ask for another dance. She was suddenly aware of what she had done, and felt guilty that she had ignored him.

But he alone commanded her attention that night, and yet it was ludicrous; he hardly seemed to acknowledge her presence. After only one dance with him, one breathtaking dance, the spell had been broken. Had he already forgotten her?

She fretted that, for the remainder of the evening, she would merely have to watch from the side as he partnered every other young, and even not-so-young, woman present.

"Elizabeth, are you feeling all right?" Anchalee asked. "You look pale."

"Yes, I'm fine, thank you. But I think I need some fresh air. I'll walk outside to the terrace for a while."

"Would you like me to come with you?"

"No, no thank you. I'm quite all right, really. You stay here and enjoy yourself. And Father says no more champagne."

Anchalee looked guilty. "Oh, he noticed, did he?"

"Yes, so you'd better be on your best behaviour from now on, or there'll be trouble."

"I can deal with Father," she stated confidently.

"I'm sure you can." Elizabeth raised her eyebrows knowingly as she walked toward the french doors that led to the wide terrace.

Outside, flickering lamps burned, and several couples stood closely together in private conversation. She looked out to the lush gardens that were landscaped with both native and non-native trees, bushes, and flowers. But she hardly saw them. What she saw instead, was his face—and in her imagination, she traced the contours of his wide brow, high cheekbones, and sensuous lips.

She had been standing on the terrace for a only few minutes when she was startled by a deep voice very close behind her.

157

"What, tired of the party already?"

She gasped, turned quickly, and found herself looking into the dark eyes she had just been thinking of. She went pale, then her face flushed with embarrassment at her thoughts of only a few moments before. "I . . . no, Mr. Taylor," she stammered. "I mean I just came out here for a little air." She tried to smile, and was sure he could sense the hammering of her heart and the quickening pulse in her neck. As he grinned, she felt that he was reading every thought that raced through her mind.

"The name's Sam. Mr. Taylor was my father."

"Was?"

He leaned on the railing beside her. "He died last year in California."

"Oh, I'm sorry." She paused and looked down. "And your mother?"

"She died when I was two. So I'm an orphan, you see," he joked nonchalantly.

She stifled a nervous giggle and then composed herself. "That must have been difficult for you, losing your mother so young."

"Not really. I never knew her. Besides, I was always the independent type."

She wanted to tell him about her own mother; about how much she had missed her when she died. But she was afraid he wouldn't be interested. There was another awkward pause and she could still feel her heart beating as if it were trying to burst from her chest. "And your family is from California?" she finally managed to ask.

"That's right. I'm a born-and-bred Los Angeleno. My father went to California to find gold."

"Oh, how extraordinary." She was delighted to discover that they had something in common. "So did mine."

"Did he find any?"

"No, but he became a photographer in California, on the gold fields. And now. . . . Well, of course, you know my father already. I was forgetting. And your father—did he find gold?"

"Nope. But he did find my mother, who he always said was better than gold. He never did get over losing her."

She felt a little more confident. "It's odd, you . . . you don't look American."

"You mean, I don't look like a white American."

"No, no . . . I'm sorry. That's not what I meant." She hesitated, embarrassed. "It's just that I. . . . Well, I imagine your father was Italian . . . or Spanish, perhaps?"

"No, he was English."

"Please forgive me for prying. You must think me very rude."

"Not at all. And if you're referring to the dark complexion," he said with amusement, "I inherited that from my mother. She was Mexican."

"Oh, I see." And although she hadn't intended it to be, she was immediately sure that her reply had sounded disdaining to him. Ashamed, she could not look him in the eye.

"Does that matter to you?"

"In what way should it?" she asked, attempting to sound as if it were a trivial matter.

"I don't know. Some people don't like half-breeds." His voice had a sarcastic edge to it, as if he were testing her in some way.

She became flustered, but then realised that the perfect response was at her disposal.

"My sister is a . . . a half-breed, as you put it."

"Of course, I'd forgotten." He smiled. "Anyhow, enough about me. Tell me about you."

She was relieved to have salvaged some dignity from the encounter. But was he really interested, she wondered, or was he just toying with her?

"There's not much to tell, really. I was born in Australia, and came here with my mother to join my father when I was a child. My mother died on the way back to England, and my father sent me to school there. When I wasn't at school, I lived with my grandparents in England. And now. . . . Well, here I am, back again in Siam."

"That explains it," he said, grinning.

"Explains what, Mr. Taylor?"

"Yesterday, when I saw you at the pier. The way you were dressed."

She considered that rather too familiar. "What do you mean?" she asked coolly.

"Oh, don't take it the wrong way, honey. You looked enchanting, but. . . ."

"Yes, Mr. Taylor?" she prompted as calmly as she could, shocked at his indecent familiarity.

"Well, you looked like you'd been dressed by your grandmother."

She turned away in embarrassment and looked out over the gardens again.

"You're right," she admitted quietly after a moment of silence. "My grandmother always chose my clothes."

"But not tonight."

"I beg your pardon?"

She almost jumped out of her skin when he then ran a warm fingertip lightly along her neckline, to the top of her breasts.

"I mean this," he said.

She could only stare at him with widening eyes, and she felt a cold sweat envelop her.

He looked out over the terrace toward the garden once more. "I'd like to see you again, Elizabeth."

She felt sick, and the heat seemed to rise up to choke her. She took a deep breath. "I don't think that can be possible, Mr. Taylor."

"Don't you want to see me again?"

"It's . . . it's not that, Mr. Taylor. It's just that. . . . Well, there's someone in England. I'm. . . ."

"I don't see a wedding band."

"No, I'm not married. But. . . ."

"But what?"

"My father wouldn't approve."

"Don't tell him. You're old enough to make your own decisions."

She was speechless.

"So you'll meet me?"

She knew she needed to see him again, and gave no thought to the consequences. "Very well," she replied impulsively.

"You can come to my hotel."

She gasped in shock. "Mr. Taylor, that's an outrageous proposal. You know well that I cannot possibly agree to. . . . Really! I've a good mind to inform my father of your . . . your. . . ." But she trailed off as he seemed to look right into her soul, his dark eyes not leaving hers.

There was a hint of a smile at the corners of his mouth. "Of course. I'm sorry. I have a friend with a house. We can meet there. Say, Tuesday at one o'clock?"

She couldn't believe what she was hearing, but still found herself nodding in agreement, as if in a trance. She knew it was dangerous, yet she was unable to refuse.

"I'll write down the address and give it to you before the end of the evening."

"But my father. . . ."

"I'll be discreet," he assured her. "Trust me." Then, with a brilliant smile, he left her, sauntering back inside, no doubt to request the company of another beautiful woman on the dance floor.

His parting words were an enigma. Could she trust him in any way? Her common sense said no, but her burning skin told her that she wanted—needed—to see him again.

❖

"Where on earth have you been?" Edward asked when she went back inside.

"Oh . . . just out on the terrace, Father. I needed some air."

"Well, I think we'll be leaving shortly. Anchalee shouldn't be out too late."

She nearly panicked. It was still early, and she didn't have the address. "Oh, Father. Couldn't we stay just a little longer?" she pleaded. "It's my first night out, after all."

He smiled, realising how much he had missed her all these years. "Very well, then. But only for a little longer."

She excused herself to use the powder room, and on the way back, in the long hallway leading to the ballroom, she saw him sitting in the shadows on one of the decorative teak chairs.

As she walked in his direction, he stood up and formally said, "Miss Fairburn," for the benefit of several other people nearby.

"Mr. Taylor," she replied, and as he brushed past her, she felt a small piece of paper being pressed into her hand.

She had no time to examine it then, but simply tucked it into her sleeve to read later.

❖ Chapter 15 ❖

Joseph greeted her at the door of his two-storey home—the same house he had lived in since coming to Bangkok—surprised at how she had changed. "Elizabeth, you've grown so." He smiled and offered his hand.

"Mr. Shaw. It seems so long since I saw you last." She took his hand in hers.

"Not at all," he said, as he ushered her into the hallway. "It seems like only yesterday you were a little girl lying on the grass with a broken heart."

"You still remember that?"

"Of course. How could I forget? It was a difficult time for you."

"Thank you for the letters you wrote when I first went away. They helped a lot when I felt homesick and missed my father."

"Were you miserable?" he asked as they went into the sitting room.

"Not so much after the first year. I got used to it. Everyone was very kind to me in England. But it wasn't the same as being here."

"And now that you're back?"

"Well, I feel like I've come home."

"Please, do sit down."

Joseph's houseboy, Simon, brought in a pot of tea on a tray and set it on the table. There was sugar in the milk jug, and milk from Joseph's own cow in the sugar bowl.

"Simon doesn't quite get it right, yet," Joseph chuckled. "But he tries, and I haven't the heart to tell him he's wrong all the time."

Elizabeth smiled at him. He was still the kind, generous person she remembered.

"How did he get an English name?"

"Well, the truth is that I had to buy Simon. He was a slave, you see," Joseph answered with distaste. "Of course, I freed him immediately, and I pay him a wage now. He wanted a Christian name when he was baptised."

"He's a convert, then?" Elizabeth asked, surprised. The missionaries still had so little success in Siam.

"Yes," Joseph replied proudly. "He was my first. Others have come and gone in the years since then. Many are Christians for a short while, then revert to Buddhism. But Simon has remained."

"Your work is still difficult, then?"

"As difficult as always, I'm afraid. I'm beginning to wonder if Christianity will ever take root in this country. The missionaries in New Zealand and Hawaii have had almost complete success. Here, we can't claim even a handful." He shrugged. "Still, it's my home now, and has been for a long time. And I won't give up the Lord's work."

"Are you ever lonely?" she asked as Joseph poured the tea. "I mean here, by yourself?"

"You mean, without a wife?" he smiled.

"Well, yes, I suppose that is what I mean."

"I've never found the right woman, Elizabeth. One cannot simply decide to marry, can one?"

"No, I suppose not. But perhaps you'll still find someone. There's time enough."

"I have my work, and that keeps me occupied."

"Of course."

"And what of you? I hear you're engaged."

James. She did not know what to think or to say about him any more. How could she contemplate marriage to one man, when she was so attracted to another?

"Well, we haven't made an announcement yet, Mr. Shaw."

"Oh. I understood from your father that you were to set a wedding date on your return to England."

"That's what he's hoping, yes."

"And you?"

"Well, in truth, I still haven't committed myself."

Joseph always seemed to have a way of eliciting the truth, but until she had uttered the words, she had not realised that that was what she thought. But it was true, and she knew it as soon as she had spoken. She had not committed herself to James, and she was no longer sure she wanted to.

"Well then, I expect you must consider carefully. And you've come far enough if you were seeking some time to think alone," he added.

She smiled politely. Joseph could not realise how far from the truth he was; for Bangkok was where temptation was at its peak. She had already decided she would not meet Sam the next day as she had promised. She could not trust herself with him, nor could she trust him with her; that was only too evident in the way he looked at her—or rather, the way he looked at every woman, she reminded herself. Her father had been right when he warned her against him.

"Elizabeth, are you all right?" Joseph asked when she fell silent. "You seem a little preoccupied."

"Oh yes, quite all right, thank you," she answered quickly. "I'm sorry. I suppose I'm still tired from the journey. And still getting used to the climate again."

"Of course. The heat is the one thing that we can always rely on in Siam."

"But Bangkok has changed so much since I was last here. Yet, it's still very independent."

"Yes, indeed. And I believe it will remain so . . . if the British and the French can be kept at bay."

"Do you really believe it's best for Siam to remain independent?" she asked, surprised. Her education in England had taught her that colonialism and empire-building were to be celebrated as the most glorious achievements of the nineteenth century.

"I do," Joseph stated firmly. "Although mine isn't a popular view among the expatriates. Of course, I'd like to see a conversion to the Church, but the people are very resistant to change. It will take time."

They talked some more, and he told her of comings and goings over the years that her father had not known of, and when they had finished their tea and exhausted polite conversation, Elizabeth stood to go.

"Well, thank you very much for the refreshments, Mr. Shaw. It's been a most pleasant afternoon."

Joseph escorted her to the waiting carriage. "I'll see you at church on Sunday, no doubt."

"Until Sunday," she replied, smiling as he helped her in.

He watched the carriage until it was out of sight, thinking to himself that she had become an extraordinarily refined young woman, and that she would make some young man a most suitable wife. In fact, he thought, as he walked up the steps to his front verandah, she was exactly the sort of woman he should have married fifteen years ago, if only there had been such a lady then. He had no doubt that a wife would have helped him immensely in his work. But it was not to be, it seemed. It was his cross to bear; his punishment for that one indiscretion so many years ago.

Edward was far from pleased at what he had heard from Elizabeth. To have a daughter married into a family with an hereditary title, which her husband would inherit, would have suited him very nicely, and it would have provided opportunity for him even in distant Siam.

He thought of the stories he had heard about Mr. Knox having secured his promotions because he was related to Lord John Beresford and Lord Ranfurly in England. Knox had originally been a soldier with no diplomatic training, yet had risen to become British consul-general in Siam, and had been knighted for his services.

Edward's father, too, had been knighted by Queen Victoria, and although in his younger days Edward had dismissed the title as inconsequential, he would now have liked one for himself—or at least the trappings and connections which accompanied the honour. If Elizabeth were to marry James, who knew what opportunities it might lead to? And she was his last hope. Anchalee was the beauty of the family, that was certain, but a half-Siamese girl could not be expected to marry into the British aristocracy. So his hopes lay with Elizabeth's marriage, and he was sure that His Majesty would accord him more time and credibility if this occurred.

While Edward had photographed the king several times with various wives and children, and was often called to duty at official receptions, he was still regarded as little more than an employee. But he wanted admittance to the inner circle, perhaps to be appointed a special adviser in some capacity, or as the sole royal photographer. In any case, and in the meantime, he would let certain people know just whom his daughter was to marry. It was sure to carry weight, assuming Elizabeth saw sense.

Anchalee heard her sister in the hallway, and stopped her as she began to run up the stairs. "How was your outing?"

"It was fine, thank you, Anchalee. But I feel quite tired. I think I'll go upstairs and rest." She gave Anchalee a weak smile and turned to continue up the stairs.

"Elizabeth? Is anything wrong? You look different."

She stopped and turned back. "No, nothing's wrong."

But Anchalee noticed the thin voice and the tight, awkward smile, which was not reflected in her eyes. Her expression appeared almost as if it had been painted on, and her eyes were unusually bright, as if she were about to cry.

"I'm just weary. I think it must be the heat. I'll see you at dinner." And she continued up the stairs.

Anchalee had an uncanny knack for seeing through people, and knew that Elizabeth had not told the truth. She went up the stairs after her, but found her bedroom door closed. Quietly crouching down, she put her ear to the door and could hear muffled sobbing.

Inside, Elizabeth lay on her bed with her face pressed into the pillow. She was deeply upset, and no matter how hard she tried to put it out of her mind, she could not. . . .

It had been a mistake, from the moment she had accepted the note at the consulate to the moment she had sat down at breakfast that morning and asked if she could use the carriage that afternoon. Edward hadn't looked up from his newspaper—it was months old, but was British, and a rare luxury. He replied distractedly, "Of course, more old friends to see?"

"No, I just thought I'd like to go for a drive," she had said. And at that point she had actually been telling the truth. Or at least she thought she had been.

She still had no intention of keeping the appointment, but she did want to get out of the house and see some more of the city, a diversion she had thought would take her mind off him, at least for a while.

She was beginning to resent the power and attraction he held over her. She wanted to forget him, and to think instead of James. Yet, when she tried to picture her fiancé's face, the image was vague. She couldn't even remember the colour of his eyes.

After lunch, she had gone up to her room to change. She asked Noi to prepare her blue and white striped cotton visiting costume. It was light and cool, with close-fitting long sleeves, a draped skirt, a fitted bodice, a bow at the high neck, a row of buttons down the front that would take the maid ten minutes to fix, even with the special button fastener Elizabeth had brought from England, and a matching dolman jacket which fell to just below her hips.

Noi helped her arrange her hair in a neat coil close to her head, and when she was dressed, she surveyed her reflection in

168

the full-length mirror. Elegant, yes, but still so dull. Why had she allowed her grandmother to buy her clothes for so long? She would love to wear the new, brighter colours that were the rage in London now, but instead, almost all her clothes were in old-fashioned pastel colours—lilac, pink, or blue—or just plain white. How could she expect to hold his attention with such dowdy dresses? "Curse the man," she said out loud. What did it matter what he, or any man for that matter, thought of her? She was engaged to James.

She picked up her white parasol, tucked a white lace-edged handkerchief into her sleeve, and was on her way. She carried a small silk purse containing a few coins, as well as the paper he had written the address on; not that she would need it, since she was not going there.

"Just go slowly up New Road, please," she ordered the driver, in Siamese. She was quickly reacquainting herself with the language, a case of necessity when very few servants spoke English.

But as they drove along in the victoria at a leisurely pace, she found it impossible not to think of the note. It was inevitable that her hands, as if of their own mind, eventually opened the little drawstring purse and extracted the simple slip of white onionskin, on which the address had been hastily written, by the look of the ink blots on it.

The place, just off New Road, was quite close to where they were. She worried that he would think her rude for not keeping the appointment—which was, after all, a lady's prerogative—and then she began to fret over what he really thought of her. He would simply move on to the next young woman if she showed no interest. Perhaps he would even forget the liaison, anyway. It was entirely illogical that it pained her to think of him with another woman, but she had been given her opportunity, and she had declined to take it.

"Driver, turn round, please," she called spontaneously. "Go back the other way." She pointed the way they had come, hardly knowing what she was doing. "I have an appointment to keep," she said to herself in English, as her heart began to beat alarmingly fast. The beads of perspiration that had already formed on her forehead ran down the sides of her face, and she dabbed at them with a handkerchief.

"*Leoh saai*—turn left," she called when they reached the side road she thought was the correct address. She would just go to the door and tell him she would not be keeping the appointment. She would apologise politely but not go in. But she would at least see him one more time.

"Wait for me here, please," she told the driver when they arrived at what she hoped was the house. It was similar in style to her father's, but was obviously quite neglected. The garden was overgrown, although she noticed that the windows on the second storey had been thrown open. Perhaps his friends had not lived there long. She rang the doorbell, expecting a maid to answer, but when the door swung open and it was Sam himself who stood there, she took a step back in surprise.

He smiled widely and his dark eyes were penetrating as he appraised her from head to toe. "I wondered if you'd changed your mind." He opened the door further and motioned for her to go inside, but she remained where she was, looking at him, again lost for words.

"Well? Please do come in."

"I . . . I can't. I'm sorry, but I. . . ."

He smiled again. "What's wrong Elizabeth? Do I scare you?"

"Of course not," she answered swiftly, suddenly irritated by his arrogant tone.

"Well then, at least come in for a cup of tea. We won't be disturbed. No one's here, not even the servants."

She looked puzzled, and a little concerned. "I thought you said your friend lived here."

"He does, but he's away in Singapore. He asked me to look in on the house from time to time, and that's what I'm doing today."

He held out a hand, which she took without thinking, and found herself in the hallway. The house smelled musty.

"It needs airing, as you can tell. I'm afraid all the furniture's covered with sheets, except for a small sitting room next to the kitchen. We'll have to sit in there."

She realised he still had hold of her hand, and she snatched it away. "Really, Mr. Taylor, I don't intend to stay. My driver's waiting."

"Well, he can wait then, can't he? They love sleeping, anyway. And I've told you before, Elizabeth, my name's Sam. Or Samuel, if you want to be really formal."

She followed him along the dark hallway, into a small but comfortably-furnished room that contained a sofa and two armchairs, a sideboard, and a low finely-carved teak table in the Siamese style. She saw no evidence of tea.

He noticed her expression as she surveyed the room. "You're right, of course. I lied about the tea, I'm afraid. But it's a little difficult to boil water when the range isn't lit. Would a glass of sweet sherry do instead?"

"Thank you, that will be fine."

He poured the drink from a crystal decanter, then a whisky for himself from another, and offered her a plate of small cakes. She took one, although she had no appetite, but she was loath to drink the sherry. She wanted all her wits about her.

"You look uncomfortable, Elizabeth," he said in a mocking tone.

"That's because I am," she answered directly, setting down the sherry, but still holding the cake, not knowing what else to do with it. He had neglected the plates.

"Well, don't be. My intentions are strictly platonic on this occasion." He sat next to her on the sofa, and she found the very proximity of him almost overpowering. It was all she could do to stop herself from jumping up and running out to the carriage. Yet she remained riveted to her seat, unable to look away.

She felt a pressing need to somehow take control of the situation, to establish some authority. "I find this meeting, shall we call it, rather an unusual way to court," she said severely.

"Be careful, Elizabeth. I can hear grandma's warnings. The old lady's still got quite a hold on you, hasn't she?"

She sat up even more stiffly. "I'll thank you not to speak of my grandmother that way. You don't even know her."

He laughed. "You're right, honey, I don't. But looking at you, I can guess."

"You're very insulting, Mr. Taylor."

"I'm sorry, I don't mean to be. I guess I've had to stick up for myself most of my life and it's given me too sharp a tongue. What do you think?" But before she had a chance to answer, he continued. "And anyway, what makes you think I'm courting, as you put it?"

"I'm sorry, Mr. Taylor, if I've misunderstood. But when a gentleman asks to meet a lady like this, it's my understanding that he's . . . . Well, he's. . . ." She blushed scarlet, unable to say what she was thinking.

"Looking on her as a possible wife?" he finished for her. "Don't get me wrong, sweetheart. You're a very attractive young woman. But I don't court anyone. I'll be straight with you. I'm not looking to get married. Those aren't my intentions toward you. I'm sorry to have to spell it out that way, but I don't want you getting any false hopes. Then again, I guess some woman some day will persuade me that it's not such a bad idea."

With a jolt, she realised what she was doing—dallying with a man her father disliked, alone, at a strange residence. And he had openly admitted that he had no decent intentions toward her. Not to mention the fact that she was already promised to another. He must think her a fool.

She stood up abruptly, and began to put on her hat and gloves, trying desperately to retain at least some of her dignity.

"Well, in that case, Mr. Taylor, I think it's time for me to leave," she stated primly.

"I hope I haven't offended you," he said, still slouched on the sofa.

"Not at all. I'm only glad we understand each other."

"Meaning?"

"Well, as I told you last time we met, I'm engaged to be married. So you see, I'm not looking to be courted either."

She wanted to leave immediately, but his legs were stretched out in front of him, effectively barring her way. "Excuse me, Mr. Taylor."

But he made no move to free her path. A smile spread across his face, and then he laughed.

She stiffened again. "If you find me amusing, Mr. Taylor, I can assure you the feeling is *not* mutual."

But he only laughed again. "No, it's not exactly amusing that I find you. Just so *very proper*," he added in a mock, upper-class English accent. Before she could retort, he jumped up and stood very close to her. "I'll walk you to the door."

She looked away. "Thank you, but I can see myself out."

"I'm sure you can."

He remained where he was, not moving an inch, and she was at a loss over what to do or say next. Then, slowly, his head moved toward hers, his arms closed round her, and before she realised what was happening, his lips were on hers, harsh, insistent, and bruising. He held her in a vice-like grip, and she felt his tongue prising her lips apart. Involuntarily, she felt her arms reach up and clasp him around his neck, and her mouth opened to his. She closed her eyes, and, just as it had that night she had danced with him, a sense of unreality swept over her. But when he pulled his lips from hers, and pressed her tightly to him, her head resting against his chest, she soon came to her senses. What was she thinking of, letting this virtual stranger take such intimate liberties?

"Let me go," she demanded, almost in a whisper. "You must let me go immediately."

He released her and she stood beside him, not daring to look into his eyes again. For if she did, she was afraid she would not be able to leave. "I must go now," she said, hastily rearranging her crushed skirt and tucking up strands of hair that had fallen during the encounter. Silently, he stood aside for her, and still without looking at him, she said, "I cannot see you again. Not like this. Not ever."

173

She turned and hurried from the room, down the hallway, and out to the waiting carriage. Sam sat down again thoughtfully and poured himself a second whisky. She'll be mine before another month has passed, he thought to himself.

❖

Outside the bedroom door, Anchalee was more than curious to discover if her sister would confide in her. She stood up, smoothed her skirts, then knocked lightly. The sobs stopped and there was a long silence. Anchalee knocked again.

"Who is it?"

"It's only me. Can I come in?"

"Just a moment." There was another interval before Elizabeth called out that she was ready.

Anchalee opened the door to find her sister seated at her dressing table, brushing her hair. But she noted that the covers of the bed were rumpled on one side and that Elizabeth's eyes were red and puffy.

"Elizabeth, have you been crying?"

"No, of course not." She spoke to Anchalee's reflection in the mirror. "It's just the air outside irritating my nose. Such a nuisance."

"But you're inside now."

"What?"

"I know you've been crying. I heard you through the door."

"Oh, so you've taken to spying on me now?"

"No, I was just worried. What's the matter?"

"I told you, nothing. I'm just . . . homesick. For England. For James."

"I don't believe you."

"Anchalee, please."

"It's a man, isn't it? Are you in love?"

"What do you mean? That's nonsense. In love with whom?"

"I can tell by that look in your eyes. It's Sam Taylor, isn't it? You've been to visit him today."

For an instant, Elizabeth's hairbrush paused in mid-air, but only for an instant. She continued brushing her hair, and her strokes were faster and harder than they had been a few seconds before.

"I don't know what you're talking about, Anchalee."

"Yes you do. I saw the way you looked at each other at the ball. And I saw you on the terrace with him. And then you met him in one of the hallways."

"How do you know all this? You *have* been spying on me, haven't you? You little devil."

"Of course not. I told you, I saw you in the hallway. You didn't see me, because you had your back to me. You've been with him this afternoon, haven't you?"

Elizabeth put down the brush. "All right, I had afternoon tea with him. There, I've told you."

She turned from the reflection to face her sister. "And you must never, never breathe a word of this to Father, or to anyone, do you hear me? If you do, I'll deny everything, and you and I will no longer be friends. Do you understand?"

Anchalee was stunned at her sister's gravity, and remained silent for a moment. "Of course I won't tell." Then she smiled as she asked, "What really happened? It was more than tea, wasn't it?"

"Anchalee, that's quite enough. I don't appreciate your insinuations."

"I'm sorry. But I can always tell."

"Well, that's good because there *is* nothing to tell. And in any case, I'll not be seeing Mr. Taylor again."

"Was that his idea?"

"No, it was mine. He's entirely unsuitable."

"If it was your idea, I don't think it would stop him."

"Now what do you mean?"

"I've heard about Sam Taylor."

"Well, I'm not concerned with anything you've heard about him, actually, because I haven't the slightest interest in him. And that's the end of the matter."

"Half the women in town are in love with him. The other half have probably already been discarded by him."

"Anchalee, that's not a fitting way for a young lady to talk."

"But it's the truth. You should be careful with him. I don't want you to be hurt."

She was forced to laugh to herself. She really was a most engaging child. But she also melted at her younger sister's concern, and she smiled gratefully. "Now I'm receiving advice about men from a thirteen-year-old, am I? Anchalee, I'm eight years older than you, and I know very well how to conduct myself with men. And, as I said before, the matter is over. But thank you for your concern. I'm sure you mean well."

"That's all right," Anchalee said, jumping out of her chair with an almost childlike movement. "See you at dinner."

She went to her own room and thought some more about Elizabeth and Sam. She could guess what he had done to upset her so much, but was certain Elizabeth would not surrender easily to a man. She was convinced that if Elizabeth had allowed him so much as a kiss, she would be very distressed. Even at her young age, she sensed the hypocrisy of a society that permitted men to act as they pleased, but which condemned women as immoral if they behaved in a similar fashion. There was something unjust in that, she knew, and on many occasions she wished her own mother were there to explain things to her.

She knew little about her mother, only that her name was Kesri, and that she had died years ago, not long after she had married Father. But no one would talk of her, or tell her why she had died so young. She reached under her mattress and took out an old, cracked photograph of a beautiful Siamese woman with her hair done the old-fashioned way, in a top-knot.

Edward had insisted that he had no photographs of Kesri, but she knew it was not possible that a photographer could have no pictures of his own wife. She had asked him some time previously if she might look through the boxes of pictures of her as a child, hoping there would be at least one of her mother—or better, of the two of them together. But she had discovered nothing. So she had waited until one day when she knew he would not return until late in the evening, or perhaps even the next day. She sneaked into his bedroom, found the studio key in a drawer in his dresser, and let herself in.

It had taken hours of searching through the boxes of dusty old prints and photographic plates. There were several pictures of young Thai women, but none had any identification on the back. Then, just as she was about to give up, she found it. The picture was in two halves, torn across the centre, as if someone—he, she assumed—had meant to discard it. On the reverse of one of the halves was the inscription "*Kesri, 1868*" in her father's handwriting. She carefully pasted the picture back together, and looked at her mother's face for the first time.

Kesri was very young—she looked to be only eighteen or so— and she was beautiful, too, with a sensuous mouth and smooth, perfect skin. And yet, she did not have youthful eyes. Anchalee saw a sadness in them, as if her mother had suffered during her short life. A man, she thought, would see only her beauty, not her sorrow.

She replaced all the boxes carefully in their original positions, and returned the key to Edward's room. She was always mindful to keep the picture hidden in her room, as she was convinced her father would be angry if he knew she had it. It seemed to her that he wanted no reminder of Kesri—he certainly never spoke of her—and he was intent on raising Anchalee as an English lady, barely acknowledging the fact that she was half Siamese.

But despite his efforts to the contrary, she had learned the Siamese language easily, and she spoke and read it as fluently as she did English. She was determined too, that she would eventually discover exactly what had happened to her mother.

❖

As she lay on her bed pondering these things, it suddenly occurred to her that the one person who might help her was her sister. Elizabeth had been only eight when she had left Siam— but that was old enough, surely, to remember people and events. She was there when Kesri was alive, and was bound to know something. But Anchalee knew too, that she would have to tread carefully. Because of the way others had reacted to her questions about her mother, she was wary of asking anything important until she had gained Elizabeth's friendship, trust, and loyalty. Perhaps this trouble her sister was having with Sam Taylor could be turned to her own advantage, she thought.

At dinner that night, Elizabeth was pale and withdrawn, and she only picked at her food.

"Elizabeth, is something wrong?" Edward asked. "You're not eating."

"No, Father, I'm fine," she answered quietly, her eyes cast down.

"Are you ill?"

She looked at him blankly. She didn't want to lie, but she couldn't possibly tell him the truth. "No, it's . . ."

"She's been suffering from some sort of irritation," Anchalee interrupted. "From the air since she was out this afternoon."

"Oh, is that all? Well, I should prescribe an early night, young lady."

He went back to his meal, and Anchalee looked across at Elizabeth, who smiled in appreciation.

April 28th, 1882

Dear Marjorie,

> *How long it seems since I saw you last, waving goodbye to me at the Liverpool docks. I have been in Bangkok for only two weeks now, yet so much has happened, I wish that I could have you here to talk to, my dear confidante.*

The city has, of course changed markedly, with innumerable modernisations, thanks to His Majesty the king, who has many innovative ideas for the development of his country. It is a particularly exciting time here at the moment, because it is the Bangkok centenary, and there are many social functions to mark the event. We attended a ball, just the day after I arrived, and only yesterday we visited the Siamese National Exhibition. Well, such a magnificent display even Europe has hardly seen the likes of, every foreigner here is saying. His Majesty has been to view it, and pronounced it quite extraordinary.

But now, dearest Marjorie, I am simply bursting to speak to you of another matter which, no doubt, in the months it takes this letter to reach you, will be resolved one way or another. I have met a man, Marjorie, and not just any man. I can see your knowing smile now, but I believe this man has completely overrun my emotions so that I can think of none other. Without divulging too much at this time, he is an American, a writer, and is also the most arrogant, insulting, yet intoxicating man I have ever met. To complicate matters, I do not believe he has any honourable intentions toward me, at least as yet. Isn't it exciting?

The problem, of course, is James. Father regards him as such a good "catch" that I shall be fortunate to be allowed to extricate myself from our engagement. I rather believe that Father is quite taken with the idea of his being married into the aristocracy, so to speak, and the advantages it might gain him. What to do, Marjorie? What to do? Nothing like this has ever happened to me before.

You will think me awfully liberal to speak of such matters, so I shall turn to my new family instead, for they are almost a new family to me since. . . .

She went on to describe Anchalee to her old school friend, as well as their house and the multi-hued tropical flowers in their garden.

She had, it seemed, made a surprisingly rapid recovery from the emotional distress she was suffering only hours earlier.

◈ *Chapter 16* ◈

On a muggy Saturday afternoon a few weeks later, Elizabeth and Anchalee decided to visit the King's Garden, near the Grand Palace, which was open to the public that one day each week. The king's band played as usual, and a large proportion of Bangkok's foreign community could be seen wandering among the spacious, well-kept grounds, which were luxuriantly planted with various tropical species, some of which were quite rare.

It was a weekly social event that both communities looked forward to. The foreigners met to trade news and gossip, or to play tennis and croquet on the lawn with the Siamese noblemen, and the Siamese public were provided the opportunity to gaze at the peculiar-looking foreigners with their eccentric fashions and habits.

"Shall we walk through the bamboo garden?" Anchalee suggested.

"Very well," Elizabeth agreed. She loved the long aisle of lofty bamboo trees, many of which were more than thirty feet tall. There weren't as many people at the gardens as usual that day, perhaps because the rains had arrived without delay that year, and the ladies were afraid of ruining their gowns in a deluge.

Elizabeth and Anchalee were delighted to have the entire 300-foot length of the aisle to themselves. They linked arms and walked along companionably.

"It feels like we're a long way from the city, doesn't it?" Anchalee remarked excitedly. "As if we could be in the jungle somewhere, having to keep a look-out for tigers and mad elephants and. . . ."

But as she was talking, she felt her sister stop beside her.

Elizabeth tugged at Anchalee's arm. "Let's turn round and go back."

"Don't be silly, he'll see." And she resisted her sister's effort to swing her round.

"I don't care, I don't care," Elizabeth insisted urgently. "Please, Anchalee, I can't face him now."

"But Elizabeth, if we turn round, he'll be walking in the same direction, and he'll surely catch up and want to walk with us. What will you say to him then? If we keep walking this way, we can merely nod and keep going."

"You're right, of course," she conceded reluctantly, and Anchalee saw that her sister had become ashen. "I can't avoid speaking to him, can I?" Elizabeth continued resignedly.

"No, you can't. Not unless you want to look foolish. And I don't suppose you want to appear that way to him, do you?"

"Absolutely not." She took a deep breath, as if preparing to dive into an icy river.

"Aha, the Misses Fairburn." Sam tipped his cap as he approached. "I wondered if I'd come across you two here today." He stood directly in their path.

"Did you?" Anchalee responded casually, neither intimidated nor embarrassed.

Sam smiled at her, and she noticed the rather obvious way he leered over both of them. Elizabeth hadn't said a word, and Anchalee nudged her almost imperceptibly.

"I trust you're well, Mr. Taylor?" Elizabeth asked, as coldly and imperiously as she could.

"Just dandy, Miss Fairburn," he replied—and they both noted the mocking tone in the comment.

Elizabeth brought the encounter to a hasty conclusion. "Well, we must be going. If you'll excuse us, Mr. Taylor."

"I'll see you round," Sam answered nonchalantly, without even attempting to linger. And he strode off in the other direction.

"You see, it wasn't so bad, was it?"

"No, thankfully. You were right."

"Don't worry, you'll see him again," Anchalee added playfully. Her sister was so obviously in love with this man that she couldn't resist the temptation to tease her a little.

"But that's just it, Anchalee. I don't want to see him again. Ever."

"Oh, and why not?"

Elizabeth still hadn't realised how her sister was mocking her. "You're only thirteen, Anchalee. I shouldn't expect you to understand. But he's just too . . . too dangerous."

"Dangerous?"

"Yes. He's entirely unsuitable for me, and would not do at all as a husband."

"You don't have to marry him. Just because you're in love with him doesn't mean there has to be a wedding."

"I'm *not* in love with him, Anchalee. I loathe him. He' s everything I despise in a man and more."

Anchalee smiled to herself, trying desperately not to break out with laughter, delighted that she had managed to fluster Elizabeth. She was thoroughly enjoying the over-reaction, which simply confirmed everything Elizabeth had been denying.

"He has no breeding at all. The son of a saloonkeeper—or some such thing—and a *Mexican* woman. No, he wouldn't do at all. It's quite out of the question," Elizabeth continued vehemently.

Anchalee made no reply, and Elizabeth quickly realised how clumsy her comment had been. "Oh, I'm sorry, Anchalee. I didn't mean he was unworthy because his mother wasn't English. I. . . ."

"Don't worry," Anchalee stopped her, smiling. "I know you didn't."

She wanted to talk about her own mother. It was on the tip of her tongue to ask how much Elizabeth remembered; to ask what Kesri had been like. But she felt it was too soon. And there was also the danger that Elizabeth would say she was too young to recall Kesri. Then the subject would be closed, and she would be no nearer the truth.

They walked on in uneasy silence, and when they reached the end of the aisle and were out in the open again, they saw that the clouds had gathered overhead, low and dark.

"Perhaps we should walk to the orchid house and shelter in there," Anchalee suggested.

Elizabeth agreed, still feeling guilty over her tactless remark, and they walked briskly to the long, two-storey greenhouse that contained thousands of lovely orchids on the ground floor, and many more varieties of tropical plants on the roofless upper floor.

As they hurried toward the building, the sky flashed with forked lightning, and rumbled ominously with thunder, a cannon roll never equalled in volume outside the tropics. A moment later, the first drops fell—each one heavy as it burst on the skin—but their timing was perfect, and they managed to leap inside just before the rain descended in sheets like a waterfall.

The orchid house was hot and humid, but there were only a few leaks from the roof, and it provided a sound enough shelter. Several other people had also taken refuge inside, although they were widely spaced apart in the 200-foot-long building. It was packed with orchids of every colour and size. Some were in hanging pots with long, tangled roots and stems of flowers that escaped the confines of their vessels to block the view along the pathway. They didn't grow in soil, but apparently took sustenance from the humidity alone. Anchalee silently wandered off, and Elizabeth—preoccupied with the beauty of the flowers and plants—remained unaware that she was alone.

As she walked on in the sultry atmosphere admiring the displays, she felt trickles of sweat running down her back. She came across one area that was even more overgrown than the rest, where a large, painted porcelain pot had been knocked over, its foliage obstructing the path further. She lifted her skirts above her ankles to climb over it, but as she did so, her foot caught the edge of the pot, and she tripped.

She would have landed on her face, had not a pair of strong arms suddenly reached out from behind and caught her around her waist. She immediately knew that it wasn't Anchalee, and when she looked down, she saw masculine hands holding her. Above them were the arms of a velvet jacket.

But she was not released when she regained her balance, and as she turned slowly, her mouth became dry as she saw that it was he who held her. She cleared her throat but her voice was still shaky. "Mr. Taylor. Thank you for your assistance. Now please remove your arms from my waist. Where's my sister?"

"She saw a friend and had to hurry off down there." He pointed back along the path, but still did not release her. "She'll be back soon."

"Well then, I must go after her. Please unhand me."

"Not on your life," he said, pulling her closer.

She tried to manoeuvre herself out of his arms, but his grasp only increased. "Mr. Taylor, please. You must let go of me this instant. Someone will see us, and think. . . ." She pushed hard against his chest in a renewed effort to escape. "Mr. Taylor, this is outrageous. Let me go this instant."

But still he refused. "No one can see us. And there's something I have to do before I let you go." And then he kissed her, passionately and urgently, and without restraint.

At first, she struggled, clamping her lips shut and pushing against his chest with her fists. But slowly she felt herself less and less able to resist. Her knees felt as if they might buckle, and finally she sank into his arms and allowed him to gently prise her lips apart as she shivered with pleasure. She knew then that she was lost to him.

"I must see you alone," he whispered.

"Yes," she agreed simply after a moment's thought, not resisting, her concern at them being seen, momentarily forgotten.

"I'll send a message to you."

"But how are we to meet? You know my father . . ."

"Shhh," he stopped her. "Is Anchalee to be trusted?"

"Yes, I think so."

"Good. Then she may be able to help us. Your father won't mind if you go out with her. Then you can meet me once you're away from the house."

The sound of footsteps and women's voices in conversation came from behind them, very close. She sprang away from him and stepped aside guiltily as two elderly European ladies walked past them in single file. She felt her whole body trembling as she realised how she could have been discovered in a most compromising position. The women both looked back at her sharply, as if to say, "Where is your chaperone, young woman?" before they disappeared along the overgrown path.

"I'll see you soon," he said as he touched her cheek briefly, sending tingles up and down her spine. He turned and was gone, leaving her alone and still trembling.

A few minutes later, from the opposite direction, Anchalee returned.

"Sorry, Elizabeth. I saw a friend from school. I had to run down to see her, or I would have missed her. I hope you weren't lonely."

Elizabeth wondered if Anchalee knew Sam had been there; wondered, in fact, if she had even engineered the meeting somehow.

"No, not at all," she replied. "Actually, I've been thinking about Mr. Taylor. There's something I'd like to discuss with you."

He hadn't felt well for weeks now, but still he tried to ignore the symptoms. In fact, if he was honest with himself, he had not been in good health for months. He had given up his nightly pipe, at first trying—and failing—to convince himself that the breathlessness and the nagging cough were a consequence of it. He concentrated all his energy on his work, as he planned to mount an exhibition of photographs taken in Bangkok. It was a rare event in Siam, for which he had been promised royal patronage. But in order to warrant the show, he needed to produce a variety of new images, from which to select the most remarkable for public display.

Despite the greater ambitions of his younger years, Edward had managed only one exhibition in his career. It was a modest but critically successful show, of pictures taken on the gold fields and in Siam, staged in Yorkshire when he had returned to England to visit Elizabeth. Perhaps because of it, he had briefly entertained the notion of returning permanently and establishing a studio in London.

But he had soon realised the foolishness of the idea. His brothers still considered him a terrible failure—rather an embarrassment to them, in fact—and his parents, elderly now but still involved in their social circles, made it clear they were not impressed by his liaison in Siam, which had produced the "other daughter".

He very soon reached the conclusion that he would be almost completely isolated if he went back to England, and he certainly did not wish to reach old age alone there, sadly reminiscing about his years in the tropics.

And so he had returned to Siam, and had laboured hard to finance the large house they now lived in, without having to make recourse to his inheritance in England.

In moments of waking torment, when the household was asleep, the certainty of his coming death would haunt him, and he would remember certain events of his past that were better forgotten. It was important now for him to finish the work for the exhibition.

❖ *Chapter 17* ❖

The message arrived in an envelope addressed to Anchalee. Inside was a smaller envelope with Elizabeth's name on it, and when Anchalee brought it to her sister, Elizabeth tore it open at once.

Be with Anchalee tomorrow, midday, at the Oriental dock. A boatman will take you to our meeting point, the typed message read.

There was no signature, but she hardly needed to be told who the author was. Neither was there any endearment or romantic connotation. It was safer that way, of course.

When Elizabeth had enlisted her help, Anchalee had seemed delighted—but now it was her younger sister, and not she, who was a little hesitant about the meeting. "Are you sure you want to do this?" Anchalee asked.

"Of course I'm sure," Elizabeth replied confidently. "It's the only way. Perhaps he'll even ask me to marry him."

Anchalee recoiled with an expression of amazement. "I don't think that's quite what he has in mind."

"What do you mean?" Elizabeth felt a tingle of unease, which she tried to dismiss as quickly as it had arisen.

"Just that you ought to be careful."

"You'll be with me. What could possibly happen?"

"Of course," Anchalee smiled. "You're right. We'll go. And Father won't think it strange if we go out together."

And he did not. Anchalee explained to Edward at the dinner table that night how she would show her sister the river and some more of Bangkok's famous temples the next day.

"That's a fine idea," Edward agreed. "But, young lady, you'll have to go back to school soon. This is your last week off with Elizabeth."

Elizabeth didn't enjoy having to deceive her father, and was glad for his sudden concern over Anchalee's education.

But Anchalee was far from impressed with the news. "I was hoping you'd have forgotten about that silly old school, Father. I really don't need to go any more," she complained.

"Nonsense, girl. You're only half educated. I don't hold with that old-fashioned idea that women shouldn't be schooled. Gives them something to occupy their minds with, instead of constant silliness. No, certainly not. You're far too young to leave."

"Too young, too young. That's all I ever hear," Anchalee pouted.

"Count yourself lucky, then. For one day you'll be too old." He could never seem to reprimand her seriously, no matter how impertinent she was, and Elizabeth was beginning to enjoy their continual sparring.

Elizabeth dressed carefully next morning, telling Noi she would finish herself, after the maid had helped her with the corset. She found that she was actually savouring the experience of preparing herself for him. She wished she had made the effort to visit Anchalee's seamstress, Mrs. Smythe, at her shop, but she would make do with what she had.

She selected a dusky pink, shot-silk gown, draped over the bustle, and falling in soft folds to the ground. It featured one of the new higher bustles, which Elizabeth thought was particularly flattering. The bodice had a double row of buttons, with a high stand-up collar and long sleeves with turned-back cuffs. She wore white silk stockings and pink silk shoes with a Louis heel, and carried a matching pink parasol. Her corset—the one with the white French lace—was the tightest she owned, and it ensured her waist measured no more than nineteen inches. The outfit was completed with a tiny straw hat trimmed with pink satin rosebuds.

There was a tap at her door as noon approached, and Anchalee entered, dressed in a simple white gown that would have made her look her age, if not for a rather low, square neckline. She looked Elizabeth over. "You look beautiful. What a fancy dress."

"Is it all right do you think?" Beside Anchalee, she now felt overdressed.

"Of course. You always seem to know just what to wear."

Elizabeth felt suddenly giddy, and she had to reach out to grip the side of her dressing table for support. "I can't believe I'm doing this. This is really going to happen, isn't it?"

"Well, only if we leave now. You're not having second thoughts, are you?"

"If I thought about it at all, Anchalee, I wouldn't dare do this. It's totally out of character for me, and it goes against all my principles."

"You can make exceptions to rules for passion," Anchalee stated precociously, and it sounded as if she had read it in a novel. This time, however, Elizabeth did not protest her sister's choice of words.

The boatman was waiting for them as the note had said. He was sleeping—as the Siamese took the opportunity to do at any time of the day—and once they had roused him, they set off in the brightly-painted craft.

They went upriver, in the direction of the old capital city, Ayuthaya, but long before they left the environs of Bangkok, the boatman turned off into a narrow series of *klongs*. It was a long time since Elizabeth had made a trip on the waterways like this, and when she had, as a girl, it had always enchanted her.

The activity here was merely on a lesser scale than that of the 'River of Kings', and as their boat progressed almost serenely on the swathe of brown water—passing clusters of bamboo-and-thatch huts amid the dense vegetation and the coconut groves—they were always alongside or within easy distance of the wooden floating houses, each with its own spirit house in front. Colourful *panungs* and *sarongs* hung from lines on almost every home.

Many of the waterside inhabitants were taking their midday meal—bowls of white rice with chicken curry or fried beef and chilli sauce—while some went about a variety of daily chores, and still others dozed in the noon heat. Impish children were everywhere in the water, and monkeys still frolicked riotously in the trees—although Elizabeth thought there might be rather fewer than she remembered as a child.

The sun beat directly down on them, and they were glad of the boat's striped canopy. It afforded little protection from the heat, but with the slight breeze in their faces from the movement of the boat, the discomfort was not too great.

As they entered a quieter stretch of the *klong*, the boatman suddenly stopped the vessel and manoeuvred it alongside a handsome, polished-teak houseboat. A maid appeared and helped them climb out, and the boatman then went on his way again. Elizabeth and Anchalee stood on the wooden verandah, and the world seemed to stand still, with only the immediate sounds of water lapping the sides of the boat, and tropical birds chattering high in the coconut palms.

The woman went round to the opposite side of the boat closest to the bank, and Elizabeth wondered if Sam were there—or even if he had decided to keep the liaison at all. The silence was disconcerting, and she began to panic at the thought of what they would do if he did not come. But then the door to the living quarters opened, and he was there, dressed Siamese-style in a silk *panung* and a white cotton shirt that was open at the neck.

"I hoped you'd come."

"I told you I would," she answered nervously. His appearance had shocked her initially, but now she found it sensual.

The woman appeared again and spoke in a low voice to Anchalee in Siamese. Anchalee disappeared round the side with her, leaving Elizabeth alone with him. He walked toward her slowly, and she could not keep her eyes from him. He held out a hand to her, and she took it, allowing herself to be led toward the open door, and into the dark interior. He shut it and locked it behind them.

He turned over the likeness again, and looked at the face of the woman he had once adored but had then cast out so heartlessly.

When he had discovered it in Anchalee's room, he had been angry with her for taking something that was not hers. But then he realised how selfish he had been. For Kesri *was* Anchalee's, as much—if not more—than she had been his, and he knew he had denied his daughter her right to a mother. It was only by chance that he had discovered she was in possession of the picture.

When she had asked to borrow the photographs of her as a baby and a child, he agreed with the provision that she must return them tidily. She had not, of course, and he knew what condition they would fall into—dog-eared, lying round her room, pushed into the edge of her mirror, or used as bookmarks—if he did not reclaim them. He made a note to let her keep her favourites but to return the remainder.

But one day in his studio, his eye had caught the row of boxes of old prints he had discarded but could not quite bring himself to throw away. He hadn't touched any of them for years, yet one was slightly out of order. The maid rarely cleaned in that area, and when he examined the boxes more closely, he could see marks in the dust on the lids. Someone had opened them recently, and it was obviously Anchalee.

She had asked for the pictures of herself only after he had told her that no pictures of Kesri existed, and—he surmised— she must have been hoping that he had overlooked at least one in the old boxes. He was more angry that, when she hadn't found what she wanted, she had taken the key to the studio without his permission—everyone in the house knew where he kept it—and looked for herself.

Could she have found what she had been seeking, he wondered? It was so long since he had seen a picture of Kesri, he couldn't remember whether he had kept any at all. He recalled, on the day she had left, smashing a number of photographic plates in anger, tearing up prints and tossing them into a fire, but keeping back the last one—although it, too, was torn in his frustration and fury. What had he done with it? Had he put it into one of the boxes, and had Anchalee found it? Did it matter? Somehow it did, and he had to know. He was possessed of a sudden urge, too, to see Kesri's face once again.

He locked the studio and went into the house and up to Anchalee's room. Where would he start? He was reluctant to rifle through her cupboards and drawers, but guessed that perhaps it was in one of her books. What was that anthology of poetry she was always dipping into? That ridiculous, romantic verse that filled her head with notions far too sophisticated and highly unsuitable?

Ah yes, there it was. He pulled out the volume from the shelf and shook it gently. He had been right. The photograph fluttered out and landed on the wooden floor. The face he had not laid eyes upon in thirteen years looked back up at him. He, in turn, gazed at her image for a few moments and then turned the print over. On the back was written, in his own hand, simply, "*Kesri, 1868*".

It was this discovery, as well as Anchalee's brooding, her regular questions, and her occasional, contrived remarks, that had brought him to his decision. Of course, when she was younger—and with her mind so preoccupied with the pleasures of childhood—there had been no effort on her part to discover the truth about her mother. But now she was maturing quickly, and so too was her inquisitiveness.

He had hoped that the photographs of her as a child would have been enough to satisfy her curiosity—at least for a while longer, or at least until she was older and, perhaps, better able to cope with the truth—but they proved only to spur her on. The situation was reaching the point where he could deter her no longer. With this growing realisation, a shadow seemed to be cast over him as his guilt returned to possess him at every turn.

Kesri had been so beautiful, and had seemed so eager and so willing to cater to his every whim. But then he would recall how she had spat on his trust in her. God had punished them both. She had been banished and barred from ever seeing her child, and he had been compelled to live with the guilt, all these years, that his actions had deprived both his daughters of their mothers.

Then Joseph Shaw had told him, less than two years later, that Kesri had died of consumption. At the time, he had believed it was her fate for murdering their child. But now he pondered the wisdom of that view. At least Anchalee would have known her mother's undoubted love, had he not banished her.

Now, also, he saw that it had been wrong of him to separate Anchalee from all knowledge of her mother. In his heart, when he looked back on his life now, he saw much wrong—and he feared he was not worthy of God's mercy. He hoped his daily prayers would save him from eternal hell.

He stopped to cough into a handkerchief—he kept several in his pocket these days—then returned the tatty photograph to the book and replaced it on the shelf. He could no longer deny Anchalee her right to know.

But equally, he knew he could not be the one to speak of her mother. The past was still too painful. There was someone else, he decided, who would be able to perform the task much better than he.

That afternoon he called on Joseph. It still surprised him that the man he had once thought of as an adversary—who had disapproved of his lifestyle—had now become something of a trusted confidant.

"She asks so many questions," he told Joseph as they sat in the garden, sipping lemon squash. "I cannot discourage her much longer."

"Why not simply answer her?" Joseph suggested. "With discretion, of course. She needn't know every detail."

"She's so eager to know about her mother," he sighed. "She's had a happy life so far, and she's wanted for nothing. But she feels a certain emptiness, I know." He paused to take a sip of his drink.

"She has an old photograph of Kesri. I thought I'd destroyed them all, but this one had been pieced together from torn remains.

It must have somehow been put into one of my old boxes, and she found it."

"Every child needs a mother, Edward. And although she may seem very mature for her age, she *is* still a child."

"It's easy to forget sometimes. I put it down to those novels and anthologies she's always reading. That romantic nonsense seems to give her all kinds of ideas. She's far too impressionable. Highly unsuitable."

Joseph blushed slightly and looked away for a moment.

Edward seemed not to notice as he continued, "But I don't want her to grow up feeling I've denied her knowledge she has a right to. It's true, I've told her very little about her mother, but I thought she'd eventually give up trying to find out."

"So, what do you plan to do?"

"Well, I must confess that's where I hope you can help me. I find that I'm still unable to think of Anchalee's mother without—emotion—let alone speak of her. To my shame, I *cannot* forgive her for what she did. But nor can I forgive myself for what I did to her. She was so young at the time, and sometimes now I think she shouldn't be blamed for what happened. And yet, I *cannot* forget it. I *cannot* forgive, Joseph, and that's a terrible sin."

"Many of us, in youth, do things we regret forever," Joseph said quietly.

"That's why I must ask a favour of you."

"By all means, if I can be of any help."

"Would you talk to her? Tell her how lovely her mother was, how beautiful she was, and how much she loved her daughter? Please don't tell her what happened—the unfortunate incident that led to her dismissal, I mean. Simply say that she and I were unable to get along agreeably together, and that we decided, for Anchalee's sake, that it was better to part. Will you do this for me, Joseph?"

Joseph contemplated Edward's request for a moment and then nodded his agreement. "Very well, Edward. Ask her to come and see me tomorrow."

Edward thanked him and they talked for some time until he had to leave for a portrait session at his studio.

Joseph continued sitting at the table in his garden after Edward had departed, and he finally decided it was indeed time to give Anchalee her mother's bequest. Although it was still six months until her fourteenth birthday, Kesri had instructed him to hand over the letter to her daughter before then if he thought it necessary or appropriate.

He went upstairs to his study and opened the safe where he kept his few valuables and private papers. There were—among other things—his birth certificate, his letter of appointment to Siam, and a picture of a young woman that was faded and yellowed now after twenty years. The early photographic processes provided poor quality images, he reflected, in comparison to those of the present day, but even so, it was a fine likeness. She still looked beautiful and regal to him, with her long, thick, wavy hair, and her *moko*—the facial tattoo that all Maori women, as well as men, wore. For a moment, he thought about what could have been, what should have been, but was denied both of them.

He put aside the picture and its painful memories, and picked up the large envelope he had come for. It was also yellowing at the edges, but the address—in the careful handwriting of someone unaccustomed to English script—was still clear.

He recalled the day, more than twelve years before, when Kesri had come to him with this letter, and he had written on another piece of paper, the script—*To Miss Anchalee Kesri Fairburn. Private and confidential. If the addressee be deceased, this envelope and its contents are to be destroyed, unopened*—for her to copy on the front. He had promised her that he would never open it or read it, nor allow anyone but Anchalee to do so. And he had kept his word. It was now time to carry out her last wish.

◈ *Chapter 18* ◈

She was almost too surprised to respond when he handed it to her. "A letter from my mother? Then she's. . . ."

"No, Anchalee, I'm sorry," he interrupted her quickly. "She died a long time ago. You've always been told the truth about that."

She turned the envelope over and over in her hands, then stared at the handwriting, touching it and tracing her name. She could hardly comprehend that it had been written by her own mother.

She had been a little put out this morning when her father had asked her to go to Mr. Shaw's house for some sort of talk. She had assumed that he had persuaded Mr. Shaw to berate her about something she was doing that Edward deemed "ill befitting a young Christian lady", and she had prepared herself for a tedious lecture. But now she was wide-eyed with curiosity.

"Before you open it," he added, "I must tell you what happened to lead to this. Yesterday, your father came to me, concerned that you were so inquisitive about your mother. I don't know why it suddenly upset him so much after all this time, but that's beside the point. Anyway, he asked me to tell you something of your mother. He considers you have a right to know, now that you're older."

"Why doesn't he tell me himself, Mr. Shaw?"

"Well, Anchalee, it's still very painful for him when he remembers your mother. And, indeed, Elizabeth's mother. He was quite upset when we spoke yesterday, and he prefers that I tell you myself."

"Does he know about this letter?"

"No, he doesn't. He and I have become friends over the years, it's true, but this was a matter of honour. I promised your mother I would speak of it to no one but you when the time came. Nobody has laid eyes on its contents but she. After you've read it, you may tell your father about it or not, as you see fit."

Anchalee, seated in his front room on the well-worn brown leather chesterfield, was mesmerised by what he was saying.

He cleared his throat to continue. "Well, I don't quite know where to begin. Kesri—your mother—was very young when she met your father. No one knew very much about her before then, except that she'd spent about a year-and-a-half with the American Protestant missionaries after somehow buying her freedom from slavery when she was sixteen. They taught her some English, and she was an extremely bright and willing pupil, although she was never interested in the religious tuition.

"Because she could speak a little English, she was employed as a servant by some of the foreign families. In fact, she worked on a kind of freelance basis, showing a lot of ingenuity for one so young. Anyway, during a party at the British Consulate, at which she was serving, she met your father."

"What happened?"

Well, she became his. . . ." He hesitated, slightly embarrassed. "Well, I'm afraid that at that time, your father was still married to Elizabeth's mother, although she hadn't yet arrived from Australia. However, when Charlotte—Elizabeth's mother—left for England later, she died tragically at sea. Your mother and father were then married, although they had a Buddhist ceremony and the union was never blessed by the Church."

"And then I was born?"

"Yes, you were born. And both your parents loved you very much."

"Then why did she leave me?"

"She didn't want to. But it was the best thing at the time."

"How could it have been?"

"Well, your parents found they were . . . how shall I say it . . . incompatible. They couldn't get along, and they agreed it was better they parted permanently. You must remember that it was very difficult for them, Anchalee. They were from very different cultures, and sometimes it wasn't easy for them to understand one another. Not only in conversation, of course, but in the way they thought about things."

"But what happened to her? Why did she never come to visit me?"

"She became very ill with consumption about six months after she left, and that's when she brought me this letter. She knew she was very sick, and sadly, she did die a year later. I was told she passed away peacefully in her sleep."

"You were told? By whom?"

"By Porntip, the maid who used to work for your family."

"I remember Porntip. Why did she never tell me anything? Why did she keep it a secret from me? Did my mother do something awful? Was she a . . . a criminal? Or a madwoman?"

"No, no, nothing like that. I suppose, my dear, that they decided it was best not to tell you anything."

"You mean, Father decided it was best," she said sullenly.

"Yes, well, perhaps the letter will explain things in more detail."

"But Mr. Shaw, you still haven't told me what she was like."

"Oh. Well, she had black hair, of course, done in a top knot, as was the style of the day . . ."

"No, no, Mr. Shaw, not what she looked like. I have a photograph of her. But what was she *like*? As a person?"

"Well, I'm afraid I didn't know her at all personally, Anchalee. So I'm afraid I cannot tell you. But I imagine she was very determined and resourceful. I hardly remember her from her time at the mission, and she was rarely seen in public with your father."

"Was he ashamed of her?"

He was now feeling very uncomfortable. "No, it wasn't that. Only. . . . Well, why don't you wait and see if she explains that in her letter, too?"

Anchalee nodded. She suspected there was much more to the story than Joseph was telling her. "And Elizabeth? Did she like my mother? Her own mother died, so it must have been nice for her to have a new mother."

"Elizabeth was very sad, naturally, when her own mother died, and I don't think she had time to get used to having a new mother. But she loved you, from the moment she first saw you. She used to carry you round with her all day."

"But she left me, too."

"She didn't want to go, either. But your father rightly decided she should be educated at home in England."

"I see. Did you know Elizabeth's mother?"

"Yes, quite well."

"What was she like?"

Joseph vividly remembered poor Charlotte and her plea for him to look after her daughter. "Mrs. Fairburn was a gracious, noble lady, and it was a terrible tragedy that she passed away so long before her time."

"You said she died at sea."

"Yes, she was on her way back to England."

"Why? Was she going away for long?"

"Well, it was said she was in need of a cooler climate."

"Oh, I see." Anchalee then fell silent for a moment before asking quietly, "Shall I read the letter now?"

"Yes, I think that's a good idea," Joseph agreed, getting up from his seat. "But first, I have something else to give you. He reached into his pocket and withdrew a small package wrapped in paper, which he held out to her.

Wordlessly, she took it, and quickly unwrapped it. It was a silver locket, old and tarnished, but beautiful to her because she knew at once that it had belonged to Kesri. She opened the clasp, and inside were two tiny pictures: her mother on one side, and herself as a baby on the other. In the corner of Kesri's picture was a tiny lock of hair. Tears filled her eyes as she slipped the silver chain over her head and tucked the locket inside her dress.

"I'll leave you here alone now," Joseph said as he left the room. "Call me when you've finished."

Anchalee again turned the envelope over and over in her hands. Strangely, she was now reluctant to open it, fearing what it might contain. It was a letter from the grave; a legacy. But it was what she had been waiting for all these years without even knowing it.

Carefully, she slit the top of the envelope with Joseph's silver letter opener, and took out a thick sheaf of pages written in the familiar Siamese script. The top sheet was dated "*January 10th, Buddhist Era 2412–1870 on the Christian calendar—at Krung Thep,*" the Siamese name for Bangkok. She unfolded the pages and spread them out on the desk before her. She was so glad her mother had written in Siamese, and not had the letter translated into English. For in her heart, Anchalee felt Siamese, not European, and she wanted to communicate with her mother in what she had always thought of as her native tongue.

She began to read, imagining as she did, her mother in this very room, so many years ago, sealing the letter. She felt Kesri's presence so strongly, it was almost as if she were not reading her words, but as if her mother had somehow materialised before her and was speaking to her in person.

It took her a long time to read the letter—pausing often to wipe the tears from her eyes and cheeks—and when she had finished, she looked up from the pages, too stunned to cry any longer. She sat for a long time, staring at the pages, their words still searing through her. Then she clutched the letter to her chest, her knuckles white. "All this time, I thought you were my friend," she cried out loud.

At first, Joseph—just outside—thought Anchalee was calling to him, but he quickly realised she was not.

He could wait no longer. In early October, Edward put his plan into action, having received assurances from his daughter—albeit rather weak ones—that she was still planning to marry James Claridge. His intention was to hold the exhibition early in the new year, and he hoped that his letter to the king would be fruitful.

❖ *Chapter 19* ❖

The sickness in the mornings, the slight thickening of her waist, the tenderness and swelling of her breasts, and the absence of her monthly bleeding—all told of the consequence of her actions. She had suspected for some time, and—bizarrely—had even welcomed it on occasion, with the hope that it would force his hand; that it would elicit from him the commitment she so desperately wanted.

It had been September when she had first given herself to him, although they had been close many times before then, in his borrowed houseboat on the *klong*. Since then, she had been stealing away—always with Anchalee as chaperone—whenever she could, at least two or three times a week. The irony of the affair was that when they met at social events, she would have to affect that she knew him only slightly, as Mr. Taylor, the American writer.

But now she felt the first stirrings of fear as she faced the reality of her situation, rather than her romantic ideals of it. But it was love, she was sure, on his part as much as hers—or she at least tried to convince herself it was so. At the height of their passion, he told her how much he loved her, how much he wanted to be with her, and how he yearned for her when she was gone. There was no mention of marriage, but she felt it must be only a matter of time.

He was busy writing another book about Siam, he had told her, and he had strict deadlines to meet. She was sure that as soon as he had posted his manuscript, he would propose to her— and she would accept, no matter what her father thought, or how strongly he objected. She would agree, in fact, even if Edward forbade it. The fact that she was carrying his child would mean only that they must marry earlier, before he had completed the book. But she would promise to give him all the time he needed to write once they were wed. She was capable of amusing herself during the days, and she would eventually be too busy caring for their child to worry about how many hours he spent at his typewriter.

James would be heartbroken, but she resolved to write to him soon to cancel their liaison. Her guilt gave her no peace, but there was nothing else for it. Edward, she knew, would be livid. He continued to pester her to set a date for the wedding, and she continued to stall him, bewildered at her own inability to tell him the truth: that she had no intentions of marrying James, or of returning to England.

She planned to tell Sam her news the next time she met him, and she prayed he would not be angry. She had dared not tell Anchalee the secret, nor had she written to Marjorie, believing it best that she carried the burden herself. Besides, Anchalee wasn't aware of what happened during her trysts with Sam. She had told her younger sister only that they talked and took tea. She doubted, of course, that Anchalee believed her, but Anchalee had never said anything to indicate she did not.

She felt nauseated again, and rushed to the basin that stood on the washstand. She vomited violently, just as there came a light tapping on the door. Anchalee opened the door and stepped into the room.

"It must have been something I ate," Elizabeth claimed, wiping her mouth with a towel. She was pale and shaky.

Anchalee stared at her.

"I'll call the maid," she said calmly after a moment or two.

Joseph was surprised when he answered a knock on the door that afternoon, and Anchalee stood alone at the step.

"Nice to see you again, Anchalee. Please, come in. What can I do for you? Is it something about school? Or the letter, perhaps?"

She looked around suspiciously, as if she expected there to be spies, then said in a low voice, "No, Mr. Shaw. Elizabeth asked me to come to see you on her behalf. She says it's a matter of some delicacy."

"In that case, you'd better come into my study." He was slightly perplexed. "Would you like some tea?"

"No thank you, Mr. Shaw. I should be going home as soon as possible."

"Certainly." He showed her into his book-lined study, which was full of heavy religious tomes, as well as a selection of the latest novels by Henry James, Thomas Hardy, and George Meredith among many others. His collection had grown over the years and he no longer felt the need to conceal his books when members of the parish visited him at home. Indeed, there were now so many that it would have been impossible to do so.

When they were both seated—he at his desk, and Anchalee in a leather chair facing it—she removed an envelope from a pocket concealed in her dolman jacket and handed it to him.

"This is a letter from Elizabeth. She said it was self-explanatory, but if you have any questions, I'm to answer them."

"But why hasn't she come herself?" he asked, even more puzzled.

"Well, she was very embarrassed. And. . . . Well, it's all in the letter, Mr. Shaw."

Joseph put on his reading glasses and opened the white envelope.

November 15th, 1882

Dear Mr. Shaw,

> *We have known each other for many years, and you have always been a good friend to me, and to my mother before me. Because of this, I should like to ask for your help with a most painful*

matter, which I have chosen to write about in this letter, rather than to discuss in person, because of its delicate nature. It concerns myself and a gentleman of my acquaintance, Mr. Samuel Taylor.

For some time now, Mr. Taylor and I have been meeting secretly, chaperoned by my sister, Anchalee. Although nothing improper has occurred, I know my dear father would not approve of these meetings, and would, in fact, expect me to marry Mr. Taylor immediately for what he would consider my indiscretions.

I am ashamed to admit the truth, Mr. Shaw, but you see, I find that after several of these meetings, my initial feelings for Mr. Taylor have cooled considerably, and I no longer believe him to be a suitable candidate for marriage. However, I do not wish to hurt his feelings, as I am positive that he feels deep affection for me and plans very soon to ask for my hand.

If you could see your way to helping me extricate myself from this unfortunate arrangement, without his knowledge, I would be eternally grateful to you. What I ask, Mr. Shaw, is that you might somehow persuade Mr. Taylor to leave Bangkok for a time.

I understand that you are seeking someone to accompany supplies to the mission in Chiengmai in the North. I know also that Mr. Taylor himself is keen to make a journey north in order to obtain more information for his book about Siam. I am sure he could be persuaded to join this expedition, which I understand is ready to depart soon. Because we cannot meet openly, he would then have only to write me a note to advise me that he was to be away for so many months.

I believe that if such a distance of time and place were put between us, I could reject any advances he might make on his return, without embarrassment to either party.

My dear Mr. Shaw, I am deeply sorry to burden you with this inconvenience, but I can think of no one else I could trust so well. You may speak freely of this matter to my sister, as she is aware of everything that has occurred, and of my intention to end this mistaken liaison.

Obviously, I would ask that you make absolutely no mention of this letter to Mr. Taylor. Because I feel so embarrassed and ashamed over this whole matter, Mr. Shaw, I would also greatly appreciate it if

you and I never mentioned it, or indeed this letter, either to each other
or to any other party, at any occasion in the future.

Your sincere and affectionate friend,

Elizabeth Fairburn

He read the letter twice before finally removing his reading glasses and putting them back in their case. "Well, poor Elizabeth has got herself into an unfortunate situation, hasn't she? I do hope he's not made any . . . unseemly advances, so to speak."

"Not to my knowledge," Anchalee lied. She had never, for one moment, believed Elizabeth's stories about what happened between herself and Sam at their secret rendezvous.

"In that case, I shall do my best to do as she asks. I agree it's best to keep Mr. Taylor away from her. Although why she ever agreed to meet him in the first place is beyond me. He is, as she says, most unsuitable."

"So you *will* help her, Mr. Shaw?"

"Of course. As I say, I shall do my best. But how shall I get word to her if I've been successful?"

"There won't be any need," Anchalee said. "The expedition leaves very soon, does it not?"

"Well, your request is most timely. It could be ready the day after tomorrow. Certainly within three days."

"Then if she receives a letter from him within two days, she'll know you've succeeded. If she doesn't, she'll know he's still here in Bangkok. As you can imagine, she's most anxious to dispense with the matter as quickly as possible. And she wishes never to speak of it again."

"I understand. She has my word that I'll mention it to no one, and that I'll never refer to it in conversation with her."

"Thank you, Mr. Shaw. She'll appreciate that very much."

205

A letter arrived for Elizabeth that day from England, and it was one she hardly dared open. It was from James, and she was convinced he would be urging her to return so they could set a wedding date.

In all that had happened to her during the last few months, she had hardly thought of him, let alone written. She would have to reply to him straight away, informing him, as gently as possible, that she no longer wished to marry him. Finally, she slit open the envelope, to find only one sheet inside. It had taken more than four months to reach Siam.

July 7th, 1882

My dear Elizabeth,

You have been away a relatively short time, yet it seems like a lifetime. Much has happened since you left, and it is my unpleasant duty to inform you of one of these events.

There is no easy way to write what I have to tell you, Elizabeth, so I shall say it directly. I have fallen in love with Lady Cynthia Asquith-Brown, and we are to be married early next year. We are a most suitable match.

Elizabeth, you know that I shall always have only the fondest memories of you, and I never meant to hurt you in any way. But for some reason I am thinking that perhaps this news will come as something of a relief to you, rather than anything else. The truth is, I feel it is time I married, and I do not want to delay any longer. My father, as you know, is in failing health, and his only wish is to see me married and settled with a family before he passes on.

I sincerely hope that this news does not come as too much of a shock to you, and with deep affection,

I remain your loyal friend,

James T. Claridge

She slowly put down the letter on her dresser, and as his words sank in, she began to smile for the first time in several days. Now, all that remained was to send a brief letter of congratulations to the bride and groom, and the matter was concluded. She sighed with relief. Perhaps this predicament was not so dreadful after all. Perhaps she and Sam could marry quickly, and—in time— people would cease counting the months between their wedding and the birth of their child. Her father would have no choice but to accept the situation since it was James, and not she, who had called off the engagement.

Sam paced up and down in his room and fretted over how Elizabeth would react when she received the letter. She would be distressed at his leaving, but it was simply too good an opportunity to miss. As Joseph Shaw had explained, his only responsibility was to ensure that the supplies reached the missionary families in Chiengmai, and he would be free to write throughout the entire length of the journey. It would provide ideal material for his book.

She loved him, he was certain of that. She was not the kind of woman who entered lightly into an intimate relationship with a man, and this had been her first. And he was forced to admit to himself that he cared for her more than he had for any woman before. Since the day he had first met her, on the jetty by the Oriental, he had known there was something special about her, even though he could not define what it was. She was not the most beautiful woman he had known. Nor was she the wittiest, nor the best lover. In fact, she had been completely inexperienced in that way, which was not generally what he liked in a woman. And yet, he wanted her and found himself longing for her company when they were apart.

He had never felt this way before, and it troubled him greatly. He wondered if he were actually falling in love with her. If he asked her to marry him, there was no question she would accept—with or without her father's approval—and he knew she would make a devoted and faithful wife. But he needed this time away to be absolutely sure. It was so strange for him to even contemplate such notions.

How could this be happening to her? The words in his brief message echoed in her head, as if he were speaking them over and over. "*I will be gone for up to six months . . . gone for up to six months.*"

"Oh, God help me!" she said aloud, throwing herself on her bed and burying her head into the pillows. It was unthinkable that anyone know of her condition, even though it would soon be impossible to conceal. She was ruined, and she broke down in a fresh series of choking sobs.

She was aware of abortion, of course, and suspected that it was available in Bangkok in some disgraceful back alley, just as it was at home. But she had heard so many horror stories and so many whispered tales—of contaminated instruments, of damage so severe that women bled to death, and of women who underwent the procedure almost certain never to bear children again—that she was too afraid to even consider it.

The likely scenarios spun through her mind. Her father would eventually have to be told, and the only possible course of action was that she be sent away and the baby be adopted out to a good family—perhaps missionaries. She would return, explaining that the extended absence was for reasons of health. No one would give the story any credence, and she would probably never marry. The best she could hope for was to become a nanny to another family's children.

She could not even envisage her father's reaction. He would never trust her again, and would never look at her with the same fondness. He was already disappointed at her failure to marry James, and he had not spoken to her in the few days since she had told him. Now he was to discover she was carrying the illegitimate child of a man he despised. A bastard child. The word rang in her ears, for that was what her child would be.

She spent the next week in misery, despairing over what would become of her. When she was no nearer a solution after seven days than she was at the beginning, there was only one thing left to do.

◈

It was in church that Joseph found her. She wore a dark dress and was huddled in one of the pews, her hands clasping her Bible, her eyes closed. He didn't disturb her at first, as he went quietly about his duties setting up for the minister's evening service. Eventually she opened her eyes and wiped the corners quickly with a sodden handkerchief. Her face was pallid, and there were dark shadows under her eyes.

He moved toward her in concern. "Elizabeth, what on earth is wrong?"

She avoided looking him in the eye and was about to say, "Nothing at all, thank you, Mr. Shaw, everything is quite in order." But she could not. Instead, she collapsed back on to the wooden pew, her tears falling uncontrollably.

Joseph rushed to sit beside her, and took her hand in his. "Elizabeth, what is it? Something dreadful has happened. Please, you must tell me what it is." He was also confused. Sam had gone, so should she not be happy?

She continued to sob. "I . . . simply cannot. I cannot, Mr. Shaw. I cannot tell you."

"Come now. It can't be that bad. You've shared your problems with me before. This one, too, can be fixed, I'm sure."

She was perplexed, then imagined he was referring to her childhood problem with Kesri. "Mr. Shaw, I cannot tell you. I . . . I cannot even imagine what you'd think of me."

"My dear, I could never think badly of you. And no matter what it is, I'm sure I can help. Why don't you come back to my house? A cup of tea will make you feel much better. Or perhaps you're in need of a sherry? You know I'm not a drinking man, but in some cases, for medicinal purposes. . . ." He stood up. "You were right to come here for guidance," he continued. "But right now, I think you may be in need of some mortal help."

She nodded, dabbed at her eyes once more, and agreed to his suggestion. He was quite possibly the only person who could help her. She had no one else to turn to. When they arrived at his house, he poured the sherry in his study, and she drank it down at once. It did seem to calm her, and although pale, she was composed, and prepared to accept whatever advice he gave her. But first, she had to confide in him.

"I'm afraid, Mr. Shaw, that I've become rather a different person of late than the girl you once knew," she began. She spoke slowly and deliberately, and he could tell it was painful for her to say the words. "I've disgraced myself in the most terrible way."

"Does this have something to do with . . . "

"Yes," she cut in before he could finish. "The cause of my trouble is a man. Or rather, the cause is my own stupidity brought about by my . . . my emotional reaction to this man."

"Are you ill, Elizabeth?"

"Not exactly, although I feel it. The truth is, I'm. . . ."

She broke down again, unable to say the words.

It dawned on him then, and he knew that she had lied in the letter. But he didn't wish to reproach her or become righteous. He wanted only to help, and his heart went out to her. "Elizabeth, I understand how difficult it is for you to talk about this. But you must answer my question. Are you with child?" he asked gently.

She looked up at him, her tears flowing again uncontrollably, and he wanted to reach out to her, to comfort her, to rescue her. She nodded, then buried her head in her hands, rocking back and forth like a frightened child.

Not knowing what else to do, he simply sat beside her on the chesterfield, and put his arms round her. She wept on his shoulder until she had no more tears to cry. He felt guilty, as if he had added to her grief. After all, it was he who had sent Sam upcountry, although it had been at her bidding. But even so—and against the Church's teachings, he knew—he still believed that marriage to Sam Taylor would not have been the best solution for her. The man was a rogue who would only hurt her and eventually desert her, he suspected.

When her sobbing eased and her tears ceased at last, he gently raised her chin to look at him, and smoothed back her hair.

"That's better. You mustn't cry any more. I will do all I can to help you, Elizabeth," he promised with rather more confidence than he felt. "But what I don't understand is the reason for the letter."

She thought he somehow knew about the letter she had received from Sam.

"He didn't know of my condition, then. Or I'm sure he would never have agreed to go. I'm sure he'd have married me, Mr. Shaw. But now he'll not return for six months or so, and it's . . . it's unthinkable that I could wait here for him in my condition. I don't know what to do."

"I'm afraid I must accept some of the blame for this," he sighed.

"How do you mean?"

"Well, as you know, it was I who suggested to Mr. Taylor that he join this expedition. If only I'd known of your condition sooner, I could have prevented him leaving."

She wondered why he thought she would know. Sam had not mentioned that in his letter, but she was too upset to dwell on details

"Please, don't rebuke yourself, Mr. Shaw. This is entirely my own doing. I have no one to blame but myself."

They were silent for a while and then Joseph spoke again. "I think you should say nothing of this for now, Elizabeth. Your father will have to know, eventually, of course, but if you allow me perhaps a short time to consider your situation, there may be something that can be done to make things easier."

She was sceptical that anything at all could save her. She was resigned to her fate, but thanked him just the same for his compassion.

When she was gone, Joseph could concentrate on nothing else. There *was* a solution, but it was such a frightening idea to put to her, that he began to worry if he could even utter such a proposal.

It was a most brilliant idea, and Edward wished he had thought of it himself. He did not, however, intend to let authenticity of authorship stand in his way. The German, Helmut Klein, had enjoyed his share of preferential treatment from high-society patrons, had staged several talked-about exhibitions, and was still ten years younger than Edward. Klein still had time enough to make a name for himself, whereas Edward did not. He had thought his hopes dashed when Elizabeth had announced she would not be marrying James. But now this golden opportunity had arisen, and he planned to take advantage before Klein could.

◈ Chapter 20 ◈

One shot and it was over. The great beast lay shuddering at Sam's feet, and then it was still. It had taken him by surprise, by the side of a river, just a half-day out of Chiengmai, and it had left him shaking, realising that it was the closest he had ever come to death.

They had left the boat to make camp where the bamboo jungle almost met the water, and he had walked into the forest along a rough path, noticing the axe marks in the dense undergrowth where other travellers had fought their way in, perhaps to pitch tents for the night or to look for wild fruit.

Fortunately, it was the cool season, and their small party—himself, two English adventurers, and twenty Siamese soldiers-cum-porters—had been spared the fevers of the monsoon, or the withering temperatures of the hot season. It was still too hot for Europeans, although it was cooler up in the hills, especially at night.

Snakes and marauding elephants were a constant menace, but the greatest fear was the silent and deadly tiger. An unwary traveller could be mauled or carried off before even having a chance to draw a gun. Sam had seen it happen on several occasions during his travels, and had once heard the story of a tiger dragging off *two* Siamese at the same time.

Still, he thought he was too wise for it to happen to him, and he was only fortunate that a frightened monkey, believing itself the tiger's prey, had screeched and scurried up a tree. By the time he swivelled, rifle aimed, the cat had begun its quick padding toward him. It was only twenty yards away, and it would have been only a second until it sprang—and he would surely have known no more.

His first shot, between the eyes, took the beast down. He fired off a second, which glanced off its head—but the cat had already fallen dead in its tracks. He was glad he had kept his marksmanship skills up to scratch, and glad too of the heavy gun he always carried on expeditions such as this. The 1876 Winchester lever-action .45/70 was the most modern weapon available for American big-game hunters, and weighed more than nine pounds. It had a range of up to 600 yards, and could bring down a charging buffalo. It had saved his life more than once.

"Good shot, man! A prize for the home hearth, eh?" Hearing the shots, one of his companions, Terence McConnell, had come running from the camp. He was followed by the other man, Sir Horatio Noone, a gentleman adventurer who was rather put out that the tiger wasn't his own kill. Both carried the Englishman's hunting gun of choice—the double-barrel .50 calibre elephant rifle, favoured because cartridges often misfired, and if this happened, the second barrel was bound to fire.

Although he carried a sportsman's rifle, Sam wasn't a sport hunter. Target practice, self-defence, and food when necessary, were reasons enough for him to carry such a weapon. And he really didn't like these two pompous Englishmen. "A prize?" he said. "I don't think so. I wouldn't want anyone to think I'd killed it for pleasure. Have it if you want."

"I say, that's jolly decent of you, old chap." Noone edged up to the animal, poking it with his foot. "Not a hunter, then, eh?"

"As I said, not for pleasure."

Noone decided his American companion was not only mysterious, but downright odd. It was quite unusual for a man to own up to being squeamish about hunting. Not that he thought Sam was any sort of coward. He had already proved otherwise.

When they had set up camp and got a good fire going, Sam filled a pot with water from the river and set it over the flames. When it was boiling, he poured it down the barrel of the Winchester. The new shotgun cartridges were a great advance, but upon firing, a large volume of smoke was released, which filled the barrel with soot. The fulminate of mercury primer in the back of the cartridge was very corrosive, and it was necessary to flush the barrel with a stream of hot water at regular intervals. Sam then took a collapsible rod with a looped end for an oil-soaked cleaning rag, and ran it up and down the inside of the barrel.

There was something immensely soothing about the cleaning process, and he sometimes preferred the ritual more than he liked having to fire the gun itself. He also ran a rag over his revolver— an 1878 double action Colt army model—which, at .45 calibre and weighing only two pounds and ten ounces, was better suited to dispatching humans than big game.

The most often-used item in his personal arsenal, however, was his bowie knife—adapted from the Scottish dirk—with its ten-inch blade and a double-edged point. It was the quickest and most effective way to deal with a serpent that ventured too close, or an intruder set on ambush because it did not alert any cohorts. Sam ran a finger along the edge of the razor-sharp blade. He would keep it beside him at night, within easy grasp of his right hand.

Later, when the others were already snoring in their bed-rolls and the Siamese watchmen were crouched in small groups, smoking, around the edges of the camp, Sam sat with his leather-bound writing pad in the light of the fires, deep in thought and writing a few lines from time to time. There could be no more hesitation. The letter had to be written. He certainly couldn't delay until he returned to Bangkok, because he believed she might not wait. He would have to risk the unreliable mail services and pay a villager well for safe delivery of the letter to Chiengmai, in the hope it would reach Bangkok before he did.

20th November, 1882

Dear Elizabeth,

Please forgive me for leaving you so suddenly and for not giving you any indication of my intentions toward you. The truth, though, is that I have only come to know my own mind since setting out on this journey.

Elizabeth, allow me to be quite frank with you, if I may. I guess I did not realize, until I departed, how much I had come to enjoy and depend on your company, for I am afraid now that I might lose you. I don't know if that is just the jungle talking, or if it has something to do with the fact that this day, I came very close to death. If not for a stroke of luck, I would have been carried off by a tiger in the forest and consumed for sure. Fortunately, I managed to shoot the beast before it could lay its paws on me, and I suppose this event has reminded me of my own mortality, and the fact that I am no longer a young man. I am more than thirty years of age, Elizabeth, and find that I now have a sudden yearning to be settled, to have a "home hearth", if you like, to quote another man's very words to me today. I would dearly love you to be part of my dream.

What I mean, Elizabeth, if you will excuse my boldness (for which you have so often chastised me), is that on my return to Bangkok, I will seek your permission to ask your father for your hand in marriage. Until then, my darling, look after yourself and think only of my return.

Your admirer,

Samuel Taylor II

She took the carriage and went as quickly as she could when Joseph's message summoned her ten days later. They had been the longest ten days of her life. So many times, she had been tempted simply to go to his house; to beg him to do something, anything. Other times she had even considered seeking out an abortionist. And she had certainly prayed that she would miscarry the baby.

Joseph seemed bright-eyed, yet nervous. He had thought long and hard about what he would do next, and had prayed for guidance. He was still doubtful whether it was the most sensible approach—or the most ridiculous notion he had ever entertained. He bade her sit beside him on the chesterfield, and she did so, staring at him beseechingly.

"Mr. Shaw, I cannot contain myself any more. I've been hoping for a miracle, wishing even that I might lose the child. I'd even dreamed that perhaps Mr. Taylor would find reason to cut short his expedition, and. . . ."

Joseph shook his head. "No. I'm afraid not, Elizabeth. And I must stress the fact that you'll have to forget about Samuel Taylor. He's somewhere in the jungles and won't be in communication for months. Your solution doesn't lie in him."

He spoke confidently—like the school teacher he was—yet he could feel the slight tremor in his hands, and knew that he was delaying what he really wanted to say.

She hung her head, and he did not want to prolong her torment any longer. He decided to ask, even if she thought it ludicrous.

"There is one solution," he offered, choosing his words carefully. "One that would save your reputation and your dignity, and would ensure that your child was born legitimate."

"I very much doubt that anything can save me now, but I *will* consider whatever you suggest Mr. Shaw."

"Please, Elizabeth, call me Joseph. We've known each other a long time."

"Yes, we have . . . Joseph. And I'm most grateful to you. What is it you suggest?"

He felt his mouth go dry and his heart beat faster. More than anything, he hoped she would not be shocked or offended. He hadn't even seriously considered the possibility of her agreement. He decided it best to be direct, and end the matter there and then.

"Elizabeth, would you . . . would you consider marriage to me?"

Stunned and speechless, she could only stare at him. After a few moments she looked to the floor, open-mouthed.

Already, he felt that it had been a terrible mistake. But an explanation was necessary, and he was compelled to continue. "I realise I'm so much older than you, Elizabeth. I'm now forty and you're. . . ."

"Twenty-one." She was still too surprised to say any more.

"Quite. But, my dear, although I'm not young, or adventurous, or handsome, I believe I'd make a good husband to you. The child we could bring up as our own, and I swear to you I'd never treat it as any less. If we were married quickly, there'd still be time to say the birth was premature. People would suspect, of course, but let them, I say. They'll eventually forget."

"But . . . Joseph, a marriage cannot be purely for convenience. There must be deep affection, some considerable feeling. . . ."

"Elizabeth, I do have a deep affection for you. And lately, I've found myself thinking of you more and more often. I admit, the idea of marriage had never occurred to me before, simply because I didn't think you'd even consider someone such as myself."

He stopped, believing he was only making the situation worse. "Perhaps I shouldn't have asked you. I've spoken out of turn. Please forgive me. This has been a dreadful error."

"Joseph, I too have a deep affection for you, although the idea of marriage to you had never remotely occurred to me either."

"Of course not," he said quietly.

She drew away and could not look at him. Tears began to sting her eyes. "I feel so ashamed. I'm a fallen woman. I've belonged to another man, and I wouldn't be fit to be your wife. Any man's wife."

"I know this has come as a shock to you Elizabeth, and I sense that you *will* decline me, but. . . ."

She tried to interject, to say something sympathetic, but he raised a hand to quieten her. "Please allow me to say that I, too, have something to confess. You see, you could equally say that I'm a fallen man."

She looked at him in surprise, not sure of his meaning.

"There's something about myself that I must tell you, Elizabeth before . . . before you finally reject my proposal," he continued, looking downcast.

Again, she tried to interrupt him, but again he hushed her.

"I've not spoken of this for twenty years, although I *have* thought of it every day. But if you were to be my wife, as I very much hope, then you should know everything about me. There should be no secrets between us."

"I'm listening," she said, intrigued.

"As you know, I grew up in New Zealand. My parents went there as missionaries and I was born there. I never felt called to serve the Church myself, but I was a firm believer, and always attended services. I wanted to be a writer, in fact, and I planned to go to England to study at university. But that wasn't to be. Anyway, I befriended a young Maori girl—a chief's daughter—whose family had converted a long time before, and whom I saw regularly at church. . . ."

"Joseph, if you'd rather not tell me this, please don't feel obliged to."

"No, my dear. Painful as it is, I want to tell you. I've spoken of it to no one else, and it's time I did. Her name was Aroha—it means 'love' in the Maori language—and I fell in love with her, although I knew that neither my father nor hers would approve of our marriage. Well . . . our affair was discovered—by my extremely pious father, in the worst imaginable circumstances—and to this day, he has never forgiven me. I receive a small income from him twice a year, but there is never any letter. My mother sends an annual Christmas note, but she's always formal in her correspondence, as if she's merely performing a duty."

"And what happened to Aroha?" she asked, touched by his story.

"Aroha was expecting our child when I was forced to leave New Zealand. Even then, my father wouldn't hear of us marrying, and I didn't have the courage to elope with her. Instead, they sent me here to become a missionary and to repent my sins.

"I wrote to Aroha every week for months, but never received a reply. Eventually, I received a brief letter from her sister, who'd been educated at the mission school, informing me that Aroha had died in childbirth, and that the baby—a girl—was stillborn.

She told me never to contact the family again; that they'd refuted the Church, and had withdrawn to their tribal *marae*."

Elizabeth saw his eyes glisten with tears as he finished the story. "I'm very sorry for you, Joseph," she whispered. "You've suffered terribly."

"But not as she did. And I felt forever after that I was responsible for her death. That's why I've never been ordained. I've never felt worthy."

"And you never wanted to be a missionary before then?"

"Well, no, at the time I didn't. I was certain I'd hate the life. But as I accepted the fact that Aroha and I would never be together, I grew to love my work. I found it gave me fulfilment. It's become much more than a penance, and for that much, I'm grateful."

He was waiting now for her answer. She took a deep breath and walked to the window, looking out at the garden. It was true, he was much older than she, but many women married men twenty years their senior. And she knew Joseph to be a good, gentle person who would keep his word and treat her child as his own. And what was her alternative? To bear a bastard child and have it adopted out, never thereafter having the opportunity to marry decently. Despite what she had said to Joseph, she believed that Sam did not really want her. Otherwise he would never have left so readily. But despite this, she still wasn't certain that marriage to Joseph was the solution to her predicament.

He began to apologise again for even contemplating the idea of proposing to her, but this time it was she who silenced him.

"Joseph, I'm grateful—more than I can tell you—for your offer, and it's far more than I deserve. But I must say that it has taken me by surprise, of course, and I feel that I need some time to think this over. Please allow me to go now, and I promise to let you have an answer very soon."

For a moment he sat without reply.

"Of course, I understand. Please take as long as you need, and I'll accept your answer graciously—whatever you decide. I only hope that I've not caused you any offence."

He fell silent again as she thanked him and left the room, still dabbing at her eyes with her handkerchief.

Next morning, Sam gave the sealed letter to one of the Siamese porters, who came from a nearby village and had always shown himself—as far as Sam could tell—to be reliable and trustworthy. He watched as the man disappeared into the jungle, supposing that he would hire a raft further downriver.

The messenger, however, ran down the track, and when he was out of view, tossed the letter away into the jungle undergrowth, pocketed the coins that *Khun* Gun—as the men had nicknamed Sam—had given him, and made haste back to his village, well pleased with himself. He hadn't seen his wives for two years, and he was tired of the nomadic life, working for these white men for next to nothing. The money Sam had given him would buy them some stock and perhaps even allow him to go into business as a trader. He wouldn't waste it on hiring a raft. It was only a letter, after all. The man could write another.

It could have been a disaster, with embarrassing repercussions. Instead, it had turned out rather well. He had taken a great liberty, and it was only after he sent the letter that he fully realised what he had done. He hoped that Helmut Klein had been too drunk to remember the night they had talked at the bar of the United Club—and had unwittingly divulged his idea.

Klein had already been well on the way to oblivion that evening, and Edward had bought him several generous shots of *schnapps* to help him along. And now, it seemed, the king's imagination had been inspired by Edward's offer of photography lessons, and he had invited him to the new royal residence at the Grand Palace—the Chakri Maha Prasad—to begin the tuition.

221

The palace had been completed only that year, to coincide with Bangkok's centenary, and Edward had not yet been admitted to the king's private chambers, although he had photographed members of the royal family at various functions during the year, and had attended several parties in the vast reception rooms.

It was a hugely imposing building, and—because of King Chulalongkorn's admiration of European culture—had been built mostly in Italian Renaissance style, although it was designed by a British architect. The roof, however—unlike any building to be seen in Europe—was traditional Siamese, with orange, green, and yellow-tiled tiers that supported three golden spires.

The most splendid room was the central throne hall, featuring magnificent crystal chandeliers, marble and gold fittings, and a beautiful, nine-tiered, white and gold pagoda-like canopy above the throne.

Edward, however, now found the pomp and ceremony of receptions held for foreign envoys and the expatriate community rather tedious. What he wanted was to see how the king really lived; to become known as His Majesty's personal photographer. And it was to this end that he had written with the offer of the lessons.

He had originally planned to use the fact that his daughter was engaged to Viscount James Claridge as a lever to attract His Majesty's attention—perhaps in the hope that he would be the guest of honour at a reception to celebrate the upcoming nuptials. After all, Claridge was distantly related to Queen Victoria, and his father had been a frequent guest in royal circles.

It had been a shock when Elizabeth had told him of James's letter. But at least it had not been she who had broken off the engagement, as he had feared, but James himself. And Edward supposed he could not blame him; a man in his position needed a wife, and Elizabeth was half a world away.

He was still reeling from the impact of the words.

"Are you serious, Joseph? Does Elizabeth know?"

"Yes, of course." Joseph smiled. "She's happy to accept my proposal, providing you give your permission, of course."

Edward was astonished. "But . . . when did all this happen? I wasn't aware of any . . . romantic courtship between you two."

"Well, I think Elizabeth and I have always been . . . quite close, shall we say . . . and since she returned, we realised—quite suddenly, in fact—what our true feelings for each other were. Yesterday, I asked her to marry me, and she agreed this morning. Which is why I've come to see you now. . . ."

"Good Lord! I'm sorry Joseph, I don't mean to appear rude. It's just that this is something of a shock. How extraordinary. Well, I mean . . . I have no objections, I suppose—if that's what she wants. I mean, what you both want."

Elizabeth, who had been listening at the parlour door, now entered the room. "It is, Father. We want to be married just as soon as possible, don't we, Joseph?"

"Well, we're both agreed on a small service and reception, so, yes, as soon as possible."

Edward, who by now sat dumbfounded in an armchair, could barely respond.

Finally, he did. "In that case, as the two of you seem intent, I think I must give you my blessing." Then, almost absent-mindedly, he suggested that the new year might be a good time for the wedding.

Elizabeth glanced quickly at Joseph.

"Well, we were hoping rather sooner than that," he said. "In fact, as soon as the banns can be read."

"Neither of us wants a big wedding," Elizabeth added. "Just a small reception here at home."

Edward was now almost completely detached from reality. "Of course, dear. I'm not a believer in long engagements myself. The banns shall be read on three successive Sundays, as usual, and I suppose you can be married the next week after that."

"Thank you, Father." Elizabeth kissed him on the cheek.

At last Edward managed to collect his thoughts. "My dear, will you excuse us?" he asked Elizabeth. "There are some matters I must speak to Joseph about."

She smiled with relief. "Of course. I'll see you this evening, Joseph."

When she had left, Edward asked Joseph to sit down.

"I'm sorry, Joseph, but I must ask you this. Is Elizabeth. . . ."

"I give you my word," Joseph assured him, "that nothing improper has occurred between myself and Elizabeth."

Edward leaned back in the chair, relieved. "Of course not. I don't know how I could even think that of you. Please forget I asked."

From the first lesson, King Chulalongkorn was entranced with the gentle art of photography, and his intelligence and creative spirit had seen him master the basics much sooner, Edward had to admit, than he had done so himself. After only a few weeks, the king was already making his own prints in a darkroom he had set up in the new palace.

During the course of the lessons, he allowed Edward to photograph him in his private rooms—both alone and with family members—eating dinner, entertaining his children, and smoking a cigar. Edward was ecstatic. It was the highlight of his career, and he was hoping the king would give him permission to use the photographs in a special exhibition he was planning.

More than anything though, Edward hoped he himself would be well enough to complete a suitable body of work and organise the event.

◈ *Chapter 21* ◈

It was true, there was no passion—she never felt her pulse quicken when she saw him—but she liked and admired him enormously, and she was sure she could be happy with him. Besides, there had been no other way.

She could hardly believe they were married. It had all happened so quickly; the nuptials that morning and the luncheon reception afterwards in the garden of her father's house. By mid-afternoon they had arrived at Joseph's own home, which was now hers, too, she found it strange to remind herself. They passed a pleasant afternoon in the garden, talking and sharing their views on everything from food to Mr. Darwin's book, *On the Origin of Species by Natural Selection*, which had created a crisis of faith since its publication in 1859, with many people questioning the importance—even the very existence—of God.

Later, Joseph appeared to doze in the shade, but she wondered if he really were asleep; wondered if he, too, were bemused by the whole event, and needed time to reflect upon it.

As she reviewed the formalities of the day, it seemed so foreign to her, as if it had happened to someone else. Anchalee's words still echoed through her mind. "Congratulations, Mrs. Shaw," she had said—and for a moment, Elizabeth had not realised her sister was speaking to her. She imagined her wedding day as if she were reading a newspaper item about some other woman's marriage:

The wedding of Elizabeth Ann Fairburn, daughter of Mr. Edward Fairburn, of New Road, Bangkok, and Mr. Joseph Peter Shaw, missionary teacher, was celebrated this day at the Protestant Chapel, Yannawa, followed by a reception for forty friends and family at the father of the bride's residence. The maid of honour was the bride's half-

sister, Miss Anchalee Fairburn; and the best man, the groom's friend,
Mr. John A. Eakin, a teacher at King's College.

The bride wore a white satin gown, ruched to show a pleated satin
underskirt, held out by a crinoline, giving the ensemble a traditional
look. She wore a long veil and orchids in her hair, but no jewellery,
except for the plain gold band given her by her husband during the
ceremony. The maid of honour wore a green satin frock in similar style
to the bride's, but without the crinoline. The gowns were made by
Bangkok seamstress Mrs. G. E. Smythe, in what was said to be a
supreme effort in the short lead-up to the wedding.

Official photographs after the 10.30 a.m. ceremony were taken by
Mr. Fairburn himself at his home studio, after which an elegant lunch
was served under a marquee in the garden. The reception was blessed
with what was, for Bangkok, an exceptionally mild day, even for the
cool season, the temperature climbing no higher than 78 degrees. Soon
after the bride and groom cut the three-tiered wedding cake at 2.30
p.m., they departed by carriage for the groom's home.

Elizabeth was brought from her reverie by the arrival of Simon,
who announced that a light supper was served in the dining room.
They went inside and sat opposite each other, making polite
conversation. But neither was concentrating on the conversation,
nor on the lightly fried fillets of fish and steamed rice—and they
both knew it.

When they were finished, Elizabeth said she would retire for
the evening, and she hoped he could not see her blush as she left
the table. He said he would follow shortly after. She put on a long
white cotton night-dress with a full, gathered and tucked skirt
that concealed her now slightly protruding stomach. Her
pregnancy was the reason, also, that she had chosen the old-
fashioned crinoline style for her wedding dress. But she hadn't
realised how ungainly a style it was, and she had been very glad
to come upstairs and change into her usual attire when they had
first arrived at his house.

She brushed out her hair, and noticed how long it had grown in
the eight months since she had arrived in Bangkok. It was almost

unbelievable to her. It seemed like a lifetime. And now here she was, pregnant, and married to a man who wasn't the father of her child, and whom she otherwise would never have thought of—even remotely—as the man who would become her husband.

She thought of Sam and his return to Bangkok. What would he believe about the marriage and the baby? She prayed for the child's sake, as well as for her own and Joseph's, that it would be blessed with her fair colouring. She wondered how she could cope with the memories if the face of the child she had to look at every day was the image of that other face.

Would he have married her if he had known? She wanted to believe he would have, but reason told her that someone such as he would not want to be saddled with a wife and child. Why had she been so gullible? Why had she not resisted more? Because she had been in love with him. Blindly in love. It was the sort of passion that came only once in a lifetime.

The door opened and Joseph entered. Sitting at the dressing table, she continued to brush her hair, hoping the long, rhythmic strokes would calm her nerves.

"My dear," he began awkwardly. "I understand that in your condition, you might not want. . . . Well, that you might prefer to sleep alone. If you wish, I'm happy to sleep in the guest room until after the baby is born."

When she realised what he was referring to, his frankness startled her. "No, Joseph," she said firmly. "You're my husband. Of course I want you here with me. You've saved my life, my reputation. I'm so grateful. . . ."

He sat on the edge of the bed. "I hope our marriage can be based on much more than gratitude. You don't owe me anything, Elizabeth. I cannot erase from my mind the fact that it was I who made this step necessary for you. Even though it was at your bequest, if I'd known of your condition when I received your letter, I should never have sent *him* away."

She frowned, and set down her brush, turning to face him. "My letter? I don't understand. . . ."

"I know you asked me never to mention it again, and I know how painful it must be to you. But we are man and wife now, and we must always speak with perfect clarity."

"But what letter, Joseph?"

"The letter Anchalee brought from you . . . explaining how you . . . you wanted to extricate yourself from his influence. . . ."

His words were a mystery. What could he be referring to? She knew of no such letter delivered by Anchalee.

"Do you still have it?" she asked, with a sense of foreboding.

"Why, yes. It's locked in my desk."

"Joseph, could I see it—again?" And noting his concern, she added, "I was so confused at the time, you understand. I can hardly remember what it was I wrote."

"Of course. One moment."

He returned quickly, and handed her a white envelope.

She opened the pages, and lay them on the dressing table before her, seeing immediately that the handwriting was not her own. She turned away from her husband as she read the lines with increasing disbelief.

In her name, it was written that she no longer believed Sam to be "*a suitable candidate for marriage*", that she wanted Joseph to help her "*extricate*" herself "*from this unfortunate arrangement*". Then the most telling words of all: "*You may speak freely of this matter to my sister, as she is aware of everything that has occurred, and my intention to end this mistaken liaison*".

She saw what had happened. Her own sister, Anchalee, had sought to ruin her; to send away the father of her unborn child. Anchalee must have guessed when she saw her sickness that morning; a morning that now seemed so long ago.

But why? What had she done to make her sister hate her so? Or, on the other hand, had Anchalee in fact not realised Elizabeth was pregnant, and merely acted in what she imagined, misguidedly, were her sister's best interests?

The letter changed everything. For, as Elizabeth now realised, Sam had not meant to leave her—and if he had not, she would have told him of the pregnancy, and he would now have been her husband.

She felt Joseph's hand on her shoulder.

"Is everything in order?"

How could she tell him? How could she reveal that this had all been a terrible mistake; that she had wanted to marry Sam with all her heart, before and after she fell pregnant? She could not allow Joseph to discover it after he had been so unselfish. It would be too cruel. But it was done, and could not be reversed. She resolved that he must never know the letter was a forgery. The other problem, of discovering why her sister had done this, could wait—but she vowed to find out the truth.

She tried to smile, tried to mask her shock and torment as she turned to look up at her husband. "I'm sorry, Joseph. You must think me so strange. I expect it's my condition—it does tend to bring on such vagueness of thought sometimes, that I hardly know where I am."

"Yes, of course." He sounded uncertain. "But you must now forget the past, Elizabeth. Close it like an unread book, and put it far away from you. We are one now, and I shall always stand by you. You know that."

Neither said another word, as she stood slowly to meet him. Then he kissed her tenderly and wrapped his arms around her. She buried her head in his neck, feeling as she always did with him, warm and safe.

"You're so beautiful, Elizabeth," he said. "I've never seen you with your hair down before—except when you were a girl, of course. That seems like a different lifetime now, doesn't it?"

He led her to the four-poster bed with its draped mosquito nets and down-filled, patchwork quilt, and they sat beside each other. He turned to face her, and she smiled to reassure him. Then he pulled back the quilt and extinguished the lamp next to the bed.

❖ *Chapter 22* ❖

King Chulalongkorn enjoyed his new pastime so much that his family and subjects were becoming accustomed to seeing him with a camera everywhere he went. And he had many willing subjects in his children, who would sometimes cheekily leap out from behind silk curtains into their father's path and demand to be photographed. It would become a life-long passion.

Edward Fairburn, however, worried him. He was a patient and courteous teacher, but then everyone was patient and courteous in the king's presence—and that in itself meant nothing. Chulalongkorn simply did not trust the man. There was something about him that led him to think that beneath his gentlemanly exterior lay a scoundrel. Discreet enquiries were made, and His Majesty paid particular attention to a story that was reported back to him regarding a certain well-known competitor of Mr. Fairburn named Helmut Klein.

The screams of agony filled the house—some high-pitched and piercing, others descending to a low moan—and the doctor could be heard urging her behind the closed door. Joseph paced the hallway outside, listening to her pain, thinking that the torture would never end.

It was three in the morning, and she had been in labour since eleven o'clock the previous morning. The doctor had emerged at one point, about five hours earlier, to tell him that it would be a long night, and that perhaps it would be best if he went for a walk. But he could not leave her. He had no idea that giving birth was like this, and as the hours dragged on, he thought of another woman, long ago, bleeding to death without him. It seemed to him so unjust that woman should have to bear the seed of man in this way.

He stopped in his tracks when the screams ceased. The silence was somehow more frightening than the noise, and he grew cold wondering if she had survived—or if she, too, had succumbed to the agony. She had filled his life so completely in the six months since they had married, that he could not imagine life without her. The silence was finally broken by the child's cry, and then the bedroom door swung upon.

Dr. Newhaven stood before him, smiling, holding a bundle wrapped in a blanket. "Your son, Mr. Shaw."

Gingerly, Joseph took the baby from the doctor and looked down at the tiny red face, the eyes shut tight, and the tuft of black hair on the crown of his head. He felt an instant love and a complete bond with this child, this son who was not his own. Then he looked back at the doctor, suddenly concerned. "My wife. . . ."

Dr. Newhaven smiled reassuringly. "She'll be fine, Mr. Shaw, just fine. She's weak, and she's lost some blood, but all she needs is rest. She's still awake. Why don't you take the baby to her?"

He was alarmed to see her looking so deathly pale, so exhausted. But she smiled when he entered the darkened room and sat beside her on the bed, taking her hand in his. She soon became drowsy, but before she fell asleep she managed to whisper, "He's your son, Joseph."

"I'll never think of him as anything else. I love him already."

"And his name will be Joseph. Joseph Edward Shaw."

It was over. Six months of work had come to nothing. The king refused to grant him permission to use any of the photographs he had taken in the private quarters of the palace.

Although the arrangement had seemed to be working rather well, His Majesty suddenly cancelled their lessons after only three months. Edward presumed that more important matters of state were demanding the king's attention, and that they would resume when His Majesty was able to spend more time at his hobby.

But no more royal summons were forthcoming in the next three months, and when he wrote a polite letter to His Majesty, enquiring after his family and suggesting they meet to share photographic knowledge, he received no reply. For some reason—he knew not what—he had been excluded.

An official note arrived one day with a palace underling, informing him that His Majesty wished it known that any photographs taken in his private quarters were to remain unpublished, and that permission to exhibit them had been rescinded due to reasons of palace security.

Shortly afterward, he heard that Mr. Klein had been appointed the official royal photographer, and had taken over the king's informal photographic lessons.

There was a sharp knock on the front door, and Anchalee ran to answer it before the maid could get there. She was bored, and a visitor—any visitor—would be a relief, even if it were Elizabeth and her pampered son. According to her sister, the three-month-old was already saying "mama", but Anchalee could only decipher ordinary baby sounds.

When she opened the door, she almost took a step back in astonishment. Then she was pleasantly surprised. The day might not be such a tedious one after all, she thought, as she greeted him with a broad smile. "Hello, Mr. Taylor. We thought you'd been lost forever in the jungle."

But Sam wasted no time on pleasantries. "Is your father home, Anchalee?"

"No, he's not, I'm sorry."

232

"Good. Then tell Elizabeth I want to see her, will you?"

"You'd better come in." She smiled sweetly, opening the door further and stepping aside to allow him into the hallway. This would be even more fun than she had imagined.

He removed his cap and strode into the parlour in front of her, as if it were his own home.

"You look like you've just got off the boat."

"You're not far wrong," he replied, turning back to her. "Got back this morning. How is your sister, by the way?"

"She's wonderful. In fact, she says she's never been happier." There was an unmistakable tone of mischief in her voice, as she showed him into the front room.

"Oh, does she now? Well, I'll have to judge that for myself. Call her down, won't you—or should I go upstairs and get her myself?"

"I don't think that would be of much use. She isn't here."

"Damn, I was hoping to see her right away. What time is she due home?"

"Oh, I should think she's home right now." She was thoroughly enjoying the game. It was the moment she had been waiting for.

"But you said she was out."

"No, I said she wasn't here."

He was only vaguely amused. "If you're trying to entertain me, Anchalee, it's not working. This is the Fairburn residence, is it not?"

"It is," she answered—and then added to his cue, "but Elizabeth is no longer a Fairburn, and no longer resides here."

"What do you mean?" he snapped, startled and frustrated with her frivolity.

"I mean that she didn't see any reason to wait for you." Anchalee whirled round and sank quickly into the sofa. "She married Joseph Shaw shortly after you left."

Her comment had the desired effect. It was the first time she had ever seen Sam caught completely off guard.

"She married Joseph Shaw! The missionary? The teacher?"

"The very same. And they have a baby now. A little boy." She paused for a few seconds. "Born prematurely."

He sat down in one of the armchairs and wondered if she were joking at his expense. It wouldn't have surprised him.

"This is unbelievable. Are you having me on?"

"Ask anyone, if you don't believe me. We could hardly believe it ourselves when she told us the news. But they consider themselves very fortunate. The baby was born so early, but he wasn't at all below weight."

He looked at her suspiciously. "All right, young missy, you've had your game. Now tell me where she is."

She went to the sideboard and picked up two framed photographs, and handed the first to him. "See for yourself. Here's her wedding picture."

He looked at it briefly, but his attention was immediately drawn to the second picture she handed to him—of Elizabeth with the baby in his christening gown.

"Is that . . . their son?"

"Yes, that's Joe."

"When was he born?"

"Three months ago, on June 30th. Only seven months after they were married. Everyone believes it's a miracle he didn't die."

She revelled in Sam's torment, not hesitating to deliver the final blow. "It's very strange though. Elizabeth has green eyes and Joseph has light blue eyes—but Joe has dark brown eyes."

"And what do you think?"

"About what?"

"Do you believe the baby was premature?"

"Of course. Why wouldn't I?"

Sam shrugged. "Well, that's that then."

"What's what?"

"Anchalee, are you always so trying on a man's patience?"

"Ah, you've finally noticed something about me. And yes, I usually am."

He picked up his cap. "Give my regards to Mrs. Shaw when you next see her."

"Oh, I shall. You can be sure of that."

"I'll see myself out."

She smiled to herself after he had left, thinking that he really was quite an attractive man.

He returned the next day, before she even had the opportunity to pass on his regards to Elizabeth. It was another duty she was much looking forward to. They went into the front room again, and she poured him a whisky from her father's cabinet. She suspected that he had been watching the house, because as soon as Edward left for a photographic assignment that morning, he arrived at the door.

"I want you to do me a favour, Anchalee."

She handed him the glass and took a seat on the sofa opposite him. "A favour, Mr. Taylor?"

"Sam to my friends, Anchalee."

"Am I a friend . . . Sam?"

"Of course. And you might be an even more valuable one if you can help me out." He took a sip of the whisky and leaned back in the armchair, eyeing her closely.

"I assume this has something to do with Elizabeth," she sighed, sounding bored.

"Yes it does. I want you to arrange for us to meet accidentally."

She looked at him, and he was sure he detected the trace of a sly smirk.

"She's a married woman now, so I'm sure she won't agree to meet you," she replied, immediately beginning to consider the best way she could arrange such a meeting.

"I know she's married, but I still have to see her. I feel I owe her an explanation for why I was away so long. Will you do it?"

She affected a show of dwelling upon his request—as if it were a terrible dilemma—and after a few moments' consideration of nothing whatsoever, she agreed. "Very well."

"Good. Now, where can we meet?"

"Well, why not here? Then she won't be suspicious. She comes to see me every Friday for the entire afternoon."

"And is your father at home during these visits?"

"Not until at least three o'clock. He has lunch with his cronies on Fridays."

"Perfect. I can arrive looking for your father on the pretence of a photographic job for my book. And be sure to ask her to bring the baby with her."

"She always brings him anyway. Why?"

"Anchalee," he sighed in a mocking tone, "you ask far too many questions for a child."

"I'm no child," she protested. "I'll be fifteen in just over three months."

He laughed at her petulance. "Well, young lady, I'm thirty-three this month, and from where I stand, nearly fifteen is merely a child."

She pouted, annoyed that he had managed to unsettle her. He would know otherwise in due course, she thought—and she was prepared to wait.

Elizabeth's quiet investigations had revealed nothing. For nine months, since she had discovered the existence of the forged letter, she had tried to work out why Anchalee had been so devious. She could not, of course, say anything that would let her sister know that she knew; and her guarded questions were met only with vague answers.

Once, when she asked Anchalee what she knew about their respective mothers, her sister had looked at her sharply, but only for a moment. Then she smiled, shrugged, and said she thought the past should remain exactly where it was.

On the surface, Elizabeth appeared the perfect wife and mother. She and Joseph had a loving relationship, and she made sure the household was efficiently run. She refused to have a nanny for the baby, preferring to spend all her time with him. Often she was unable to prevent herself gazing at his face—aware that every time she did so, she saw his father's reflection.

Joseph was as good a husband as any man could be, and—thankfully—was never demanding. Night after night, while he slept soundly, she lay beside him wide awake, hot with anger, and cold with disbelief at what had befallen her. Meanwhile, she visited her sister once a week, and continued her secret quest.

On Friday, Elizabeth arrived as usual with Joe, and he smiled and gurgled as soon as he saw his aunt. He seemed to have a special liking for Anchalee, but she could not understand why. She never gave him any encouragement.

Elizabeth pushed the beautiful English perambulator into the front room and adjusted Joe's white *broderie anglais* quilt that had once belonged to her mother—and which had, in fact, covered herself when she was a baby.

"We just missed the rain, by the looks of the sky," Elizabeth said. It was the monsoon again, and it rained heavily almost every day.

She managed to get Joe to sleep, and they sat in the front room, with a pre-lunch sherry, when there was a knock at the door.

"Are you expecting another guest for lunch?"

"No. But Father did say someone might call about a time for a photographic session." Anchalee went out to open the door, and Elizabeth heard her talking in the hallway.

"Oh, do come in. Elizabeth will want to say hello."

Elizabeth stood and turned to greet the visitor, and then nearly collapsed back into her chair when she saw him. She felt as if her legs would buckle under her.

He stood in the doorway and then walked toward her. "Hello, Elizabeth. It's been a long time."

"Sam . . . Mr. Taylor. I didn't expect to see you . . ."

"No doubt," he cut her off curtly. "I've only just returned from Chiengmai."

"Well, I'll go and see how lunch is progressing," Anchalee said breezily, smiling as she walked out.

Elizabeth sat down again and quickly reminded herself that she had nothing to feel ashamed of or nervous about in front of him. After all, it was he who had abandoned her. There was silence for only a moment before she spoke coolly. "You left without much warning."

He sat down and her words seemed to disarm him slightly, although there was little hint of contrition in his voice.

"I sent you a letter."

"A letter!" She sank back into the sofa. "It was less than I expected of you."

"At the time I had no choice," he argued. "You know that it was impossible to visit you here."

"If it's possible now, why was it impossible then?" she retorted.

"That's unfair," he protested. "Besides, nothing was resolved, and I said I'd see you when I returned. And I told you in the next letter what my intentions were. You didn't think me worth waiting for?"

"What do you mean, your next letter?"

"The one I sent during the expedition—it should have come here via Chiengmai. You did receive it?"

She shrugged, puzzled. "I don't know what letter you're referring to. All I know is that you left, informing me with a rather vague letter, and leaving me to. . . . Well, anyway, it doesn't matter now."

But he was distracted, and barely seemed to be listening to her. "*Damn the man!*" he almost shouted, seemingly to himself. "Damn him to hell. Jesus, can't anyone be trusted? I should've known better."

He then realised where he was, and seeing her alarmed expression, moved to the sofa and sat beside her. For a fleeting moment she thought he was going to take her hands in his, but he did not.

"I'm sorry, Elizabeth. Excuse my outburst."

For a few seconds he simply looked at her, and she felt the magnetism once more. She was desperate to tell him the truth; desperate to tell him they had been tricked into a life apart. Yet she knew she could not. From now on, their relationship would, of necessity, be one of formality and distance; a veneer to disguise their real feelings and the tragedy of being forced to live their lives without each other.

He had spoken of his "intentions". She had no doubt that if he had known she was pregnant, he would have married her. But if she had known he meant to marry her on his return, would she—could she—have waited for him, despite the baby? Could she have thumbed her nose at conservative society, borne a bastard child, and be called a harlot, if it meant one day getting him back?

But no. She realised only too well that she would never have done that. She lacked the courage—and she was ashamed to admit to herself that social appearances had taken precedence over her love for him.

She knew she must be rid of him. "Please, Sam. I think it's best that you leave. I made a terrible mistake and I have a new life now. I'm happy with Joseph—no doubt you already know of our marriage."

"Yes. But why, Elizabeth?"

She glared at him as sharply as she could. "Because . . . because I love him."

"I don't believe you."

"Well, it's the truth. And it's really of no consequence to me whether you believe it or you don't."

He suddenly noticed the pram in the corner of the room, and she watched as he stood and went over to it.

She tried to deter him. "He's asleep. Please don't disturb him."

He looked down at the sleeping baby, and all he could see were closed eyes and black, wispy hair. "Very dark, isn't he?"

She sensed the bitterness in his voice, and was so certain he would see the truth. She could feel her hands shaking. She held them together tightly in her lap.

"It's only baby hair," she said nervously. "It will lighten in a few months when his real hair grows in."

"Really." He walked slowly toward the sofa and stood before her. "Can you swear to me, without any doubt, that this is Joseph's son?"

She looked up at him and then hesitated for only a fraction of a second before replying confidently, "Yes, Sam. He's Joseph's son."

He stared intently into her eyes, and she looked back unflinchingly—so afraid that he would see through her.

At last he spoke. "Then we have nothing left to discuss."

She shook her head slowly, still looking into the brown eyes she had once fallen in love with. She knew she was still in love with him—that a part of her would always love him—but now it was hopeless, and she prayed that she would take this secret with her to the grave.

Without another word, he turned and walked away, and she heard the front door open and close, and then his steps down the path becoming fainter and fainter. She sat transfixed, as if she had been turned to stone, until Anchalee appeared again.

"Has Sam gone already?" her sister asked, in a clear expression of disappointment.

"Did you know he was coming?" There was irritation and suspicion in Elizabeth's own enquiry.

"Of course not." Anchalee noticed Elizabeth's displeasure, and then paused to affect a sudden realisation. "I'm sorry. I shouldn't have asked him in. I thought you wouldn't mind, now that you're married, of course."

"Mind? Of course I don't mind. It doesn't matter." Elizabeth looked away, as if to dismiss it as a triviality. And she hoped she had given no indication of the depth of her discomfort.

Elizabeth was quiet during dinner that night. She looked pale as she simply pushed the food round her plate.

"Not hungry?" Joseph asked.

"Just tired, that's all." She put down her knife and fork. "Joseph—truthfully . . . are you . . . are you happy with me?"

His eyes widened in surprise. "Elizabeth, what an extraordinary question. Of course I am. You know that. I couldn't be happier."

She seemed to relax a little, and then she took a deep breath.

"Joseph, I think there's something that might make you even happier than you are now."

He looked slightly perplexed.

"A child, Joseph, of our own. Yours and mine."

"But we already have. . . ."

"Joseph, I'm going to have a baby."

"You mean. . . ."

She was smiling now, and crying at the same time. "Yes, I'm expecting. Isn't it wonderful?"

It wasn't the only time she saw Sam that week. A few days later, he was at her own house, and she was alarmed when Simon ushered him in. She didn't need to utter the question, as the expression on her face told Sam all he needed to know.

"Don't panic," he said immediately in the lazy, almost insolent manner she knew so well. "I'm here to see *your husband*. About the mission to Chiengmai. I have my report to give him."

"Oh, of course." She had almost forgotten that his part in the expedition had been at Joseph's instigation. "I'll call him down."

"There's no need." He raised a hand. "The boy's going."

"Well then, please sit down."

"Where's the baby?"

"Joe," she answered with emphasis on his name, "is asleep in the nursery."

At that moment, Joseph entered the room. He and Sam exchanged an uneasy greeting which was little more than a mere acknowledgement of each other's presence, and Elizabeth could feel the underlying tension. She excused herself hurriedly and wondered how her husband felt.

Joseph led Sam to his study and sat behind his desk. Sam sat in the leather chair opposite as Joseph eyed him closely and wondered what he had been saying to Elizabeth. He was also a little piqued that Sam had simply arrived at the house unannounced.

"I gather the mission was a success, Mr. Taylor."

Sam wondered how much Joseph knew of his affair with Elizabeth. And had Joseph purposely sent him upcountry in order to leave the way open for him to marry her himself?

"A complete success, Mr. Shaw. Your people up there are well settled now."

"I'm most grateful. The entire mission is grateful. Your fee will be forwarded to you in due course. Did any other matters arise from your journey?"

"The mission families gave me a bag of mail to send on for them. I've already taken it to the consulate." From an inside pocket he extracted an envelope addressed to Joseph, and passed it to him. "The rest you'll find in my report."

"Thank you. A written report will be most helpful."

Sam stood to go, and said curtly, "I must offer you my congratulations on your marriage. And on the birth of your son."

"Oh, well, thank you again. Both events are indeed a great joy to me." Joseph then quickly changed the subject. "Would you be available for further excursions to the North in future?"

"Only if you don't want me back in Bangkok in a hurry."

"Oh?"

"I'm returning to the North very soon—for some time I expect. Joining up with a government expedition to charter the Siamese boundaries. Might even look into the teak trade while I'm up there and join the Borneo Company."

It was a venture he would not pursue, but he said it to gauge Joseph's reaction. The man's obvious relief at the prospect of being rid of him told Sam all he wanted to know.

"I see." Joseph smiled slightly for the first time. "Well, in that case, I wish you *bon voyage*, Mr. Taylor."

Sam nodded, saying he would see himself out—leaving Joseph hoping that this new expedition would, indeed, be a lengthy, if not permanent one.

She felt unusually tired as she sat resting in the window seat in the front room, and he asked if she would like him to stay with her. But she told him no; that he should go on to his mission meeting. She was also suffering from cramping pains in her back. She had been lucky not to have any morning sickness with this pregnancy, and so could not understand why she felt so awful now. She was past the first three months, and should be feeling fine.

Nevertheless, her cheerful air reassured him, and he kissed her goodbye, promising he would be back in time for an early dinner. She sat for a while before going upstairs, as the gripping pains in her stomach intensified.

When he did arrive home at four o'clock, the house seemed unnaturally quiet. Then he remembered that Simon had the afternoon off, and the only other servant—the cook-cum-housekeeper—would be out the back working in the kitchen.

Elizabeth was not in the front room, and he thought she had decided to take a nap before dinner. He was right. When he climbed the stairs and entered their bedroom, he saw her lying on the bed, peacefully asleep. He was surprised to see she had been so tired she had not changed out of her dress. He sat beside her and pushed back the strands of hair that had fallen across her face, noticing that her forehead was damp and there was a sheen of moisture on her skin. Her breathing was shallow and fast, and she was perfectly still.

"Elizabeth?" he whispered, beginning to feel alarmed. "Elizabeth, wake up. What's wrong?"

Thinking that perhaps it was simply his imagination—that she was only perspiring because she was fully-clothed—he decided to loosen her skirt and blouse. He turned her gently on to her side to undo them. As he did, he gasped in shock and sprang back from the bed. The back of her dress and the quilt were saturated with blood. She was unconscious, not asleep, and he knew the child was lost.

❖ Chapter 23 ❖

Chiengmai, Rose of the North

Chiengmai is the principal city of Upper Siam—or Lanna as the old kingdom was known—and is enclosed by ancient battlements dating from the thirteenth century. The town itself has broad streets, hundreds of glittering temples, and a population of around five thousand. The people from this part of Siam consider themselves Lao.

The city is set beside the Mae Ping River, on fertile land framed by mountains and forests. It has been isolated from Bangkok for so long that the people of Chiengmai hardly know the country's capital exists— and indeed, they have had separate rulers and considered themselves a separate entity through much of history. Bangkok certainly plays no part in their lives, and being more than 400 miles distant through some of the most difficult terrain I have ever encountered, I can understand why.

There are, as yet, no railways, no telegraph, and no reliable postal services between Chiengmai and Bangkok (a telegraph line between Bangkok and Saigon in Cochin-China opened, after much pressure from the French government, on July 16th, 1883), but with modernizations being uppermost in King Chulalongkorn's mind, changes will come quickly. With them, the country will gain much, of course, but something of its unique character, born of complete parochialism, particularly in Chiengmai, must surely be lost in the process. It is this uniqueness, this stunning character that I have found in my travels, that I would like to help preserve in some small way by telling my readers how it is in 1884, and how it shall never be again.

He wished he were still there. But he had been away for nine months—as long as he dared—and his editor in New York would be screaming for his next chapter by now. He returned to Bangkok to find several letters, months old, from his publisher. Each one noted fine sales for his last book, and entreated him to be quick about providing new material while his name remained clear in his readers' minds.

It would take him some time to write enough for a new book, but in the meantime, his publisher would take each new chapter and sell syndication rights to newspapers and periodicals in America and Britain, thereby ensuring a steady income for them both. Eventually, the work would be republished in handsome, leather-bound book form.

He had made good progress in the two weeks since his return. There was much he could not write, of course, lest it offend Christian sensibilities. He was well aware that most readers in America and Britain would thoroughly disapprove of some of his activities—and because he was a popular author whose work was often serialised in family magazines, he had to consider this readership if he wished to continue receiving the substantial quarterly royalty cheques.

He put aside the pages and leaned back in his chair so that the leather creaked. It was early evening at the run-down Oriental Hotel, and he could already hear the Scottish merchant seaman in the next room singing to himself, the bottle clinking as he poured himself another whisky.

The Oriental was managed by a former mariner, and so attracted sailors who had heard of it from other seamen, perhaps as far away as the Caribbean. It had a chequered history, and by the condition of it these days, Sam didn't think it would remain in business much longer. The original hotel had burnt down in 1865, and the current building was a particularly utilitarian, two-storey, wooden rectangular design with verandahs on each level, and an exterior staircase.

Sam had ceased renting houseboats or houses in his vain attempts at domesticity. He had lost his sudden desire to settle almost as soon as he had acquired it. Perhaps it had been only a whimsical notion borne of his desire for one woman. He wanted to be ready at a moment's notice for a new adventure, for if he remained in one place for too long—especially here—he was sure he would be consumed with thoughts of *her*, and of his stupidity in losing her.

Not that the memory of her had prevented him from seeking subsequent conquests. There had been many, and he had taken physical pleasure in women wherever it was to be found, and whenever he felt the inclination. There were plenty of jaded expatriate wives seeking excitement in their otherwise tedious lives, not to mention the missionaries' daughters, and the exquisitely delicate Siamese women. Throughout the country he had been offered daughters for a night or forever—whichever he saw fit—and he did not object. But a night or a week almost always sufficed before he tired of them and moved on. On one occasion he had even won a girl in a gambling game at the home of the chief of Chiengmai, Chao Luang Intanon.

He picked up the pages of the manuscript once more, and read on, taking up his gold-nibbed fountain pen to make corrections.

The expedition was launched on January 16th, 1884, an auspicious date according to King Chulalongkorn's astrologers. Among the party there were Louis Leonowens, English head of the king's cavalry; surveyor James McCarthy, an Englishman on loan from the Indian government who had returned from three years' work in the Siamese jungles only in November past; and myself, of no particular talent, save that of being able to record the journey for posterity.

During the dangerous Northeastern expedition, McCarthy—with a staff of seven young Siamese surveyors and the Bangkok harbourmaster's twenty-one-year-old son, George Bush—was to map the boundaries of the Siamese and French holdings. It was an important task to the Siamese in terms of national security and diplomacy, and quite a measure of the respect given McCarthy and Leonowens in a country that has been notorious for its past distrust of foreigners.

Our route was made perilous indeed by tribes of warlike Haw invaders from Yunnan in China—and Leonowens's orders were to

protect the surveyors by driving out or eliminating the Haws if necessary.
To enable Leonowens to accomplish this, His Majesty provided two
hundred infantrymen. Unfortunately, from the outset, it was obvious—
even to a person such as myself, untrained in military disciplines—that
most of these men would be of no use in the event of a battle. Leonowens
had not trained them himself, and was not at all sure what particular
training they had undergone, but it certainly did not appear to be in the
art of warfare. The arts of sleeping, eating, and gambling, however,
they appeared to be well acquainted with.

Sam smiled as he remembered the expression on Captain
Leonowens's face when he decided to encourage the troops by
organising target practice. They had passed through some Meo
hilltribe villages beyond Nong Khai, and were heading toward
Chiang Khan in their pursuit of the Haws, who were said to be
only a day or two's march ahead. . . .

. . . . But the sight of the sacked temples and burned houses, and
the stories of villagers—men, women, and children—murdered without
mercy, had unnerved the men so much that they would run off into the
forest, forgetting their guns, at the slightest unexplained noise. They
did not consider this cowardly or uncourageous. To them it was merely
common sense. Most had wives and children at home. Siamese families
are very close, and even the men are as devoted to babies and children
as the women—and they had no intention of being killed in the line of
duty.
So, target practice was arranged, and it was a disaster. Leonowens
was at first livid, and then shocked into disbelief, as he discovered the
sad fact that most of his men had never before fired a rifle. When he
demonstrated for them, expertly hitting his target with the first shot,
most of them fell to the ground, terrified of the explosion. He retired to
his tent in disgust.
Later, he picked out the best of them—around thirty who had at
least fired a gun before—and sent packing the remaining 170 to await
them in the Lao province of Luang Prabang.

Sam too, had been reluctant to involve himself in much of the fighting—he would rather have observed from a hillside above and written his impressions for dramatic passages in his book—but his passive approach, however, was not always possible; for it was evident that Leonowens needed all the assistance he could muster.

We were sure—Leonowens, myself, and the tight band of thirty men who had become his devoted followers—that we would soon be embroiled in battle. The Haws were less than two hours ahead, and we were gaining rapidly. McCarthy, by the way, calmly continued his own surveying duties—using our camp as his base, but often disappearing with his small team for days on end, and upon his return, rarely commenting on anything more than the weather, or what birds and other animals he might have seen along the way. Never have I seen a man so suited to the task at hand, so dedicated and so unfazed by the myriad physical discomforts of the tropical jungle. I could tolerate these for months at a time, but McCarthy could endure up to three years at a stretch without, apparently, feeling the need for contact with civilization.

We had, so far, managed to avoid much hand-to-hand fighting, because with our limited resources, Leonowens had decided it was best to rely on scare tactics, and to chase the marauders over the borders wherever possible. However, they were becoming suspicious of our actual number, we could tell, and one night, a small band doubled back from their camp, half a day to the north of us, and infiltrated our own jungle bivouac. Three of them crept in past the watchmen and would almost certainly have murdered us in our beds.

Leonowens, sleeping in a bed roll two feet from myself, has, however, a sixth sense regarding such things, and just as two advanced—one to strangle him, the other to smother me—he leaped up, his pistol at the ready, fired a shot, and mortally wounded the man before the other could turn round. At the same time, my grip instantly tightened around my knife, and I sank the bowie deep into the man's chest. His eyes widened in the shock of one who realizes he is about to die. He fell to his knees, and then, sickeningly, on to his chest where the knife had still protruded. He was dead within seconds. The third, on hearing the shot and the groan of the man I had stabbed, managed to flee, and disappeared into the jungle. His escape was unfortunate for us because he would report back that we were, indeed, a small camp, and not the army they had suspected us to be.

It was decided, after that encounter, to run down this particular band, and to engage them in full battle. We pushed on with our elephants for the next two days through the jungle, which the Haws had laid with sharpened bamboo snares. These inflicted some serious wounds in some of the soldiers' feet, which slowed us considerably.

Our elephants too, were overloaded and exhausted, and the crossing of rice paddies became a laborious trial. The men had to make a sort of woven bamboo mat for the elephants in order to allow them passage across the paddies. It looked hopeless at first to myself and Leonowens, but this ingenious invention actually worked quite well.

We negotiated a heavily-jungled mountain range, and when we reached the town of Muang Ngan, we found it nearly deserted except for one small boy, shivering in terror, who attempted to hide under some pig carcasses. He told us—once we had reassured him that we were the king's men and would not harm him—that most of his village had fled in terror when the Haws arrived, but that many had been killed, including his parents, whose poor bodies lay side by side outside their shack.

The boy had tried to run, but twisted an ankle, and had to hide in a large water jar until the invaders had passed on. Surprisingly, he spoke to us in French, and told us that two foreigners in the town—French missionaries—had escaped. The boy looked so morbid when we made to leave, that he begged to be taken along with us. Leonowens agreed, adopting him as a kind of mascot for the force.

The expected battle did not eventuate that time. The Haws apparently decided that a confrontation was best avoided, and had broken up into small groups, retreating on their fast ponies back over the borders. Meanwhile, once we reached Ta Tom, we sent the elephants back to Nwang Kai without us. They had completed their task and *were now more of a liability than anything else. Since we had consumed most of the heavy goods we carried with us in the order of tinned condensed milk, coffee, cookies, and salted meats—we were now travelling comparatively lightly, and so had less need of the elephants as porters.*

Apart from our weapons, which were the heaviest items, each man carried in a canvas bag, his bed-roll, pillow, and mosquito net, plus a blanket for the cool Northern nights. Each man also had a small tent, although we used them only if it was raining; a lamp with a supply of oil, as well as candles; a medical kit with bandages, quinine, and fruit salt for stomach disorders; and a set of clothing fit to be worn in a town or amongst mixed company. Leonowens and I carried water filters and used them religiously, although the Siamese seemed content to drink directly from the rivers.

It was well known in Bangkok now that Leonowens was something of a hero, after effectively chasing the Haws from Siam. After his success, he returned directly to Bangkok to marry Caroline Knox, daughter of British Consul Knox. The wedding took place on August 29th, 1884.

To those in the city, the expedition—in its retelling—had become a glorious adventure. But Sam knew just how perilous it had been, and he had feared for his own life several times—if not at the hands of the Haws, then from disease or misadventure.

The swirling waters on the Mekong had resulted in Leonowens's and McCarthy's launches colliding one night. They had moored the boats and decided to sleep in them, but McCarthy had awoken to find that the stern of Leonowens's vessel had turned and rammed his own. They subsequently had great trouble to separate the two, and so avoid being swamped and drowned.

In addition, when Leonowens's group had rejoined the other men in Luang Prabang, it was to find most of them laid low with jungle fever, contracted from the swamp adjacent to their camp. McCarthy and most of his party were also stricken—despite Leonowens immediately moving them to higher ground—and young George Bush was a sad fatality. The dour McCarthy took all these events in his stride, commenting little, and always eager to proceed with the job at hand.

As Leonowens headed back to Bangkok and the hardy McCarthy planned to continue his surveying in the district, despite the onset of the rainy season, Sam decided to reacquaint himself with Chiengmai. Without the occasional thrill of military engagement, he found the arduous daily climbs entailed in cartography to be rather monotonous. He needed a bath, a strong drink, and a woman—not necessarily in that order.

A British vice-consulate was established in Chiengmai with the signing of a new treaty in 1883, and Mr. Edward Gould—a veteran of eleven years' service in Bangkok—was appointed to the position, arriving in the Northern outpost in May, 1884. I knew Gould slightly, so decided to visit him and see how he was coping.

Sam smiled to himself again. He had never liked or admired Gould in any way—and the feeling was mutual, he was sure. Sam found the tall, thin British parson's son to be supercilious, uncompromising, and obsessed with his own importance. And he imagined Gould found him, in turn, to be lascivious, undisciplined, and far too swarthy for his liking. Gould was a fool and a bore. What Sam wanted, however, after the rigours of months in the jungle, was some sport—and he thought Gould's flounderings might amuse him.

But first, I decided to call on the chief, or prince of Chiengmai, to pay my respects. I had met Chao Luang Intanon when I was last in the city, and we had got along exceedingly well. He is a complex character, but a most wonderful host, and I enjoyed several evenings at his home. He served sumptuous feasts, and his guests were entertained with performances of classical Siamese dancing—whose uniqueness and graceful beauty is unequaled in the Orient—as well as exhibitions of the peculiar Siamese form of boxing, in which the pugilists are permitted to use the fists, as well the legs, feet, and elbows to overcome an opponent.

The prince resides, with a number of wives, in a palace magnificently decorated with great chandeliers, gilded screens, and silk-draped chairs (although the Siamese themselves rarely sit in Western-style chairs, preferring to crouch or kneel on the floor. This is, no doubt, partly because inferiors are required to keep their heads below those of their elders and superiors at all times). Siamese houses of the wealthy often have front rooms decorated in European style, in which they receive visiting Occidentals. However, these rooms are a façade, and beyond them, where the Siamese live, one finds a more traditional scene.

Sam, in fact, felt the chief was rather a kindred spirit. His *"number of wives"* was, actually, a harem of beautiful concubines, headed by the principal wife, Chao Radchabut, whom the other women appeared to be very much afraid of. The evening entertainment began with Siamese boxing bouts, on which the assembled guests gambled furiously. The classical dancing Sam enjoyed more for the sight of the slim, beautiful women—some of whom came from nearby Burma and Laos—than for the art itself.

The prince made it clear that Sam could have his choice of the women, or several at once if he so desired, and he had accepted the offer, on one occasion enjoying the company of seventeen-year-old Burmese twins for several pleasurable early-morning hours. Only when they began to chatter and to ask him questions in broken Siamese did he tire of them, and send them away.

However, the real business of the evenings began after the dancing and boxing, when dice games were played by the Siamese noblemen and wealthy visitors. The games continued until daybreak, with seemingly endless supplies of money—replenished frequently from each nobleman's heavily guarded stashes—brought by servants who attended, throughout the night, to the gamblers' every need.

The Siamese are not, as a rule, great consumers of alcohol, although they do distill a potent rice liquor called samshu *that can have a debilitating effect on the unacquainted. I had always assumed that the people of the region would consume great quantities of tea, having seen many areas of land in the surrounding mountains covered in the crop. McCarthy, however, informed me that the tea grown here—some wild, some cultivated—is not drunk, but rather chewed, much like tobacco in the United States, or betel nut in other parts of Siam. The tea leaves are harvested, steamed, rolled, and then buried with salt in the ground. A wad can be sucked all day, and is apparently an excellent stimulant.*

It had been a magnificent adventure—superior to anything he had read in a novel—and there was still much to write. But he felt there was something missing in his life. He needed to discover again the *true* soul of an adventurer, but to do that, he knew he must do something about the cause of his decline: Elizabeth, and the child he was convinced was his son.

❖ *Chapter 24* ❖

He eyed her with something approaching lust, and knew that he would have to maintain a tight rein on himself to avoid any indiscretions during the course of the evening. She was maturing into a voluptuous young woman, and he could barely keep his gaze from her.

"I can't believe how much you've grown, Anchalee. You look five years older."

"No, just a year. I'll be sixteen in a few months."

She went over to her father's cabinet. "May I pour you a drink, Mr. Taylor? Scotch?"

"Yes, you may. And you know it's not *Mr.* Taylor. Sam will do just fine."

He continued to leer at her in admiration as she poured him a generous measure of whisky, and a sherry for herself.

"So what have you been up to while I've been away, Anchalee? Or must I call you Miss Fairburn, now that you're so grown-up?"

"Anchalee will do just fine." She handed him his glass. "We Siamese don't care much for surnames, you know. Too recent an addition to our identities."

He laughed out loud. "I'd love to be here for your father to hear you say that. So, you consider yourself Siamese, rather than British?" he asked, mockingly.

She scowled, and answered him petulantly. "I was born here, and I have as much Thai blood as British. So yes, I do." She was serious, and she gave a disparaging sneer of frustration as she sat next to him on the sofa.

Her low-cut, green silk dress revealed a deepening cleavage, and she felt his glances sweeping over her body. He had been away with a group of men for a long time, and she was only too aware of how much power she could have over him. She planned to use it.

He leaned back and rested one arm along the back of the sofa. Despite her confident maturity, which was as transparent as his crystal glass, he harboured a suspicion that this one might be tougher to crack than her elder half-sister. But there would be only one way to discover that for certain.

"Rather a daring neckline for one so young, isn't it?" he remarked suggestively.

"Do you think so? This was made for Elizabeth, but she thought it inappropriate in her condition, so she gave it to me."

She swept a delicate finger slowly along the neckline, which served only to emphasise the swell above her bodice—and he knew she was teasing him with her feigned innocence.

She looked at him, and his eyes followed hers as she surveyed her body. "I had to have the bodice let out, and the waist taken in, but otherwise it was just right."

But the dress itself was of no interest to him whatsoever. His eyes still lingered over her breasts, and he imagined her without the frock at all.

When she looked back at him, he caught himself.

"Ah . . . Elizabeth. Is she . . . is she expecting again?"

"Yes. Due in May, she thinks. She's so brave to try again."

"What do you mean?"

"She lost the last baby. It was just after you left. She and Joseph were distraught. She's desperate for them to have a large family."

"Well, you must pass on my condolences. But they're happy together?"

"Very much, she says."

"And the child—the boy?"

"Young Joe's fine. He's walking now, of course. And he's the image of his father." She looked away in mock distraction.

Sam said nothing for a moment, and shifted on the sofa to a less compromising position away from Anchalee—lest Edward enter the room and notice Sam's enthusiastic attention toward his daughter.

"Speaking of fathers, where's yours?"

"Oh, he'll be down soon. The maid went to tell him you were here. I think he'll be most interested to hear more about your adventures. Although I'm sure he won't be told the whole story, will he?"

"And what would the whole story be, young lady?"

"Oh, you know, all the details not considered suitable for polite conversation. Especially those concerning the fairer sex." She raised her eyebrows in a knowing expression, and emphasised the last word ever so slightly.

He laughed out loud again. "You're a wicked young lady. Someone needs to teach you to hold your tongue."

"I've tried," Edward called out jovially as he strode into the room. "But I haven't been very effective."

Sam stood and they shook hands.

"Anchalee, why didn't you tell me Mr. Taylor had arrived?"

She looked slyly at Sam out of the corner of her eye. "I told the maid to tell you. She must have forgotten."

Edward noticed the glass of sherry on the table beside her. "And I've told you about helping yourself to the liquor. You may pour a drink for a guest, but you may *not* pour one for yourself. You're still too young."

"Father, I wasn't drinking it. I only poured it for appearances."

"Yes, but it's still unseemly for such a young girl to have a glass of sherry, whether or not she drinks it. You may do so when you are married, or when you're twenty."

"Father, I'm not a child any more. I'm almost an adult," she pouted.

"Yes, yes. I'm only too well aware of that."

Sam smiled to himself during the encounter, but quickly straightened his expression as Edward turned back to him to apologise. As they went through to the dining room, he glanced at her and shook his finger in playful disapproval—but she simply dismissed his smirk with a scowl.

During dinner the two men talked of the North, and of their respective adventures in various parts of the world. Anchalee was bored with their one-upmanship and was forced to stifle a yawn on more than one occasion. She was barely able to say a word all evening. Only when the meal was over did Edward address her directly, and then it was only to say that he and Sam would retreat to his study for cognac and cigars. His cough had seemed to improve lately, and he had taken to the occasional after-dinner smoke once more.

He then had the gall to say that she may sit at her needlework in the front room. "Or perhaps you should like to retire early," he further suggested, much to her chagrin.

She gave him a sneering smile. "I'll be in the front room, Father. Reading. Something *interesting.*"

Half an hour later she sat curled up in the window seat of the front room, immersed in a novel she had borrowed from Elizabeth. Edward maintained that novels were not suitable reading material for young girls—only further encouraging their silly notions of romanticism—but she ignored him, as usual, and read them anyway. Joseph had a wonderful collection, and Elizabeth said she could help herself to whatever took her fancy. This particular novel, a new one about pirates and adventure on the high seas, was called *Treasure Island*, and her father would have deemed it particularly improper—probably just for the sake of berating her, she thought.

"I thought adventure stories bored you." His voice beside her made her jump.

"And I thought you were smoking cigars or something with Father."

"I told him I needed the water closet."

"Well, this isn't it, *is it?*" she responded provocatively, suspecting—quite correctly—that he had made the excuse to her father so he could see her alone.

"Never mind that. I wanted to ask you something."

She looked up at him through long lashes. It was an airless evening and she felt a bead of sweat work its way down her temple.

"Well, what is it?"

"It's about Elizabeth."

"Oh, her." She thought she had been making progress, and made no effort to conceal her disappointment.

"Yes. Do you think you could possibly arrange for me to see her one more time? There's something I need to ask her."

"I could. But it wouldn't do any good. She'd refuse to see you."

"How do you know?"

"I've already asked her. I mentioned that you'd returned from Chiengmai, and asked her if she'd like me to arrange a meeting between you. She said no. Most definitely not. In fact, she said that she never wanted to set eyes on you again." She looked him straight in the eye, to dispel any doubt in his mind—of which there was plenty—that she was telling the truth.

He sighed. "Well, I suppose it's for the best."

"She really is very happily married. I'd advise you to forget the past, and forget her. You don't want to cause any *trouble*, after all, do you?"

He had to stifle his laugh in case Edward heard him from the study. "And what would you know about such matters?"

"More than you might imagine." She looked down at her book again, as if to dismiss him.

He ran his eyes over her once more, and then sat on the sofa and loosened his collar. "How old are you again?"

She did not look back at him. "I told you, fifteen. I'll be sixteen in a few months."

"Fifteen going on twenty-five," he joked, knowing well that it was not far from the truth. It was becoming increasingly difficult to deny to himself that he wanted her.

"Won't my father be wondering where you are?" she said dismissively.

"What do you think he'd say if he knew I was in here with you?"

"He'd probably scold me for leading you astray."

He wanted to roar with laughter, but was able to prevent himself from doing so as he stood to return to the study. He found her sharp tongue almost as seductive as her slim, but voluptuous figure. "Perhaps I'll see you at the King's Garden this weekend," he added with a hint of suggestion.

"Perhaps. But don't count on it."

"Who's counting on it?" he added with a grin as he left the room.

She smiled to herself. It was proving easier than she had anticipated, after all.

Physically, he seemed to have rallied. The grating cough and the weak spells became fewer, and he attributed them to some other illness. Perhaps they were due to the worry that accompanied the high ambitions he held for his photographic work, and also the fear of eventually being discovered—for he was sure, to his shame, that the king now knew him to be a cheat. He accepted that his photographic aspirations would likely not be realised, and he wanted now only to enjoy his family. With Elizabeth happily married, and Anchalee his constant and witty adversary, he wanted for little.

Business had not been so good lately, anyway, and he began to notice some members of the expatriate community—always those he suspected of never having liked him anyway—look at him with disdain, make snide comments, or simply ignore him. He knew he had done wrong, but still he could not bring himself to admit it, or to go to Klein and apologise. Instead, he carefully put into storage the wonderful photographs of King Chulalongkorn, knowing that they would never be seen publicly in his own lifetime, but that perhaps one of his descendants would be able to make use of them.

He was strolling toward the orchid house, and she saw him before he saw her. It was a perfect opportunity. She turned to her father, who was chatting with an acquaintance, an English businessman who supplied him with photographic equipment.

"Father, I'd like to visit the orchid house."

"Of course, my dear. I won't be a moment."

"Father, I'm quite able to go by myself. Why don't you stay here and talk to Mr. Brightman? I shan't be long."

He nodded his approval, turned back to his friend, and she hurried off in the direction of the enclosure.

The air was heavy inside, and she wished she could take off her shoes and stockings and walk barefoot. It was so much of an inconvenience to have to wear the ludicrous English fashions. They were so uncomfortable, and so obviously unsuitable for Siam. When she was married, she thought to herself, she would dress as she pleased—not "like a young lady" as her father continued to insist upon. Or perhaps she would go about the house naked, even. She was sure her husband would not mind.

She wondered which floor he was on. Likely the upper terrace, as it was open to the air, and cooler. She was right. He was sitting halfway along on a cast-iron two-seater, and he raised his bowler hat to her as she strolled slowly toward him.

"Fancy meeting you here." He smiled knowingly.

Her plain, deep blue dress of shot silk was now clinging to her uncomfortably. But even without the intense humidity, it would still have accentuated every curve of her breasts and hips. And it did not escape his notice.

"Why don't you sit down and cool off?"

She did so, sitting just a little less than would be considered a respectable distance from him on the bench, and he caught the aroma of rose water and something sweeter on her moist skin.

"I didn't come because you'd be here," she told him. "Father decided we should have a day out."

"Did you follow me in here, then?" he asked, amused.

"Of course not. Why should I want to follow you?"

He simply smiled, and gazed directly into her startling green eyes.

"How on earth did you emerge into the world with eyes like that?"

She held his gaze without blushing or looking away. "Courtesy of my father. Or hadn't you noticed?"

"I can't say the colour of Edward's eyes has ever intrigued me." He then lowered his voice and leaned toward her. "If we weren't in such a public place, I believe I'd be forced to kiss you."

She looked away, as if entirely disinterested. "Well, I don't see anyone here."

"Are you daring me?" He looked around, and then back at her, smirking.

"Not at all," she replied. "I've no desire to be kissed by such an old man."

"Old! You watch your tongue young lady. I'll teach you a lesson if you're not careful." He suddenly grabbed both her wrists and pulled her into his arms, kissing her hard on the mouth.

She yielded for just a second, then wrenched free of his grasp and stood up.

"Excuse me," she said brusquely, "I've already learnt *that* lesson. You'll have to speak to my father if you wish to see me again. Goodbye." And with a toss of her head, she walked briskly away, leaving him amused and pondering the fact that he desired her so wantonly.

He had never thought of her as a prospective conquest until very recently. She had always been the little sister, engaging and undeniably beautiful, but far too young to consider romantic involvement with. But now—as was only too evident—she was a woman in almost every sense but age. But even then, she would be sixteen soon, and that was an age when many girls married.

Elizabeth was lost to him now, and he was certain of how seriously she would take her marriage vows. She would never leave

Joseph. Yet, she was still the woman he dreamed of. While he had been away that past year, he had thought seriously of no other woman but her, and he had hoped that somehow, when he returned, he would discover her free again.

His thoughts wandered back to Anchalee. She was young and wild, but he had dealt with perilous situations before—and only too recently at that. His thirst for adventure had not been slaked, and the prospect of a dangerous liaison with her filled him with excitement. Here was a challenge he could not resist. She had dared him brazenly—and he was certain he could tame her.

◈ *Chapter 25* ◈

Elizabeth felt a rushing in her ears as her legs buckled under her and the room fell into darkness. The next thing she recalled was waking up on the couch with Joseph fanning her face and reviving her with smelling salts.

"Elizabeth, are you all right? Shall I call for the doctor?"

"No, no, I'm quite well, really. It's just . . . it's just my condition. It sometimes unbalances me for no particular reason." Her pregnancy was showing now, at five months, although her generously-cut skirt did much to conceal it.

"I think you should rest here for an hour or so before we go home," Joseph suggested.

She still felt slightly disoriented, and she struggled to remember what had happened before she had fainted. It was Anchalee's sixteenth birthday—January 10th, 1885. There had been a meal, a cake, candles, then. . . . Then it all came back, like a horror story, and she realised she would have to feign her congratulations for the sake of appearances.

She wanted to cry out what she now knew to be the truth— that her sister had always wanted Sam, and had plotted for years to tear him from her, and eventually to marry him herself. But she knew she could not reveal anything without hurting too many others.

Her father knew nothing of her relationship with Sam, but how much pain would this bring to Joseph, having him so close? She wanted only to go home, but she could do nothing to arouse her father's suspicions. Or indeed, Anchalee's. But what could she possibly say?

Anchalee ushered the men from the room. "Go to your billiards game, and let poor Elizabeth have some peace and quiet."

When they had gone, it was she who spoke first, sitting beside her sister and wiping her brow with a damp cloth. "I do hope it wasn't the announcement of my engagement that upset you."

Elizabeth attempted to smile. "No, of course not. Why should it have been? Our . . . friendship . . . was long ago. And anyway, it was of little consequence."

"Well, it has worried me that perhaps you still. . . ."

"That was more than two years ago, Anchalee. I'm a wife and mother now, and I love my husband. I have no feelings toward Sam, one way or the other."

"Then you don't mind?"

"Of course not." She managed to smile, but the expression masked a storm of emotions—shock, disbelief, anger, and a sense of betrayal—that swirled within her. But she would never give Anchalee the satisfaction of knowing that she had caused her such pain. She wondered why she had not seen the reason for her sister's deception before. "When is the wedding to be?"

"February 20th. And since you've been so gracious, and so kind in your good wishes, would you be my matron of honour?"

It was impossible. She could not bear that responsibility, and she had to make an excuse quickly. "I . . . I'd love to, of course. But in my condition, I can't guarantee my health, and I wouldn't want anything to spoil your day. Perhaps you should choose someone else."

Anchalee sighed. "There's no one else I'd rather have. You're my best friend as well as my sister."

In the billiards room, Joseph and Edward discussed the same subject.

"Are you sure he's a suitable choice for Anchalee?" Joseph lined up his cue and sank another ivory ball.

"No, of course I'm not absolutely sure. But you know how headstrong Anchalee is when she wants something. She's almost impossible to discipline. A trait she has inherited from her mother, I'm certain of that. Do you know, Joseph, she had the audacity to tell me that if I didn't agree to the marriage when Sam came to ask for her hand, she'd elope with him, or—worse still—she'd simply live with him without benefit of clergy. Joseph, she simply doesn't care what English society thinks of her. There was nothing I could do but give my consent."

Joseph paused for thought before taking another shot. "I must agree that she's certainly wilful—and probably a little reckless, too. But she does look happy. Then again, the emotions of the young can be fickle."

"Indeed," Edward agreed, sipping his port. "But at least if she *is* married, I shall no longer have to worry about her. And even though I don't entirely approve of Sam, he *is* eighteen years her senior. She needs an older husband. I fear that a younger man simply couldn't control her."

"He doesn't strike me as the responsible type. Where is he tonight, anyway? One would have thought a newly-engaged man would be present at his fiancée's birthday dinner."

"Well, that's true enough. But Anchalee says she told him he needn't come, apparently. I don't think family dinners are his particular interest. And she said he had to work on his manuscript."

Joseph wore a doubtful expression as Edward continued.

"I admit, I once thought him a scoundrel. But I've come to know him better lately. He's a talented writer, of course—and yes, he's more than rakish, but I believe that's merely the result of an adventurous spirit." He laughed to himself. "In fact, dare I say it, I almost see something of my younger self in him sometimes. It's a rare man who could capture Anchalee's attention for long, but I think they're of similar character. And I'm certain he has enough substance to hold her."

"Perhaps it's for the best then," Joseph concluded as he prepared the table for the next frame, and Edward mistook his strained look as merely concentration on the game—and the effects of the afternoon port. Joseph rarely drank, but had consumed four glasses already.

266

The old sailor from the next room wasn't such a bad sort after all, Sam thought hazily. The two were propped up on stools at the United Club bar, and—after their tenth whisky—Sam had told him groggily that it was his engagement celebration.

"Hah! Then we huv tae hae one mair wee dram, laddie," the old salt drawled, ordering "two large doubles!"

"An nain ay yer waterin' doon tricks wi' 'em," he slurred in addition to the bartender. "Marriage! A fine institution."

Sam nodded heartily. "Are you married, Jock?"

"Hah! Ye wouldnae catch me fallin' intae that trap." He leaned close to Sam and looked at him with squinted eyes. "Dae ye love her, man?"

"No. I love another."

"Hah! Then that's all reet, laddie," Jock bellowed. "She willnae be able tae get the best ay ye. This calls fae one mair drink!"

Two hours later, things were even less lucid to Sam. He excused himself, leaving Jock—who actually seemed to have sobered up—to entertain another drinker they had met at the bar. Sam lurched into a rickshaw waiting outside, and soon found himself stumbling up the stairs to his room at the Oriental. The next morning he would not remember how he got there.

At the time, however, all he could think of was her. As he drunkenly tried to visualise her face, he realised that he had failed her, and would likely never have her again. He fumbled to insert the key in the lock, and then turned back to the stairs and vomited over the railing.

February 20th, 1885

Dear Marjorie,

   It is my sister Anchalee's wedding day, and I have been compelled to tell them, falsely, that I cannot attend the ceremony owing

267

to my present condition. I write this letter to you at the very moment the nuptials take place. Anchalee was disappointed, of course, when I made my excuse, but although I am actually quite well, I feel that I simply cannot go through with it, and I do not wish to spoil her day. I will explain all this, dear Marjorie, but you will first want to know what she wore—and having said goodbye to her just before she set out, I must admit that a more stunning bride was never seen. The dress was of white silk with a straight skirt, a large bow at the back, and a fitted bodice with a high-buttoned neck and leg-of-mutton sleeves. She wore a plain white tulle veil without any other decoration on her head, and carried a bouquet of white orchids. We are, of course, far behind you by the time the latest fashions reach us here, but we do our best.

And now to my explanation, Marjorie. I must tell you, my dear, that the man she has married, Samuel Taylor, is the very same I wrote to you of some time ago with respect to myself. I must tell you also, that when Anchalee made her announcement, I was filled with grief and heartache; and my despair has hardly diminished since then.

As you know, Marjorie, he had departed on that long expedition to the North of Siam, and believing myself abandoned, I married Joseph. I can hardly believe, upon his return, he chose my own half-sister, of all people, as his wife.

Everyone says they make a delightful couple, and I can hardly make comment about the difference in age between them, my own husband being so much older than myself.

We continue to pray for a happy event around April. . . .

She put down her pen, wishing she could write the truth to Marjorie. She had told her friend that although she had married Joseph in the despondency of her abandonment, she loved him deeply nonetheless. She had made no mention of her pregnancy to Sam, but knew that if Marjorie were there in person, the other would soon ascertain the true nature of her secret.

But she could not, and Marjorie was herself married now, and quite possibly pregnant too. She folded the pages and put them into her writing compendium. She would have to finish the letter another day, for the wedding party and their forty guests would be back to the house soon, and she would have to go downstairs, at least for the cutting of the cake.

Her pregnancy had also furnished her with an easy way to excuse herself from becoming involved in the wedding preparations—and she was glad she had managed not to see Sam during the weeks leading up to the day. She no longer even knew what she felt for him. She had grown to love Joseph dearly—for his kindness, his gentle ways, and his acceptance of her child as his own—but there was no passion in her marriage. She accepted that as the price she had to pay for her sin. And she wondered time and again what Sam would have done had he known of her condition before he left for Chiengmai. She thought she would never know.

She lay on the bed in the guest room with the blinds drawn—and the clock told her that by now, they would be man and wife. Physically, there was nothing wrong with her. This pregnancy had been much easier than the last, and she felt confident now, at six months, that she would not miscarry. She prayed that she had not inherited her mother's weakness after all.

When she heard their arrival downstairs, she sat up on the bed. There was no avoiding it any longer. She would have to put on her new turquoise silk dress, and offer her felicitations to the happy couple. And from now on, whenever she wanted to see her father, there would be the chance she would see him—for he and Anchalee were to live there until they built a house of their own.

Somehow, she managed to tolerate the company and hold her emotions in check, and it was a great relief to her to be able to keep up appearances. She found, however, that she could not face up to Sam. There was nothing to say to him other than offer her brief congratulations, and she did not try to elaborate beyond that simple courtesy. She glanced at him on only a few occasions during the course of the afternoon—a dark figure in his black morning coat and grey striped trousers—and each time she did, she turned away quickly to engage someone in conversation, or see that their drinks were refreshed.

At one point, when it seemed as if he would come over to her, she made to seek sanctuary in the bathroom. But it was not necessary, for at that moment, his best man, Louis Leonowens—newly married himself, and so full of good cheer—came across to slap his friend on the back, put a glass of champagne in his hand, and propose yet another toast.

Elizabeth then found she was able to drift away and climb the stairs once more to her former bedroom and wait for Joseph to take her home.

She never did finish the letter to Marjorie. The next day, she tore it up, knowing that she would not write again soon. She felt as if she were deceiving her old friend, and she felt it better to maintain her silence.

It was a stiflingly hot April night, and she awoke soaked in sweat. As she had done the previous night, and the night before that, she prayed that her child was safe. For that past week, she had felt no movements within her. But the baby was due any day, and it had been such an uneventful pregnancy, she had not wanted to alarm Joseph by telling him. Neither had she wanted to worry Anchalee, now pregnant herself.

Her back ached and she could not even lie down comfortably. The hot season had sapped the energy from her, and there had been no respite from the unbearable temperatures. Even at night, it rarely fell much below eighty degrees.

She had begun to wish she could go back to England. For despite her initial joy at returning to Siam, she realised bitterly that the last three years had brought her little happiness, and much pain. True, there was Joseph, but had circumstances not been what they were, she would never have married him. How different her life might have been had she married James. There would have been no guilt, and no Joseph. But then, there would not have been Joe, either—and she could not wish for that.

She sat up and reached for the glass of boiled water beside her bed, but as the first strong contraction gripped her, the glass slipped from her hands and fell to the floor, smashing on the polished wood.

Joseph bolted upright. "Elizabeth. What's happened?"

"I think you'd best send Simon for the doctor. The baby's coming."

❖

Twelve hours later, as he again waited in the hallway, Joseph was reminded of that last time, when Joe was born. Then, as now, Elizabeth's moans had abruptly ceased. Then, he had heard the baby's cry. But now, he heard nothing. Perhaps she was still in labour, or perhaps she had fainted. He prayed that hers would not be the fate of so many other women in childbirth.

Dr. Newhaven, looking tired and pale, emerged from the room soon after the silence, drying his hands on a towel. Joseph rushed toward the open door, but the doctor closed it behind him and motioned him to stop.

"Mrs. Shaw is in a satisfactory condition," the doctor informed Joseph before he could put the question. "A fortnight or so's rest will see her substantially recovered physically."

And the baby. . . ." Joseph's voice trailed off as he saw the look of regret on the doctor's face.

"I'm sorry, Mr. Shaw. The baby was stillborn. There was nothing to be done. A little girl."

Joseph hung his head in grief, and agonised as to why such another innocent life had been taken from him. When he went in, Elizabeth was propped up in bed, her face blank and so white, her eyes closed. She opened them and looked dully at him as he sat beside her on the bed. "I'm sorry," she whispered weakly. "So sorry."

He could not look toward the little blanket-wrapped bundle in the crib. But he had to be strong. He held her cold, dry hands in his.

"Don't blame yourself. The doctor said it couldn't be helped."

"No, it's my fault. My mother was the same. That's why I was her only child. The doctor says I probably inherited the weakness from her."

"Then there must be no more children."

"No, Joseph, no! I want to give you children, more than anything."

"I would rather have you than ten children. I won't put your life in danger. Besides, we have one perfect child. He is enough."

"But Joseph, he's not your. . . ." She caught herself before her words could be more hurtful.

Joseph put a finger to her lips. "I could never love a child more than I love Joe. He is ours—yours and mine. And that's all that matters."

"There is such goodness in you, Joseph," she whispered.

"Let's be happy with what we have. With Joe. From now on, we must be extremely careful. You know what I'm speaking of."

On a breezy, cool-season day in December that year, Anchalee gave birth to her first child after an easy, six-hour labour. The baby was a seven-pound girl with chubby red cheeks, and a thatch of dark hair on top of her head. They called her Kesri, after her maternal grandmother.

◈ *Chapter 26* ◈

She twisted nervously at a handkerchief as the carriage trundled along New Road toward Edward's residence, where they were to celebrate Christmas midday dinner. It was an occasion she could not make an excuse to be absent from—and besides, she owed it to Joe, now two-and-a-half, to give him a joyful day surrounded by his family. It was the first Christmas he was old enough to really participate in.

Since the wedding in February, she had actually seen little of Sam or Anchalee, or even of her father. Edward's health worsened considerably since then, and he had been receiving visitors and clients at home, instead of going out himself. Strange, after having such high hopes for his work a few years ago, he had suddenly seemed to lose all interest. She supposed it must be his health problems. For a time, the cough had seemed to improve, but after the wedding it had returned, worse than ever—though he insisted it was nothing to worry about.

Then there was Charlotte, whom they had named and buried the same day. The birth, only a fortnight previously, of Anchalee's daughter, had brought back the pain of losing her own children. She had not seen the baby yet; today would be the first time. She had previously excused herself with a cold, saying that she did not want to pass it on to either Anchalee or little Kesri. But Christmas she could not avoid.

As they progressed along New Road, the driver suddenly pulled the coach over, leapt down, and crouched by the side of the road. Joseph looked out of the window, craning his neck to see the road ahead. Every other Siamese within sight had done the same as the driver.

"It's the king!" Joseph told them excitedly. He opened the door and helped Elizabeth out, then picked up Joe as they stood respectfully to watch the scene.

The king's *barouche*, drawn by six horses, was approaching. Behind was a procession of horsemen, followed by the carriages of his wives and children. It was quite unusual for the monarch to ride out in his carriage so early in the day, Joseph thought. Like many wealthy Siamese, he rarely ventured out until late in the afternoon, when the heat of the day was beginning to dissipate. Joseph surmised that this early jaunt was indeed because it was Christmas; that His Majesty wished to acknowledge the day for the benefit of his foreign friends. Indeed, high-ranking members of the diplomatic community were invited to dine at the palace later that day.

As the king passed, Elizabeth and Joseph bowed their heads, noticing that within the four-seater carriage with him were several of his older sons. It took a full fifteen minutes for the royal procession to pass, and only when he was sure it had, did the driver jump back into his seat and they were off again.

Anchalee bustled them inside to the front room, where she had pinned up Christmas decorations found in an old box in the cupboards under the stairs. Elizabeth vaguely remembered the streamers and baubles from Melbourne, and which must have come on the ship with herself and her mother all those years ago. Extraordinary items to have brought to Siam, she thought.

Edward sat in a chair near the window but did not stand up to greet them—and Elizabeth was shocked to see how thin he had become, and how grey his skin looked. He was fifty-seven but looked at least ten years older. His voice, however, was just the same, and he smiled brightly when he saw his grandson. Kesri was asleep in her crib at the back of the house, watched over by the maids as they prepared the Christmas dinner.

Joe ran up to him, clambered on to his knee, and they played together. A moment later, however, Edward began to cough. The fit was so bad that Elizabeth was forced to lift Joe off him.

Anchalee hurried back into the room with a glass of whisky. The coughing subsided, and he put away his handkerchief—careful not to allow his children to see that it was spattered with blood.

"Have you called the doctor about that cough?" Elizabeth was deeply worried. "It's not getting any better."

"Nothing wrong with me," he replied, as if unconcerned. "Just can't seem to shake off this cold." But he did seem to improve after the whisky, and some colour returned to his face.

Sam stepped into the room then, and if Elizabeth had expected any tension between them, it did not arise. He shook Joseph's hand, and knelt down to say hello to Joe. She almost gasped when she saw the two of them close together. The likeness was alarming, and she was certain that it was obvious to everyone in the room that they were father and son. They both had the same dark wavy hair, the same dark brown eyes and olive skin, and the identical cheeky grin. Of course, Edward was the only one present who, she knew for certain, was not aware of the truth. Anchalee and Sam, she more than suspected, had already confirmed in their own minds what was so evident. But she worried mostly that her father would notice—and that the shock of the truth, if he were to discover it, would send his health into further decline.

Sam stood up and poured champagne that had been cooling on ice specially brought from Singapore. He seemed perfectly content, and she could scarcely believe he had once been her lover, and was the father of her son.

As they chatted and sipped champagne, she realised she was staring at him. When he returned her gaze, she felt the colour creep up her face, but—for a moment—still could not avert her eyes from his. She knew him well, and with that look—the way his eyes met hers, and the tilt of his head—she sensed he had not forgotten. It unnerved her, and she forced herself to look away, knowing that he must have seen the longing in her eyes. There could be no secrets between them. He took great interest in Joe, and she was convinced he knew the truth. Indeed, anyone who half suspected it, need only look at the boy for their suspicions to be confirmed.

The maid entered the parlour then, announcing in Siamese that dinner was served. To her discomfort, Elizabeth found she was seated opposite him. Yet to have asked to be moved would only have been conspicuous. She ate almost nothing of the first course, a hearty vegetable soup, and remained mostly silent during the conversation. When everyone had finished, and even Joe's bowl was clean, she had still taken only a few mouthfuls, and had then set down her spoon.

"You've barely eaten anything Elizabeth. Are you unwell?" Edward asked. He looked much brighter than he had done when they arrived.

"No, not at all. It's delicious." She made an effort to swallow two more large spoonfuls.

"I'm teaching Noi to cook more English food," Anchalee said. "The chilli doesn't seem to agree with Father these days."

"Nonsense!" Edward protested. "She mollycoddles me."

Elizabeth smiled at him fondly, grateful that he had broken the tension. She was glad of something to take her mind off the man sitting opposite her. The main course was a feast of roast pork, corned beef, duck, and a huge fish—stuffed, baked, and presented on a platter. The room buzzed with conversation, and Elizabeth ate only because she didn't wish to draw attention to herself. She hardly tasted the food. Flamed pudding and custard followed for dessert, and they then withdrew to the parlour for coffee, fresh fruit, and port. The tropics were not the place for such heavy food, but no one could deny that it had been a magnificent English dinner. And it would have been almost a sacrilege not to have celebrated Christmas with a traditional meal. The men loosened their collars and rolled up their sleeves. Young Joe had eaten too many chocolates, and expended so much energy opening his presents that he had fallen asleep in the window seat.

As they were sipping coffee, Edward was suddenly stricken by another attack. His face reddened, and he didn't seem able to catch his breath. It had worsened over the previous few weeks, and the frequency of the attacks had increased. There was an overwhelming atmosphere of unease in the room. Anchalee held a glass of port to his lips. She hardly dared face up to what it meant. Again, he attempted to dismiss it, and grabbed a napkin to cough into. But when the spasm subsided, he seemed almost to collapse, dropping back into his chair in exhaustion, the napkin slipping to the floor in front of him. Elizabeth went to pick it up, and gasped when she saw it. Silently, she held it out to Anchalee. All were quiet, except for Joe, who had woken up and begun to cry.

Elizabeth broke the silence. "Father, why didn't you tell us about this?"

"I'll be fine . . . in just a minute." There were specks of blood on his chin.

"I had no idea it was this bad," Anchalee said.

"Didn't want to worry you," Edward continued. "Doctor says nothing can be done. Just have to hope for the best." He sat up straighter and smiled. "Why all the long faces? It's Christmas, let's enjoy ourselves." Insistent that he was fine, and that they not fuss over him, he took Joe on his lap and his grandson soon settled down.

Elizabeth poured more coffee and tried to convince herself that it was merely a chest infection—that he would simply have to put up with it until it passed, and that he would make a recovery. But deep down, she feared that she was fooling herself. She knew what it meant. It was consumption, and it would eventually claim him as it did so many others.

It must have been a particularly bad day for him, because he said he would not go with the rest of the family to the afternoon Christmas service. He was emphatic that they all go on without him, that he would be fine by himself. But Elizabeth was equally determined that she would stay behind with him.

The house was quiet after the others had gone out to the carriage, and she sat talking to him for some time until he decided to take a nap. She helped him up to his room, closed the drapes, and told him she would be back to check on him in half an hour.

In the parlour, she too decided that an afternoon nap would be expedient. She lay back on the *chaise longue*, but just as she was drifting away, the sound of the door opening disturbed her.

"It's all right, Noi, you can clear the dishes away later," she called, thinking it was the maid.

"I don't think I'll be doing that," he joked, leaning in the doorway.

She sprang up, wide awake. "I thought you'd gone to church. Did you forget something?"

"You know I'm not a church-goer. Told them I was going for a long walk, to work off that big Christmas dinner."

She self-consciously smoothed her skirts and composed herself on the seat. "Oh, really? And what did Anchalee say about that?"

He walked slowly over to one of the armchairs.

"She knows I'm not religious. I'd only get restless and walk out during the service anyway. She doesn't want to be embarrassed in front of the congregation by such a heathen. Anyway, she only goes herself to please your father."

"Quite," Elizabeth replied condescendingly, but now a little unsettled as she realised that—except for her father, upstairs asleep, and the maids, who were probably taking an afternoon nap, also—she was alone in the house with him.

"The boy's growing fast," he said suddenly. "Why did you name him Joe?"

She had anticipated this. "It's his father's name of course."

"Shouldn't the boy's name be Sam, then?"

The words were like a slap to her face, and she felt as if the breath were leaving her body, as if her sins had crept up on her and were trying to strangle her.

"What? Whatever makes you say that?"

"Elizabeth, admit it. He's my son. He's the image of me, anyone can see that. This story of him being premature is nonsense."

"How can you say such a thing? It's simply not true." She was desperate now, panicking. "There's dark blood on Joseph's side of the family . . . Maori, actually. That's why Joe is dark. And I believe my great-grandmother had jet-black hair and olive skin."

He stood up and stepped toward her. "Don't lie to me, Elizabeth. You and I both know the truth."

She felt tears pricking her eyelids. "Sam, for pity's sake, can't you see what you're doing? The hurt you could cause? He's Joseph's son. Joseph's the only father he knows. To admit anything else would be . . . immeasurably cruel. It would help no one. Let the past remain in the past." She felt the back of her throat constrict with a sob. "I cannot say any more."

She buried her head in her hands, and then, unexpectedly, he knelt beside her and gently took her hands in his, forcing her to look at him.

"If I had known. If you had only told me. I would have . . ."

"Don't. What's done is done. We cannot change it now. Don't you see that? I love my husband, I swear to you I do. There's no better man on earth. And you're married to my half-sister. You and I must remain apart—forever."

"But we're not apart. I'm your brother-in-law. Can't we at least be honest with each other? I don't want to take Joe from you, or to cause harm to anyone over this. I know Joseph is a good father to Joe, and I accept it. I'll be happy just to watch him grow up— even if he knows me only as his uncle. But please Elizabeth, admit to me now, once and forever, that Joe is my son. Then I promise you, I'll never mention it to you again, if that's the way you want it."

His voice was earnest, and she relented. "Very well. . . . It's true, Sam. Joe *is* your son. And Joseph knows it."

"Why didn't you tell me you were expecting, Elizabeth? I can't understand. . . ."

Should she tell him? That her sister, now his wife, had designed their estrangement, only so that she could wed him herself. But what service would it do anyone to tell? It could not change anything. They were both now married; there were innocent children to think of; and her father, in his illness, did not need to suffer the stress of a family crisis. She would have to tell him only a half truth.

"Before I could tell you, you'd gone—and there was no way to contact you—you know that. The shame of bearing an illegitimate child was too much. I couldn't bear the thought of my child a bastard—of myself a fallen woman. When Joseph made his proposal it was as much a shock to me, as it was to you when you returned." She paused to retrieve a handkerchief from her sleeve and wipe the tears from her eyes. "But I could do nothing else. There was no other way. I had to accept."

"I understand. But you know, the most ironic thing of all is that I'd decided that when I returned I *would* ask you to marry me." He sat beside her. "Can we forgive each other, Elizabeth?"

"Forgive? There's nothing to forgive. We're both to blame. We're simply victims of circumstance." And she wanted to add, "Anchalee's meddling."

She paused. "But just . . . just knowing that you . . . that you would have. . . . It's a comfort, that's all. I'm sure we can be good relatives, even friends."

"You in your marriage, and I in mine?"

"That's the way it must be, Sam," she whispered. "I think you should go on your walk now. They'll return soon, and who knows, if the maids saw us in here together. . . ."

He took her hand a last time, and—a moment later—left without saying anything. She stood and walked to the window as he went.

❖ *Chapter 27* ❖

It was a lengthy document, written in Siamese, and—judging by the thin and yellowed paper—quite old. His wife's maiden name was written on the envelope in childish script, and at first he thought it likely an old letter from a girlhood friend, or some such. Had he seen it elsewhere, he would probably have dismissed it— would not even have bothered to discover its contents—except for the fact that he had not found it where one might expect to find such a thing; that is, in the box where she kept her other correspondence tied with ribbons. It had been so deliberately hidden, in a place where he would never think to look—for anything—so that he was sure it was something important; something she wanted to keep from him.

But why? He knew just about everything there was to know about her—or so he assumed. She had been a young girl in her father's house when he had first met her, and that had continued to be so until they were married. What secrets could she possibly have? She had always had a vivid, if immature and girlish imagination, and had always been somewhat influenced by the romantic novels she read. But to the best of his knowledge, she did not keep a secret journal, not being much interested in writing herself.

Lately, however, he had noticed a change in her. She had become fiercely protective of Kesri, and spent hours talking to her in Siamese and telling her nursery rhymes that she could not possibly comprehend. She also spent hours at the little Buddhist shrine she had insisted on setting up in her dressing room. Edward would have been disappointed—but not at all surprised—for he had done his best to ensure that she was brought up as a Christian.

But her father was confined almost constantly to his room now, and since Anchalee ran her own household, she could, as she had said to Sam, do as she pleased. When not with Kesri, she was often lighting incense and paying respect to the Buddha. Sam hardly considered himself a Christian, and he didn't care one way or the other what religion his wife followed, but he was concerned at the amount of time she spent alone.

One day, he came home much earlier than expected—from the United Club, where he been to meet Leonowens, who was to tell him of his latest adventures over a few drinks. Louis had left the king's employ to become a Borneo Company agent at Raheng and Paknampho. Although there was now a fortnightly mail service between Chiengmai and Bangkok, via Moulmein, and a telegraph service between the two via Raheng, Louis liked to travel back to the capital periodically on important business.

The telegraph service was particularly unreliable. He had returned briefly in late 1884 to apply to his boyhood friend, King Rama V, for permission to log a teak forest—the Mee Tuen—that he had found above Raheng. Permission was granted, and Leonowens became the first foreigner to lease a forest in Siam. Others followed soon after.

But Louis had arrived at the United that day, breathless and excited. "I'm to be granted an audience this afternoon, Taylor," he said, slapping his friend on the back. "So I must be away very shortly. Can't miss an appointment with His Majesty, can I! Come and visit us in Raheng!"

Well, Sam smiled to himself when Louis departed for his audience after only one quick drink, he had only been brushed aside for the king, after all. He ate lunch alone that day, finished his whisky, and went home to surprise Anchalee—thinking that he could probably interest her in an afternoon tryst. Anchalee had, he pondered thankfully, a most un-Victorian appetite for sex—and he had not found it necessary, even once, to seek pleasure elsewhere. That, at least, had remained constant, even after the birth of Kesri, and it was still something of a surprise to him that he had managed to stay faithful to her.

He let himself into the house quietly, knowing that the maids would all be asleep at that time in the afternoon. If he were lucky, Anchalee, too, would be already napping in bed. She always slept naked, and he loosened his collar in anticipation as he climbed the stairs. As he moved up the hall, however, he heard her voice, low and muffled. He thought he would have to wait until Kesri was asleep, but when he looked into their daughter's nursery, the baby was already tucked into her crib. Who was she talking to? He pushed open the door to their bedroom, and saw that her dressing room door was closed. She continued talking beyond it, and he could just make out the occasional phrase or two. "I won't fail you," he heard, ". . . for what she's done . . . I promise."

It crossed his mind that perhaps she was having an affair; that behind the door was his wife with another man. There was nothing for it, but to put his eye to the keyhole.

He was relieved to see no one else in the room, but frowned when he saw what she was doing. She was on her knees before the shrine, with a thick envelope clutched to her chest, uncharacteristic tears running down her face.

She stood, lifted the Buddha image, placed the envelope in the hollow of its stand, then replaced the idol carefully. She then knelt on the floor again, brought her hands to her forehead and lowered her head to the ground three times before the shrine.

He left the room quickly and went downstairs.

She found him in the living room twenty minutes later, reading a newspaper and smoking a cigarette. She helped herself to one from his silver case and lit it.

"Your father wouldn't approve of your smoking," he joked.

"In case you hadn't noticed, I'm no longer Daddy's girl," she replied, sitting on his knee and blowing smoke into his face.

She wore only a thin silk *sarong*, and one side had dropped open, revealing her breast, heavy with milk. He circled her nipple, and it responded instantly. She stood up then, allowing the garment to fall in ripples to her feet. She was magnificent, he thought, and the slight rounding of her belly—the result of her recent motherhood—only served to increase the desire in him. She turned and walked from the room, and he followed a minute later, knowing the game well, wondering where he would find her. She rarely favoured their bed for love-making, and would often tease him by hiding, heightening his anticipation.

A few minutes later he found her—it was never very difficult—spread across a trunk in the boxing room under the stairs, lying on her stomach, with her long hair sweeping to the floor. She was pretending to read a book. As he entered, she glanced sideways at him.

"Did you want something, Samuel?"

"You know what I want 'harpy'," he smirked, undoing his trousers but not even bothering to take them off.

He hadn't forgotten that other matter—but it could wait.

A week later, unable to restrain himself any longer, he had confronted her with what he had discovered. She stood on one side of the bedroom, fists clenched in rage, and he on the other holding the sheaf of papers. They could not raise their voices too much, because Edward and the servants were downstairs.

"And what gave you the right to go through my personal papers and to steal my property—the only thing I have left of my mother?" she hissed at him. "You bastard, I hate you!"

"Well, you certainly didn't marry me because you loved me, did you, Anchalee?"

"What would you know about love?"

"Not as much as you know about hate and vengeance, it would seem."

"You don't know what you're talking about."

"This is all the evidence I need." He waved the pages at her.

"How do you know what's in it? It's in Siamese—a language you're hopelessly inept at," she spat.

"I had it translated. And the translator did an excellent job. Your mother's dying wish—that you should repay Elizabeth for some imagined crime. The ravings of a madwoman!"

"How dare you speak of my mother that way? Elizabeth ruined her—Elizabeth killed her."

"So, you married me, hoping she'd be consumed with jealousy."

"That's right. And you're Joe's father, aren't you?"

Sam looked startled. "How do you know that? I believe Joe's birth certificate names Joseph Shaw as the father."

"That means nothing," she countered. "I know everything. I'm not as ignorant as you seem to think. You're the father of that child, and anyone who has eyes can see it plainly. I know, Joseph knows—everyone knows. Everyone except my father, and I'm sure the shock would kill him if he did. Perhaps that would make Elizabeth happy—to have killed both my parents. I'll bet she just wishes I'd drop dead as well, so she can have you. You're not fussy after all, are you?"

He stepped up to her, and grabbed her tightly by the arm. "You little bitch. Don't you think you can make a fool out of me, because you never will. I'll always have the last word."

"Let go, you're hurting me," she said through clenched teeth.

"Not until you listen to me. I didn't find that letter by rifling through your belongings. I have better things to do. I came across it by accident."

"By *accident*? Where I put it? And it has my name on the envelope, not yours." She jerked away from him. "Have you been spying on me, you disgusting voyeur? Can't you leave me alone for one moment?"

"It's time you started showing me some respect. I'm your husband—or had you forgotten?"

"How could I forget?" she said scathingly, "when you prove the fact to me so often? Anyway, it's none of your business. This is between Elizabeth and myself. Or do you still care for her more than you dare admit? I've seen the way you look at her."

"And that's none of *your* business. In any case, your plan hasn't worked out the way you'd hoped. Elizabeth is happy—she loves Joseph. And he's a better husband to her than I ever could have been."

Her eyes narrowed. "Yes, but wait until she discovers the truth about why she isn't married to you."

"What do you mean?"

"Her marrying Joseph was a result of my plan too." She wanted to hurt him now, and she allowed a moment of silence to pass as she went to sit on the edge of the chair next to the doorway. She was stealing herself to run, should he become violent with anger.

"I forged a letter from her to Joseph, asking him to think of some way to make you leave so she didn't suffer the embarrassment of having to put you off herself."

"You did *what?*"

"You heard me." She had never seen him this wild. His eyes were menacing, and she had no idea how he would react. "Joseph sent you to Chiengmai to get rid of you. And she thought she'd been abandoned—pregnant and unwed. Until Joseph became the good Samaritan and married her himself. That, I didn't plan."

"Did you know she was pregnant?" His voice was low and threatening.

She stood next to the door, her head held high, with a scathing look on her face. "Yes."

"You disgust me. You're not fit to be related to someone like Elizabeth. And to think she loves you, trusts you. . . ."

"So you see. It's I who's having the last word now."

"I wouldn't count on that," he retorted. "You've punished Elizabeth, but she's at least in a loving marriage. On the other hand, *you* are destined for a long and loveless marriage that you'll regret from now on."

"Nonsense, I'll divorce you."

"No you won't. Not without my consent—which I'll never give."

"A Siamese court will grant me one, with or without your consent."

"No," he said, standing calmly over her. "You like to think you are Siamese, Anchalee, but in the eyes of the law you're an American subject now that you're married to me. And before that you were a British subject. Siamese laws don't apply to you. They never have. Does the truth hurt?"

He threw her mother's letter to the floor and left the room, brushing past her and leaving her feeling as if there were rocks in her stomach.

She sat down again, stunned. What hurt most was the realisation that she would not have divorced him, even if it were possible. She was doubly bitter because she did care for him, but knew that he would never feel for her as he did Elizabeth.

As she sat expressionless, staring at the papers strewn across the floor, she pondered her future. He would remain her husband, if that was what he had to do to punish her, but it would be a marriage in name only, for she would never sleep with him again. He would find out how strong her own loathing could be. She resolved to drive him into Elizabeth's arms again. And what would transpire when Joseph discovered his wife having an affair with her brother-in-law, the father of her child?

She went to the nursery, where Kesri was sleeping soundly. She touched her tiny hand and gently stroked her soft, downy cheek.

A week later they were invited to the Shaws' for Saturday afternoon tea and croquet on the lawn. For the sake of appearances they agreed to behave as if everything were normal. Sam decided it would do no service to Elizabeth to burden her with her sister's betrayal. He warned Anchalee that he was watching her closely, and would not allow her to do anything to further hurt Elizabeth.

The sisters sat in the shade—Anchalee holding Kesri, and Elizabeth trying to keep Joe in her sight. There were snakes in the long grass at the edge of the property, and he had not yet acquired the sense to avoid them. Elizabeth had once found him poking at one with a stick, and it was fortunate, on that occasion, that the serpent was not of a venomous species. But Siamese cobras were common, and whenever Joe was playing in the garden, Elizabeth lived in constant fear of him being bitten.

"The mosquitoes are dreadful this year," she said to Anchalee as she scratched again at her ankle. Both had been bitten a number of times already. "They're actually biting right through my stockings. I can remember my mother sitting with a large paper bag tied round her legs. Perhaps we should revive that practice."

Anchalee made no reply, and Elizabeth suspected that she and Sam had had a disagreement.

"Anchalee, is something wrong?" she ventured.

Elizabeth had finally been able to make peace with herself over the fact that Anchalee had stolen Sam from her. Talking to him at Christmas had actually been a relief to her, and she had decided the best thing she could do was to try to re-establish her relationship with Anchalee.

But her younger sister looked distracted and disinterested.

"Anchalee?"

"No, nothing at all," she answered.

"You seem pre-occupied."

Anchalee smiled, but the expression was not one of warmth. "Being a mother is tiring," she offered. "I didn't realise quite how exhausting it would be."

"Don't worry. It's not so unusual to feel an emptiness. Men simply can't understand why we feel that way. You're so fortunate to have such a beautiful girl. And before long, I'm sure you'll find you're expecting again."

Anchalee merely nodded, but didn't reply, or even smile. It wasn't likely she would bear Sam another child, she thought bitterly, when they were no longer even sharing the same room.

Then a thought crossed her mind. Perhaps Elizabeth would have another child to him when their affair began. For she was sure it was only a matter of time. She could see it in their eyes when they looked at each other. She took heart at the idea, and Elizabeth mistook her smile for one of a brighter mood.

He was dying, he knew it, but he was not ready. He had always imagined himself in old, old age, reflecting on a long and eventful life, entertaining his grandchildren with stories of old Siam. But not this decrepit, premature infirmity at a time when he should still be full of vitality.

He felt pathetic in his slippers, unable even to smoke his pipe any longer. Although he appeared a sickly, old grandfather, in his mind's eye he was still the adventurous young photographer with a host of experiences still to live. But time was escaping him. As his condition worsened, he had thought a lot—and at least all was prepared and his affairs were in order. He had seen to that, with Mr. Harbeck's help.

His daughters believed he wasn't really conscious of much that went on around him any more. But he had learned more about his family in the previous few months than he had known for years when he was fit and active. Somehow, his senses seemed to have sharpened, and he had become more aware of the gestures, expressions, and feelings behind their words.

He supposed he had been a shallow man throughout his life, and would be remembered as such. Until recently, he had never felt the need to analyse his life or any of his actions and their consequences. But now; now that he had all the time he did not want, he saw things more clearly.

He saw, for example, a streak of vindictiveness in his younger daughter, where before he had seen only girlish spirit. He saw a sense of loss in his elder daughter; and he saw his grandson, Joe, growing into the image of his father, Sam.

Oh yes, he knew Sam was Joe's father. That would surprise them. It was one of the first things he had realised. When one had more time to look and to ponder than anything else, one often came to the correct conclusions.

Such matters did not overly concern him, however. It was for them and his future descendants to resolve themselves. Not to mention, he thought wryly, the sins of their father. For he had sinned, he knew.

It was not in his nature to regret, but now that he could foresee his end, he wanted to confess. He wanted absolution; wanted to leave in the knowledge that he had declared his wrong-doings. If only to ease his conscience, peace would be a fine thing indeed.

❖ *Chapter 28* ❖

It had begun. She could see it in their secretive glances whenever the two families were together; in the way his fingers lingered when he passed her a drink. But what she did not know of—and what would have surprised even her—was the suddenness of the affair. It had started at the consulate ball, only a few nights after they had spent the afternoon in the Shaws' garden complaining of mosquitoes and snakes. She had made an excuse not to attend the ball, but encouraged Sam to go alone.

When Elizabeth first greeted him at the ball, she had been nervous. But he asked her to dance while Joseph was busy talking to friends across the room, and before she could reply, he had whisked her away. His arms encircled her for the first time in more than three years. "You're as beautiful as ever," he whispered.

And she did look wonderful. The fitted, pink satin gown accentuated her figure, which at twenty-five had filled out attractively. Her hair was brought up softly and coiled around the top of her head, and she wore a double choker of pearls, and long white gloves.

As they danced and he drew her closer, she thought of how much had happened since they had first danced together. It seemed like an eternity. For a while she felt as she had then. But Joseph wasn't far away and he was likely watching their every move. She pulled away from his embrace a little but he drew her back and quickly whispered that he wanted to see her alone outside the ballroom.

"I don't think I should answer that," she said, extracting herself from him and returning to Joseph. A few moments later, however, she excused herself and walked down the long hallway toward the ladies' restroom. Only, she did not turn into it, but instead continued along the passage until she reached a curtained-off alcove. She stepped in and closed the curtain, her heart beating, her breathing shallow, and her hands trembling. She knew exactly what she was about to do.

A few seconds later the curtains opened quickly and then closed again. Without a word he took her in his arms, and his kiss was deep and longing. She did not pull away. He moved behind her, and—as he kissed her neck—his hands roamed from her waist to caress her breasts.

He wished he were touching her bare skin instead of the tight satin, but he could feel the warmth of her body through it as she arched her back against him. Much as he wanted to, it was impossible to undress her there in that small space. Instead, he gently guided her down on to the cushioned seat, and knelt between her legs as he raised her skirts and kissed her smooth milky-white thighs.

I can't let this happen, she repeated to herself, but her thoughts were lost—without any pretence of refusal or resistance—as she felt him stroke her gently, intimately. She relaxed against the cushions and forgot everything but him.

Later, when she returned to Joseph, he noticed a faint sheen on her forehead. She lied, naturally, when he expressed concern at her absence, asking if she were unwell.

"Sorry. I ran into Caroline Hooper in the ladies' room, and you know how she can talk. I couldn't get away!"

It was true, she had seen Mrs. Hooper in the ladies' cloakroom—although she had not actually spoken with the woman for longer than two minutes. At that moment, Sam had passed them with a beautiful young woman, the daughter of a naval captain, on his arm.

"Actually, Joseph, if you don't mind, perhaps I *am* a little tired," she said suddenly. "I think I should like to go home after all."

But Anchalee knew none of these details. She knew only that sometime between February and the current month, April, the two had become lovers again. But as much as she wanted now to create a crevasse between them—one that would last their entire lives—she could do nothing while Edward was still alive. He had always been good to her, and she loved him dearly. She wanted him to be at peace when he died—for he *was* dying, and they all knew it.

The consumption had deepened in the four months since Christmas. The coughing fits were more frequent, and the blood soaking his sheets and his handkerchiefs more voluminous. He was confined to bed most of the time, although once or twice a week, she sat him by his window so he could look down at the garden he had always enjoyed so much. His hair had turned white and his speech was slow. He now looked twenty years older than he was. But he never complained, and one day by the window he said to her, "I've had a good life, Anchalee. I've known love and happiness. I only wish your mother were here today. I regret. . . ." But the remainder of what he wanted to say was lost in a spasm that sent him back to his bed. When it subsided, he was too exhausted to talk again.

April was the hottest month of the year, and the oppressive heat further depleted his strength. His appetite had all but disappeared, and he would take only weak chicken broth or a few spoonfuls of rice. One morning, Anchalee simply found him dead in bed. He looked quite peaceful and composed. Beside him was the beginning of a letter in a weak, spidery hand. It began, "My family, do not judge me harshly for. . . ." and broke off. He had either paused for thought, or at that moment had left them forever. She imagined he meant to say something about her mother, and perhaps Elizabeth's. She tore up the page and threw it away.

She sat in the chair by his bed for more than an hour, staring at the walls. For a long time, when she was a child—not so long ago in years—it had been just Edward and herself. Until Elizabeth had returned. And now, excepting their children, Elizabeth was the only living relative she knew of. He had been her last link with her mother, even though he never spoke of her. She was still only seventeen, but felt much older. She always had. And with the death of her father, she felt that her childhood was finally behind her.

The funeral was held a few days later. Joseph gave a special reading, and Sam attended church for the first time since he had married Anchalee fourteen months before—and for only the second time since his childhood. They stood apart, neither a comfort to the other. Elizabeth clung to Joseph's comforting hand.

Then there was his will, which his solicitor wanted read that same afternoon. Elizabeth would rather have waited. It seemed so final. Nevertheless, Anchalee had agreed that Mr. Harbeck would speak to them after the wake. Elizabeth didn't imagine the will contained much more than the disposal of the house and some personal possessions. He seemed to have had no other assets, apart from his photography business, which had dwindled away to almost nothing before his death, anyway.

As she sat on the sofa in the parlour, sipping a cup of tea and listening to the subdued conversation around her, she caught Sam's eye. He glanced quickly toward the door, and she knew what he wanted her to do. Despite her grief, she felt the blood rush through her veins at the thought of him. She then felt a surge of guilt. Could she do this at her father's funeral? But she was desperate for him; desperate to escape from the morbid gathering.

He had already left the room, confident she would follow to meet him in the old studio, which her father had not used for more than six months before his death, and which had become one of their places of rendezvous. She told Joseph she needed to get some air, and when he offered to go with her, she insisted hastily that she preferred to be alone.

Anchalee watched from across the crowded room as first her husband, and then her sister, slipped out to the back of the house. Did Elizabeth have no shame? Could she defile even her own father's funeral with her infidelity?

Sam waited for her in the darkroom off the studio, and she let herself in with the spare key they kept hidden under a rock in the garden. Twenty minutes later—they dared not exceed that limit— Sam returned to the house, his absence hardly noticed, he thought, while Elizabeth sat in the garden looking out toward the river.

As always, after she had been with him, she felt utter remorse, and agonised over how long she could continue deceiving Joseph. She had prayed for the will to resist Sam, to tell him it must stop, but each time he touched her, her resolve vanished. She knew it was unforgivable, but she could not help herself—even as she felt herself sinking lower and lower into a well of lies and deceit.

She did not, however, feel any guilt at all about Anchalee. Although she had tried to let the past be, when their affair had started again she had been reminded just what she had lost because of her sister. She had even tried to raise the subject with Sam, but he had placed a finger over her lips, his other hand caressing her back, and she had lost herself once more in their passion.

Joseph found her sitting alone on a two-seater cast-iron bench. He sat beside her and took her hand. She said his name as if she were about to tell him something, and he turned to her. But no sooner had she spoken than she stopped and told him it was no matter.

Sometimes she wanted to confess to him, but she could never find the strength to utter the words. She meant everything to him, and it would surely ruin him if he were ever to discover her adultery. How would she even begin? Had she been about to tell him? She wasn't certain exactly what she had meant to say. She knew only that after today's encounter, she felt more shame and regret than ever before. Somehow she had to end it. Joseph was too good a man to deserve the trauma she would bring on him if he discovered the affair.

Anchalee called from the window that lunch was served, and Joseph stood and brushed his trousers with the back of his hands. They were covered in leaves and twigs from the trees. The garden had become overgrown and neglected during Edward's last weeks.

He offered his arm to her and she walked inside with him, accepting more condolences from the many people who had gathered to mourn her father.

The guests departed soon after lunch, and Elizabeth, Anchalee, Sam, and Joseph waited for the solicitor in the dining room. At two o'clock exactly, Mr. Harbeck arrived. He expressed his regrets at Edward's death, put on his gold-rimmed spectacles, and began to read from the document before him.

The first part of the will was straightforward. It bequeathed the house and contents, except Elizabeth's mother's belongings, to Anchalee. Elizabeth was to take anything of Charlotte's she wanted, and there was a sum of cash allocated to her. Then there were several small bequests to friends and trusted employees.

Mr. Harbeck continued reading. "I should like to bequeath the remainder of my estate, which consists largely of moneys in cash, to be equally divided between my grandchildren, Joseph Edward Shaw and Kesri Taylor, and held in trust until each attains the age of twenty-one, or upon marriage, whichever is first. In the unfortunate event that either child should pass away before reaching his or her majority, the money is to be donated to a charity organisation nominated by his or her mother or guardian, as the case may be." He removed his glasses and looked up from the paper. "Are there any questions so far?"

Anchalee spoke up. "Yes, Mr. Harbeck. How much money is to be in trust for the grandchildren? I can't imagine my father's cash reserves amounted to much."

"On the contrary, Mrs. Taylor, Mr. Fairburn was a very wealthy man. Particularly since he preferred to live from the earnings from his photographic business, rather than deplete his inheritance."

There were astonished looks all round the table. "His inheritance?" Anchalee continued. "His father died years ago, and his mother last year. I didn't think they left much, except the mansion in England—but his brothers refuse to sell."

"Not his parents, Mrs. Taylor. In the 1860s he inherited a very large sum of money from his grandparents, who bequeathed their substantial estate not to their children, but to their grand-children—as he himself has done. I believe he was in Australia at that time, and made a trip home to England to settle those financial affairs."

"I remember!" Elizabeth exclaimed. "Now it makes sense— why he left, and was gone for so long."

"Quite," Mr. Harbeck said, clearing his throat. "And the money remained untouched by him. As you all know, I'm sure, he was not an extravagant man. It seems he preferred to work for a living and to forget that he was, in fact, independently wealthy."

"So exactly how much do the trust funds contain, Mr. Harbeck?" Anchalee asked again.

The solicitor cleared his throat once more, embarrassed. He disliked surprising clients, even with good news. "Approximately 300,000 pounds, Madam."

There was a collective gasp.

"That means Joe and Kesri will each inherit 150,000 pounds," Elizabeth remarked almost imperceptibly.

"No, Mrs. Shaw," Mr. Harbeck said, even more embarrassed. "I meant 300,000 pounds *each*."

There was stunned silence.

"Additional interest accrued—over the next twenty years and eight months in Miss Taylor's case, and eighteen years and two months in Master Shaw's case—will substantially add to the capital; in fact, will exceed it."

He went on as they remained speechless. "There *is* one provision, however. In order to make claim on the funds, each child will be required to present him- or herself at the London offices of Harbeck & Sons in person at the appropriate time. Mr. Fairburn has not authorised any transfer of funds from England to overseas, except by the recipients in person."

There were questioning looks from the family members. Was there a catch?

"That is the only provision," Mr. Harbeck announced in reply to their unvoiced question. "Mr. Fairburn, I believe, was keen for his grandchildren to know something of their heritage; to visit England, if only once during their lives."

Thinking the reading was at an end, they began to talk excitedly among themselves. Mr. Harbeck cleared his throat once more, and they looked at him again, expectantly.

"There is one final bequest, and I'm afraid it's a . . . a secret clause."

"A what?" Sam asked.

"Yes, it's for Mrs. Elizabeth Shaw to hear only, and I'm afraid I shall have to ask the rest of you to leave the room."

Yet again there was a shocked silence, and eventually the others slowly pushed back their chairs and walked out.

Mr. Harbeck closed the door behind them, turned back to Elizabeth, and looked over his glasses at her. "I expect you think this rather unusual, Mrs. Shaw," he said quietly.

"To say the least, Mr. Harbeck."

"Yes, of course. But I'm afraid I'm not at liberty to divulge very much to you today."

"Whatever do you mean, Mr. Harbeck?"

"Well, in fact, this clause is actually a short letter to you from your father—which perhaps you should read yourself." He opened a sealed envelope that had been attached to the back of the will, and handed her the single page which was dated six months previously, October 31st, 1885.

My Dear Elizabeth,

> *As I write this letter, I know that I shall die soon. And although at this point you are aware of my illness, the gravity of it I must keep from you for as long as possible, given your present condition. . . .*

She paused and took a deep breath. Since he had written this final letter, she had indeed given birth, but his grandchild had been lost once again. How disappointed he must have been. First his wife, and then his daughter had failed him. She was only

relieved that he never knew the depths to which she had sunk.
She read on.

*The fact that you are now holding this letter in your hands means
that I have indeed passed on, but do not grieve for me, my child, for I
have had a full life, and my children and grandchildren have brought
me more joy than I perhaps deserve.*

*Elizabeth, I must assure you that I have never forgotten your dear
mother. She was my first, and, despite everything, my only true love.
Nor have I forgotten how my selfish actions forced her to leave us,
forever. I have always felt that in so doing, and then in my sending you
away from me, I deprived you of something precious that could not be
replaced. Although I know your grandmother did her best, I realise
that I denied you your mother's true and lasting love.*

*Elizabeth, my love, this is not the only thing to have haunted me.
These last months, I have had time enough to reflect on the mistakes I
made in my life, and I must tell you now of the reasons why I left
Australia for England so abruptly, and—as it transpired—so
permanently, in early 1867. Indeed, it is also the reason why I ventured
to Siam, and—as a consequence—why it is now your home.*

*You know of course, that the main reason I returned was to oversee
some financial matters, which you now know to be my inheritance
from my grandparents. I was, naturally, eager to ensure that my
brothers did not appropriate my share. Another reason, I have to confess
to you, was to escape, at least for a while, from an increasingly difficult
marriage to your mother; one which had become full of guilt and
disappointment.*

*But there is one other reason, Elizabeth, which you shall discover
for yourself in due course, that compelled me to leave you and your
mother in Melbourne for so long. It has been kept all these years, since
1867, in a bank vault (but not in my father's and brothers' bank, you
understand) in England.*

*This package has personified all my wrongs and all my evils. And
because it has represented such ugliness to me, I have prayed all these
years that one day I could do something to change it; that the evil might*

eventually be turned to good. I have arranged for Mr. Harbeck to wire his head office in London on my death, and to request that this package be sent to you. You will know what to do with my last bequest, my daughter, I feel sure. I ask only that you keep this matter a secret until the time is right, and you will know when that is.

Your loving father,

Edward

She turned the page over, wanting—needing—more. But there was nothing.

"Mr. Harbeck, you must tell me immediately what this is about. It has frightened me to death. What can it be?"

"I'm so sorry, Mrs. Shaw. What little I do know, I've sworn under oath to keep confidential. Mr. Fairburn wanted to do this in his own way. I'm afraid you'll just have to wait until the package arrives. It's being shipped, I believe, as we speak."

He stood, shuffled the papers in his folder, and put them into a well-worn brown leather briefcase with "*Harbeck & Sons, 1820*" embossed in a corner in small gold letters. "I shall be in touch soon. Good day to you, Mrs. Fairburn."

After seeing the solicitor out, she went, ashen-faced, to join the others in the drawing room.

"Well?" Anchalee asked, agitated. "What's the big secret?"

"A . . . a family matter," she stuttered.

"I'm family."

"No, to do with my mother and myself. Just a letter, really. Nothing of interest to anyone else."

Her reply was so obscure, and her condition so distressed that no one urged her to divulge any more. And she vowed to herself that she would not—until she knew for herself if it were possible do so.

◈ Chapter 29 ◈

Anchalee could see no reason to delay much longer. While her father had been alive, and before his will had been read, she feared that perhaps he could have disinherited her, or even Kesri, if he discovered the truth. Not that she had harboured the least idea of the fortune her father owned. *That* had been a genuine surprise to everyone. But now that Edward was gone, and Kesri's inheritance was assured, it was time to act.

Still, one thing disturbed her. She liked Joseph a great deal. He had always been kind to her—and, indeed, to her mother—and she regretted having to do it. She justified it by forcing herself to believe it was her duty to tell him. He had a right to know.

She went to see him three weeks after the funeral, on a day when she knew he would be alone. It was a Thursday afternoon, when Elizabeth was always out, helping at the Library Association, which had been established by a group of American women in Bangkok in 1869, and which was the expatriate society's major source of English books.

The look of astonishment, of disbelief, and of utter despair on his face when she told him, was something she would remember for the rest of her life. For a moment she wavered when he asked her in a barely audible voice to repeat what she had told him. Her words had sent him reeling, and—for a moment—she considered telling him she had been mistaken; that she had not meant what she said.

"Joseph, I believe that Sam and Elizabeth are having an inappropriate liaison. An affair, in other words."

"But how. . . ? When? I don't believe it!"

"I didn't want to either, Joseph. But you must believe me. It's the truth. I've never been more certain of anything in my life—and I've never been so repelled by anything more. But I can't deny the truth any longer, nor have I the right to keep it from you."

Slowly, as if suffering from some infirmity, he sank into a chair in the front room where they were talking. He spoke quietly, as if defeated. "Are you absolutely certain of this, Anchalee? It would be a dreadful mistake to make. . . ."

"I've made no mistake, Joseph. Mark my words. I ask only that you confront Elizabeth with this, as I shall confront Sam. Then you'll see."

"But how could this happen? I . . . I trusted her. Trusted her completely. . . ." He stopped in mid-sentence, his voice breaking.

"I'm sure you don't wish to know the sordid details, but they've been meeting secretly. . . ."

Joseph held up a restraining hand and shook his head slowly. "You're right, Anchalee, I don't want to know the details. But tell me one thing. How do you know this for certain?"

"My husband kindly told me himself," she lied.

"Why would he do that?"

Her eyes filled with melodramatic tears. "We had a dreadful quarrel, Joseph. I'd suspected him of having an affair for some time, but I was quite prepared to forgive him . . . especially if he promised me it meant nothing. I'm a mother now, and I cannot. . . . Well, I cannot attend to him as much as I used to. Forgive me for speaking so frankly. Perhaps he felt lonely.

"Joseph, I could have turned a blind eye to some ridiculous interlude with a servant, or some married woman I didn't know. But my own sister! He seemed so proud of himself. He even said—and I don't want to believe this, perhaps he was just angry—he said that he'd married me to get to Elizabeth! Can you imagine?" She pretended to dab at her eyes with a handkerchief. "There's no question of divorce, Joseph. I won't countenance that. But I

302

thought it my Christian duty to inform you, as my brother-in-law."

"So what now? What shall we do?"

"I'll leave that up to you. But it must not continue."

"Of course not."

"I'm sorry to be the bearer of such hurtful news. Would you like me to stay with you for a while?" She did feel guilty, seeing his pain—but, after all, she was not lying about the affair.

"No, no thank you," he said, almost as if he were in a trance. "I think I'd like to be alone. This has been a terrible shock."

When she had left, Joseph sat with his head in his hands. Had he made a mistake in marrying Elizabeth? He had done his utmost to please her, and obviously it was not enough. He suddenly flared with anger. Damn the man to hell. He picked up the cut-glass vase from his desk, filled with stems of purple orchids, and threw it with all his strength at the wall. Anchalee heard the smashing glass as she closed the front gate behind her. Then he knelt on the floor and cried.

She decided not to consult Dr. Newhaven—the family physician, who had advised her never to have another child—for fear that he would ask awkward questions. Dr. Daniels, an American who was not acquainted with the family, was new in Bangkok, and she needed, more than anything, to be discreet. In the event of a false alarm, word was less likely to circulate that she had even suspected she was pregnant. But she was expecting the worst, and her fears were now confirmed.

"Congratulations. You are indeed expecting a child," the doctor brightly informed her.

Fear gripped her like a collar of ice, and if she had been standing, she would have fallen to the floor. "How many months?" she managed to ask, feeling nauseated.

"About fourteen weeks, as far as I can tell," he replied. "Maybe more, maybe less. Any previous complications? You say you have one son already."

There was no reply. It was too late even to cajole Joseph into marital relations and to once again pass off the child as his.

"Mrs. Shaw? Are you feeling ill?"

She gathered her wits and tried to present an appearance of normality. "No, Doctor. I'm quite well. What were you saying?"

"I was asking if you had had any complications in your previous confinement?"

"Oh . . . no, no. Everything was perfectly normal." She hadn't told him about the other pregnancies.

"Good. Then you can expect your child to be born in November, Mrs. Shaw."

She thanked the doctor, saying wearily that she would return for an appointment the next month, while already searching desperately for lies and excuses. The irony was that she and Sam had ended the affair. She realised, however, that she must have conceived almost as soon as it had started.

After the funeral, they had met only once more in the old studio.

"It isn't right, Sam," she had told him. "I *cannot* live with myself. To give into these . . . these desires is a sin, that's all."

At first he tried to convince her to continue their liaisons, but his efforts were half-hearted. He too, eventually realised the futility of it. "You're right. I didn't think it could last—not really. It's too intense, too dangerous."

"Sam, we're not free to indulge ourselves. It can lead nowhere, except to ruin. And Joseph. . . ."

"Say no more." He gestured impatiently and turned away. "I understand completely." And he was gone.

In the three weeks since that last meeting, she felt as if she had been spinning like a top that had fallen. And in those weeks of dizziness and confusion that followed, she began to suspect the truth—but still denied to herself that it could be possible. She had even blamed her lack of menstruation on the grief caused by her father's death. Her cycles had never been regular, anyway.

But now it was confirmed, What were her choices? Tell Sam and abscond with him? Would he abandon his own wife and daughter to go with her when it was most likely that the child would die before it was born? The notion of terminating the pregnancy was out of the question, the thought of it almost more frightening than admitting the truth to Joseph.

With a dread greater than any she had experienced before, she realised there was indeed no other solution. She must tell him and suffer the consequences. He was a gentle, good man, and he would not act violently toward her, she had no fears of that. But he would be crushed by her betrayal, and he would surely never trust her again.

Their marriage was ruined, for she was sure he would never forgive her. She could barely comprehend her own stupidity; that she had not considered the likely consequence of their affair. It infuriated her, too, that Sam had so completely blinded her to reality—not once, but twice.

All too soon, the carriage drew up at the house, and reluctantly she walked up the path. In another few minutes, her life would change forever.

Perhaps she could delay telling him. Another day? An hour? A few minutes more before the axe fell? But it would gain her nothing.

Joseph opened the door, and she was so mired in her own misery that she did not see the look of torment on his face. If she had, she would have known immediately. He followed her into the front room and she turned to him, without taking off her hat or gloves. There were already tears in her eyes as she prepared to say what had to be said.

"Joseph, I have something to. . . ." But the words died in her throat as he told her to sit down before she could even begin.

She did as he asked, and when she looked up at his face, she saw something she had never seen there before: desolation, darkness, and above all, desperation; the look of one who had been betrayed by the person he loved most.

"My God, you know, don't you?" she whispered, wondering how he had discovered it.

He nodded, looking down at her. "Anchalee came this afternoon. She knows, too. He's admitted it, and it was she who told me."

"Joseph, I swear to you it's over," she cried—realising he was speaking only of the affair. The worst remained to be said, and her tears began. "I beg you to believe me. I love you, I love you."

She slipped from the sofa and grasped his trouser legs with both hands. He disengaged himself and stepped away, leaving her on the floor, looking up at him pathetically.

"How could you do this to me—to us, Elizabeth?"

Tears coursed down her face now, and she lay on the floor and beat it with her fists. "I don't know, I don't know," she moaned. "I ask God to strike me down; to punish me, for there's no greater sin."

For Joseph, the tragedy of it all was worst. To have saved her from the devil's arms, only to see her fall back into them once more. Was it not his failure, too—for not foreseeing the danger?

"Get up, Elizabeth," he said, and helped her on to the sofa.

She tried to control herself, although her body still convulsed as she sobbed. Her face was ashen now, and she was consumed with fear. "There's more than you know, Joseph. More than anyone knows. . . ."

"I've already told Anchalee that I don't wish to know any details."

"You must know," she insisted weakly, and then forced herself to continue. She would tell him the worst, but would still not reveal the fact that they were married only because of a letter forged by Anchalee. She could not do that to him. She felt as if her lips were almost fastened together as she fought to say the words.

"I'm expecting his child." And then she hung her head as her tears fell to the floor.

Joseph's legs seemed to crumble beneath him and he sank slowly into an armchair, his head buried in his open palms. As he fell back in the seat, his cry of, "No," was little more than a strangled groan. Then there was silence.

When he spoke again, it was mechanical. He felt numb and drained of emotion. "Elizabeth, you could die. Are you certain of this?"

She spoke rapidly through her tears. "Yes. I've just come from the surgery. A new doctor. He . . . Sam . . . doesn't know," she added hastily.

"When?"

"In November. But Joseph . . . I'll leave. I'll not shame you with this. It's God's punishment and I must suffer it alone. You must want rid of me now. I'll pack my things. I can go back to England. I'll take Joe with me."

"Elizabeth, I cannot contemplate this so quickly. And I cannot accept what has happened, either. But I'll pray, for the strength to find forgiveness. Only God can be the judge." Then he looked at her incomprehensibly again. "Why? Why in God's name have you done this?"

"Joseph, I cannot explain myself. I knew it was wrong, I knew what I was doing . . . and I was somehow blind to anything else."

"Do you have any idea of the misery you've caused? The shame I feel, the failure? Yes, for it's my failure, too. I too have been blind." He seemed almost to be speaking to himself, and she did not interrupt.

"In the last few hours, I've asked myself why I married you. I told myself at first that I was doing it for you. A long time ago, I promised your mother I would watch over you. I told myself it was a Christian act to save a young woman's reputation; to save her from ruin.

"But I see now that I didn't do it for you at all. I did it for myself. Because of the guilt within me. And because I wanted a life like other men. I believed that because I'd saved you from disaster, it would ensure your loyalty. I was wrong."

She saw now how completely her actions had destroyed his faith in human nature. "What will happen to us, Joseph?"

He looked at her with empty eyes. "I don't know. I must pray for guidance. I think we must spend some time apart."

She stood up. "I'll pack my suitcase."

"No. You have nowhere to go. A woman and a child alone— a hotel is not suitable. People will talk, and that's the last thing I want." He shrugged, too broken to talk any more.

She watched as he walked slowly from the room. He was gone, and she would not blame him if he never returned.

Joseph walked along New Road to the riverbank in Yannawa district where the Protestant chapel stood, and where he knew he would find Reverend McFarland. It was the same church in which Joseph had consoled Elizabeth three-and-a-half years before.

Europeans seldom walked along the road, as they would arrive at their destination covered in dust or splashed with mud from the numerous puddles. There were pot-holes everywhere, and so many vehicles traversed the street erratically—victorias, trishaws, rickshaws, and food carts—that it made strolling uncomfortable and an inconvenience.

But Joseph did not care, and he waved away the bemused rickshaw pullers who continually stopped beside him, calling out cheerfully, "*Pai nai?*"—Where are you going? In fact, as he walked, Joseph had already decided where he was going—and it was further than any of the rickshaw pullers could take him.

Reverend McFarland had been urging him to visit the American mission at Petchaburi for some time. "Quiet and peaceful," he had said of his old home of several years, and it seemed to Joseph as good a place as any to seek solace from his torment.

The reverend could see that Joseph was under some sort of strain, but asked him no questions when he said he wanted to leave for Petchaburi immediately. He simply made the arrangements and offered to take over the younger man's classes at King's College while he was away. Reverend McFarland was also headmaster of the college—established in 1878 at Nantha Uthayan Garden, Suan Anan district, Klong Mon, for sons of the nobility—but his work at the boarding school was part-time. He had not wanted to spend too much time away from home, and he combined his scholarly duties with other missionary responsibilities at the church.

The newly-arrived Reverend W. G. McClure and his wife at Petchaburi would be grateful of his company, the reverend assured Joseph. "Perhaps you'll like it well enough there to stay a while," he added hopefully.

It was simple enough to recruit able young missionaries for Bangkok, but it was quite another matter to find those willing to travel beyond and take up the Church's work in jungle outposts where Europeans were rarely seen. Many missionaries did not endure long in such places. They would arrive, full of enthusiasm and idealism, only to leave within two years, once the difficulty and discomfort of the life took its toll.

Petchaburi was not terribly isolated, and the mission had high hopes for it. The town was 100 miles southwest of Bangkok, and was becoming increasingly popular as a resort—frequented by foreigners as well as the Siamese—where it was possible to revive one's spirit and delight in the fresh air and more sedate pace of life. The king himself had a palace there, where he and his court spent part of every hot season.

Joseph was the only passenger on the roomy houseboat, which was just as well, because he didn't think he would be pleasant company for anyone at that time. The six oarsmen rowed throughout the night, and to his surprise, Joseph slept well. He arose in the morning to eat a few mouthfuls of plain steamed rice, but refused the crew's offer of chicken curry and fish sauce, not because he could not stomach the spicy Siamese food—his constitution had become remarkably resilient over the years—but because he had no appetite for food. Despite the emptiness he felt both physically and emotionally, fasting would enable him to think more clearly, he thought.

Moving downstream, however, his anguish would occasionally recede into the background as he gazed out appreciatively at the serenity of life along the river. They passed by men in small fishing boats, children frolicking in the river, and mothers tending to their laundry—and it all seemed so uncomplicated to him.

A large white bird seemed to fly with the boat, flapping from tree to tree with a raucous "ark, ark" each time it took off. As far as he could see beyond the river were rice paddies—the bright green seeming almost unnaturally verdant—and every now and then, a small thatched hut on stilts.

On reaching Petchaburi in the early evening of the second day, Joseph was amazed to find it a sizeable town of 20,000 people, with a number of double-storey brick houses, a leafy main thoroughfare, a substantial market, and numerous glittering temples. The sparkling royal palace, built by King Mongkut, stood on a hill overlooking the town.

The only foreigners were the two missionary families—and Reverend McClure was pleased indeed to welcome Joseph, and to show him the church. "We could do with a fine teacher such as yourself, Mr. Shaw," he said. "And the company of your family would be a very welcome addition too."

On the third morning of his stay, Joseph awoke renewed, feeling as if some of the burden at least had been lifted from his shoulders. He knew now what he must do, and there could be no turning back. It was time to return to Bangkok and make arrangements. If only Petchaburi were further away, he thought to himself as the houseboat drew away and his friends waved goodbye from the landing.

They sat like strangers, stiff and formal, in the front room when he arrived home. She had received no correspondence at all from him since he had left the week before, and she had been afraid she might never hear from him again.

It seemed now that he was no longer a defeated, sunken man. He held his head high and he spoke with a strong, unwavering voice. "For more than three years now, you've been my life, Elizabeth. You, and then Joe. It wasn't difficult for me to accept that you'd been with another man before I married you—as you know, our situations were quite similar, and I couldn't condemn you for making a mistake, as I, too, had transgressed. And you and I had not the slightest hint of an understanding before that time. I believed you'd learned the same terrible lesson I had. I don't believe myself to be a harsh or unforgiving man. It's not in my nature. But this . . . this has tried me beyond all else. . . ."

"You're right, Joseph. And I cannot ask you again to . . ."

"Let me continue. I don't want to cast you out, Elizabeth. You're my wife, and I'll see us through this, despite everything. Together, we must pray for forgiveness; for your life—and that of the innocent child. That will be enough. If the child lives, I shall accept it, as I accepted Joe. After all that's happened, I find I cannot stop loving you. I . . . I could not go on without you."

"It's more than I deserve." She began to weep, hardly daring believe that he meant to stay. "But how can it work, Joseph, we're bound to see them again?"

"We must wait and see," he replied simply, adding nothing else as he left the room.

He had a proposal for Reverend McFarland.

Joseph was more than surprised to receive the message from Sam asking to meet him at the United Club. He had no desire to see the man again, but he reluctantly agreed. It would be as good a time as any. He was not fond of the United Club either—and rarely went there except occasionally to peruse the foreign newspapers on the long tables in the reading room upstairs.

Joseph arrived first, sat at a small wooden table by the door, and ordered a lemonade from the bar. He didn't stand when Sam entered, nor did he return his greeting, but merely nodded to the chair opposite. Sam understood Joseph's bitterness.

A bar attendant brought Joseph's lemonade and took Sam's order of a gin and tonic. Joseph then suddenly looked directly into Sam's eyes. "I know everything. Everything, including the fact that you're Joe's father." When Sam did not comment, he continued. "You seduced Elizabeth when she was an innocent girl . . ."

"Now hold on," Sam interjected. "It takes two, Joseph. I never forced Elizabeth to do anything she didn't want to do, then or now. I intended to marry her. I didn't know she was expecting, and when I returned, she'd married you. I was astounded."

"I'm not saying she wasn't partly to blame. But you were older, wiser to the ways of the world. And now. . . . Well, I suppose this isn't the first time you've had to deal with an angry husband," he sneered. "But she's your own wife's *sister*, man." He cleared his throat, and seemed to change tack. "I'm not here to discuss the past. What was your reason for this meeting, anyway?"

"To tell you—actually, to show you—something that I'm sure you ought to be aware of. In fact, you have a right to know of." He paused for a second. "You know, Elizabeth and I had already agreed to end our . . . to stop seeing each other, permanently?"

"And did you know that, once more, my wife is with child by you?"

Sam's head snapped up sharply. "What?"

"Do you know that another pregnancy could kill Elizabeth, and the child?"

"No, she never told me. I knew she'd had some problems, but I never knew it was that serious." His voice was subdued.

Joseph, in contrast, was tense and angry. "Now do you see what you've done? Your dalliance comes at a high price, as such things always do."

"Elizabeth is—was—no 'dalliance' for me," Sam responded quickly. "I told you, I wanted to marry her. I loved her, for God's sake."

"Keep your blasphemous tongue to yourself." Joseph felt his temper rising, but managed to restrain himself and keep his voice down. "I'd hoped you intended to discuss this civilly."

"I'm nothing if not civil."

Damn him! Even now there was mocking irony in his voice. The man had no conscience whatsoever. "Elizabeth wasn't so fond of you after she became pregnant with Joe. It was she who asked me to send you away. She wrote to me, saying she no longer cared for your attention, and she begged me to intervene."

Sam leaned on the desk toward Joseph. "Well now, it seems that you don't know everything."

"What do you mean?"

"That letter was forged by Anchalee. Elizabeth wrote no such letter, and to this day knows nothing of it. It was Anchalee who wanted me out of Elizabeth's way."

"What?" Joseph slapped the table, so that several people at the bar turned to look. He brought his voice down almost to a whisper. "This is outrageous. It doesn't make sense. How can you say such a thing?"

"Because it's the truth. Confront Anchalee with it if you don't believe me. It *was she* who brought you the letter, wasn't it?"

"Well, yes. But that doesn't mean. . . . Anyway, what earthly reason would she have for such deception?"

"I'm afraid there's much more to Anchalee than you know, Joseph. Much more." He leaned back in his chair. "Anchalee's not a meek little girl. She's a woman with a generation of hate behind her, and she's carrying out a vendetta against Elizabeth as revenge for something she thinks happened years ago."

Joseph had never heard anything so extraordinary in his life. Then he remembered their wedding night, and how vague Elizabeth had seemed, asking to see the letter, reading it as if she had never before seen it. Which of course, she hadn't. She must have realised what had happened, and yet still had not told him. Was he the only one who didn't know, then? He sat silently and waited for what Sam had to say next.

"Do you know about the letter her mother wrote her?"

"Yes. I gave it to her. Kesri gave it to me for safe-keeping just before she died."

"And do you know the contents of that letter?"

"No, of course not. It was personal correspondence. Nothing to do with me."

Sam took a sheaf of papers from his coat pocket and put them on the table in front of Joseph.

"Then I suggest you read this English translation of that letter, and see for yourself how it concerns you—or rather, Elizabeth. I'll give you some time. I think you'll need it." He then took his drink and walked out to the garden, where he lit a cigarette and looked over to the tennis games on the club's courts. He was greatly disturbed at the revelation of Elizabeth's pregnancy.

Joseph did not feel comfortable about reading the letter, but his curiosity would not allow him to ignore it. He was desperate to know what it contained, and what Sam meant. He had always thought of Anchalee as an uncomplicated, if somewhat spirited young girl—although it had shocked him when she had announced her engagement to Sam. He took up the pages and began to read.

January 10th, Buddhist Era 2412 (1870)

My dearest daughter,

I had always hoped to see you again; to return to you when you were older and you could make up your own mind about me. I would have loved to have seen you become a beautiful young woman, as I am sure you now are. Unfortunately, I have learned recently that this life for me will soon end.

Do not feel sorry for me, Anchalee, for you know that I shall be reborn to a better life. My only regret is that I shall not see you again. That is why I have written this letter, on this, your first birthday, because I cannot tell you myself what you need to know, and what, I guarantee, no one else can, or will, tell you.

Perhaps you do not even know my name, or anything about me. You will know, I suppose, only as much as your father has chosen to tell you, which may be nothing. But I trust Joseph Shaw to keep his word to me, and to give you this letter unopened. I beg you not to reveal its contents to anyone else, but to do what you feel necessary.

Even if your father has told you everything he remembers about me, there are things he did not know. I will explain everything about myself in this letter, as honestly as I can, so that you really know who your mother was.

At the time of writing this, I am nearly twenty years of age, and my husband, Edward Fairburn, has forbidden me to see you again. This is the penalty I must pay for something I did, which, in your father's eyes, was a crime, but in mine, was an act of love for you. You will discover what it was soon enough. But first, let me start long before I knew your father.

I was born in February, BE 2392 (Christian era 1850). I have never known the exact date, as records were not well-kept in those days, and my parents could not read or write. They were slaves of a wealthy Krung Thep (Bangkok) family, and so the date of my birth may be in their records, I do not know. In recent years, I have celebrated my birthday on February 1st.

I too was born into slavery, but, unlike my parents, was determined to escape that wretched existence. I would rather have died than spend my life at the beck and call of someone else.

When I was about twelve, I began to notice that men looked at me in a way they had not a year earlier. I was maturing early, and had almost a woman's figure. I was a little taller than most girls, and had fuller breasts, and my skin was smooth and unmarked by the smallpox scars that disfigured so many. Among the men who noticed me was the master's nineteen-year-old son. He was already married with three wives and a number of children, but still I felt his eyes upon me whenever he visited his father's house, which was often, as his own house was within the same compound.

I had an idea that perhaps this man could help me in some way, so I began to tease him, but making sure no one else noticed. As I poured water for him, I would lean over a little further than normal so that my breasts would brush against him. I did not really understand what I was doing, but neither did I dislike the feeling of his skin on mine. I smiled at him shyly, and lowered my eyes whenever I saw him.

One day, as I was washing clothes in the klong, I was suddenly grabbed from behind and pulled into the bushes on the bank. A hand was clamped against my mouth, and I thought I must surely be murdered. But then I was allowed to turn round, and I saw that it was him. He was laughing, and I pretended to be amused too. What happened next was my first experience with a man, and I closed my eyes tightly and did not cry out when the pain came.

When he was finished, he said he would send for me to visit him at his house. He asked me if I would like him to ask his father to give me to him. He did not mention marriage, of course, and I knew that I would remain just a slave. I decided that while he was infatuated with me, I had some power, and I also knew his first wife was very jealous. I had seen her looking at me sometimes when she noticed her husband's interest in me, and I knew she did not like it. She did not mind how many wives or slave girls or concubines he had, as long as none were as beautiful as she. But I was more beautiful, and also three years younger, and she viewed me as a threat.

I told him I did not want to displease his first wife, and that perhaps he and I could meet secretly. I agreed to sleep with him whenever he required, and he agreed to pay me for my services. His slave would come to me with his summons, day or night, and I never complained. The son was not a bad man, although he expected so much of me, and I worked hard to earn my money. In fact, we became friends gradually, and he told me he believed slaves should be given a fair chance of earning their freedom. He enjoyed my company for about three years, during which time I bore him two sons, both of whom died of cholera a year apart when they were but infants.

When I was fifteen and growing too old for his tastes, a new slave girl came to the house. She was thirteen and he fell for her immediately. He told me my services were no longer required, but I did not mind because I had enough money to buy my freedom from the master. Like my sons, my parents had also died of cholera—the previous year—so I was free to go where I pleased and had no responsibilities. But I had no way of earning a living, except to beg or to become a concubine, and I did not want either. I was still beautiful, and my figure was firm and youthful, even though I had borne two children. I dreamed of becoming the first wife of a wealthy man, but knew that as a former slave who had already had children, the best I could hope for was to become a minor wife while I was still young and desirable.

But then another opportunity presented itself. In the slum where I lived, on the river near the port, I heard talk of the white-skinned farangs, who were all said to be very wealthy, with so much money they could buy whatever they liked. I had seen some of these strange creatures walking in the markets. They were always dripping with sweat and they talked so loudly in their ugly languages.

Some of the women in the slum where I lived said the farang men loved the Siamese women, and some had even married them. Farang men had only one wife, who had all her husband's riches and attention for herself. They had concubines, of course, but they were usually kept hidden away, and did not receive any honour or respect. This sounded strange to me, and I wondered if being the wife of a farang would be too exhausting, not having any other wives to share the burden. But it did not really deter me.

I decided that the only way I could make a better life for myself was to know one of these farangs. They were ugly, it was true, but I would rather have married an ugly farang who was wealthy, than a handsome Siamese man who had nothing. I decided the best way to meet these men was to learn more about them and their language. In those days, only the king and a few noblemen were reputed to be able to converse with them. I was sure it would not be so easy for me, but I had heard that ex-slaves were sometimes taken in and educated by the farang missionaries.

One day, I got into my little boat—it was practically the only thing I owned, and it was so old and worn, it was likely to sink at any time— and rowed upstream until I reached the American mission. I hid my boat under the landing and arrived on their doorstep, explaining that I had used all my money to buy myself out of slavery, and that I had nowhere else to go.

The missionaries always tried to accommodate young people such as I, because they imagined their charity would buy our devotion to their religion. Most Siamese who went to them later realised their stupidity and embraced Buddhism once more.

The missionaries were very strange, but their religion was even stranger. Some could not marry; others could. It was very confusing at first, and seemed too ridiculous to take seriously. Anyway, I stayed with them for eighteen months, and during that time I tried very hard to learn English. I even learnt to read and write a little. But more important, I learned to read and write Siamese, and discovered I had a natural ability to learn fast.

I worked as a servant at the mission when there were visitors, as a way of repaying my board in kind. I even hoped that I might marry one of the young missionaries, but I soon discovered they were interested only in marrying Christian women, and I could not bring myself to convert to their religion. It was too strange, and I could not accept it, or even pretend that I did. I met Joseph Shaw at the mission, although I think he hardly remembers me from that time.

The only employment for a woman such as myself was domestic service, but I knew I would still be little better off than I was as a slave. So I did something that I think few, if any, Siamese had done before. I hired myself out as a temporary servant to foreign households when they needed extra help for their dinners and parties. Usually they borrowed friends' servants for their functions, and the servants themselves did not benefit. But with my new scheme, I was my own mistress, and the harder I worked, the more money I made.

I was in great demand when foreigners realised I could understand some English. I knew how to cook proficiently, and I could remember most of the strange recipes for their bland dishes without the need for translation. I worked many nights at balls and dinner parties, and also afternoons at women's lunches, teas, and card games. I still lived in my hovel in the slum, but I saved the pittance they paid me and hoped it would not be long until I found a man who would keep me in style.

Months passed, and although I knew I was still as attractive as ever, and always took care with my appearance, no one seemed to notice me. I began to loathe serving them. Then, one night at the British Consulate, I saw Edward, your father, and I think he fell in love with me the moment he saw me. We spent that night together, like husband and wife, and a few weeks later, when he had rented a house, I went to live with him.

The house was like a palace to me. It was the first time I had ever slept in a bed, and the first time I had not had to work from dawn to dusk for someone else. I cooked and cleaned for Edward, but in the evenings we dined together. He promised that soon he would hire a maid, so that I would no longer have to work in the house.

Then his wife, Charlotte, arrived from Australia with their daughter, Elizabeth, and my new life changed. I had always known about Charlotte, and accepted that she would be the first wife. I was not upset, but when this woman arrived, she treated me like a slave, ordering me around from morning to night. Worst of all, I was not to have my own room upstairs as I had thought, but was sent out to live in the servants' quarters and had to pretend to be a maid.

Edward was ashamed of me and had not told Charlotte who I was. He sometimes came to my room at night, but he left as soon as he had satisfied himself, and I slept alone on a bedroll on the hard floor. The daughter, Elizabeth, was treated like a princess, and she also gave me orders—she, who should have been made to treat me with the respect I deserved as her father's wife. I could have accepted that from a boy—

after all, mothers must obey their sons and their husband's sons by other women—but not from her.

When I discovered I was pregnant with Edward's child, I was very excited. I thought the news must surely please him so much that I would be restored to my former place. After all, Charlotte cruelly withheld herself from him and refused to have another child. But his reaction was the opposite to that I had expected. He told me I must pack my things and leave. He would care for me and for the child, but I was never to live in his house again. So I was pregnant without a husband— even though he did provide for me quite well, and I had a comfortable houseboat on the river. But I was so lonely, so alone. When the baby arrived, you my darling Anchalee, my friends laughed at your nose and your green eyes. But I did not care what they said, and I thought you were beautiful. I loved you from the moment I first held you, and I was determined that your life would be better than mine; that you would have everything that I had not; and that you would want for nothing. Somehow, I had to get us both back to Edward's house.

He visited us regularly, but I told him nothing of my hopes. His new maid, Porntip, was a friend of mine, and I knew she would help me. He still had not told Charlotte about me, or you, and so I decided it was time she knew. I asked Porntip to bring Charlotte to visit me, and I told her that Edward was the father of my child. She was so shocked she nearly fainted, and then she demanded Porntip take her away. Shortly after, she went away to England, and I once more went to live with Edward.

My happiness would have been complete, had it not been for Elizabeth, who did not go with her mother. Elizabeth was spoiled and badly behaved. She never accepted me, but I realised, only when it was too late, just how devious she was. Charlotte must have told her to spy on me, and she continued this even after the news came that her mother had died at sea.

I had not wished such suffering on Charlotte, but I was not sad to know she was never coming back. Elizabeth was jealous of the affection her father had for me, and she wanted me gone. Even though she was only a child, she already had a sly and secretive nature.

One day, she was spying on me, hidden behind the curtains in the front room, and she saw me take a small piece of silver from a cabinet She noticed me take another piece shortly after, and she decided to tell her father I was stealing from him.

You may wonder yourself, my love, what I was doing. The truth is that I was in need of money that Edward could not know about. I was pregnant again, and it terrified me that he would be angry, as he was the first time. I was also worried that when I had lost my attractiveness in pregnancy, he would take another wife, and my place, and yours, would be lost. I wanted you to have everything. I did not want you to have to share with many brothers and sisters. After all, his reaction to my first pregnancy had been awful, so I did not want to displease him again and risk your future. I could not let that happen. I decided to destroy the baby.

I knew of a farang doctor who had a secret surgery in Chinatown where he performed such operations. But it was expensive, and the doctor expected to be paid first. I took the silver pieces to a pawn shop in Chinatown, and I swear I would have recovered them as soon as I was able.

Meanwhile, Elizabeth told Joseph Shaw what she had seen, and they both went to Edward. I do not blame Mr. Joseph for that—there was nothing else he could do. Edward had his assistant follow me, and so discovered what I had done. He said he would never forgive me, that he no longer loved me, and that I must leave him forever. But he also insisted that he would keep you, Anchalee, and that he would bring you up as his daughter should be, and that you would want for nothing as long as I stayed away. I had no choice. I had to agree. And so I went. The fancy clothes I wore sometimes while I was Edward's wife were of no use to me now, but I kept them, as well as a small silver locket he had given me when we first met. I want you to have the locket, and I have instructed Mr. Joseph to give it to you with this letter.

As I write these words, I wonder how you will look when you are grown and you are reading this. I have discovered that I have a fatal disease. A farang missionary doctor who was kind enough to treat me, explained to me that it is called consumption, and that I have only a *year or two left to live. I know now that I shall never again see my little daughter; never see you grow up, marry, and have children of your own. I will die a broken woman. But, my dear Anchalee, I shall live through you. It is you who must make my struggles and my death worth something.*

Elizabeth must pay for her treachery; for her cruelty to me; and for depriving you of your mother. Only you can decide how she must be punished. But the one who caused so much unhappiness should not be allowed to find happiness herself. For the sake of your poor mother, who will be long dead by the time you read this, I ask you to remember what has happened; to never forget that your sister, Elizabeth, is the cause of our lifelong separation.

When Sam returned to the bar, it was to find Joseph staring out the window. He was speechless as he handed the pages back.

"So you see, Joseph, at the time you married Elizabeth, she was still in love with me." Joseph looked sharply at him, but Sam quickly continued. "Still, that's not the point. We were discussing Anchalee. She was determined, Joseph—so she set out to marry me, to hurt Elizabeth by flaunting the man who was once her lover.

"Anchalee knew I was Joe's father—from the beginning, I know—and having married me, she then decided that if she brought Elizabeth and me into constant contact, there was a good chance the old flame would be rekindled. It was . . . as you now know, and Anchalee picked her time to tell you, thinking you'd surely separate from Elizabeth, but knowing also that she'd never agree to let me go. Anchalee's plan was simple, Joseph—that Elizabeth would end up alone."

He stopped to light another cigarette. "She's a devious and evil little bitch, Joseph, believe me. It's insane. A ridiculous vendetta over something that probably never happened. That letter, to me, is pure fabrication. Or at least Anchalee's mother misunderstood the situation. Elizabeth was only eight or nine years old at the time! How could a child that age be so cunning and vindictive? Having read that letter, and knowing Anchalee as I do now, as far as I'm concerned it's a case of like mother, like daughter. They're both wilful and jealous bitches."

Sam took another sip of his drink, put his cigarette to his lips, and sank back in his chair. He seemed to calm a little. "But anyway, she realised early on that this revenge scheme had failed . . . because Elizabeth truly loves you." At this, Joseph looked up again. "She was—and is—happy with you, Joseph. And you've made her more content than I ever could have. It's to your credit you've decided to stay with Elizabeth. In similar circumstances, I can't say as I'd do the same." He paused. "And the child. . . ?"

"Will be brought up as my own, of course."

"Of course," Sam said, almost bitterly. "I know the hurt I've caused, Joseph, and it's not like me to seek sympathy—or deserve any—but it's ironic that I've lost out in this, too."

"How exactly?" Joseph sneered.

"I have a wife who despises me, and the woman I love, and our son, and our unborn child, belong to another man. I suppose you'd tell me it's God's punishment for my sins."

"Something like that," Joseph replied. For a moment he felt almost sorry for the man, but then he came to his senses.

"So where do we go from here?" Sam asked.

Joseph was still shocked by the revelations, and needed time to ponder them. But he believed, more than ever, that his plan was the only solution.

He looked directly at Sam. "I think, under the circumstances, that our two families must be parted indefinitely. We must all pray for the courage to forgive each other, but there's no possibility for a relationship between us in future. We're better off completely separated."

Sam hesitated, but then nodded. "It's the only way, I guess. Elizabeth's adamant she wants to save her marriage to you, Joseph." He sighed, then shrugged. "But how will we do it? Bangkok's a small place for foreigners. It would be difficult to avoid each other, unless we became hermits."

"I've thought of that. And I have a solution."

"Why didn't you tell me?"

"I wanted to spare you."

"Spare me? *Spare* me? Elizabeth, if only you had told me the letter was not your doing. If only you had trusted me. . . ."

"Joseph, it was our wedding night."

"All the more reason to be honest; to confide in me. I'd not have thought badly of you."

"I thought it was too late; the damage had been done; her plan accomplished. What purpose would it have served?"

"I could have helped, could have done *something*. And who knows, all this might have been avoided."

"I still cannot believe it of her. That she planned everything, using you as some sort of pawn. . . ."

Despite his distress at her affair, Joseph was sorry for her. "If it weren't for her interference, you would have married Sam."

"Then I do have something to thank Anchalee for," she told him. "I've found true love and goodness in you, Joseph, that I could never have had with him. I know that now."

He looked down, and he was sure they could go on together. "We'll not see them again. There's no other way."

Her eyes filled with tears, but she nodded in agreement. She still could not believe what he had told her about Anchalee. And she could not help it—but she had to address the matter with her sister.

18th May, 1886

Dear Anchalee,

I can hardly comprehend what Joseph has told me, but he is not a man to stray from the truth, and so I must believe him. I did not come to see you personally because I was not sure you would listen to me, but please, I implore you, read this letter in its entirety before discarding it.

Anchalee, what your mother wrote about me in her letter simply is not true, and you must, above all, believe me when I tell you that I never meant to do her harm. I am not, by any means, saying that she was lying. I am sure Kesri believed she was telling you the truth, but I am afraid that she misinterpreted that unfortunate event.

I give you my word that I never intended to spy on Kesri. What I saw that day was purely an accident, because I was already in the room, reading behind the curtains, when your mother entered. I intended to surprise her, but then I saw her take the silver and was afraid that she would berate me if she discovered me there. We hardly knew each other, and I was often in fear of her moods. I admit that I did not trust her, but I was a child, Anchalee; I had no conception of wickedness.

After my mother died, I confess that I did believe that Kesri was partly responsible. It is true, Charlotte was many miles from Siam when she passed away, but I could see only that she had left because of your mother. In my child's mind, I reasoned that if she had not had to return to England, she would not have died on that ship.

Anchalee, my mother loved Father so much, and she suffered hell for him. There were many miscarriages and great pain, and yet she did not 'withhold herself' from him, as the letter alleges. She was like me, Anchalee. The doctors had told her there should be no more children. She and Father were both afraid for her life. Then he met Kesri, who was so willing, so young, and so beautiful.

You must understand that Charlotte's values were those of a Victorian lady. She was deeply shocked when she discovered Father's relationship with your mother, and when he refused to give up Kesri, she could not bear such a betrayal, as she saw it. She conceded bitterly, but gracefully. She would never have been able to marry again, because she would not have considered divorce, and would have lived the rest of her life alone, even though she had a husband and a daughter across the seas.

We both lost our mothers, Anchalee; both tragically, and both long before their time.

It might perhaps come as a surprise to you that I know you forged the letter that made Joseph send Sam away, therefore ensuring we did not marry. I saw the letter on our wedding night, and realised immediately what had happened. I thought, when your engagement was announced, that your only plan had been to win Sam for yourself. That, in itself, was bad enough, but I had no idea that there was so much more behind your actions.

You have done me great wrong and great harm, Anchalee, but how can I blame you when I myself am not blameless? I am so ashamed of what I have done that I sometimes wish I could be swallowed whole by the earth. I shall never forgive myself. This will be the last time I shall write to you, but I hope you find peace one day in your life. It is the best either of us can hope for.

Your sister,

Elizabeth Ann Shaw

Anchalee folded the letter and felt a hollowness she had never experienced before. There was no satisfaction and no success. And yet when she thought of Elizabeth carrying Sam's child, she was cold with jealousy. For despite herself, she had come to realise that she cared more for him than she ever imagined she would. Now, with the prospect of losing him because of his disgust at her, she found that she wanted him more than ever. She looked out the window with tears in her eyes. "I've fallen in love with him," she cried aloud. "And he'll never love me as he loves her."

After what she had done, she could not hate Elizabeth. But still, the gulf between them was too wide now to bridge. There was too much unhappiness, too much deceit, and too many betrayals. They would be strangers and that was the way it had to be.

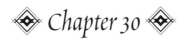

❖ Chapter 30 ❖

2nd June 1886

Dear Mr. Shaw,

This letter is to formally confirm your appointment to the Presbyterian Mission station at Chiengmai, Northern Siam. As discussed and agreed, you will leave Bangkok as soon as Mrs. Shaw is able to travel—most probably in late November or early December.

The journey, as you know, is unpredictable, and can take up to three months or longer, but we presume, at that time of the year, it will take about two months, by river and elephant. Dr. and Mrs. McGilvary will expect you early in the New Year.

May I personally commend you, Mr. Shaw, for your brave gesture in volunteering to take up residence in our most remote station. Your skills as a teacher will be of immense benefit to the community, to be sure. However, let me also reiterate how much we here in Bangkok shall miss your gentle manner with our students, not to mention your excellent Bible readings in the church each Sunday. God speed.

Yours faithfully,

Rev. S. G. McFarland,
Principal,
King's College.

Elizabeth had not objected to the move to Chiengmai, believing it for the best, and even as a penance. Joseph did not intend it as a punishment at all, however. It was simply the only way, in his mind, for them to survive as a family.

He had, at first, wanted to leave immediately, but he understood that the journey would be even more perilous for a woman with child. And with Elizabeth's delicate condition, he might very well be sending her to her death. It was safest to remain in Bangkok for the five months or so until the birth. He would attend to business while Elizabeth stayed home with Joe, resting and preparing herself for the ordeal to come. In August they sent some of their furniture on ahead of them, so it would be ready in their house in Chiengmai.

Joseph had decided to go to the North no matter what happened—even if, God forbid, Elizabeth should pass away in childbirth, as he feared she might. If that dreadful possibility did actually happen, he determined that he would still go with Joe, and would try to raise the boy with love enough for two parents. He would never marry again.

Until this latest episode, he could easily forget that Joe was not his natural son. The reminder served to make him strive even harder to love the boy as his own, never to hold the identity of his real father against him. But he could already see something in the boy's eyes at times that unsettled him. It was a dogged determination, a stubborn streak that, he realised, came straight from Sam Taylor.

Joseph wasn't afraid of the journey to Chiengmai, although its perils were well-known in Bangkok: jungle fever, tigers, poisonous snakes and rampaging elephants, and bandits and river pirates who thought nothing of slaughtering an entire family for a mere gold watch. He believed that God's will would be done, and if they were meant to come through the journey unscathed, they would. Besides, he had been most interested in the work of the Chiengmai mission station since the McGilvarys had opened it in 1867. He had met Dr. McGilvary twice in Bangkok—in 1873 and 1881—and had been intrigued by the man's experiences, and inspired by his courage. But he had not thought it fair, after he married Elizabeth, to isolate her from Bangkok and her family, especially since she had been away at school in England for so long. He had kept his interest to himself.

But at least they would not have to endure what the pioneering McGilvarys had experienced when they first journeyed north. He remembered Dr. McGilvary telling him about conditions in Chiengmai when he had first arrived with his wife, Sophia, and their two children, in 1867. Because of a misunderstanding with the chief of Chiengmai, after a four-month journey they arrived to find that the land and timber for a house that had been promised was not to be provided at all. They were forced to camp in a public *sala* for a year, their every move watched by intrigued locals who had never seen Europeans before.

"But let me assure you," Dr. McGilvary told Joseph when he had visited mission headquarters in Bangkok a few years previously, "that they were very much more afraid of us than we were of them. They believed us at first to be evil spirits, I suppose, and we heard mothers warn their children to stay away, otherwise they might be eaten by us! Eventually, though, they came to accept our presence—especially when they saw how our medicines could help them. Some even began to enjoy our Bible readings. Our first converts came from that time, and I do recall that year fondly, despite its hardships."

After nearly a year, the McGilvarys finally received materials to build a house, but it was mainly bamboo, and for more than three years, they and their fellow missionaries—the Wilsons, who had arrived in February, 1868—had to live in fragile dwellings that provided little protection from the elements.

Now, of course, they resided comfortably in fine teak houses, and Joseph was assured that a similar residence would be provided for his own family. The Edict of Religious Toleration in 1878, issued by the new Siamese resident high commissioner, Phya Thep Worachun, on behalf of the king of Siam, had guaranteed that

Christians would be permitted to practise their religion, including observance of the Sabbath, without harassment or persecution.

But first, there was the birth. Joseph found himself wishing, early on, that she might lose the child naturally. It would certainly be less of a threat to her own health. He had severely admonished himself for such thoughts, and had prayed for the poor child's soul—but still, the thought persisted. Life would be so much more tolerable without the reminder every day of her infidelity. He could forgive, but he could hardly forget. Horrific visions sometimes came to him of her in his arms, and he tried to blank them out.

He toiled harder than ever, taking on extra work in some of the city's slums, teaching the children there to read. He had been an avid pupil himself of the Siamese language, and his patience over the years had been rewarded. He was fluent in the language, and could read and write it more than adequately. It was most useful in his slum work, where English was of no use to impoverished children who would have no contact with wealthy foreigners. It was better they became literate in their own language.

King Chulalongkorn had visited Europe, and was impressed with the standards of education there. He had made great efforts to improve it in Siam. A Department of Education had been established around 1880, and primary schools in Bangkok had many thousands of pupils.

But the poorest children could not possibly hope to attend. Most were already required to supplement their parents' incomes if they were even to eat, and it was these children he hoped to reach. Their lot was in stark contrast to the lavishly-dressed sons of noblemen—with their retinues of servants—whom he was accustomed to teaching.

But he found the slum children to be quick and willing learners. He would spread out a blanket on the dusty ground, and the children would crowd around. There were never enough pencils or paper to go round, but those who missed out were content to use their fingers to trace the Siamese characters in the dust. They loved listening to the stories he told from the books he borrowed from the school—most of which were translated from foreign folk and fairy tales—and even their parents would crowd closer to listen when they had time.

In mid-October, when Elizabeth was swollen and almost immobile, she was surprised one day to take delivery of a heavy wooden box from England. She had—in the tumult that had swept through the family after Edward's death—almost forgotten her father's last, and secret, bequest. Anxiety once again overwhelmed her, and she could not decide whether to welcome it, or wish it condemned to the bed of the ocean.

It was about the size of a large hat box, but extremely heavy, and it sat—where she had asked the maid and delivery boy to open and leave it—on her drawing room floor beside the *chaise longue* she was resting on. She tentatively lifted the lid, and inside saw a well-wrapped package and an envelope. She decided to open the envelope first.

For the third time in their marriage, Joseph longed for her screams to end. She had gone into labour three weeks early, and this time was no easier than the others.

Once again, her pain ceased abruptly—only on this occasion, the silence was followed by a tiny wail.

"Thank the Lord!" Joseph cried in relief, but he soon began to wonder why he heard no more sounds from Elizabeth or the baby, and why it was taking the doctor so long to emerge. He paced the floor, praying she would live.

When Dr. Newhaven finally came out of the room thirty minutes later, he anticipated the question Joseph dared not ask.

"Your wife will recover," he told him, and Joseph let out a long sigh. "She's lost a lot of blood, but she is relatively comfortable."

"And the child, doctor?"

"It was a girl, Joseph."

"Was? I heard her cries."

"I'm sorry. I did everything I could to save her. She cried once, and then she simply stopped breathing."

The doctor, who was also a family friend, took off his glasses and rubbed his tired eyes with the back of his hand. He put a hand on Joseph's shoulder and said simply, "I'm so sorry."

Elizabeth lay there, her eyes open but unseeing, staring straight ahead. Beside her, in the little crib Joseph had made, was a tiny bundle covered with a clean white pillow case.

"Perhaps it's for the best," she whispered.

"It's God's will," he replied. But when he looked at her expressionless face, he knew he would regret those words for the rest of his life.

As she awoke, she tried to sit up, craning her neck so she could see into the little crib by the window. It was empty, and the netting, the lace cover, and the white pillow were gone. Where was her dead child? She heard raised voices from somewhere in the house; voices that sounded angry.

Slowly and painfully, she struggled to get out of bed.

"In the name of goodness man, do you not think you've done enough?"

"I must see her. I cannot live with myself otherwise," he slurred. "Do you have no compassion?"

"How can you even dare to speak of compassion?"

"For God's sake, it's my child who has died."

For Joseph, it was as if he had been stabbed. The smell of stale whisky on Sam's breath permeated the room, and made him even more repugnant in Joseph's eyes.

"How dare you come into my house like this, you drunken wretch. You disgust me. You're not fit to be a father, much less a husband. You've destroyed her life, Taylor. And with it mine, and that of our son."

"Your son?"

"Yes, my son. You may have sired him, you devil, but I'm his father. Now get out!"

Sam took a step toward Joseph, his hands at his sides, open palmed, entreating. "Just one minute with her. Let me at least tell her how sorry I am. . . ."

Elizabeth came into the doorway just as Sam stumbled backward and slumped to the ground.

"Joseph, what's wrong? What's happening?"

For the first time in his life, Joseph had hit another human being. All the anger, the frustration, and the degradation Sam had brought out in him, swelled within him until it burst and erupted like a poisoned pustule. And Sam, who had already been swaying in his inebriation, had fallen like a fly.

Joseph stared at the unconscious man, and then at his wife in her white nightgown, silhouetted in the doorway.

"My God, Joseph, what have you done? What have you done? You've killed him!"

But Sam came round quickly and began to laugh as he rose to his feet—a guttural, bitter laugh that Joseph and Elizabeth would remember for years. He felt the first rush of blood from his broken nose, and pulled a handkerchief from his pocket and held it to his face. He turned as he stumbled out—his laugh ceasing and his mouth twisted with the pain—and said, "Well done, Joseph. I was wondering when you'd do that."

November 10th, 1886

Dear Sam,

I do not know how to start this letter, only, I suppose, to say goodbye. Joseph regrets yesterday's events, and is ashamed of himself for his outburst. But you should never have come. My only hope is that you can leave the past be, and that you can continue life with your family, as we shall also have to do.

You know that in a short time we will be leaving for the mission at Chiengmai. I know you have travelled there several times before and have a great fondness for the place, but I beg of you, I implore you, not to return. Please do not tempt fate. It can only make things worse.

I know what you said to Joseph about the child, and I confess that I had not given you credit for such paternal feelings. I should have known better, for despite your insensitive exterior, I know you are a man of substance and of deep feelings. And that is why I am writing to you, without Joseph's knowledge, concerning Joe.

Joseph is right when he says that he is, and will be, the only father Joe will know, but that cannot negate the fact that you are his true physical father, and I have decided that it would be more than cruel for you never to know anything of his life. Yet I cannot permit you to seek information from us, nor can you see him as he grows up.

My solution is that I shall write to you once at the close of each year, in which I shall tell you of his progress. The letter will be disguised on the envelope as being from a business associate of yours in Chiengmai, named Mr. Dian Cecht. The irony will not be lost on you when I tell you he is the Irish god of healing. You see, a British education has been of some benefit to me!

I ask of you one more thing. Please destroy this letter when you have read it, for it can serve no purpose but to incriminate us if discovered. Correspondence from Mr. Cecht will be disguised so as to appear inconsequential, but you shall understand plainly its meaning. These you may keep or destroy as you see fit. That is all, Sam. Please do not try to contact me or to reply to my letters.

Elizabeth Ann Shaw

Part Three

February 1904 – May 1905

◈ Chapter 31 ◈

Modern Bangkok
by Samuel Taylor
Photography by Kesri Taylor and Edward Fairburn

Prologue

Foreigners were still calling Bangkok "the Venice of the East" when I first arrived in the 1870s. Now, in 1904, the daily life of the city is concentrated as much on its roads as on its river. But it is still the stately Maenam Chao Phya, the "River of Kings", that gives Siam's capital city its character, its charm, and its wit. And it is still this river that provides access to the rest of the country, for there are no roads beyond Bangkok.

In thirty years, Bangkok has transformed from a medieval city, hundreds of years in development behind the United States and England, to one that is preparing to join the modern world of the twentieth century. There are roads and railways, electric tramways and lights, telephones and a telegraph service, a reliable postal service and daily steamers to Singapore and Hong Kong and one of the East's finest race-courses. There are three banks, several fine hotels run by Europeans, a French hospital, a British nursing home, and plenty of European, British, and American doctors.

The city's official population is around 500,000, including 800 or 900 Europeans and Americans, or "farang", as the Siamese call them. Only a decade ago, the postal roll gave the city's population as 169,000, with 300 Westerners. Besides the official inhabitants, there are many thousands more who live in makeshift slums, and who are not therefore counted in any census.

The foreigners who come here have changed in nature since the early days of modernization when I first arrived. Then, there were many like myself, who were hungry for adventure, eager to experience a different culture, and keen to see things few other white men had seen. Now, they are mainly businessmen and diplomats. Of course, the missionaries are still here, and although they made valiant efforts through much of the last century to persuade the Siamese to convert to Christianity, only a few have given up Buddhism. The converts are, anyway, mostly Chinese rather than true Siamese. I am pleased to note that through all its changes, upheavals, advancements, and opening to the outside world, Bangkok is still as Oriental, as essentially Siamese, as it always was.

Samuel Taylor
Bangkok, 1904

Before he could go on to read over the first chapter of the final draft of his new book, he was interrupted by a knock on his office door. Kesri entered with a pile of photographs—some taken as far back as 1868—and put them on the desk in front of her father. "Here's the last of Grandfather's Bangkok prints."

"Thank you. How's your own work going?"

"I'm still developing my latest photographs today. But they should be ready for you by tomorrow morning." She smiled across at him, and he marvelled again at this beautiful, delightful daughter.

Her long black hair fell past her shoulders, and—naturally—she had inherited the dark complexions of both her father and her mother. She was slim, much taller than Siamese women—and most Siamese men too—although of more European than Siamese build, with long legs and a narrow waist. Her large eyes tilted up at the outer corners as her mother's had, but the most fascinating thing about them was that they often appeared to change colour—from a mysterious jade green to a clear honey brown, depending on the light, or even her mood. She had inherited much of her mother's beauty, but where Anchalee had been sophisticated and knowing, there was a sweetness and innocence about Kesri that her mother had never possessed.

"What are you thinking of?" she asked her father.

"I was thinking about your mother, actually. And how much like her—but not like her—you are."

"It doesn't seem a year already, does it? I still come home expecting her to be here, dressing for a ball or making sure the table's set correctly for a dinner party."

"She certainly loved the social occasions. She always did, from the time I first met her. She was only about thirteen then."

Kesri sat on the edge of his desk, eager to hear more. She loved hearing his reminiscences of the early days.

"And was she really allowed to go to a ball at that age? How did she persuade Grandfather to allow it?"

"Your mother had a way of getting what she wanted. When she set her heart on going to a ball, she wouldn't take no for an answer from Edward."

"She must have been very mature for her age."

"Yes, she was, you're right. And I'm glad to see you're not your mother's daughter in that respect."

"It's funny, you know, I always think of her as happy and. . . . Well, laughing and dressed up for parties, wearing her sparkling jewellery and her beautiful gowns. I can't seem to remember her being really sick for very long at all."

"Well, she didn't want to admit, even to herself, that it had finally got a hold on her too. It killed her mother and her father. She nursed Grandfather until he died, so she knew exactly what was in store for her. She needed enormous strength just to keep going as long as she did." He looked up to find Kesri's eyes filled with tears.

"She wouldn't want us to be sad, sweetheart."

She managed a weak smile. "Oh, by the way, there's a letter for you. Mr. Cecht has written from the North." She retrieved an envelope from the bottom of the pile of prints and handed it to him. "I haven't seen that name for quite some time. Strange isn't it? I always remember it, even though he hardly ever writes. And he has never come to the house, has he? He must visit Bangkok from time to time?"

"Not to my knowledge. He prefers to stay away from the city. Business upcountry."

"Well, I'll be getting on with that developing."

He waited until she had closed the door behind her before tearing the letter open. He had not heard from Elizabeth since December, and he hoped nothing was wrong. There was a reliable postal service now, both within the country and overseas, so it was unlikely that letters would have gone missing. In fact, the fortnightly service to Chiengmai had come as early as October 1885. But it was a long and difficult journey then, making the post somewhat unreliable and often late, with postmen having to trek through the jungle at the end of the journey to reach the Northern city.

With the beginning of rail construction in 1891, the mail service improved each year. The first line, between Bangkok and Paknam, had opened in 1893; Korat had been reached in the Northeast; and a line was progressing steadily north to Chiengmai. Sam loved facts and figures such as these, and he went to much effort to record them in his travel work. In recent years, however, his adventurous spirit had waned slightly, and his journeys had become few and far between.

Nevertheless, he had found a way to continue writing in the same spirit—and at the same time release his creative and emotional feelings without having to travel—by becoming an adventure novelist. His books—with their main character, Thomas Yearby, and his travels throughout Asia and the Pacific—drew upon all his own experiences, and already extended to ten volumes. Each new one was eagerly awaited by a British and North American public hungry for travellers' tales, both tall and true.

He was disappointed to find inside the envelope only one thin sheet with a single paragraph of writing.

1st February, 1904

Dear Mr. Taylor,

> *Just a note to inform you that our esteemed colleague, Mr. J., will be in Bangkok on his way to us in late February. He intends, against our advisement, to spend some time in the capital before proceeding to us. He is, nevertheless, well informed as to whom to avoid in the city, and it is our fervent hope that he will not have to contend with any unwelcome advances from certain unsolicited influences.*
>
> *I remain, sir, a colleague with your own best interests in mind,*

D. Cecht, esq.

Was she really so afraid of his influence after so many years? What did she imagine he would do? And what, he asked himself, would he do if he indeed came face to face with the son he didn't know—in fact, would not even recognise? Did he even want to meet him? He had Kesri, and she was the joy of his life. And he had discovered, over the years, that fatherhood suited him, and that he *was* a good father.

But in truth, he was curious. Joe was a man now, and he would have liked to have seen how he had grown. But he had to admit also that he no longer really thought of him as a son, and that if they ever were to meet, he had no idea of what he would say.

Elizabeth had been true to her word, and had kept him informed over the years, but now that Joe was an adult—it would be official on his twenty-first birthday that June—he supposed she might not write again. In his mind, she was still the young woman of their youth, and he hardly ever thought of the fact that she was now forty-three. After decades spent in the tropics, where the sun was not kind to fair skin, she could be expected to look that age, and more.

He went to put the letter in the bottom drawer of his desk with the others, and was compelled to pick up the pile and leaf through them. Certain ones stood out from the others; the ones that marked milestones in the boy's life. But there was never any word of *herself*. She never gave him an inkling of how she felt; how she coped; if she was happy; or if she ever thought of him at all.

December 1st, 1890

Dear Mr. Taylor,

You may be interested to hear that my young charge, Master J., is soon to be sent to England to ensure that he has a broad and liberal education. At his young, impressionable age, my associate and I feel this is for the best, although we shall miss his engaging countenance.

We believe Harrow is a most suitable public boarding school, and shall monitor his progress with eager anticipation. We are hoping Master J. may continue at Oxford or Cambridge, with a view perhaps to joining our company at some later date. We also feel it will be of immense benefit for the young man to grow up around suitable cousins and acquaintances at home, as certain possible future influences in our adopted homeland are a concern to us.

Our work continues in the North, but we do not seem to make many sales. Still, persistence is all. I hope your family is well. Regards and best wishes for Christmas.

Yours,

Dian Cecht

December 1st, 1895
Oriental Hotel, Bangkok

Dear Mr. Taylor,

By the time you read this, I shall be on my way to England, for the first time in thirteen years. My mother passed away

342

recently, and I am returning to settle the estate and also to see our young friend, who has been there for five years and is pining for Siam.

He is at an age when he believes he knows better than his elders, but we maintain that England is the best place for him until he attains his majority and can decide his own path. He is a bright student, though rather a dreamer, becomes easily bored or distracted, and is never satisfied with remaining in the one place, or so his school reports inform us. He is, I should say, quite like his father in these respects, and I believe you have made that gentleman's acquaintance on one or two occasions.

Please forgive me, sir, for not informing you earlier of my arrival in Bangkok. You may have assumed that in such an event, we could conceivably have met for some small conversation. However, with my grief at my mother's death being quite current, and recalling the other business that has occurred historically, you will appreciate my detachment.

Yours,

D. Cecht

December 1st, 1901

Dear Mr. Taylor,

I should like to inform you of Master J's graduation at Harrow, and his acceptance by Oxford University for the coming academic year, where we have persuaded him to read classics, which we feel a suitable degree for a young gentleman. He may then continue in the study of some profession, perhaps in theology, we dare to hope, in order that he may enter the Church in due course. Thankfully, he shows, as yet, no hankering for an early marriage.

Yours faithfully,

D. Cecht

March 15th, 1903

Dear Mr. Taylor,

> *Please accept my sincere condolences on the passing of your wife. I am so dreadfully sorry. I should have liked to have met her again.*

> *Your friend,*

> *Elizabeth*

Sam smiled at this last one, despite its sad memories. In her distress at Anchalee's death, she had neglected her *nom de plume*. He perhaps should not have kept it, but he had been touched, because it was the first time she had revealed something of herself to him.

That brief note of condolence was the only letter he had received between the 1901 correspondence and the one that day. He supposed she had read of her sister's death in the *Bangkok Times* when it had arrived in Chiengmai several weeks after the obituary was published. It must have been a terrible way to learn of such news. He had wanted to write himself, but she had forbidden him ever to contact her, and he had decided, finally, that he could not risk breaking the frail line of communication he still had with her. He wondered, if she had been in Bangkok, would she have attended the funeral?

Thoughts of Anchalee crowded in then. After the turmoil that tore the two families apart, she seemed to settle down. She forgot her quest for revenge against her sister, and Elizabeth's name was not mentioned in their house for a long time. And although they continued to share the same house, they led separate lives and slept in separate bedrooms for the next three years. She approached him more than once, but he always rejected her advances, still angry with her for what she had done to Elizabeth—and angry with himself for his part in the events. He found temporary solace in brief, discreet affairs with other married women—to which she turned a blind eye—and over those years, his anger gradually dissipated, until it was finally gone. Companionship between them sprang from the simple need to bring up their daughter.

Then, one night in 1890, she simply moved back into his bedroom, without explanation or excuse. He did not ask her to leave. From that day they lived as a normal, married couple, and found that their relationship was a reasonable one, after all—although she stressed the fact that she wanted no more children. Kesri was enough to worry about, she told him, and they were careful.

Sam still indulged in the occasional passionate, short affair from time to time, but as the old century drew to a close, he seemed to lose heart for these romantic entanglements. He came to realise that he was searching for something that did not exist—another Elizabeth—and that it was better to concentrate on finding happiness where he could, in his own home.

The last four years were the happiest. They grew close and became true friends, although they never mentioned the dreadful first years together. Until one night, as they lay in bed together, she revealed how she had fallen in love with him even as she plotted against Elizabeth. "I couldn't see my love for you because I was blinded by my ridiculous obsession. And by the time I realised, it was almost too late. It took a long time to get you back." He had held her close then, and for the first time, felt he really loved her as a husband should love a wife.

She must have known then that she was sick, because the signs became unmistakable a short time later. He had found her, only to lose her to a cruel, painful death. When she died, he truly grieved for her, and for the years they had wasted. The house was so empty without her.

But then there was Kesri to think of. The shy girl of a year previously was blossoming into a lovely young woman, who was also becoming a talented photographer. She had been interested in the art ever since she had found the key to her grandfather's locked studio at the back of the house. But his old cameras were far too heavy and complicated for her to use, and they had been superseded many times by more advanced inventions.

Sam was delighted at her interest, and he visited Mr. J. Antonio's Charoen Krung Photographic Studio on New Road, opposite the Banque de l'Indochine, to purchase a new box camera, complete with accessories, a supply of film, and a book about photographic techniques and developing—which he presented to her on her sixteenth birthday.

She quickly mastered the mechanics, and in no time was experimenting with new artistic interpretations of her own—and visiting Mr. Antonio's shop herself to discuss what she had learnt. Her prints were so accomplished, that Sam was using some in his new book on Siam, along with historic pictures taken by Edward. He thought it was probably the first book to feature photographs by a man and his granddaughter in the one volume.

She had no recollection of her grandfather, of course—she had been only a baby when he died—but she felt she knew him through his pioneering work, which she greatly admired. Some of the images he had captured in the early days in Siam would be used in books and shown in museums for years to come. There were boxes and boxes of them, and she planned eventually to catalogue and preserve them all. She had even found one of the king's father, King Maha Mongkut—taken in 1868, according to the inscription on the back—at Hua Wan, where he had apparently journeyed with a large entourage to view an eclipse of the sun. It was one of the last ever photographs taken of him before he died.

Sam picked up the prints and leafed through them. She had a good eye for what would reproduce well, and had picked only the most suitable images. As he began to ponder which ones to include or omit, she knocked and came in again, another print in her hand.

"Forget one, did you?"

"No. This wouldn't be suitable for the book, but I just wondered who it was."

She held out the fading print and, as he took it, he immediately recognised the subject.

"She's very beautiful. Who is it, Father?"

Sam gazed at the picture of the young Elizabeth; the poised twenty-one-year-old he remembered vividly. It was how she had looked when he first saw her; head held high, but with a look of wide-eyed naïvety in her eyes.

"Don't you recognise her?" Kesri prompted.

"Yes. It's your Aunt Elizabeth."

"Ah, the one we mustn't speak of." She wondered yet again why he had been reluctant to tell her. "What really happened, Father? Why won't you tell me?"

Sam sighed. "Like I said, it's a complicated story, and I'm not sure that it should concern you."

"But they're my relatives—the only relatives I know. Or, rather don't know. They must come to Bangkok once in a while. And I'd love to go there to visit them. It would be an adventure for me. Think of the photographic possibilities! What could have been so bad?"

He made a show of busying himself with his papers, and spoke as if it were of little consequence. "It was . . . something between your mother and Aunt Elizabeth. As I said, nothing that concerns you."

"But it's been so long. It must have happened when I was a baby, because I don't remember ever seeing Aunt Elizabeth, Uncle Joseph, or cousin Joe. And Mother's no longer with us. If it doesn't concern me, why should I not see them? Don't you think the feud has gone on long enough?"

"There's no feud, Kesri. Things are just better left this way."

"But Aunt Elizabeth didn't even come to Mother's funeral."

"There's a lot you don't know, but it all happened a long time ago. And believe me, it's better left unspoken now."

"But what if I meet them socially? By accident. I'm bound to one day. Like the king's garden parties? Who knows when they could be there? People would think me most odd if I pretended not to know my own family. Everyone knows everyone else . . . you know that. They'd all be talking behind my back if that were to happen. Father, it would be so embarrassing."

It had occurred so long ago, that only a few long-term expatriates remembered. People came and went, and had long ago stopped gossiping about the rift, or speculating over its cause. There were new and more exciting scandals concerning younger, fresher beauties.

Even so, Sam considered what she said, and understood that she was right. He also understood her desire to be accepted, aware that she felt part of neither one world nor another—and at her age, that was a very confusing thing.

He didn't think there was much chance Elizabeth or Joseph would be in Bangkok, but suddenly recalled that young Joe would be—very soon, if not already.

He could only hope she did not come across him. He could not tell her, for if he did, she would undoubtedly go searching for him, forbidden or not.

"Well, yes, that's true," he agreed at last. "You must be polite, of course. Then there'll be no cause for gossip. But you're not to get involved with them, Kesri—in the unlikely event that you do meet any of them."

"Involved? Father, I doubt I'd even recognise them. Please, just agree that I may introduce myself, if I do meet them some time."

She should be studying law, he reckoned, for like a good barrister, she had left him with no argument.

"I suppose there'd be no real harm in that—for social appearances. But I'm not keen on the idea. And don't expect them to encourage any contact, either."

She kissed him on the cheek and skipped out. "I'm going for a fitting for my dress," she called as she left. "You remember? For the party next week."

He sat for a long time after she had gone, staring at the photograph of the girl who had been not much older when he first met her than his daughter was now.

He wondered how she had aged, how she looked now. He tried to fill in the lines of maturity that the years would have added, but it was impossible. He could think of her only as a radiant young woman.

He lit his cheroot and went to the window, looking down on the well-kept garden and wondering if he would ever see or speak to her again. Anchalee had thought he would. On her deathbed, her last words as she faded were of her sister. "Tell Elizabeth . . . that . . . that she . . . was right. Tell her our mothers. . . ."

But she had died before she could finish the sentence, and Sam still agonised over what she had meant to say.

Meanwhile, at Mrs. Smythe's Tailoring Shop—now run by her Siamese daughter-in-law—Kesri tried on the white high-necked dress, and looked with satisfaction at her reflection in the three-sided mirror. She hoped her father wouldn't be angry.

The garden party had a Victorian revival theme, and guests were invited to dress in the costumes of late last century. She had found this beautiful old dress of her mother's, and decided it was made for the occasion. It needed loosening slightly, but was otherwise perfect on her. Some of the guests who were recent arrivals to Siam would have to have new costumes made, but Kesri was proud to be wearing an original.

Mother must have been quite young when she wore it, perhaps about the time she attended that first ball, Kesri thought. It must have trailed on the ground, too, because it was just the right length for herself—reaching to the tips of her shoes—and Mother had been shorter, she knew.

She had also found a matching white and pink-trimmed parasol in the trunk, but had not been able to recover the hat that completed the ensemble. Instead, Mrs. Smythe's daughter-in-law had made her a new Victorian-style bonnet that framed her face prettily with white silk roses and little bows.

On the Saturday of the party, Kesri dressed carefully, asking her maid to help her put up her long dark hair under the bonnet. She wished she had curls, or at least some wave in her hair, like her friend, Janie. But her hair was perfectly straight, and required a lot of coaxing with pins to stay in place. It was the bain of her life, for although she had inherited the straight hair of the Siamese, it was not thick and strong like theirs, but fine and brittle, making it difficult to style. Still, she and Noi eventually managed, and as she stood back to admire herself in her full-length mirror, she smiled.

"I do look like I belong in the last century, don't I?" she remarked in Siamese. Anchalee had been determined that her daughter spoke both English and Siamese fluently.

"You do, Miss Kesri. Your father will be proud to escort you." Noi was much more comfortable with Kesri than she had been with Anchalee. She had been a young girl when she first came to work for the Fairburns in 1879. She was middle-aged now, and Kesri treated her with kindness and respect—almost like an older friend—encouraging her to voice her opinions, and never to bow down and kneel on the floor before her. Noi loved her for it, but did, in turn, make sure she was always properly respectful toward Kesri. Indeed, it was not difficult for Noi to keep her head lower than Kesri's, for the mistress of the house was a good six inches taller than the maid.

"Do you remember Mother wearing this dress?" Kesri asked hopefully. "It must have been for an important occasion."

Noi pretended to busy herself by adjusting the neckline. How could she tell her that this dress had never belonged to her mother. She didn't want to lie, yet was unable to tell the truth. "I'm sorry, Miss Kesri, I can't seem to remember your mother wearing it at all. But I'm getting old and forgetful."

"Nonsense, Noi. You look younger every day." She swirled away then, down the stairs and into the parlour, where Sam was waiting. He had shaken out one of his old morning suits for the event, and the coat, waistcoat, and striped trousers were only slightly tighter than they had been twenty years before.

"Well, Father, here I am," she announced.

When he saw her, he was almost dumbstruck. She was lovely in the white gown, but it was not pride in her that rendered him speechless. It was something about the dress that made him feel uneasy; something that stirred his memory like a whirlpool. Where had he seen a dress like this before?

"I did it to surprise you, Father."

"Did what, Kesri?"

She twirled once more before him. "Don't you recognise it? It's an old dress of Mother's. It hardly needed any alterations, either. Isn't it perfect?"

A long-forgotten, once cherished image was forming in his mind. But he was sure that image was not of Anchalee. "Where did you find this gown?" he asked.

"In a trunk in the studio. The lid had so much dust on it, I don't think it had been opened for twenty years."

Then it became clear. The young woman in the white dress, in a boat on the river, with her father and young sister. It was Elizabeth, the first time he had seen her. The beguilingly innocent girl she had been before she was his mistress. The dress was the one she had worn that day, he was sure. It must have been left there, Sam thought, when Elizabeth moved to Joseph's house all those years ago.

Kesri stopped twirling, concerned at the distant look in her father's eyes. "What's wrong, Father? Don't you like it?"

He was sorry for her disappointment. "No, it's fine. It just . . . just brought back memories, that's all."

"You're angry I didn't ask permission."

"Of course not. You look wonderful. But we'd best be away now. You don't want to keep all those young men waiting, do you?"

◈ *Chapter 32* ◈

She watched him, pretending not to, and tried to move deftly closer to his circle. She was determined to discover who he was, and how she could meet him without appearing to have shown too much interest.

When she stood only a few feet away from him, talking to Janie, he happened to look in her direction—and their eyes met. She couldn't look away as he half-smiled, then, realising they did not know each other, raised an eyebrow. She turned away quickly then, her cheeks burning, knowing he had caught her out. He was twenty or more, and handsome in a way that her father must have been when he was that age.

The garden party, in the grounds of Vimanmek Palace, the king's magnificent, new Dusit Park teak mansion, was held simply to take advantage of the last of the days of the cool season, when temperatures were still pleasant. During the hot season, most foreigners found the heat and humidity too draining to spend much time outdoors.

Every foreigner in town seemed to have been invited. The king was so generous and hospitable, he would simply have his minions inform the various foreign embassies that there would be a party, and the guest list would be left to their discretion. Consequently, the gatherings were always an interesting mix of Siamese noblemen and army officers, foreign consular staff, Danes from the Siamese navy, travellers, doctors, government advisers, missionaries, school headmasters, judges, industrialists, plus the occasional entrepreneur or teak trader in town for business or relaxation before returning upcountry.

The king, the first queen, and several of their children circulated as if they were merely one of the crowd. There was little formality, and His Majesty himself was particularly liable to wave companionably to a foreign friend and stroll over for a chat.

The minions were always unnerved—often distraught—by the lack of protocol, not knowing whether to follow their monarch closely, or to keep their distance. The royal umbrella-bearer sometimes had a most difficult task keeping up with his sovereign, and his anguish was clearly evident whenever the rays of the sun were inadvertently permitted to fall upon the royal visage.

Queen Saowapa, although tiny at just under five feet tall, was a commanding presence, and many of the guests were as eager to speak with her as they were with the king himself. She had married him in 1878 when she was just sixteen, and had borne him nine children, the last in 1893. Two years later, she was elevated to the status of first queen, when her eldest son, Prince Vajiravudh, was pronounced heir to the throne. When she was young, she had been known as a great beauty, and although she was still attractive, it was her aura of authority that most attracted people to her.

It was well known that she had the ear of the king—and in fact, it was due to her that the women of the court were now permitted to mix with the foreigners at social functions. Before her time, the ladies of the court had been largely excluded, although a few old-timers still remembered the days of King Mongkut and the eclipse at Hua Wan, when some of his consorts had participated in the festivities.

Nowadays, the courtesans were present at many of the royal excursions, including picnics upcountry, trips to the palace at Bang Pa-In, and sailing on the royal yacht. The king had even appointed Queen Saowapa as regent while he was away in Europe in 1897, the first time a woman had held such a post in Siam.

But Kesri was not concerned with the royal meanderings. She didn't even notice when His Majesty joined her father and his group some way off. And she had long since drifted from the conversation with her friend.

"Kesri. Are you listening to me?" Janie nudged her. "Or are you too busy making eyes at Romeo over there?"

"What? I don't know what you mean, Janie." She was mortified that she had been so obvious.

"Of course you do." Janie giggled. "And don't look now, but he's coming our way."

"He's what?"

"'Bye." Janie walked away, grinning widely. "I'll be getting some punch."

"Janie, wait. You can't. . . ."

But she was gone—and an instant later, the young man was standing in front of Kesri. His eyes were a startling shade of green, not the brown she had expected.

He held out his hand. "I don't believe we've been introduced. I'm Joseph Shaw. Everyone calls me Joe."

"Oh dear," she exclaimed unintentionally, and took a step back as she let go of his hand. "Then . . . I'm your cousin, Kesri Taylor."

He was silent for a moment as the news sank in.

"Well, we meet at last."

She began to relax. "I'm only amazed we haven't met before now. You live in Chiengmai, I know, but you must have visited Bangkok from time to time."

"Oh, I can explain that," he replied, grinning. "I've not even been in Siam for years. I was sent to boarding school in England when I was very young, and then I went up to Oxford to start my degree—I was reading classics. Spent a year there, but got a bit tired of it. Just didn't seem . . . practical, I suppose. So I'm taking a year off to try to decide what I want to do. Mother wasn't very pleased, needless to say."

"And what about your father—Uncle Joseph?"

"Oh, Father's a good old stick. Said it was up to me, and whatever made me happy was fine by him. But he's hoping I'll go back next year." He leaned closer and said conspiratorially, "Actually, if the truth be told, I think he'd rather like me to become a man of the cloth. Or at least a missionary, like him." He grinned again, and she saw there was no chance of that.

"So what will you do? Will you go back?"

"I expect so. I'd like to be a barrister eventually, I think. Something useful. Perhaps even come back here one day to help establish a law school."

Janie arrived back with the punch, but seeing the two so obviously enjoying their conversation, she went off to talk to some other friends, thinking that it was hardly like Kesri to show much interest in boys. She was usually too involved in her photography, but she hadn't brought her camera today.

"And what about you, Kesri?" Joe asked. "I've heard very little about you from my parents, as you can imagine."

"Yes. Well, actually there's not much to tell. I was educated here, mostly by private tutor, which was very tedious, and now I help my father with his books."

"Really? Are you a writer?"

"No, I'm taking photographs for him."

"Talented as well as beautiful." He laughed, making her blush. "Wasn't our grandfather a photographer?"

"Yes, I use his old studio. All his photographs are still there. I wish you could see them."

"Not much chance of a family reunion in the near future, I'm afraid."

"Do you know what went on all those years ago? I'm dying to find out."

"Not really. My parents won't tell me anything except that it was something between my mother and your mother."

"My father, too. It must have been awful to divide the family for this long."

"Oh, I don't know. Some of these family feuds go on so long, everyone forgets what the argument was about, and they simply hate each other. Like the Montagues and the Capulets."

"Janie was just saying that . . . oh, it doesn't matter."

She smiled, embarrassed. "Anyway, *Romeo and Juliet* is my favourite play. . . ."

"Kesri, let's agree that we'll end this feud. That you and I won't continue it, at least."

"Excellent! I agree. Let the Montagues and the Capulets be friends once more."

"Sealed with a kiss," he said, and before she could stop him, he had taken her hand and raised it to his lips.

Instead of pulling away, she looked at him, noticing again how green his eyes were.

"I'm sorry. You must think me quite rude." He at last released her hand, worried that he might have offended her.

"No . . . it's just that you have my mother's eyes."

"No, I have *my* mother's eyes."

"Then, they must both have the same colour. Must come from our grandfather, I suppose. I found a photo of your mother when she was very young. She's beautiful."

"Yes, but I've heard from certain parties—not my parents, you understand—that your mother was the true beauty of the family."

"She *was* beautiful, even when she was very ill, to the end."

"I'm sorry to hear she passed away."

"It was so unfair. She was young—only thirty-four."

"I vaguely remember going to your house. The person I remember most, strangely enough, is your father, Uncle Sam. I don't know why, but I have a clear picture of his face in my mind."

"He hasn't changed much. A little grey at the temples, a few more lines on his face. I've always thought he was the most handsome man in the world."

Joe feigned disappointment. "Are you sure?"

"Well, perhaps there are some who could equal him," she teased. "And speaking of my father, he's here somewhere. If I see him, I'll have to leave you. He won't want to be introduced, I shouldn't think. And, while we're on the subject of parents, are you not supposed to be on your way to Chiengmai, to see yours?"

"I should be. But I'm to have a slightly longer spell in Bangkok than anticipated. I've been recovering, you see—from a mild bout of jungle fever."

She looked alarmed. "Oh dear. . . ."

356

He smiled. "Not very serious, and I'm better now, I think. The result of a childhood bout that seems to recur from time to time. The climate, I suppose. Anyway, the doctor thinks it wise for me to rest for a few more weeks before setting off up North."

Joe was serious once more. "Kesri, is there any way I can see you again? I mean, alone? I realise it would have to be without my parents or your father knowing. I'll be here until the doctor says I can travel."

She was taken aback, and suddenly nervous. But equally, she wanted to see him again more than anything.

"I . . . I don't know." She wasn't certain it could be achieved. "If only it were possible. But I can't think of a way."

"Think hard, Kesri, please. I'm determined this thing between our parents won't stop us from being friends. It's ridiculous."

"I'm determined too. But I don't. . . ." Her eyes brightened. "Well, I don't know if it would work, but. . . . Well, you could come to my studio."

"Your studio? But it's in your house isn't it? I'd never get past the front door."

"You wouldn't have to. There's a back entrance from the *soi* behind the house. No one would see you. And no one disturbs me there—especially if I have a sign on the door when I'm in the darkroom. I could show you Grandfather's pictures."

Joe thought for a moment, then nodded. "Why not. Let's live dangerously, eh?"

"Come on Wednesday afternoon," she said boldly. "Father's usually out then, anyway. Here's how to get there. . . ."

Meanwhile, Sam looked across the lawn, through the crowds, to where Kesri was talking to a young man. He could not see who the boy was, as he had his back to Sam, but he could see Kesri laughing and chatting comfortably, as if she had met him before.

They had been talking for some time, and Sam wanted to excuse himself and wander over to her for an introduction. But that was impossible under the circumstances. The king was still in his circle, and it was unthinkable that he excuse himself and leave.

A few minutes later, he noticed Kesri and the boy parting. She smiled, and the young man took her hand briefly before walking off to another group of friends some distance away. The king too, took his leave of Sam's group and moved on.

Kesri breathed a sigh of relief that Joe had left when she spotted her father walking toward her. When he asked who her friend was, she was evasive. "Spying on me, Father?"

"Of course. I become very protective when I see my daughter so obviously interested in a young man. Someone special?"

"Not at all, I just met him." She changed the subject quickly, trying desperately to prevent her face glowing bright red. "Hey, I bet I could beat you at croquet."

"You? A mere slip of a girl beat the champion of Bangkok himself? We'll see about that, young lady."

From a safe distance, Joe watched them stride away together, arm in arm. Sam was tall and well-built, and he certainly did not fancy getting on the wrong side of him.

But he had never met anyone like Kesri before. The girls he had known in England were either impoverished, upper-class snobs looking to catch a wealthy, eligible bachelor, or study-bound intellectuals hell-bent on proving that women were the equal of men. His few intimate encounters had been only fleetingly satisfying, and he had lost interest quickly. They all seemed to want marriage, or money, or both.

But she was different. He warmed to her personality even more than he did physically—which was strange because she was an exceedingly beautiful young woman. He wanted to be near her, now that he had finally met her.

It was two o'clock on Wednesday afternoon, and she had been pacing the studio floor since noon. They hadn't agreed an exact time because he was uncertain when he would finish a meeting regarding a shipment of supplies for the mission.

She had thought of nothing but him since the garden party. He promised he would come, but what if he had changed his mind, decided it was not worth the risk after all? She felt so strange, so different. Nothing like this had happened to her before. It was not just that she was attracted to him. There was something else; something she could not fathom. Was it love at first sight? How ironic that he was the very person her father would want her to stay away from most.

There was a light, hesitant tap on the door, and she rushed to open it, her heart beating fast. She hurried him in, closed the door behind them, and they looked at each other as they stood apart, awkward now to find themselves completely alone. Anything could happen, and no one would know.

But Joe was almost frantic with worry that Sam would walk in and find them. "He'd be livid if he found us alone here. I'd have to explain myself, and then what. . . ."

"Tell him you're a client come to see about some portraits."

"You have clients?"

"Well, I might soon. You can be my first."

The curtains were drawn, and candles burned on the old wooden table. She busied herself pouring lime juice and setting out a plate of scones with jam, and the tension soon disappeared as they sat on the sofa together and looked through the old photographs. They laughed and talked like old friends, and it was as if they knew each other through and through.

When it was time for him to leave—because Sam would return home soon—they were strangers no more. As they said goodbye, he took her hand in his, and she didn't want him to let go.

He visited as often as he could after that, sneaking up reluctantly and furtively from the back *soi* like a fugitive, even though she assured him that her father was out—and would not recognise him in any case. But still, Joe was not entirely convinced, and he fretted continually that they would be discovered.

Of course, she couldn't resist taking photographs of him, and he would help her develop them in the darkroom. He could have taken advantage of her on those occasions, but was always a perfect gentleman.

Kesri didn't know it, but Noi had seen Joe heading along the back path toward the studio on a number of occasions—and she knew that he did not emerge for hours. She saw the infatuation in Kesri's eyes, but she was loyal to her mistress, and told no one of the liaisons.

Sam too, recognised all the signs. It was obvious his daughter was in love. But with whom? He always accompanied her to dances and other social functions, and she had not seemed attached to any one particular young man more than another. She had her share of admirers, but it seemed to him that she made little effort to encourage any of them. The rest of the time she spent alone in her studio.

It had crossed his mind that it might only be in her imagination, and was not reciprocated; that she merely dreamed of someone she had met. But her behaviour and the look in her eyes were not those of a girl with an innocent obsession. He knew women well enough, and her demeanour suggested she was confident and sure of her love.

He could ask her directly, of course—and perhaps she was waiting for him to do just that. If she were really in love, and if the young man were suitable, he would have no objections. She would be nineteen in December—a time when most young women were beginning to think of marriage—and Anchalee had been only sixteen when they married. He decided he would ask her gently—at an opportune moment—if there was anything she would like to tell him.

If he climbed the stairs too quickly he would find himself breathless by the time he reached the first landing. Sometimes there was a tightness in his chest as if a vice were crushing him. He had told no one about it, and went on with his daily tasks as best he could.

He was sixty-two now, had lived in the tropics for more than forty of those years, and had been fortunate never to have had any of the serious diseases—consumption, jungle fever, or cholera—that had killed so many of his friends. Several missionaries had drowned, and others still had become chronically ill and were invalided home. Many were separated from their families for long periods, as exhausted wives took their children and returned home, some never to see their husbands again.

He considered himself lucky that he and his family had so far remained fit and healthy. Elizabeth and he had been careful never again to put her in danger of becoming pregnant, and—in truth—Joseph these days was simply not energetic enough for regular intimate relations with his wife. She did not seem to mind.

He could no longer accompany the great Reverend McGilvary on his upcountry tours, despite the fact that the reverend was a good fourteen years Joseph's senior. The old man was a legend in the North, famous for his jungle treks on a gigantic elephant, which gained him access to villages where Europeans had never before been seen. Joseph had accompanied him and his equally adventurous daughter, Cornelia, on an 81-day tour in 1890 to Lampang and Phrae, southeast of Chiengmai, where the reverend baptised a Siamese convert; then up to Nan; to remote Chieng Kong; as far north as Chiengsen; and then down to Chiengrai, where he established a new church. McGilvary was popular wherever he went, and his procession of elephants was both feared and admired, serving to scare away bandits who might have robbed—and perhaps killed him—if they had not been so awestruck.

Joseph did not join the 1891 trip to Burma, which he still regretted because the reverend had planned to continue on to Muang Sing in Laos. That section of the expedition was cancelled, however, when Joseph's replacement, Mr. Phraner, became seriously ill. There were also reports of bandits in the jungles ahead, and so they turned back.

Neither was Joseph able to travel with McGilvary on his five-month tour to Yunnan, in China, in 1893, because he was needed at the mission in Chiengmai. But he did take his place on the 1897 trip to Muang Sing, during which the reverend—as usual—busied himself distributing scriptures, and spoke to the people in their own language about the word of God.

After 1898, in his seventieth year, McGilvary ended his extensive mission tours when the French government finally refused him permission to carry out further work in Laos. He was greatly disappointed, but he continued to visit villages around Northern Thailand, and Joseph was often his willing companion.

Joseph liked nothing better than to sit at night around a campfire on the banks of the Ping or Kok Rivers, and listen to the old man's stories. But it was not all reminiscing. McGilvary was still full of energy, and had many plans for the future.

Never before considering himself an adventurer, Joseph was amazed to find himself not at all anxious or afraid during these journeys. He believed that if robbers, or jungle fever, or a tiger were meant to take him, they would—wherever he went. But he also felt that God had too much work for him still to do to allow him to be taken this way.

But a year-and-a-half previously, he had returned from a week-long village tour exhausted as he never had been before. "I don't know what it could be," he told Elizabeth. "I don't feel terribly ill, yet I don't feel well, either. And this aching in my legs. . . ."

She smiled and took his hands in hers. "Joseph, it's nothing, I'm sure. Just that. . . . Well, you're getting old, dear. You're not forty any longer, or even fifty. You can't live like a young man forever."

"But Reverend McGilvary. . . ."

"Is a walking marvel," she finished. "You don't need to try to keep up with him. We all age at different times, Joseph, and to tell you the truth, I *have* thought you looked tired lately. You need a rest from all this. Perhaps . . . perhaps we should make a trip home—to see Joe. You've never been on furlough—not in all these years."

"Home? Elizabeth, I've never even been to England in my life. It's hardly my home. The only home I have is Siam. No, no, I'm needed here. You go again if you want to, my dear."

Now, in April 1904, he knew his travelling days were over. He simply did not want to make a great effort to go anywhere, particularly during the hot season, which seemed to be more stifling than ever. He was happy in Chiengmai, as he had been from the moment they arrived. He felt it was yet another chance in his life—the third chance, to be precise—to start anew, away from the ugliness of what had happened in Bangkok. He still taught at the missionary school, and helped with the Church's many administrative duties. He planned to retire in three or four years.

Elizabeth again broached the subject of visiting England, and he had finally agreed, although the idea held little appeal for him. She had endured much over the years, had given him all the best years of her youth, and had been devoted to working for the mission's charities at a time when many young women of her class would have enjoyed a rich social life. Now, he felt she deserved more comfort. And once he had retired, too, he knew it would sadden him to be sitting, useless, in a rocking chair in Chiengmai, while other younger missionaries took over the work he loved.

There was nothing for him now in New Zealand, so there was no question of his wanting to return there. His parents had died long ago, still bitter at their only child's youthful error. They left nothing to him, but donated all their worldly goods to the Church. Not that he had wanted, or expected, to inherit any money. But it would have been nice to receive a few family mementoes, or even a piece of the beautiful wooden furniture—made of the 35,000-year-old native *kauri* timber—that he remembered from his childhood.

◈ *Chapter 33* ◈

For two weeks, their entire time together, he had been a gentleman in every respect—making no attempt to even kiss her. Perhaps that was why, despite her growing love for him, his words still came as something of a shock

"Marry you? I don't know what to say. We can't possibly. The family. . . ."

"Hush," he said, taking her into his arms. He kissed her eyelids and the top of her nose. "Don't you love me as much as I love you?"

"Of course I do. I've loved you from the moment I first saw you. I feel as though we were made for each other. We belong together. You seem to know everything about me; everything I think and feel."

"Then marry me."

"But the family. Father would never agree."

"How do you know?"

"Because I know the way he feels about your parents. Because he's told me I mustn't have anything to do with you. He's hardly going to let me marry you."

"But from what you've said, he's a reasonable man. If you explained to him that you love me, that we're not interested in the feud, that we intend to put an end to it, whether they like it or not, I'm sure he'd agree. Once we're twenty-one, they can't prevent us anyway."

"But I'm not twenty-one for nearly three years."

"No, but I am. Or will be in three months. I'll be an adult, and they'll have to listen to me."

"I don't know if I could bear it if Father wouldn't give his approval. I don't want to go against him. He's always been so wonderful to me."

He smoothed her long, straight hair, and wiped a tear from her cheek. "I know. Don't cry, sweetheart. He'll surely listen to you. And after you've explained everything, you'll have his blessing for certain."

"But what about your parents? What will they say?"

"Well, I *would* like their blessing too. But Father's stubborn. Although he talks of forgiveness, I don't think he always practises what he preaches. Although Mother sometimes has some influence. Perhaps I should tell her first, and let her speak to him."

"Are you sure we're not too young? And what about Oxford?"

"Come with me to England. With my inheritance, we'll have no financial concerns—whether our parents agree or not."

"And my inheritance equals yours. It's perfect. Thank goodness for Grandfather."

"It doesn't matter. I'd still want to marry you, anyway. Even if we were cut off without a penny and our parents disowned us. Don't you see? You're the most important thing in my life now. Oxford, my career, even my parents don't come before you. I love you, Kesri."

He kissed her then in a different way, and she responded as his hand moved to her breast. She felt a ripple of warmth along her spine, and she gave herself up to its pleasures as she sank into his embrace. When she made no protest, he raised her skirt and caressed her thigh through her silk stockings, and then his fingers moved along the fabric until he reached her skin where the stocking ended, and together they sank to the floor.

The pictures of Joe were her first formally-posed portraits, and she had pinned them up around the room, trying to choose the best one to be enlarged and framed. He wanted to present the picture to his mother on his return to Chiengmai, and thereby open conversation about her.

As she stood back from one of the pictures, there was a knock at the studio door. Although she wasn't expecting him, she assumed he had decided to come anyway, and skipped over to answer it. As she swung the door open, she was caught completely by surprise. "Oh . . . Father. I wasn't expecting you."

"I can see that. But you look as if you were expecting someone." He smiled and moved past her into the studio before she could make an excuse to keep him out.

"And here he is, no doubt." He walked from print to print, looking closely, as Kesri held her breath. The young man looked familiar somehow, but Sam was sure he did not know him. He did, however, recognise something of himself in the features. He thought of Joe, and then dismissed the notion that it might be him. He was sure they had not met. "So this is the young man, eh?"

"This is who, Father?" she tried to ask in a surprised manner, but then quickly gave herself away when Sam remained silent as she continued without being prompted. "I'm not sure what you mean. He's just a client, who wants a portrait for his mother, that's all. They've turned out quite well, don't you think?"

He laughed. "You're not a good liar, my dear. You don't have to keep this a secret from me. He looks like a respectable young man. Why don't you tell me about him?"

He looked closely at one of the shots. Again, he was sure he had seen him before, but could not recall where. And he wondered, once more, how he could have missed the developing relationship between them. He looked at another portrait—the only one in which the boy was smiling—and he felt as if he should know his name.

She poured him a glass of lemonade, nervously considering what to say or do. After a few moments' thought, she accepted that she could not keep it from him. He knew, and she would have to tell him eventually.

"Why don't you sit down, Father, and we'll talk."

He sipped his drink, waiting for her to begin.

"You're right," she began. "He *is* someone I care deeply about. We met only a few weeks ago, but we feel as if we've known each other all our lives."

"Are you in love with him, sweetheart?"

She looked down, embarrassed. "Yes, Father."

"And does he feel the same?"

"He does. He's told me many times. In fact, he's . . . he's asked me to marry him."

"Kesri, then why haven't I met him? Why hasn't he come to the house and told me about this? I don't even know who he is." He paused, waiting for an answer, but she gave him nothing. "Who is he, Kesri ? Why are you so reluctant to tell me?"

She looked at her hands in her lap, not at him.

"Because I'm . . . I mean, he's. . . ."

He suddenly feared the worst. "You're not in trouble, are you, Kesri? You're not. . . ."

She tensed a little. "No, Father, nothing like that." She prayed that she wasn't.

"I'm pleased to hear it. Now, tell me his name, sweetheart."

There was another silence. "I'm afraid to," she finally admitted. "You won't like him. And you won't give your consent."

"Kesri, I don't even know him. How can I not like him, or agree or disagree?"

"Because . . . because of his family."

"Are they good people?"

She nodded.

"Then I'm sure I won't disapprove of them. It doesn't matter if they're not British or American—if they're Siamese—if that's what you're worried about. Kesri, think of your own mother. My own mother."

"They're British."

"Then what's the problem? Who is he?"

"He's . . . he's. . . ." She swallowed hard, and then said it. "He's my cousin, Joe Shaw." She bit her lip nervously and looked across at him.

His face was ashen. He looked as if his life had flashed before him in the split second before death seems certain. And in a real way, it had. Of course. He recognised the face in the photograph because it was himself. His daughter wanted to marry his son—her own half-brother—his own flesh and blood. Neither had any idea, and they could not imagine the consequences. It would be incest—if it wasn't already. It was horrific.

"I knew you'd be angry, but. . . ."

When he spoke, it was as if he were pleading. "You can't be serious, Kesri. Tell me you're not serious." Never in his worst nightmares had he imagined this happening.

"Father, I *am* serious. But I knew you'd disapprove. I'm sorry to have deceived you."

"Deceived me?" he said quietly, still reeling from the shock of what she had said, but unable to tell her the true reason for his horror. He remembered the young man now from the party.

"Kesri, You know how I feel about this. How could you do this to me? How could you do this to yourself? He's your *cousin*. Your *first* cousin besides."

"First cousins marry all the time, Father. There's nothing shameful in that. And Joe and I have decided that this family feud is stupid. We won't continue it. It must stop. It all happened so long ago. How can you continue it for so long?"

"There's a lot you don't know, Kesri. And there's so much I can't tell you."

"But it doesn't make any sense." She choked back her tears. "It's not fair that Joe and I be punished for something that happened twenty years ago between Mother and Aunt Elizabeth."

"It didn't concern only them, Kesri. It involved all of us. You must believe me. You can't marry Joe. You *cannot* and you *will* not. It's impossible, and that's my final word on the subject."

Tears of frustration ran down her cheeks. "I thought you'd understand. I thought you'd listen to reason. That you'd want me to be happy. Can't you understand? I love Joe, and he loves me. We. . . ."

"No!" Sam roared, leaping to his feet. "I forbid you to see him again, do you hear? You'll not see him or speak to him, and you have no hope in hell of marrying him. Have I made myself clear?" He was desperate now.

"No!" she returned defiantly, also jumping to her feet. "I'll never give him up, never, do you hear? I love him, I love him."

He grabbed her by the wrist before she could flee from the studio. "Kesri, don't force my hand on this. If you don't agree to end this now, I'll send you to finishing school in Europe, and while you're gone, I'll arrange your marriage to some suitable man, and your inheritance will become his property."

He had never imagined himself talking this way to her— intimidating her—and he hated himself for it. He loved her, but this was a situation of utter despair for him. He had to prevent it.

Indeed, he *had* never before spoken to her like that, and she was horrified. "You wouldn't do that, surely? How could you threaten me like that? How could you?"

"I've never been more serious in my life. Mark my words, Kesri. This is no idle threat. This is a promise."

She pulled her hand away and looked at him with disdain. "You really would, wouldn't you? You'd ruin my life, just to continue this ridiculous family argument that has nothing to do with either Joe or me." She turned and hurried for the door. "I'll never forgive you for this. Never!"

He took several deep breaths and tried to calm himself; tried to prevent himself from ripping the portraits to shreds. But then he found himself staring at the photographs, unable to tear his eyes away from the son he had never known, with his own dark wavy hair, his own expression in the eyes. But there was something else, too: a compassion about the mouth, and the way he held his head. That was from his mother, Sam thought, and then he wondered if she ever thought of him, and if she had the least idea what their son had unwittingly become entangled in. Was it possible that he had written to her of his intention?

Kesri was right about the feud, but what else could he tell her? The truth would be devastating. Even now, he realised it was better for him to suffer the torment of his daughter despising him, than to have her despising herself—scarred for life—if she knew the truth. If he could prevent her from seeing Joe, she would eventually recover from the heartbreak. She was young—time would heal— and she would soon forget him.

At least she wasn't pregnant—so he presumably hadn't made any physical advances toward her. He hadn't been able to bring himself to ask her that outright; could hardly bare to think of it. She had never lied to him before, and he still trusted his daughter at her word, even after her deception.

He should not have. For in her room, where she had thrown herself on to her bed, she was already planning their next meeting—and how she could continue to see him without her father's knowledge. They would have to find a safer meeting place, now that he knew what Joe looked like.

She wished her father had had a telephone installed, so she could have called and left a message for him at the mission where he was staying. The first telephones had appeared in Bangkok eighteen years previously, and it was becoming commonplace to have one, particularly among the foreign community. Sam, however, maintained that the irregular service was worse than useless, especially during the wet season, and that if one had a telephone, one would come to rely on it—but in Bangkok, it was liable to be out of order more often than not.

She hurriedly let him in and locked the door when he arrived at the studio the next day. "Did anyone follow you?"

"Follow me?" he asked, puzzled. "No, of course not. Why?"

"Father knows. I had to tell him. He saw the photographs, and he's forbidden me to see you again."

"My God, do you think he's watching you?"

"I suppose not. It's probably safe. Joe . . . he says he's going to send me away to Europe if I don't stop seeing you. He's serious. He doesn't make idle threats."

"I take it he wasn't impressed when he discovered who I was?"

"He wouldn't listen to me at all, or even discuss it. He wasn't interested in how I feel. I thought he was going to hit me. I love you, Joe." There were tears in her eyes, and she sank on to the sofa. "I don't know what we'll do."

He sat beside her and put his arm round her. "Don't worry. We'll elope."

"*Elope!*" She couldn't believe it. It was impossible.

"I've got a plan. You know it's my birthday in June, and to claim my inheritance, I have to appear at the London solicitors in person? You too, when you claim yours. Well, I can be perfectly plain to my parents about leaving for England. I'll tell them I'm going back to varsity as well, so I'll have to leave very soon. I just won't tell them I'm taking you with me. I shall have to go to Chiengmai first to see them, of course. But it won't be for long."

"Joe, you can't be serious. It would never work, and it wouldn't be right."

"Kesri, listen. We'll ask the captain to marry us on the ship as soon as we sail. He won't refuse us if we say we're already living together and you're expecting our child. He'd be honour-bound to do it. Before we reach land again, you'll be Mrs. Shaw, and no one will be able to do anything about it."

How could she contemplate such a thing? The prospect of leaving her father and sailing for a land she had never seen before was frightening. Siam was all she knew.

◈ *Chapter 34* ◈

He was working at home that day, and found himself alone in the house except for Simon, who was still with them after all those years. Elizabeth had gone to play bridge with friends; a rare afternoon off from her good works, and one of her few pleasurable indulgences. Simon looked in to say he was going out on an errand, and if Joseph wanted anything, he was to call Kob—Simon's wife of ten years, who was employed as the maid. Kob was busy in their own quarters—the bamboo cottage Joseph had built at the back of the house—attending to their five children. Over the years, as Simon's family grew ever larger, the servants' quarters had become far too small.

Joseph stretched his arms in front of him and looked out the windows to the lush, tranquil garden beyond. There were banana palms, heavy with fruit, which Kob would deep-fry with lime juice and sesame seeds as a special treat for the children; there were hedges on which mauve flowers climbed; and there were banks of low bushes with bright orange blooms.

He decided on a nap before Elizabeth returned at five o'clock, and stood wearily from his desk and went into the hallway to climb the stairs. He really was feeling unusually tired, and had to pause for breath halfway up. Perhaps he should ask Dr. McGilvary for a tonic, he thought, and then decided that it could wait until tomorrow.

Just as he neared the top, he suddenly clutched his chest. The pain was more gripping than usual, and as the tightness increased, he gasped for breath. He grabbed at the banister in an effort to support himself on the final step, missed his footing, and—with everything seeming to happen slowly—realised he was going to fall. His arm did not respond when he lunged to catch hold of the banister again, and then he hit the hard wooden stairs, rolling over and over, down and down—for what seemed like an eternity—to blackness.

When Elizabeth returned home two hours later, it was to find Simon, Kob, and their children huddled together on the porch, all silently waiting for her. She hurried up to the house, immediately aware that something was wrong. "Whatever's happened, Simon?"

"Madame, the Master—he sick, sick. Doctor with him now."

She rushed inside, and when she called for him, Dr. McKean, an American who lived nearby, appeared at the top of the stairs.

"Doctor, what's happened? Has there been an accident? What's happened to Joseph?"

His expression told her that it was serious. "You'd better come into the front room, Mrs. Shaw. I'm afraid I have some rather bad news for you."

She sat on the old chesterfield with a great sense of foreboding.

The doctor took off his glasses and sat opposite her. "Mrs. Shaw, I'm very sorry to have to tell you that Mr. Shaw passed away this afternoon. It was his heart, I think. Just suddenly gave out. He didn't suffer for long, Mrs. Shaw. Simon found him at the bottom of the stairs. He must have fallen during the attack."

She looked at him with glazed eyes, shocked. "There was . . . there was nothing you could do?"

"He was already gone when Simon found him, I'm afraid. When the heart gives up, we're helpless. I'm so sorry, Mrs. Shaw. Is there anything I can do?"

"No. No thank you, Doctor. Is he . . . is Joseph upstairs?" Her voice was quiet and calm.

He nodded. "Would you like to see him?"

"Yes. I think I'd like to go up alone, thank you."

When she entered the room, she at first thought the doctor had been mistaken. Surely Joseph, lying on the bed so serenely, was only asleep? She leaned over him, touched his cheek, and kissed his lips. But he was already cold. He had been much older than she, and she had always feared he would probably die before her. But he was still relatively young, and she had never really imagined herself a widow so soon.

Joe had written to say that he had arrived in Bangkok, that he would come to Chiengmai soon, but that he wanted to return to England as soon as possible. That would leave her alone, and the thought terrified her.

She looked again at the face of her dear husband, and the past came once again to haunt her.

"Oh Joseph, I wronged you so much. I hurt you and caused you great suffering," she cried. "But you always forgave me and loved me, despite everything."

She took off her hat and shoes then, and climbed up on the bed to lie beside him one last time. One last time before they buried him in the warm earth of his adopted homeland.

It was unpleasantly hot, with not a breath of wind nor a cloud in the sky on the day of his funeral. During the service, most of the more than one hundred mourners managed to find shelter under the trees, but Elizabeth stood stoical in the blazing sun, watching as the coffin was lowered into the ground. She stepped up to the graveside, let the single white orchid she had picked from the garden he loved so much, slide from her fingers, and then Mrs. McGilvary led her away and into the waiting carriage.

She had sent a telegraph to Joe at the mission in Bangkok the day after Joseph's death, and Joe had left early the next morning, even though he knew he would miss the funeral. In the searing heat of the season, a body had to be interred almost immediately. Although travel had improved markedly within Siam, it still took Joe two weeks to reach Chiengmai.

Kesri received a hastily-scribbled note from a courier with instructions to deliver it to her hands only. The note said simply, *"My darling, something awful has happened that may see our plans postponed. I received a telegraph to say my father died, and my mother, of course, is distraught. I must leave for Chiengmai at once, and she may need me for a while. Nothing else has changed. I love you. Wait for me. All my love, Joe."*

Tears came to her eyes as she read his news. She wanted to be there to comfort him, to hold him. The note read almost matter-of-factly, but she knew how much he had loved and respected his father, how much he had looked up to him. He too, would be devastated.

"I shall stay with you, Mother, as long as you need me," he promised, as they embraced. "I can postpone the trip to England for the moment."

She smiled gratefully. He had always been a wonderful son, and he was there for her now, never disappointing her. She was proud of him.

"I've decided to go back to Bangkok," she told him. "There's nothing for me here now. And in due course, I think I'll probably retire to England. But there's still work to be done. Your father wanted to do so much, and I should like to continue at the mission for a year or so, until I get used to the idea of being alone. Bangkok will be easier for me, I think."

Even the prospect of seeing Sam again—perhaps unintentionally, perhaps not—did not concern her now. She was tired of hiding from her past.

Joe agreed with her. "Mother, that's a wonderful idea. It's best for you. And you won't be alone. I'll be there as long as necessary."

She smiled then, for the first time since Joseph had died. "Nonsense, dear. You have your own life to lead. Don't forestall it on my account."

There was an obituary in the newspaper and she told her father over breakfast.

"Yes, I heard yesterday," he said, without looking up from a letter from his publisher he was reading.

"You knew and you didn't tell me?"

"It doesn't concern you," he said coldly, and made no further comment. He certainly did not tell her that he had received a telegraph from Elizabeth herself.

If only you knew, she thought. But now they would not be leaving for England as planned. She had already started to pack a trunk in her studio, but would now have to unpack it again, in case it was discovered. Then an idea occurred to her. Joe had said that his father was the party most likely to be opposed to their marriage. Now that he had passed away, perhaps there would not be such strong objection from his mother. Perhaps Joe could at least solicit approval from Aunt Elizabeth against her father's stubborn refusal.

In Chiengmai, Joe had arrived at the same conclusion. He decided to tell his mother, hoping that when they returned to Bangkok, maybe she could do something to convince Sam. But Elizabeth's reaction was exactly as Kesri had described her father's.

When Joe told her of his intentions, Elizabeth went deathly pale and buried her head in her hands. "Joe, this is a nightmare. I must have misheard you. Please tell me I did."

Joe was almost equally as shocked at her reaction. "No, Mother, you're not mistaken," he answered quietly, beginning to worry that whatever the secret, it must be serious. "I love her deeply and I intend to marry her. I know about the family feud, and I don't care. *We* don't care."

"There's no feud." She clasped her hands together in her lap so tightly that the nails dug into her palms. "You know nothing; nothing about what happened."

"Then tell me about it. It was nearly twenty years ago, Mother. For goodness' sake, it can't be that bad."

"I can't tell you what happened. I can't . . . not now. But believe me when I say that you *cannot* marry Kesri."

"Please, Mother, hear me out. Why must Kesri and I be punished because of something that happened so long ago? I thought you'd understand."

Again, her head fell into her hands in despair. "Oh, Joe. I understand too much."

"Then when we return to Bangkok, will you at least go to see Uncle Sam and talk about this with him? Tell him how much I love Kesri, and how happy I shall make her—if only he'll give me the chance. Will you talk to him?"

Slowly, she raised her head again to look directly at him. "Yes, very well. I think that's what I must do. It sounds like this has gone far enough and there's no other choice."

When they arrived back in Bangkok, Elizabeth wasted no time. After settling in at the Oriental Hotel and cleaning up after the long journey, she went directly there—having written to Kesri, but not Sam, in advance.

Kesri had been expectantly looking out of the front room window for over an hour, and when she finally saw her walk up the path, she instantly recognised her from the photograph. She was older, but the refined beauty that had set her apart in youth was still striking. Indeed, hers was the kind of mature loveliness that improved gracefully with age.

Kesri opened the door and was suddenly nervous as she spoke to her for the first time. "Aunt Elizabeth. Please come in."

Elizabeth—almost in panic herself at the prospect of meeting Sam again after nearly twenty years—had never thought of herself as an aunt. She had, after all, never been addressed as such—either in writing or in person—and had never known Kesri. The lovely, innocent young woman before her had much of her mother's looks, she thought, but there was also a softness about her features, a sweet prettiness that was not Anchalee.

Despite the fact that she had come to ensure that her son would never see Kesri again—and that it would surely break the girl's heart—she smiled warmly and genuinely at her niece. She took her hand as she entered, and they embraced briefly. "Kesri, you look so lovely. It's wonderful to see you after all these years. You know I've come to see your father. Why don't you tell him I'm here."

"Where's Joe?" she asked.

"He's taking care of some business at the mission—for his father. Before he goes back to England."

She wanted to ensure that the two of them were kept apart as much as possible, and had asked Joe to settle some of Joseph's affairs. She was certain it would keep him busy until his departure in the next few days.

Kesri showed Elizabeth into the parlour, and then went up to Sam's study, tapping on the door before she walked in. "Father, you have a visitor."

He looked up from the novel he was working on. "I'm not expecting anyone. Who is it?"

"It's someone you know. Aunt Elizabeth."

"Elizabeth . . . here?"

"Yes, Father. She's waiting in the parlour."

His face was a calm surface that concealed a maelstrom of emotions. She could not imagine what he was thinking, but knew from his silence that the news had disturbed him greatly.

Eventually, he spoke, and he sounded uncharacteristically apprehensive. "Kesri, would you . . . would show her up here, please? And have Noi bring us some tea."

"Yes, Father." And she almost ran from the room.

He waited, rooted to the spot. It was almost eighteen years since they had spoken, and now she was here. What would he say to her?

All too soon, there was another tap on the door, and there she was before him. At first glance she looked almost the same as she had when he last saw her. But then he noticed the lines etched round her mouth, the faint circles under her eyes, and the pale cheeks that had once been rosy. He went toward her, stopping an arm's length away.

She saw that he was not much changed. He was as handsome as ever; his dark hair still thick and wavy, and greying only a little at the temples. But the young adventurer with the fire in his eyes had mellowed at fifty-three. He looked comfortable, settled, and satisfied, as if he no longer cared to burn up the world's trails with his energy.

There was a long silence between them until she spoke first. "I had to come, Sam."

"I was sorry to hear of Joseph's death," he replied quickly.

"Thank you. And Anchalee, too. I wanted so much to come to her funeral."

"Yes, I know. But please, sit down." He indicated the leather sofa by the window. "It's been a long time, Elizabeth. This is something of a surprise. I had no idea you were in Bangkok."

"It's a shock to me too, Sam. But I've moved from Chiengmai permanently now. There's no reason for me to stay, now that Joseph has gone. I'm at the Oriental until I can find a suitable house. Joe's at the mission."

"Yes, of course. And what made you come today?"

"I think you must know the answer to that," she said hesitatingly. "Joe. And Kesri."

"I guessed as much." He sighed deeply, and then raised a finger to his lips as he nodded toward the door.

She understood what he meant. "Sam, this is a catastrophe. They really believe they are going to marry, and they're adamant no one will stand in their way."

"No, not any more. Kesri gave me her word she would never see him again."

"Nevertheless, that hasn't altered their feelings or their plans."

He was shocked that Kesri would disobey him, and he realised now that their attachment was more serious than he had thought.

"Have you told Joe it isn't possible?"

"Of course."

"But have you told him *why?*" He leaned forward from his chair opposite her.

"No, I couldn't."

"I couldn't tell Kesri, either."

"But we must tell them now, Sam. We must."

"Why? If we can keep them apart and just forbid the marriage, that should be enough."

"Sam, I'm afraid they'll do something rash. I'm worried they're going to elope."

That possibility had not even occurred to him. "But the marriage would be invalid. They're brother and sister, for God's sake."

"That may be the reality, but no one knows it except us. Officially, in the eyes of the law, they're only cousins—which isn't illegal. It could happen. And Sam, we can't afford to take the chance that they'll do this without our permission. Has it occurred to you that your daughter could become pregnant with her own half-brother's child?"

He shook his head. "I asked her. There's been no . . . physical contact. I have to believe that."

"That may be, but if they did run away, we couldn't apprehend them soon enough to stop it. It could be too late."

He thought for a moment, then looked up at her again, defeated. "You're right, Elizabeth, there's no other way. They must be told. Today."

Elizabeth was afraid of what it would do to Joe; to discover in the same breath that not only was the woman he loved his half-sister, but that the man he had known as his father all his life was, in reality, his step-father. She wished Joseph were still alive to guide her. Then again, she was glad he would not have to witness Joe's reaction to the truth.

"We probably should have told them a long time ago," Sam said. "After all, as Kesri herself says, it's not that unusual for cousins to fall in love and marry."

"But we didn't realise they even knew each other."

"I know, but we were fooling ourselves to believe they wouldn't meet at some time. The foreign community is small. It's difficult to avoid people, even if you want to. Even though you've lived so far away, you would have spent at least a short time in Bangkok."

"You're right. But it's too late for regrets now."

She stood and walked to the window. "It's . . . it's nice to see you again, Sam. Despite these circumstances." Then she looked at him directly. "I didn't think I ever would. Not like this. . . ."

He walked toward her then, and took both her hands in his. "The people we could have hurt by continuing even the vaguest of friendships are gone now. Sadly. Let's help each other through this crisis. And then. . . ."

"And then?" she asked, realising with a jolt that he still had power over her—and that through it all, even though she had despised him at times and tried to push him from her memory, she still cared for him.

"Then we can be friends, I hope." He released her hands.

She lowered her eyes. "I hope so too."

"This will be a terrible shock to Joe, won't it? To find out that Joseph wasn't his father."

Elizabeth looked up again, tears pricking her eyelids. "Oh Sam, you don't know how much Joe loved and respected him. Joseph was wonderful when Joe was small, and he never once referred to, or even alluded to the fact that Joe wasn't his son. They were father and son in every way. It may ruin him to discover this. In one day, he'll lose the woman he wants to marry, and his own identity. Not to mention what he'll think of me."

"Wait, Elizabeth. There *is* another way. A way by which Joe wouldn't have to be told the truth. If you're agreeable, I think it may work."

He motioned her to sit down again, and she did so, eager to hear anything that might lessen the pain she was about to inflict on her only child.

◈ *Chapter 35* ◈

Kesri, of course, had put her ear to the door as soon as Elizabeth entered the study and closed it behind her. She had, however, heard nothing of their conversation. The teak was thick and solid, and they had kept their voices low, precisely because they knew she would be eavesdropping just outside.

When she entered the study at her father's call, she found him and Aunt Elizabeth sitting on the sofa together. Any hopes she was entertaining of them relenting, faded completely when she saw her father's grim expression.

"Sit down, Kesri. There's something we must discuss with you. Something that will change the way you feel about Joe."

Puzzled, she did as he asked and sat on the chair opposite them. "Nothing will change the way I feel," she said resolutely. "I love him, and he loves me. It's as simple as that. As simple as two people falling in love."

"Falling in love is rarely simple, Kesri."

"Why? Why can't you accept what has happened and put your old feud to rest?"

Sam glanced at Elizabeth. She nodded almost imperceptibly. "I think I can say that there's no feud between your aunt and me. There never was, as you will see shortly."

Kesri looked from one to the other, now even more perplexed. "But I don't understand. Then why. . . ."

Elizabeth stood up. "I think this is best discussed between the two of you, in private. I wanted to be here, Kesri, just to tell you that you must believe everything your father tells you, and do exactly as he says. In this, we are united. He will tell you some things that will hurt you, but they're things you must know—for they concern your future, and Joe's future. They also concern the past." She paused. "I shall go now. I can see myself out." She motioned for Sam to remain seated as he made to get up. "And please, Sam—Anchalee—if there's anything I can do to help. . . ." But her voice cracked, and she turned and walked from the room, closing the door softly behind her.

"Father, has something happened to Joe?" She looked alarmed.

"No, Kesri. Joe's fine. But now we must talk about this love you think you feel for him, this desire you think you have to marry him."

She was becoming impatient with him. "It's not just something I *think* I have. It's something I *know* I have. I feel deeply for Joe, and nothing you say will change that. Not even if he were a murderer, or anything else." She was red with anger, frustrated with his inability to treat her as an adult. But she was also very afraid of what he would tell her. Not certain that she could face it yet, she defiantly got up to leave the room.

"I've had enough of your orders. I'm going to marry him, and I don't care what you say."

Before he could stop her, she had fled the room. She closed her bedroom door behind her, and sat on the bed, shaking with fury. What could she do to make him understand? She had never known him to be so stubborn, especially where she was concerned. But on this matter, he was resolute. She thought again of Joe, and she yearned for him. He had been away for so long, it seemed, and she needed to be with him.

She remembered the last time they were together. It had seemed such a natural thing to happen, and she felt no guilt. When she recalled his intimate touches on every part of her body, she shivered. Her only thought as he entered her for the first time was that this was the man she would spend her life with—and she would not have cared if they had conceived a child then. As events had transpired, she was glad they had not. But she longed to feel him within her again, the two of them locked in an embrace that felt as if it would never end.

But now there was an impatient rapping on her door, and—without waiting for her to invite him—Sam came in. He was clearly under great strain. "Kesri, you must listen to me," he began.

She hated to defy and hurt him this way, but she could not relent. "It's no use, Father. My mind's made up. With or without your blessing. I don't care what you say."

"Would you care if I told you Joe was your brother?" he said quietly.

She faltered, instantly frozen—a look of astonishment, horror, and disbelief on her face. "My what?" she finally whispered.

She stood up and moved toward him, staring at him as if he were speaking a foreign tongue. Fear had now completely overwhelmed her, and she was shaking as she asked in panic, "What do you mean, my brother? What do you mean?"

When he told her to sit down, she remained standing, unable to move. He took her by the shoulders and guided her back to the side of the bed, sitting down beside her.

"Kesri, the reason I've been absolutely opposed to this relationship between you and Joe—so abhorred by it—is not because I dislike Joe or his parents. It's because such a relationship between you is *not* possible. You see, a long time ago, Elizabeth and I were . . . very close. Intimate. It was before I knew your mother well. . . ."

Her face was a mask of death; her eyes wild and disbelieving.

"Kesri, sweetheart, your aunt and I were in love, and I was planning to marry her. But then I was called away at short notice for an expedition to the North, and when I returned, she was already married to Joseph. They had a baby son, who everyone said had been born premature. I was suspicious at the time, and when the child was still very young, I realised the truth. Elizabeth had been expecting my child when she married Joseph. You see, she believed I'd deserted her when I'd done no such thing. It was all a dreadful mistake. Actually there was more to it than that, but I don't. . . .

"Anyway, Joseph nobly agreed to marry her, and to bring up the child as his own, to protect her reputation. It was the most selfless act I've ever known a person to perform."

Kesri was very still, and when she spoke, her voice was almost inaudible and seemingly not her own. "And the child. The child was Joe?"

"Yes. The child was Joe. I'm his father, Kesri. And he's your half-brother. He knows nothing of this, sweetheart. He still believes Joseph is . . . was . . . his father. I think it would destroy him if he found out the truth."

"The king is married to several of his half-sisters," she said.

"What's that?"

She looked toward him, but her eyes were unfocused. "King Chulalongkorn has married some of his half-sisters. The Siamese kings always have—because there aren't enough women of high enough station for them to marry." She was calm, trying to make it right.

Sam knew that she was in shock. It had been a traumatic realisation, and he understand her anguish. Her words meant little—he knew she was simply reacting to the dismay of the truth—but he did remind himself that she was part-Siamese herself. Despite the fact that she had been raised, for the greater part, as a Westerner, there could be no doubt that the country of her birth, and its culture and customs—quite distinct from his own—had influenced her to a great degree. Perhaps it was not quite the same for her.

He took her in his arms and said sympathetically, "I think that's different, sweetheart. I'm so sorry to have to tell you this. But you can see now, why it could never have been."

She broke down then. "Why in God's name did you not tell me this before? Oh Father, I know, I know. I didn't mean it. I can't marry my own brother."

"I should have, I know. But I didn't realise it had gone this far, until today."

"Does Joe know yet?"

As he suspected, she had not heard him before. "That's another thing I want to talk to you about, Kesri. You must know that if Joe ever discovers the truth of this, it would be. . . . Kesri, he must *never* know. And you must do as I say—and what Elizabeth asks. For Joe's sake."

By the time he left her alone, she was inconsolable. Face down on the bed, weeping uncontrollably, he could do or say nothing to comfort her—and he would never know the true depth of her torment. He decided to leave her until she cried herself to sleep, resolving to send her away from Bangkok at the earliest moment— hopefully that same day, so that Joe had no opportunity to see her.

May 15th, 1904

My dearest Joe,

You will probably have begun to realise by now that I will not be meeting you today. I have decided against eloping with you. I have searched my soul to find my true feelings, and I know now without a doubt that I cannot marry you, either now, or at any time in the future. I am afraid that I have come to realise that I simply do not love you in that way. I love you as a wonderful person, as someone I respect and admire, as a dear cousin, but not as I should love a husband. To go through with our plans would be to live a lie, and I cannot do that to you.

I know how much this letter will hurt you; how you will not want to believe it; how you will want to come running to me to try to change my mind. Please do not, if you truly care for me. My mind is set, and for you to try to contact me at this time would only bring us both more pain. In any case, by the time you read this, I will be away from Bangkok. I cannot tell you where, and it would be futile for you to try to follow me. I am truly sorry for the hurt I have caused you.

Please, Joe, go to England as you had planned, but go without me. Do not look back, and do not wish for something that cannot be. Look to the new life you shall have, and the happiness you shall surely find. I should like to think that at some time in the future, we could become friends, as cousins should be. I give you my word that this is wholly my own decision, that these are my true feelings, and have nothing to do with my father's influence.

Your affectionate cousin,

Kesri Taylor

She sealed the letter and gave it to her father. When the time came, he would send it with a messenger—telling the boy, "It's for Mr. Joe Shaw only. Deliver it into his hands and no one else's—to where she had promised to meet Joe.

It was the hardest thing she had ever done. It would leave him distraught, but she hoped it was forceful enough to convince him to continue the journey to England alone. Nevertheless, now that it was done, she felt as if a weight had been lifted from her. She had truly been in love with Joe. She had truly felt passion for him. But those feelings had been taken from her so suddenly that she was even wondering now if they had ever been real.

What they had done together filled her with grief and distress. The memories tortured her, and she quickly stifled them. She was lucky. When she imagined what would have happened had she conceived, she almost writhed in agony.

Now that she knew the truth, her heart did not ache for lost love, but she grieved for the pain he would feel. And she agreed that he should be spared the awful truth. Then perhaps, one day, he would feel he could befriend her without embarrassment.

She missed his company already, and she knew with certainty that she would not develop romantic feelings for anyone else in the near future. It just seemed too tragic when she reflected on what it had done to Aunt Elizabeth, to Uncle Joseph, to her own father, and now to herself and to Joe. It was not worth it. Better to find some other purpose in life, she thought; some useful occupation or goal that brought reward to the soul. Not a romance that ended in shreds and destroyed those involved.

She had finally discovered the secret that her father would not divulge to her for years. But at what price?

Only the day after arriving in Bangkok, despite being preoccupied keeping Joe busy with trivial matters, she managed to find a house on Sapatoum Road near the Belgian community— which was not inconvenient because she had learned to speak French quite well as a girl, and had often met French missionaries in the North. She always enjoyed the chance to speak the language whenever she could.

The house was a modest two-storey, wooden building, with slatted windows and a verandah that had been added by the previous occupants, a Belgian legal adviser to the Siamese Ministry of Justice, and his wife.

Over the years, she had acquired an impressive collection of Northern Siamese crafts—including lacquered pots etched with gold leaf, lengths of silk in brilliant colours and patterns, and exquisitely-painted paper umbrellas—and she had always made wonderful decorative use of her treasures, so that within a few days, the house was starting to look like a home. Their servants had once again moved with them—Simon happy to be back in Bangkok, and Kob excited to live in the city and to give their children more opportunities for education and employment.

Joe wondered if she really would return to England one day. He was amazed at her strength of character, at the way she had seemed to rally after Joseph's death. She was still somewhat quiet and withdrawn, of course, but that was to be expected.

He was also surprised that she had not raised the question of the relationship since her meeting with Sam, but he guessed she had other things on her mind. Unfortunately, that talk with his uncle had not persuaded her—or him, by her accounts—to change her mind, so he had simply made no comment, and continued with the original plan to elope.

He had not seen Kesri, but assumed that their escape—agreed before he left for Chiengmai, and consolidated with further messages since—would go ahead as planned. In a few short days, they—he was sure—would be on their way to England. His mother, believing that he must hurry back to continue his education, had assured him she would be fine by herself, and did not need him to stay on. He assumed that when they were married, their families would have to accept it. And when the first grandchild arrived, he was sure that both Mother and Uncle Sam would give their blessings. Soon she would be his bride, and she would lie beside him every night. She might even be pregnant by the time they reached England.

Little did he know that his messages sent to her since his return to Bangkok had already been intercepted by Sam. Indeed, that they would never have reached her anyway, since she was at Bang Pa-in with family friends.

Elizabeth bustled into his room one afternoon, tutting disapprovingly when she saw the way Joe was packing his trunk. She waved him away. "Joe, you should have let Kob do this. You're absolutely hopeless. Where's your mind these days? You can't pack those trunks like that. Anything breakable will be smashed to bits, and your clothes will all be completely crushed. Go and get Kob, will you? She and I will do it between us."

Joe waited at the docks, ready to board a boat that would take them out to the ship. He had said goodbye to his mother at home, telling her it would be easier on her if she did not come to see him off. Surprisingly, she had not objected.

Kesri was late, but he was not yet concerned. Perhaps she was having trouble getting away, or perhaps her father was late leaving home for his club. They had plenty of time. It couldn't have been her luggage causing the problem. She had agreed to pack only one small bag instead of a trunk, to avoid arousing the suspicions of the servants when she left. He would buy her enough to make do in Singapore, and when they reached England, an entire *trousseau* to make up for not having a proper wedding. Money would not be a problem. He ran a hand over his jacket pocket once more, feeling within, the small gold band he had bought for her.

An hour later, she had still not arrived. Time was getting short, with the boat waiting to leave. He paced the dock with increasing anxiety.

The boy raced up to Joe, thrust the letter into his hand, and then disappeared again. Joe was now almost frantic. The last passengers were boarding the steamer, and if she did not arrive within minutes, it would leave without them. He ripped it open and read it, while the boatman continued urging him to hurry.

He scanned the letter quickly, unable to believe it. Was it some kind of joke? Perhaps she was hiding, and in a moment would appear, giggling, and hugging him. But it could not possibly be. It would have been too cruel.

As he read the letter a second time—slowly so that each word stabbed at him—he began to grasp that it was true. It was her handwriting, not a forgery. She was not coming, and his heart sank to his stomach. His shoulders sagged, and there was a great constriction in his throat and chest, as if the life were being squeezed out of him.

The boatman called again, and Joe was torn in two. He could not make her marry him against her will; he could not force her to love him. She was very young. Had he overestimated her feelings? Had he seen in her a maturity that simply wasn't there? He guessed that she had finally been unable to disobey her father.

The boatman was now in a frenzy. He jumped from the boat and tugged at Joe's sleeve, almost begging him to jump aboard. Joe looked one more time toward the temples of the city; toward where she was. Then he turned and looked down the Chao Phya River, to where the steamer was lying midstream. In another instant, he leapt into the waiting boat, and a short time later went straight to his cabin on the ship and locked the door.

He could not see Siam as he left, and through his tears he could barely face up to the truth that she was lost to him.

❖ *Chapter 36* ❖

Sam showed Elizabeth into the front room. "I haven't seen you for nearly two months—since Christmas. Why don't you visit more often?"

She smiled and shrugged. "I'm much busier with Joe gone than I ever expected to be." She took off her gloves and hat—a large-brimmed affair of the type that had become so fashionable—and set them beside her on the sofa. Sam poured her a sherry and they talked about various acquaintances.

"And how is Kesri?" Elizabeth asked. "I understand she's become very involved with charity work."

"It's a full-time occupation for her these days. It's not pleasant work for a young girl. But she's happy to feel useful, and I'm glad for her. Time enough yet to find a husband."

"Is there no young man in her life?"

"None," he replied. "Oh, plenty ask for her, but she's not interested in any of them."

"She will be, when she's ready. She's only nineteen, after all—hardly an old maid yet. People are getting married much later nowadays. Don't worry about her. Let her make the most of her freedom while she has it."

"You're right, I shouldn't worry. And how's Joe? Is he doing well at Oxford?"

"Absolutely marvellously. Actually, he's the reason I've come to see you."

"Oh?" For the first time he noticed her eyes were sparkling with happiness.

"I've received a letter from him, in which he gives me the happy news that he's engaged to be married."

"That's wonderful. So he really is over the . . . disappointment of last year."

"He assures me he is—and that he's very much in love with a Miss Victoria Crossley. A lady *graduate*, no less!"

"Interesting. What's her field?"

"She intends to become a doctor. You see what I mean, Sam— we women are catching up with you men. Look at Kesri and her photography."

He smiled. "And when is the wedding?"

"In August, before university starts for the year. And that's what I wanted to talk to you about particularly. Joe has asked that perhaps you would like to accompany me to the wedding."

She took a sheet of writing paper from her bag, and unfolded it. "As he says, '*Uncle Sam is my closest male relative, and it would be an honour if he would consent to escort you to England for the nuptials*'."

She looked up at him, concerned at what his reaction would be. "He doesn't know anything, of course, Sam. But it seems as if he's forgiven us for our opposition to. . . . Well, you know. . . ." Her voice trailed off as she awaited Sam's answer.

He needed to think for only a moment. "Very well, I'll do it. And I'll look forward to travelling with you, Elizabeth. There might even be a story in it. You never know."

To be present at Joe's wedding, even though Joe would never know their true relationship, would be the closest he could come to acting as his real father. The irony of him being considered a sort of surrogate father was not lost on Sam, either.

"It really seems as if this will all work out for the best," she said. "At least, I hope so."

"I hope so, too. But there's something else I'd like to see happen to finish this thing finally."

"And what's that?"

"I'll tell you on the ship."

She did not tell him then, but she too had decided that it was time to lay to rest the final ghost from the past. Their conversation had convinced her. It would be the act that would finally free her; the last constraint on her life as an independent woman; and the end of her guilt, pain, and responsibility.

Indian Ocean, May 1905

She had not felt so relaxed or so well-attended in years—perhaps ever. The new super-liners were the last word in luxury. The vessel's interior was fitted with highly-polished dark mahogany panelling, delicate white and gold trim on walls and ceilings, and electric lamps throughout. A magnificent, stained-glass dome rose over thirty feet through the ship's two decks, and there was a stylish drawing room with walls of carved satinwood and cedar, and an elaborate mantelpiece over the fireplace. Her luxuriously-appointed suite, next to Sam's, consisted of a sitting room and bedroom, and the whole gave the impression of an exclusive, very expensive hotel—which, of course, it was.

She and Sam had, for the first time in their lives, developed a comfortable friendship. She discovered a sensitive, caring side to him that she had never known existed. And he discovered a quick intelligence about her that he had never noticed when they were lovers. They dined together each night, walked on the promenade deck, then said goodnight with a gentle handshake and retired to their respective cabins. She owed it to Joseph's memory, she continually reminded herself, to forget what had passed between herself and Sam so long ago. But it was impossible.

One evening, after a wonderful meal, when Sam had been at his most charming, and they had lingered for an extra glass of wine, she found herself unable to sleep. Eventually, she did, but it was only to dream of him. They were on a house-boat together on the Chao Phya River, drifting, oblivious to where they went. Then the lights of London twinkled ahead of them, and he turned to her and smiled, his eyes crinkling at the corners. He reached for her, and she floated into his arms, and he began to remove her clothing, piece by piece, on the open deck of the boat.

She awoke, trembling and shivering, even though there was a slick of perspiration on her brow. After more than two decades, she still wanted him, still yearned for his body beside hers. She realised that—even through her marriage—she had always held some of herself back. That was the part that had belonged to him, and him alone. She deeply regretted the affair—it had not been right in any way, for any of them—but her feelings for him, she now discovered, had never changed.

The next night, she dressed with even more care than usual, in a low-necked, white silk dress. She smiled to herself as she thought how shocked her grandmother would be to see her now. "Never be a slave to fashion," she had said. "Never drop a neckline purely because everyone else does. It won't suit you."

It might not have suited her then, but it did now—and she felt she had earned the right to dress as she pleased. She had become her own woman, and the light of confidence shone from her eyes. Her hair was pinned up softly, and she wore elbow-length white gloves on her slender arms. In the dim lighting, she could have passed for thirty. She was still slim, her face still smooth with only a few light lines, and the dark circles and weariness of the last year had vanished.

When he met her in the lobby, his gaze swept over her and lingered below her bare shoulders. She felt flushed and excited, almost like she had that first time so many years ago. When dinner was over, they danced again—his warm hand on her back, his breath brushing her neck as he held her close—and the years spun away.

She allowed herself to imagine them once more as the young adventurer and the innocent girl, captivated by each other and unable to let go. But she allowed it to go no further. They were no longer those people, and she was wiser now. There had been so many hard lessons, so much left unsaid, and so much pain over those years. And yet he was still the man she wanted after all that time.

Instead of leading her back to the table, he steered her toward the doors and out to the deck, where the breeze was blowing gently, and where couples were strolling, some with champagne glasses in hand. She breathed deeply as they walked in silence. Toward the bow, he stopped and leaned on a rail, looking out into the blackness, as if deep in thought. She leaned against the rail too, facing inward to the ship. He then moved closer, first winding his fingers around hers, and then pulling her gently toward him. She went willingly, her arms reaching around his neck, and they kissed gently for the first time in many years.

Soon she pushed him away a little, and looked around, flustered. "Sam, stop. What will people think?"

"I don't care," he answered, then took her hand and led her along in the direction of their cabins. She offered no resistance.

Inside, he opened the door of her suite, and she was at first disappointed when he took her hand and raised it to his lips—thinking he would only say goodnight as usual. But then he stepped into the room with her, closed the door, and kept her hand, kissing the soft, sensitive skin between each finger.

As they kissed, they removed each other's clothes until they lay scattered on the floor around them. She stood naked with her legs apart—not timid, but revelling in his admiration—as he knelt below her, his tongue tracing its way over her smooth, white stomach. He moved down between her thighs, and she almost cried out in pleasure, running her fingers wildly through his hair. He stood then, turned her away from him, wrapped one of his legs around hers to steady her, and was soon within her. When he withdrew and turned her to face him once more, they both sank to the floor, continuing their quest among the rustling silk of her fallen clothes.

Hours later—after they had slept—they lay awake in each other's arms with only the distant sound of the waves crashing against the side of the ship to break the silence. When Sam spoke, what he said surprised her.

"I may be moving house when we get back to Bangkok," he told her suddenly.

"Really? Why is that?" It seemed such a strange subject to talk about there and then, she thought.

"Well, the house was Edward's, as you know—and was left to Anchalee and me. But there are so many memories there. Too much history. I want to make a fresh start when I marry again."

There was an awful sinking feeling inside her. She should have realised. "So you're thinking of remarrying?" She felt self-conscious, and moved away from him, wrapping the sheet more tightly about her.

He made no attempt to stop her. "As soon as possible, yes."

"I'm sorry, I had no idea. I would never have asked you to come if I'd known." And would never have given herself to him again if she had. She didn't want to cause another woman the same pain she had so many others by indulging herself with him.

"Elizabeth, you and I have known each other a long time. We've been through so much, and I once caused you so much anguish. I owed it to you to come to England."

Was that why he had agreed? Because he thought himself in her debt?

"So that's what you meant when you said there was one more thing that would make your happiness complete."

"What?"

"That you wanted to marry again?"

"That's right. But I didn't think you'd remember I'd said it."

"Had you met her then?"

He seemed to find that amusing, and grinned slyly in the way that had always both attracted and repelled her at the same time. "Yes, I'd met her then. I'd known her for years, in fact."

"Do you mind if I ask you who she is?"

"I'll tell you on one provision."

"And what's that?"

"That after tonight, you agree to share my cabin with me for the rest of the passage."

Was that all he saw her as? Someone to satisfy his physical needs while he was away from the woman he was to marry? After all this time, did he still think of her only as a woman to toy with? She sighed deeply, not angry any more, but disappointed.

"I'm surprised you could ask me that, Sam. You know I won't agree."

He didn't object as she left the bed and began to dress, and he watched and waited until she was finished.

"Are you against sleeping with your husband then?"

She turned quickly back to him. "What do you mean?"

He was smiling broadly now. "Haven't you guessed?"

"Guessed what?"

"It's you. She's you."

"Who's me? I don't understand."

He got up, reached for his silk robe, and strode up to her. He pulled her gently to him, then stood facing her with his hands on her shoulders. "It's you, Elizabeth. You're the one I want to marry. I've fallen in love with you all over again. Or perhaps I never stopped loving you. And this time, I don't want to lose you."

She said nothing, so amazed was she by the revelation.

"We're both free now," he continued. "Free to do what we should have done years ago. Only now we can—without hurting anyone. Say yes, Elizabeth. Just say yes."

As he spoke, his grip on her shoulders had increased so that it was almost painful. But she hardly noticed. Her initial confusion turned to disbelief, then—as she realised he was serious—she could not reply. She looked into his eyes.

Seeing her faltering, he felt the need to allow her some space. "I've tired you, I know. What with . . . before . . . and now this. Please think about it, Elizabeth. I love you, and we belong together."

Later, in her bed alone, she could not sleep, despite her fatigue. She did love him, she knew, but it was the freedom holding her back. Marriage was no longer what she wanted or needed from him. She had been taken care of by others all her life. Now that poor Joseph was gone, she was completely herself. She had no man to look after her now—but did she need one? With Joe away, she had proved to herself that she could survive alone.

What had happened tonight was different. It was something that she felt had to be done. It was desire, yes—but it was also a way of closing one chapter of the past, and moving on to the next. She was not even sure of what she would do yet—but it would be a decision she alone would make.

Explaining it to him the next day was much harder. She knew he would do his utmost to convince her—but she was prepared.

Nevertheless, when she told him, to her surprise, he seemed to accept it without question, and his final plea was one of happy resignation. "I'd give you every freedom, Elizabeth. I'd never try to possess you."

"Yes, but don't you see, that's just it. I don't want to even be in the position where someone else can choose to 'give' me my freedom—or not. I want to be in charge of my own destiny. I've finally become independent, Sam—and I like it. What happened between us . . . just happened. I don't regret it. Please say you don't, either."

"Of course not."

"But it cannot, and will not, ever happen again. I love you, Sam—I can say that with honesty. But I'm no longer *in* love with you. I've gone beyond that. Now I know that we'll be friends, and that this time, it's right, and good, and it will last forever."

He took her outstretched hand, and together they looked out from the deck across the vast ocean, and he knew their love affair was over. But in its place was the greatest friendship he had known, and that was enough. He felt old, and wise, and fulfilled.

"Well, let's go to a wedding anyway—just for the hell of it." he said, grinning. "Our son's wedding."

◈ *Epilogue* ◈

The young woman lifted the dying child so he could sip weakly from a glass of water she offered him.

"You must see he gets enough fluids," Kesri told the boy's mother, who—she noticed—was several years younger than herself. "Try not to use river water. But if you have to, make sure you boil it properly first. Fifteen minutes, at least."

The mother shrugged with hopelessness. "There's no other water until the wet season. We used our stored rainwater months ago. And there's usually no wood for a fire."

It was a familiar story, and Kesri felt powerless to help the hundreds, probably thousands, of people who died of cholera because they drank the filthy water from the *klongs* and river. She gently laid down the child on the dirt floor of the lean-to shelter and covered him with the rags that were all his mother could provide. At least it was not cold, and no one froze to death here, she thought. But the boy would die soon, anyway—probably that night.

She excused herself quickly and went out, so the boy's mother would not see the tears in her eyes. Once outside, she breathed deeply and tried to compose herself. In a few more minutes she would have to visit another fetid shack, and then another after that. She would see similar tragedies in all, and would be powerless to help any of them. All she could do was try to make the dying comfortable, and hold the hands of the grieving.

"It doesn't get any easier, does it?" an older woman emerging from another bamboo-and-thatch hut said kindly. She came over to Kesri and put her arm around her in consolation.

Fanny Knox looked part-Spanish with her fine, dark features, but was actually the daughter of Sir Thomas Knox, who had been

401

British consul in Bangkok in the 1860s and 1870s. Unbeknown to Kesri, he was the same man her grandfather had met all those years ago when he first came to Siam.

Fanny's story was legendary in both expatriate and Siamese circles in Bangkok, but had probably been embellished in its telling over the decades. Fanny herself preferred to talk only of the present, and her work in helping the city's poor and ill.

As the story went, Fanny had left Siam for a number of years to be educated in Europe. She returned in 1875 at the age of nineteen, and soon fell in love with a Siamese nobleman, Phra Pricha, who was a widower and fourteen years her senior. Phra Pricha was a member of the wealthy and influential Amatayakun family, and was also a personal friend of King Chulalongkorn. Such was his status, that when he discovered gold in his province, he had not retained the workings for himself, but had presented them to the state.

At the same time, however, Sri Sriyawongse, the then powerful chief minister, who had been regent until King Chulalongkorn reached maturity, decided that Fanny should marry his grandson, Nai Dee. The match was politically important for Sri Sriyawongse, and Sir Thomas agreed to the union, forbidding Fanny to see the man she loved, Phra Pricha. Fanny, however, refused to obey her father, and she and Pricha were married at his house in Bangkok, without either her parents' blessing or presence. The couple then travelled to his upcountry estate in Prachin.

Meanwhile, Sri Sriyawongse, his plans thwarted, was determined the two should not be allowed to live contentedly. Within weeks of the wedding, Pricha was summoned to Bangkok, where he was arrested and charged with—among other things— insulting the king by marrying without his permission, mismanaging his estate, embezzling state money, and mistreating and murdering workers in the gold mine. He was found guilty of the crimes, and—amid debate over the fairness of his trial and his alleged guilt—was eventually executed at Prachin. This despite—surprisingly—Consul Knox's best efforts to save him by requesting that Chulalongkorn appoint new, unbiased judges in the case. The king could not oppose the cabinet, however, but did insist that Phra Pricha receive a fair trial.

Fanny escaped to Europe with her and Pricha's baby son— and with his two children from his previous marriage. She could easily have remarried, or spent her time in quiet retreat in England, as befitted her status, but instead, Fanny embarked upon a bizarre plan to help the French in Cambodia annex Siam—and so, she reasoned, abolish the corrupt system that gave men such as Sri Sriyawongse such unjust power.

But Fanny mellowed with age, and when Sri Sriyawongse died in 1883, she decided that revenge was not the answer. She returned to Bangkok and rented a small house off New Road. King Chulalongkorn even granted her an annuity in acknowledgement of the injustice her husband had suffered, and she then decided to devote the remainder of her life to helping the poor and those she felt were unfairly treated in Siam.

Kesri had heard her father tell Fanny's story, although she did not dare talk to Fanny herself about it. Indeed, Sam had known Fanny since she was young, because her sister, Caroline, had married his old friend Louis—who, in fact, had initially wanted to marry Fanny herself. Caroline died in 1893 when she was only thirty-five, and Louis had remarried in 1899, to a young Australian woman named Reta. Sam still saw Louis and Reta from time to time, although they had just been on a long trip to England and Canada.

They walked silently to their next case until Fanny noticed that Kesri still looked disturbed. "Still thinking about that child?"

"Actually, I was thinking of you," Kesri replied. "How do you do it, Fanny? Day after day, year after year. Doesn't it make you feel despondent? It's so hopeless."

"It's not hopeless at all," Fanny retorted rather too firmly—so that Kesri jumped slightly.

She continued more softly, realising that her harsh response was unwarranted. "Even if we cannot stop many of them dying, Kesri, even if we can bring only comfort and a shoulder to cry on, that's something. I believe we're bringing real help to these people."

"I'm sorry," Kesri said. "Of course we are. And I love the work, I really do. I'm just having a bad day."

"Why don't you go home early. Forget about all this for a few hours. I can see you've got other things on your mind."

"You make me feel so guilty for admitting I have. Compared to these poor people, my problems are slight."

"Do you want to talk about anything, my dear?"

"There's nothing to say, really. It's just that it's a year ago today that. . . ." She stopped and turned away.

The distant look in Kesri's eyes told Fanny all she needed to know. "Did he break your heart, dear?"

"No, actually I think I broke his. But it was just not possible for us to be together. My feelings were changed when I was told about something that happened before I was born—something that neither of us could have known about. But it meant we could never be married."

"Our lives very rarely go the way we plan," Fanny said gently. "But you'll see, good will come of this if you let it. Perhaps it already has. If I'm right, it was that experience that sent you to me, was it?"

She nodded. "Actually, it was my father. And I'm glad he did. I have some purpose now."

When she arrived home, she found a package waiting for her in the parlour. It was so heavy that at first she thought it might be a shipment of her father's new novel. Then she saw that it had not come from overseas, but from Bangkok itself. Perhaps he had left it as a surprise for her while he was away. He had been gone only four days, but already she missed him.

He had asked her to go to England with him; not, of course, to attend the wedding—that would be unthinkable—but simply to visit. She turned him down, however, preferring to continue her work, and telling him that she would go to England when she had to, in another eighteen months or so, but not before. Besides, she did not care to be reminded of her half-brother and what he had meant to her.

Today, however, she had not been able to put him out of her mind—given that it was a year ago to the day that he had left. The anguish, for her, was still very real, and it would be a long time yet before she would recover her spirit.

Sam had not been happy at her insistence on staying in the house with only the servants. He had suggested she stay with Louis and Reta, or some other older couple, but she had been adamant, and he eventually acceded. He felt he could not deny her much, after what she had been through, and he could trust her not to use his absence as an opportunity for further romantic interludes. In fact, he was positive nothing of that kind would occur for a long time to come, if her mood and demeanour were any indication. And that was not surprising. She seemed to have regained her good sense, and there was always Miss Knox, with whom he had already had a quiet word, to keep an eye on her.

She ripped open the package, and inside found an envelope, and a square, wrapped box. Inside the envelope was a letter from Elizabeth.

May 10th, 1905

My dear Kesri,

You will be surprised indeed to receive this delivery from me, and the mystery of it will be revealed to you shortly in both this letter, and in the contents of the other envelope. The package itself, which I am sure you are anxious to open, contains a legacy from your grandfather, Edward Fairburn, originally bestowed on me when he passed away.

As he requested in his will, I have always kept the contents of this package a secret; no one knows of it, including your father. To be honest, I have never known what to do with it, but my father said in his letter regarding it, that I would know what to do when the time was right. I think that time has come, Kesri, and I believe you are the right person to have it.

As you will discover, this legacy does not have a noble history. Please be assured, however, that the fact I am now passing it on to you, is no reflection on your own dear self. What you will find in this package was gained as the result of a gross error of judgement by my father. It was a sin he fully acknowledged and regretted at his death, but did not feel able to admit or atone for in his lifetime. I have even made discreet enquiries in Australia, and have discovered no information about the other party concerned, so presumably there are no other heirs or claimants.

Anyway, my dear, please read the enclosed material carefully, try to forgive your grandfather, and use this treasure wisely, so that out of such misadventure, some good may come.

Your loving Aunt Elizabeth

Under the wrapping of the second package was a large tin box, about eighteen inches square, and the same in depth. She levered open the lid—it was too heavy to lift out of the surrounding package—and peered inside.

The huge gold nugget, encased in quartz, as it had emerged from the ground, was positively the last thing she had ever expected to see, and the brilliance of it overwhelmed her. She had seen similar pictures in books, and had once seen a real gold nugget at an exhibition, but never anything like this. She ran her finger along its rough surface.

The second envelope lay on top of the huge nugget, and it had already been opened—presumably, she realised, by Elizabeth.

Eager to understand—and imagining that her aunt must have felt exactly as she did now—she reached inside and took out a letter and a very old newspaper article. She unfolded the clipping, and saw that it was the front page of the *Melbourne Argus*, dated 8th October, 1866, making it nearly fifty years old. One of the articles had been circled in ink.

BARMAID DIES IN BALLARAT FIRE
ALLEGED GOLD NUGGET MISSING;
FRIENDS BLAME THIEVES

Ballarat, Oct. 6—*A young woman died in a domestic blaze in Bridge Street last night, the house well alight and its sole occupant deceased by the time the volunteer fire brigade arrived. The woman was:*
Celia Mary Marsden, *26, employed as a barmaid at the Grand Royal Hotel.*

Miss Marsden, a Sydneysider who had been in Ballarat for five years, was believed recently to have found gold on her claim, in the form of a nugget reportedly weighing some thirty-five pounds gross. The gold was not found in the house after the fire, and colleagues of Miss Marsden are claiming it to have been the motive for thievery, the culprits, on having been discovered by Miss Marsden, then setting the house alight before making their escape.

An inspection of the bedroom where the conflagration originated, however, has revealed it was probably the result of a smouldering cigar, presumably. . . .

She did not want to read on. Had Grandfather been a thief— or worse? She turned to the old letter.

To whom it may concern,

> *That you are now reading this letter means I have passed away. At the time I first lodged this treasure with my London solicitors, Harbeck & Harbeck, the year was 1867, and I was a young man expecting a long life ahead of me. But now, as I write this, it is late 1885, and I know that I shall soon die.*

My solicitors, as directed by my will, have been ordered to dispatch this package soon after my death to my daughter, Mrs. Elizabeth Shaw, even though I feel almost certain that she will not wish to retain this bequest, but will, as I have suggested in a separate letter to her, pass it on to someone, perhaps your good self, who will use it for some good purpose.

From the moment I acquired it, this gold has been as heavy a burden upon me as if I were wearing it around my neck like a millstone. The accompanying newspaper article will tell you that it is associated with an event which I now bitterly regret. However, I beg that you do not judge me until you have read this, my own explanation of that unfortunate time. My hope is that you will conclude, that while reprehensible, there was nothing malicious in my actions.

The gold nugget, discovered by myself and Celia Marsden—the woman mentioned in the article—actually weighs twenty-eight pounds and four ounces, of which I am assured that, after separation, around twenty-three pounds of pure gold will be retrieved, the remainder being quartz. While it is worth only a small fortune, when compared with that which I have bequeathed my heirs from other sources, it is most important to me that it be used in such a way as to cancel out the evil of its acquisition. The events I will describe happened long ago; long before I came to see the true path my life should take, and before ever I listened to, and heeded God's word. You must now forgive me for having to speak so frankly in the following explanation.

In the newspaper item accompanying this letter, you will read that the young woman in question, Celia Marsden, died in a suspicious fire, and that it was widely believed that the person who stole the gold nugget was responsible for her death. I confess, here and now, that I was the intruder who broke into her house that night, but must state absolutely that I was not responsible for the fire. I also regret to say that Celia was more to me than a business acquaintance; and the circumstances of our meeting will be explained in due course.

At that time, I was at the Ballarat gold fields working as a photographer. I also prospected occasionally, although I must say that I was never serious in that endeavour, since my photography provided me with a comfortable income. For me, it was more of an adventurous diversion, at which I never expected any success. It was on one of those occasions, however, that Celia and I discovered this gold together. Needless to say, we were both astounded at our good fortune, and we entered into a verbal agreement, as I shall explain, about what we would do as a result of the find. Celia did not honour that agreement, and I went to her house that night merely to retrieve what I saw, at the time, as rightfully mine.

I, a young man with a troubled marriage, was besotted with Celia, and fell for her artfully-practised charms like a fool. I was blinded to her true nature, and although I had heard rumours that she was nothing better than a prostitute, I did not care to listen. To me, she was exciting, vibrant, and dangerous, while my own wife forever consumed me with guilt for my causing her the pain and disappointment of numerous pregnancies, in which all but one of our children died or miscarried. Our beautiful daughter, Elizabeth, survived, and I should, to my greater shame, have been content with that. But I was not, and when I met Celia, I could not help myself.

I did not realise it then, but Celia actually despised men, and would exploit them for whatever she could gain. Still, as I confessed earlier, when I first met her, at the Grand Royal Hotel, Ballarat, I was infatuated with her, and we immediately formed a liaison. She told me that she wanted to try her hand on the tailings at the Sovereign Hill gold fields, and even though I did not think it appropriate for a woman to become a digger, she was adamant, so I purchased our equipment and we staked our claim. Each day she had free from her work as a barmaid at the hotel, she would be there, working on the fields as hard as any man. I had fooled myself into thinking that I was in love with her, and that we would eventually run off together—with I deserting my wife and child.

With hindsight I know that it could never have worked, and would have led to my complete destruction. I have asked myself time and again, would I really have gone with her? Or would I have seen sense? I knew very well that if I went through with this outrageous and nonsensical plan, my family in England would disown and disinherit me. I would be left without a penny, and would have to rely on my own resources. I was doing well with my photography, and earning enough to keep Charlotte and Elizabeth. But whereas Charlotte was a frugal woman who did not want for fancy clothes and jewels, I knew Celia would require much more to keep her happy.

Anyway, that is by the by. One day, when I was with her on our claim, we did indeed find gold in the form of the sizeable nugget you now see before you. It was strangely isolated, with little other gold around it in the section we had dug, and I prised it out with a pickaxe while she was above, rinsing tailings in a pan and finding only flecks of gold dust. I truly believed that the find was a portentous omen that would enable me to start anew with Celia. I trusted her, and gave it to her for safekeeping.

Almost immediately, however, she began to behave differently towards me. I had heard stories about her gentleman callers, but she had always maintained they were just friends, which I suppose, in a way, was more accurate, for she cared for none of them. I had wanted to keep our find a secret, until we could leave safely with it, but she could not prevent herself from announcing it to all and sundry. I soon heard, from other parties, that she intended to move on and start afresh somewhere else, perhaps to open up her own establishment in Sydney. Her plans very obviously did not include me, and eventually she pretended not to know me, refusing to answer her door when I called.

I was furious, but mostly, I suppose, it was my self-esteem that was broken. I had been useful to her, but was now discarded, and she already had a new acquaintance to replace me. I felt extremely foolish, and more than a little stupid for having contemplated renouncing my inheritance and my family for her. It was then that I decided to steal the nugget one evening while she was in her usual drunken stupor.

On the night in question, the fire had started to smoulder before I even reached the house, and as I was removing the gold from her room, it flared up. I assume that it had begun as a result of her falling asleep while smoking a cigarette or cigar. I beg you to believe me when I say that, although I tried, I could do nothing at all to help her. It was too late for anyone to save her, and I had to escape quickly to save myself.

It is true that it was a cowardly act that I did not remain to call the fire brigade, and nor did I ever own up to taking the gold. After all, it was I who had found it, and half of it was mine.

Celia had no family or dependants, and certainly would not have left a will at her young age. Thus, I knew that if I did confess, the gold would have been confiscated by the government, who had already robbed the poor diggers blind with their licence fees, before the brave Eureka stockade stand in Ballarat during the fifties. In addition, I would surely have been charged with theft at least, and perhaps with murder if they did not believe my story.

A detective did visit me at my lodgings in Ballarat, referred by some rogue from the hotel who had been acquainted with Celia before I, and so had a grudge to bear me, but I was able to persuade him that I, an English gentleman, had no reason for an attachment to such a common woman, and that I knew her only slightly as the hotel barmaid. Fortunately, he believed me, and a small gratuity helped him to do so.

Although I was determined to keep the gold for myself, it was clear to me that I could never use it in my lifetime, not only because of the increasing guilt and remorse I felt with its association, but also for the practical reason that I lived in fear of some connection being made if I ever attempted to do so. It was most propitious that I had to return to England at about the same time, and so I took the nugget with me, and deposited it with my solicitors there.

All my life I have regretted such a grave error of judgement as taking up with that woman. However, now that I am an old man, and staring at death, I have decided that some good must come of this cursed find. I ask only that it be used to finance some project of charity to others, preferably in Siam, my adopted homeland, where there are many who could benefit.

Edward Benjamin Fairburn

She ran a finger over the nugget once more. It was dazzling, like a golden honeycomb caught in the sunlight. Now that she knew the whole story, she did not think ill of her grandfather. It was so long ago, nearly half a century. And she knew just what to do with the gold.

January, 1906

There were already a large number of women waiting outside when she arrived to open the doors. Many carried sick babies, others were ill themselves, and still others were simply curious. Local women around New Road—and from much further afield— had quickly learned that you went there to see Khun Kesri if you were destitute; if you needed to see a doctor but could not afford to pay; if your children needed vaccinations; or if you were being bullied or abused by your husband or anyone else. She had persuaded several respected Western doctors to work *gratis* at the centre, and graduates and interns from the Medical School and College in Bangkok, established by King Chulalongkorn, were also willing volunteers.

Kesri taught the women about the dangers of consuming contaminated water and food, and she taught young girls to sew, to speak English, and to read and write Siamese. Fanny Knox was always willing to give advice, and at the beginning, Kesri would have been lost without her.

She had offered Fanny the role of director of the centre, but the older woman had kindly declined, saying that she preferred to work independently with the students in Bangkok who would one day become its policy-makers. At twenty, Kesri often felt overawed with such a venture. But she also felt, even more strongly, that this was her vocation, and that the sins of the fathers—and indeed, her own—were truly being redeemed.

The carriage stopped outside the house, and a woman got out. She stood for a while, observing the women and children waiting outside, and the activity all around it. Moments later, her niece appeared at the door and walked down the garden path to greet her. They embraced and then walked back up the path to the house. Beside the front door, on the wall, was a small brass nameplate. It said *Ban Si Thong*, Golden House. Kesri waited expectantly for her aunt's reaction. Elizabeth simply smiled, nodded, and took Kesri's hand. Then the two women went inside together. There was much work to be done.

❖ *About the Author* ❖

Caron Eastgate James is a journalist who has worked on
newspapers and magazines in New Zealand, Australia and
Thailand. She lived in Bangkok from 1990-1993, and from
1997-1999, and currently resides in Melbourne.
A New Zealander by birth, she has also lived in England and
the United States. She holds a Master of Arts degree in literary
studies and hopes one day to complete a PhD. *The Occidentals* is
her first novel, and she intends to write two more in the series
to complete a trilogy.